Just One of the Groomsmen

Just One of the Groomsmen

CINDI MADSEN

Entangled Publishing, LLC
2614 South Timberline Road
Suite 105, PMB 159
Fort Collins, CO 80525
Visit our website at www.entangledpublishing.com.

Amara is an imprint of Entangled Publishing, LLC.

Edited by Stacy Abrams
Cover design by Hang Le
Photographer Simonkr/iStock
Interior design by Toni Kerr

Print ISBN 978-1-64063-431-2
ebook ISBN 978-1-64063-430-5

Manufactured in the United States of America

First Edition June 2019

AMARA

*To the great group of guys who made
high school more fun,
from poker games for Mtn Dew to
checking cows & riding four-wheelers,
& even for occasionally forgetting I was a girl*

CHAPTER ONE

The houseboat came into view and Addie's excitement level went from its already high seven to a solid ten. An emergency meeting had been called, and all the guys were going to be in attendance. Every single one, including the guy she'd been dying to see for so long that she'd almost worried their sporadic phone calls, texts, and messages were the only way they'd ever communicate again.

Addie pulled up next to the sleek compact car she'd have to make fun of later—right now it meant that Tucker Crawford was here in the flesh, and within a few minutes, the rest of the gang would be as well.

She wasn't sure why Shep had called the meeting, but it took her back to high school, when so many of their evenings and weekends were spent here at the Crawfords' houseboat.

Lazy afternoons and countless poker games; impromptu parties that usually got them busted for one thing or another; and nights spent celebrating team wins or commiserating over losses, whether it was the high school team that the guys had all played for, War Eagle football, or the NFL, on which they were a house divided—it'd led to some of her and Tucker's most heated exchanges.

The scent of cypress trees, swampy lake water, and moss hit her as she climbed out of the beater truck she often drove, and since she was hoping for a minute or two with her very best and oldest friend before everyone else showed up, she rushed down the pathway. "Tucker?"

"Addie?"

She heard his voice but didn't see him. Then she rounded the front of the boat, where the chairs and grill were set up, and there he was.

Even taller and wider than she remembered, his copper-brown hair styled shorter than he wore it in high school, although the wave in it meant there were always a couple of strands that did their own thing.

A laugh escaped as she took a few long strides and launched herself at him, her arms going around his neck. "I'll be damned, you actually made it this time."

Using the arm he'd wrapped around her lower back, he lifted her off her feet and squeezed tight enough to send her breath out over his shoulder. "I'm sorry for accidentally standing you up a few times. It's stupid how hard it's been to get away this past year."

"That's what happens when you go and become some big city lawyer."

Despite working at the law firm for nearly two years, he was still one of the junior attorneys, which meant he ended up doing all the time-consuming research for the partners, and even their calls and texts had slowed to a trickle. Before that, law school had kept him plenty busy, and while she wasn't usually the mushy hugger-type, she didn't want to release him yet, just in case she had to go another five or six months without seeing him.

She pulled back to get another look at him,

taking in the familiar blue eyes, his strong, freshly shaven jawline, and— "Holy crap, dude. When did you get so jacked? Is lifting bulky legal files muscle building? If so, maybe I should start recommending it as part of my clients' therapy regimens."

His gaze ran over her as well, most likely assessing the ways she'd changed—or more likely hadn't. "Isn't it about time for a new sweatshirt?" He yanked one of the frayed, used-to-be-black strings. "That one's looked ratty since our first year of college."

She gasped and shoved him. "Hater. Just because *my* Falcons made it further in the playoffs than your Saints did last season. And don't even try to tell me you've thrown out your beat-up baseball cap that practically grafted itself to your head during high school. Or maybe you don't wear it anymore so you can show off your fancy-pants forty-dollar lawyer haircut."

She reached up and ran her hand through his hair, loosening the hold the gel had on it.

Much better.

There was the boy who'd once landed her in detention because he'd dared her to put superglue on the teacher's whiteboard markers while he distracted him with a question. The boy who'd challenged her to a deviled-egg-eating competition at the town festival and then moped about her beating him—to this day, the sight or scent of a deviled egg still made her stomach roll.

He grinned, every inch the laid-back Tucker Crawford she'd grown up with once again, and just like that, all seemed right in Uncertainty, Alabama.

"Crawford? Where you at?" Shep's booming voice hit them a few seconds before he, Easton, and Ford rounded the corner and stepped onto the back deck.

"Murph!" they yelled when they saw her, and then they exchanged high fives, shoulder punches, and a few bro-hugs on their way to give Tucker the same treatment.

Addie saw the rest of the guys around town here and there, but it was harder to get together now that everyone had careers and other obligations.

Funny how in high school they couldn't wait to get older so they could do whatever they wanted, and instead they ended up having less free time than ever.

Shep placed two six-packs of Naked Pig Pale Ale, the best beer in all of Alabama, on top of a big planter that only held dirt, since the neglected plants had shriveled up and died long ago. "Before we get this party started, I guess I should let you know what we're celebrating."

The hint of worry Addie had felt since receiving the urgent text evaporated. The message had been so vague—typical guy, although her mom and sister accused her of the same thing.

Addie sat on the edge of the table, and when Tucker bumped her over with his hip, she scooted. The table wobbled, and Tucker's hand shot out and gripped her upper arm as she worked to rebalance herself.

He chuckled. "Guess we're heavier than we used to be."

She scowled at him. "Hey! Speak for yourself."

"Right. It must be all my jacked muscles."

Addie rolled her eyes. That's what she got for giving him an accidental compliment.

Every single one of her boys had egos the size of pickup trucks, and the many girls who'd fawned over them through the years didn't help any.

Shep raised his voice, speaking above the din. "So, you guys might recall I've been seeing Sexy Lexi, going on almost a year now."

"How could we forget?" Addie quipped. "You talk about her nonstop." She glanced at Tucker, who'd yet to meet Shep's girlfriend, thanks to busy schedules and his last canceled trip. "Seriously, we go to get a beer and watch the game, and it's Lexi this, Lexi that."

Shep didn't frown at her like she'd expected, grinning that twitterpated grin he often wore these days instead.

"She's actually very lovely," she added, then curled her hands around the table. While his Southern belle girlfriend worked to hold it at bay, Addie didn't think Lexi was her biggest fan.

She hated always having to downplay her friendship with the guys in order to not upset the balance of their relationships. Hopefully a little more time and getting to know each other, and Lexi would understand that Will Shepherd was more like a brother than anything.

All the guys were, and thanks to the fact they'd both stayed closer to home the past few years, she and Shep were even more sibling-like than the rest.

It wasn't the first time her friends' girlfriends were wary of her, and she doubted it'd be the last. Sometimes she worried she'd get left behind, just because she'd had the audacity to be born a girl.

Being the only girl in a group of guys was merely a technicality, though. It wasn't that she didn't have female friends or that she didn't know a lot of great women; it was that she'd grown up with these guys and forged memories and they liked to do the same things she did.

It was why she'd gone by "Murph" more often than Addison Murphy, or any other variation thereof. Thanks to her love of comfy, sporty clothes, she'd been voted "most likely to start her own sweatshirt line" in high school.

A title she was proud to have, by the way.

Easton had been voted "most likely to end up in jail," and ironically enough, he was now a cop, something they all teased him about.

Which reminded her…

"Don't let me forget to make fun of your prissy car when this meeting is over," Addie whispered to Tucker.

He opened his mouth, assumedly to defend himself, and Shep cleared his throat.

"*Anyway*, last weekend I asked Lexi to marry me." A huge smile spread across his face. "And she said yes."

Not at all what Addie had been expecting.

Marriage was such a big step, and it took her a beat or two to process.

But happiness radiated off Shep in waves, the guy who'd once rolled his eyes over "whipped dudes" long gone.

She was glad he'd found someone, even as a tiny part of her wanted to press pause on this night while they were all together, before everything changed in their group yet again.

"You get to bang Sexy Lexi for the rest of your life?" Ford held up his hand for a high five. "*Bro.* I remember when you had to work your ass off to score her number at that bar in Opelika, and Easton and I had that bet about whether her amazing rack was real."

"*Bro*, that's gonna be his wife," Addie said.

"Yeah, have some respect," Shep said. Then he put a hand to the side of his mouth and stage-whispered, "They're one hundred percent real. I told you guys that, right?"

"Only, like, one hundred percent of the time you talk about her." Addie smiled.

This was the one downside of being the only girl. Sometimes things got a little too TMI about the women they were sleeping with or hoping to sleep with.

Everyone continued to offer their congratulations, and after a few claps on the back and obligatory jokes about balls and chains, Shep said, "I want you guys to be in my wedding. To be my groomsmen."

Addie's stomach dropped.

"You guys" usually included her, but she knew the word "groomsmen" didn't. "*Ha!* Y'all are gonna have to wear stuffy penguin suits and take hundreds of pictures. Have fun with that."

Shep looked at her, and a sense of foreboding pricked her skin. "Before you go celebrating too much, you're in the wedding party, too, Murph. I told Lexi I wanted you as one of my groomsmen."

While his girlfriend—make that fiancée—was

pretty patient and understanding of Shep's crazy, out-there ideas, she was also *extremely* girly.

"I'm sure that went over about as well as coming out as a vegan in the middle of Sunday dinner."

"She understands you're just one of the guys," Shep said, and a hint of hope rose up.

She hated that she'd immediately felt left out, the same way she used to when a group of girls would show up at the bar and suddenly she'd be alone, no one to help with game commentary.

"But she's also more traditional, her family even more so," Shep continued.

"I understand," Addie said. "I don't think I'd look very good in a tux anyway, and my own mother would probably die twice over it."

Since Addie hadn't been on a date in a depressing amount of time, Mom had also recently given her this whole spiel about dressing up once in a while, and how men wanted to feel needed, so to make sure not to act so assertive and dominant all the time.

Like she didn't want to feel needed?

She'd just prefer a possible significant other want her the way she was, not because she donned a dress and acted helpless.

"Which is why…" Shep straightened, his hazel eyes locking on to her. "Lexi and I came up with a compromise. You'll be a groomsman in name and when it comes to all the usual pre-wedding stuff, but in order to be part of the wedding party, you're gonna have to wear the same dress and shoes as the bridesmaids." The rest of the words came out in a fast blur, like he hoped if he talked fast enough she might miss them. "And you might have to dress up one or two other times."

The guys burst out laughing.

"Murph in a dress and heels," Easton said. "That'll be the day."

Addie picked up the nearest object she could find—a weather-warped coaster—and chucked it at his head. It bounced off, and, if anything, only made him laugh harder.

The table shook, and when she glanced at Tucker, he had a fist over his mouth in an attempt to smother his laughter.

"You too?" Was karma punishing her? Was this what she got for being comfortable for most of her twenty-seven years?

"Please, Addie," Shep said. "I know it's not your thing, but I can't imagine you not being part of this." He shot a challenging glare at the group of them. "And spare me the jokes about actually caring about my wedding. I never thought I'd be this happy, but I am, and I need you guys with me on this."

This time, the "you guys" definitely included her.

Which made it that much easier to say, "I'm in. I'll do whatever you need me to."

• • •

Man, it was good to be back in town, even if only for a quick weekend.

Tucker had been working hours and hours on end, thinking that eventually he'd have enough experience and clout to slow down a bit. It never slowed down, though, his workload multiplying at an impossible-to-keep-up-with pace.

Now that he was seated around the poker table with his friends, though, all felt right with the world.

"You're bluffin," Addie said when Easton threw several chips into the pot. She matched his bet, and then they laid down their cards, her full house easily beating his pair of aces. "Read 'em and weep, sucker."

She shoved the sleeves of her two-sizes-too-big hoodie up her arms as she leaned over the table to gather her winnings. Her familiar movements were nearly second nature, as much to him as her. She flopped back in her chair and reached into the bag of Lay's for a different kind of chip.

Her knee came up to rest against the table, rattling everything on top and boosting the time-machine effect, and she wiped her fingertips on her frayed jeans before reaching for the newly dealt cards. Her neon-colored gel sneakers, the one new item in her outfit, reminded him of all her lectures on how important the right shoes and changing them often were for your joints.

He cracked a smile again at the thought of her in a dress and heels, bouquet in hand. The image still didn't compute. It was kind of like animals wearing human clothes.

It just wasn't right.

It wasn't that they'd *never* seen Addie wear a dress; it was that she loathed them with a hatred he withheld for things like paperwork and blind refs who ruined games.

She'd once slugged him in the shoulder for even mentioning her dress-wearing at her sister's wedding. The skirt had been long and baggy, and the real tragedy was that she couldn't toss around the pigskin.

So then they'd *both* had to sit there with their hands folded in their laps for what seemed like forever and it was boring as hell, an emotion he'd rarely experienced around her.

"Your poker face is crap, Crawford. I know you're thinking about how funny it is that I just agreed to wear a freaking bridesmaid's dress, and if you don't want me to jam that beer you're drinking where the sun don't shine, I suggest you wipe the smirk off your face." She pointed her finger around the table. "That goes for all of you."

"I appreciate you going along with it," Shep said. "I told Lexi that you'd probably slug me just for suggesting it."

"Lucky for you, you were too far away and wearing that lovestruck grin that makes me take pity on you."

"When someone basically says thank you, maybe don't follow that up by insulting them." Shep placed three cards, face up, in the center of the table. "Just a suggestion."

"This is why so many guys in town are scared of you," Easton said with a laugh.

She clucked her tongue. "They are not."

The other half of the table nodded.

Tucker found himself nodding even though he hadn't lived in town for the better part of two years. It'd been like that since high school, with Addie intimidating anyone who dared cross her path, and the selfish part of him was glad no one had come in and swept her off her feet.

Not that she would ever let some guy do the sweeping. A few had probably tried, with her completely oblivious. With her dark-brown hair that was forever in a ponytail, the smattering of freckles across her nose, her big brown eyes, and the fact that she was cool as hell, it was surprising she'd stayed mostly single.

Ford pinned her with a look. "Addie, when dudes come in to see you for physical therapy, you tell them to stop crying over something your grandma could do."

"Well, she could! My nonna is tougher than most of the crybabies who come in and whine about having to put in the work it takes to get over their injuries. Telling them my grandma could do it is motivating."

"Not to ask you out," Ford said, and snickers went around the table.

"Very funny. Being scared of me and being undateable are two different things."

"You're hardly undateable," Tucker said, the words similar to exchanges they'd had before.

"Yeah, but it's nearly impossible to find someone who doesn't already know too much about me—or me about him—and even if I manage that, then I introduce him to you guys, and things unravel pretty quickly after that."

"Maybe with one of us gettin' hitched, we'll be less intimidating." Shep dealt the turn and they started a round of betting.

"I'm sure it's me," Addie muttered. "Now, do you guys want to talk about my pathetic dating life, or do y'all want me to finish taking your money?"

"Wow, what great options," Tucker deadpanned. "Not sure why anyone would be scared of you. Couldn't be all the threats."

She turned those brown eyes on him and cocked an eyebrow. "Listen, city boy. Maybe you can just flash your shiny car and some Benjamins to get your way where you live, but here we still live and die by the same code."

He leaned in, challenge firing in his veins. "And that is…?"

"Loser buys beer next time. And/or acts as designated driver."

"And sleeps on the breakfast bar," Easton added, jerking his chin toward the hardwood bench they'd taken turns crashing out on at one time or another. There were only so many sleeping spots in the houseboat. Winner and runner-up got the bed, and third place landed the couch.

"Oh, man." Shep rubbed his lower back. "I don't think I've recovered from the last time I passed out there." He dealt the last card, revealing the river, and Tucker watched for everyone's reactions.

The guys folded after he doubled the bet, and then it came down to him and Addie.

"Poker's so much better with all of us here," she said.

"Trying to distract me?" Tucker asked. "'Cause it won't work."

She laughed. "No, just telling the truth. We've tried to play with people from everyone's respective jobs, or some other rando who wants in when they hear we play poker, and it always sucks. And it's never as interesting with just four."

Ford shifted forward in his seat. "Remember Buck? That guy never shut up."

"And thanks to you"—Tucker gave Ford's shoulder a shove—"we already have the loudmouth position filled."

Ford flipped him off and then let out a loud burp. "He also scratched his balls even more than Easton does."

"Hey," Easton said. "When you've got balls this size, they require constant adjustment."

Addie took a swig of her beer. "Buck wasn't as bad as that Yank Shep brought over. That dude didn't even know how to play."

"That Yank happens to be my cousin," Shep said. "And it's not like I wanted to bring him. My mama insisted, and it was easier to drag him along than argue with her."

"We explained the rules over and over"—Easton reached across the table to grab the potato chips—"and that dude still didn't know whether to check his ass or scratch his watch."

Whenever Tucker came home, he noticed the extra twang in his friends' voices—not to mention the more colorful sayings—and he knew by the end of the night, he'd pick it right back up, his own accent thicker for a few days before the city smoothed it out a bit.

"All right, let's see what you got," Tucker said, and he and Addie placed their cards on the table at the same time.

Then she proceeded to take the last of his chips.

They played until everyone was sober again and

Addie had pretty much cleaned them out. One by one they left, save the two of them.

"Are you staying here at the houseboat tonight?" she asked as she gathered her keys off the table outside. "Because you know that my door is always open, and I even have a bed that doesn't sway."

That was Addie's way of offering him a place to crash without making him feel homeless.

His parents had divorced his junior year of high school, which was extra fun in a small town where everyone gossiped about it. The next hit came when the bank foreclosed on his childhood home, leaving him feeling completely uprooted, something he'd only ever confessed to Addie.

It didn't help that Dad sold nearly everything so he could move towns, and Tucker had to beg him to hold off selling the houseboat.

Halfway through law school, Dad claimed he needed money too badly to wait any longer, so Tucker drove to Uncertainty, took out a loan against the small plot of land his grandfather had left him, and bought the houseboat himself. He'd nearly paid it off, although he'd already seen repairs that would need to be made whenever he found spare time—so probably about three years from now.

"I like it out here on the lake," he said, "and I don't mind if my bed rocks a little."

"Dirty," she teased, and he laughed.

Although now he was thinking about how long it'd been. Work was getting in the way of every single aspect of his social life. If he loved his job, it would be one thing, but he was giving up a lot for a future of making a lot of money—right now he still had plenty of bills and student loans to worry about.

A smile curved Addie's lips as she ran her hand over the deck railing. "I love this mini-house and all our memories here."

"Yeah, those were definitely the good ol' days."

He folded his forearms on the railing and looked out over the water. It'd been a long time since he'd been able to kick back and joke with people who understood him. A long time since he'd felt so relaxed. While being with the whole gang was a blast, Addie had always been his go-to when he needed advice or wanted to get more real.

Certain things couldn't be communicated over the phone, and no matter how hard they'd tried to keep in touch, it just wasn't the same as in person, and now he was out of practice.

So he stuck to simple. "Tonight was the most fun I've had in a long time."

"Me too. Like I said, poker's not the same without you. Same with football games, whether we're both cheering for Auburn on Saturdays, or if you're spending Sundays being an annoying ass who talks trash about my team." She set her jaw. "Even you have to admit that the Falcons had a good season last year."

"I admit nothing."

"Stubborn," she muttered. As if she wasn't equally as stubborn. She sighed and lightly punched his arm. "Night, Crawford."

He returned the gesture. "Night, Murph."

She turned to go, but then abruptly spun around and wrapped her arms around his waist. "I understand that your job is demanding, but don't be a stranger."

He squeezed her back, noticing that her hair smelled fruity, like maybe strawberry or raspberry, or something berry, anyway.

"At least with Shep getting married you've got another excuse to come down and spend more than a weekend," she said, and something deep in his gut tugged.

"Yeah, it's good to have an excuse." What he wanted was an excuse not to go back to his cold, generic apartment and mind-numbing job.

Back to his serious life where he'd have to feel the loneliness he was doing his best to pretend didn't exist.

What he wanted more than anything was to return to his friends and the town he loved, and he wasn't sure how he could possibly go back and be satisfied with his old life after tonight showed him everything that was missing from it.

CHAPTER TWO

Four months later

Addie tossed clothes out of her old dresser, trying in vain to find something to wear. She'd gone straight from a hectic day at work where her boss was on a rampage to her parents' house to check on her grandmother, and now she didn't have time to go home to change.

She'd already texted Lexi and asked her to pick her up here, too, and considering she was on her way to her very first bridal shower and had no idea what to expect, her nerves were stretched to the fraying point.

Yoga pants were good enough for her and her clients, but since she knew the unconventional decision to have her as a groomsman had already made her the problem child of the wedding party, she was making an effort to keep Shep's bride-to-be happy.

She wasn't sure why she thought she'd have better luck with her high school wardrobe. It was all jeans, old baggy T-shirts, and cozy sweatshirts.

Ooh, this is where my AU Tigers sweatshirt is.

Her mother had tried getting rid of it several times thanks to the bleach stain on the front, but it used to be her favorite. Not dressy enough for tonight, but it was going in her take-home pile.

Next time Tucker comes back to town, I'll show

him that I own more than one sweatshirt.

Of course it was equally as ratty as her Falcons one, and wouldn't get as big a rise out of him, so then again maybe not.

These jeans are on the nicer side. Addie shed her yoga pants and slipped her feet inside the legs of the jeans. She tugged until they were halfway up her thighs.

Where they might remain forever.

One thing was for sure, she wouldn't be getting them on without ripping the denim and losing the ability to breathe.

As she bent to pull them off, her bound legs caused her to wobble. She fell backward, hitting the bed before thumping her way to the floor.

"*Ouch.*"

The door swung open, and she grabbed the quilt off the bed to cover herself the best she could, in case it was Dad and they both ended up scarred for life.

Instead, her sister stepped inside and looked down at her, forehead all scrunched up. "What on earth are you doing?"

"Getting a harsh reminder that I'm not the same size I used to be in high school," Addie said. "When did you get into town?"

"Just barely." Alexandria extended a hand and helped Addie off the floor, and she gave her sister a quick hug.

Alexandria was six years older, and while they didn't have much in common, they were blood, and they cared about each other, despite being so opposite.

For example, if anyone tried to call her Alex, she'd freeze them to death with her icy glare, whereas Addie would do about the same if anyone used her full name.

Obviously Alexandria was the girly, pretty one. The one teachers asked Addie why she couldn't be more like, same as her mom had countless times before.

Her sister had followed the typical life plan. College, marriage, motherhood. At least that last one meant Addie didn't get as much pressure from Mom and Nonna Lucia about wanting grandchildren. "How long are you staying?"

"Just the weekend."

The only edge Addie had over her sister in all things "should" came from the fact that she still lived in Uncertainty, and her sister had moved a whole state away.

Her family had been so upset, asking if they'd done something wrong, because how couldn't you want to stay in Uncertainty, Alabama, where everyone knew everyone, and that somehow entitled them to being all up in your business?

Addie sat on the bed and tugged at the denim encasing her legs. "I wish I knew you were coming. Maybe then I could've gotten out of this bridal shower thing I have to go to."

Alexandria gaped at her as if she'd suddenly grown a unicorn horn. "*You're* going to a bridal shower?"

Finally, the pants came free and Addie sighed in relief. "It's for Shep's fiancée and I'm one of the groomsmen, so…"

"You didn't even go to *my* bridal shower, even after I— Wait. Groomsmen?" The concern on Alexandria's face only grew. "You're a groomsman?"

Addie assumed Mom would've told her, or that someone else in town would've, since word spread like butter on a hot biscuit round these parts.

When the elderly postwoman heard the news, she'd sighed and told Addie that no guy would ever see her as a girl if she didn't at least *try* to act like one. There'd been facts about cavemen and certain things being in men's DNA, but after the hunter versus berry-gatherer mentality part, Addie tuned out.

She'd gotten good at tuning out, even though a few remarks always poked their way in and jabbed at her.

"Don't worry, I'll be wearing a bridesmaid's dress to the wedding."

"Well, good to know that Will Shepherd can get you to do something I never could." While the words had a gentle ribbing vibe, a hint of genuine indignance swam under the surface.

Offense pinched Addie's gut, especially after she'd sacrificed her comfort the day Alexandria walked down the aisle. "I wore a dress to your wedding."

"No, you wore a skirt, and you got it dirty playing ball with that Crawford kid before we could get all the pictures I wanted."

Mom had tried to make her and Tucker sit like good little statues. It'd worked for a while, but when Tucker told her he couldn't take it anymore, they'd snuck to the park for a game of catch, and the rest of the guys showed up.

Good times.

"Anyway," Addie said, not wanting to rehash the many occasions she'd disappointed everyone, "I have nothing to wear. Suggestions?"

The bibbed overalls in her closet caught her eye, and she tugged them away from the rest of the clothes. Comfort was king, so that was one of the fashion trends she'd been totally on board for. Too bad it didn't last, although someone said overalls were coming back around. "Maybe with the right shirt—"

Alexandria slapped her hand off the miles of baggy denim. "For goodness' sake, I have a dress you can borrow."

Addie wrinkled her nose. "A dress?"

"What were you planning on wearing?"

"Nice jeans and a dressy-ish top with—"

"Come on, we'll need to hurry." Alexandria didn't even slow enough for her to grab the discarded yoga pants.

She dragged a pants-less Addie into her room, plucked a dress out of her suitcase, and tossed it at her head.

Addie lifted it to examine it. "Pink lace? Why did you even pack a dress, and what makes you think I can pull off pink lace? This looks kind of short, too."

"When's the last time you shaved your legs?" Alexandria asked.

"Recently-ish."

She tossed a razor, and luckily Addie's reflexes were better than her ability to rock a dress, because she whipped up her hand and caught it before it could hit her in the chest. Then her sister was shoving her into the adjoining bathroom and instructing her to shave her legs—"all the way up, I mean it"—while she went to work curling Addie's hair.

And Addie vowed to never ask her sister for help again...

If she even survived the night.

• • •

The town sign proudly welcomed Tucker to Uncertainty—kind of ironic, considering his current predicament.

Thanks to the townsfolk being loud and proud about how their tiny town came to be, everyone learned how back in the day, the people who'd first dwelled there filled out an application for township. Since the settlement was on the shore of Lake Jocassee, and the citizens weren't exactly sure whether their town fell in Alabama or Georgia, they'd filled out the form with "We remain in Uncertainty."

When the township was granted, it was under the name Uncertainty.

So basically, it'd been named by mistake, and oh how the locals loved telling that story to anyone who wandered through.

Seeing as how the townsfolk also liked changing history to suit their whims, a case could be argued for reasonable doubt, although he certainly wouldn't be undertaking it.

He might not be doing things like paying

necessary bills, or having enough money for luxuries like groceries, either, but he was doing his best not to think about that.

Totally failing, too.

This might be the stupidest, most reckless thing I've ever done.

Considering his history of bad ideas that landed him in hot water, that was saying something.

Tucker slowed as he rounded the bend of the road leading into the heart of town. A group of women stood around a car, and the tense postures made him think something was wrong.

When a tall, skinny brunette looked over her shoulder and saw his car, relief flooded her features. She took a few steps toward him, her tall heels and the gravel road making her wobble as she waved her hands, signaling for him to stop.

Which he'd been planning on doing already.

He pulled up next to the vehicle. None of the women looked familiar, so maybe not everyone in town would know that he was back by the time evening fell.

Not like it mattered. They'd find out eventually, and besides, what was done was done. While it'd been impulsive and ill advised, he couldn't bring himself to take it back.

Ever since that night at the houseboat when he and the rest of the gang had played poker, he couldn't stop reminiscing on the good times and fixating on how miserable he was in the city. Working his job.

He hadn't told a single soul he was coming back, deciding to just show up and surprise them with the news.

Now he was thinking everyone was going to wonder why the theatrics.

Speaking of theatrics, the woman who'd flagged him down was gesturing wildly outside of his window, talking even though he couldn't hear her. He cut the engine and climbed out.

"Oh, thank goodness you came along. We were on the way to my friend's bridal shower and the vehicle broke down and…" She placed her hand on his arm and he took in her delicate features. Pretty, and even with the heels, he had a few inches on her. Not that he was going to take advantage of her stranded situation, but maybe afterward he could get her number. "I'm so glad you're here."

The other two women turned to stare at him, and he flashed them a warm smile. "No worries, ladies. I'll help however I can. How about you tell me what happened and we'll take it from there."

He froze when he caught sight of the bare legs sticking out from underneath the hood. The pink skirt was hiked high on her thighs, and the overlapping accounts of what'd happened as they were driving out of town faded to the background.

He'd always liked girls on the more athletic, curvy side, and this girl's toned legs were quite a sight to behold. Add in that she was lying on the ground in her dress, no hesitation, and she seemed like his type of girl.

"I don't think she knows what she's doing," the pretty brunette said.

"I *do* know what I'm doing. It just takes more than two seconds to check things out, and I don't have the parts to fix it hidden in the nonexistent pockets of this dress."

That voice.

Tucker tensed, thinking he was hearing things. He took another look at the sexy legs and strappy sandals. It couldn't be who he was thinking of.

Then again, if anyone would lie underneath a car in a dress, it'd be—

She slid out from under the vehicle and he let out an accidental "*Gah!*" even though his brain had been trying to tell him it would be Addie.

Since he'd just checked out her legs, his brain had also tried to insist it wasn't.

"Tucker?"

He nodded. As if it wasn't clear.

A smudge of dirt marked her cheek, her hair hung in loose waves around her face, and she looked so different, he still tried to make her into someone else.

His body finally caught up with the mental overload situation and he extended a hand and helped her to her feet.

"Murph," he said, because right now he needed an extra barrier or five between his mouth and his thoughts so he didn't go saying something highly inappropriate about her thighs. That'd make things even weirder and they needed to get back to normal, stat. "I've seen you bent over a hood or underneath a car many a time, but I've never seen you do it in a dress. I gotta say, it's rather eye opening."

That was a little too true. Logically he knew she was a girl, but at the same time, he had no idea.

"I highly suggest you keep your smart-ass

comments about me being all gussied up to yourself."

His gaze dropped to the sandals again, just to make sure he hadn't imagined them.

They were flat but lacked the support she always insisted upon—she sure as hell couldn't play sports in those things, and that was one of her footwear requirements. When his eyes reached hers again, she gave him a deadly look, half daring, half threatening.

Working to get things back to normal, he said, "Let me guess, or you'll introduce me to your right hook."

One corner of her mouth twisted up. "Nah, not for you."

He grinned, about to joke that he liked feeling special.

"You'd get my jab. Right to the nose."

He laughed full out, and then the brunette, who was apparently the leader of the group, cleared her throat. "We're on our way to the Magnolia House in Montgomery, and we've got reservations. How long is this going to take?"

"It's a broken water pump belt," Addie said. "Which means we're gonna need a tow truck."

The pretty brunette crossed her arms and turned to him. "Aren't you going to double-check to see if she's right?"

"Hell no. She just threatened to use her jab, and she throws a mean punch—trust me, I've been on the other end of one before. Besides, if Addie says that's what's wrong with the car, that's good enough for me."

Addie straightened a few inches—she'd always

struggled to feel confident around other women, as opposed to being a total ball-buster around the guys.

This was the first time he got a glimpse of why.

The short, dark-haired girl who had only blinked up until now started hyperventilating—or close to it. "But it was all planned, and it took so long to get a reservation there, and I'm so sorry, Lexi. This was supposed to be your special day and now it's ruined."

Tucker glanced at the curvy platinum blonde wearing the red dress, glad he hadn't checked her out, although she was definitely pretty. Just not his type. "You're Lexi? As in Shep's fiancée?"

"Right. I guess it's on me to make introductions." Addie gathered her hair in one hand and pulled it over her shoulder, and the brusque, slightly irritated way she did it made him think she wanted it up in her usual ponytail. "Lexi, Tucker. Tucker, Lexi."

"It's so nice to meet you!" Lexi surprised him with a hug. "I've heard so much about you that I feel like I know you already."

She introduced him to Melanie and Brittany, the one he was currently debating whether or not to ask for her number.

He probably should so he could scrub the memory of Addie's legs out of his mind and replace them with another set.

But his thoughts returned to being back home and his jobless situation, and it wasn't like he wouldn't have time later, what with her being part of the bridal party.

Besides, save Addie, the stress level seemed to be

growing by the second.

Tucker dug his keys out of his pocket and extended them to his buddy. He wouldn't trust many people with his vehicle, but they'd learned to drive together on the back roads of town, and she could pull a truck out of a tailspin like nobody's business.

Good thing, too, or the cop would've busted them for doing donuts in the parking lot of the formerly abandoned grocery store.

"Take my car," he offered. "I'll take care of this one."

"That would be amazing," Brittany said, her hand going to his arm again. "If we hurry, we can still make it." She gave him a flirty smile that made it clear any advances would be welcome, and then the three women headed toward his car.

"Are you sure?" Addie spun the keys around her finger, the jingle filling the air. "You know how long it takes to get Ray out here."

"I'm sure. You go. This way I get to save the day."

"Oh, sure. *I* crawl under the hood while wearing a stupid dress, but *you're* the hero."

"Speaking of, you've got…" Tucker plucked leaves out of her hair and then tugged on the ends. "I don't think I've seen you without a ponytail or bun in decades."

"What I'm hearing is, you want to be reintroduced to my jab."

"I'm just saying, you look…nice." Putting that out there felt weird, and now he thought he should've just let it go. The dress was still throwing him off.

He longed for that ugly-ass Falcons sweatshirt.

She smoothed a hand down her hair and tugged at the hem of the skirt, clearly uncomfortable. "My sister forced me into her dress. She's responsible for the hair, too. Luckily I was running late enough that the only makeup she could force on me was a swipe of mascara. I feel ridiculous, and we're going to this frou-frou restaurant, and I just don't fit in."

The loud honk of a horn made her jump, and she daggered a glare at the car.

"And now I might kill the tall, Type A one. Do you think Lexi will care if I downsize her bridal party?"

He chuckled and clapped her on the back. "I have faith in you."

"That I can take her out?"

"That you can make it one night out without offing her. Especially since I was kind of hoping you'd put in a good word for me."

Addie rolled her eyes. "You want me to pass her a check yes or no note, you girl?"

"You threaten me, but then you go and insult me like that, and I have no choice but to point out that *you're* the one wearing the dress. You girl," he couldn't help but add, even though he should've resisted.

The whole point in mentioning Brittany was to help him forget about Addie's legs and redirect his thoughts to the tall brunette. Who also had nice legs. He thought, anyway.

Right now, he couldn't exactly recall.

Addie blew out her breath. "Okay, fine on the no-killing thing. You can pass your own damn love notes, though. So are you in town for a bit, or—"

The horn honked again and she curled her fists.

"We'll talk later. You better go. Just one more thing…" He hesitated, but wouldn't it make him a jerk if he let her go to a fancy restaurant with dirt on her cheek?

He used his thumb to wipe at the smudge.

She batted his hand away, scowling at him like he'd lost his mind, and took over rubbing the spot. "I'm a mess." She shrugged. "What else is new? Anyway, talk later."

"Later."

When she turned to go, he noticed the dirt on her butt, even as he fought against focusing on the shape of it. That dress definitely needed to be baggier.

"You might want to also, uh, brush off your butt. Need help?" he asked before he thought better of it. That'd be weird as hell, mostly because he was thinking too much about it now.

He'd never offered to brush dirt off any of his friends' asses before, and he sure as hell didn't plan to ever again. Why did everything feel off today?

Oh, probably because you have no idea what you're doing with your life and Murph's walking around in a dress. It made him feel like he'd come back to some alternate universe.

That's it. I'm not in Uncertainty. I'm in Bizarro World.

CHAPTER THREE

Addie kicked off her sandals the second she stepped inside the door. She jumped when she turned and came face-to-face with Nonna Lucia, who was dressed in all black, a gardening spade in one hand, a six-pack of flowers in the other.

"Nonna, what in Sam Hill are you doing?" Earlier today she'd called to say her new meds made her woozy, which was why Addie had come over to check on her. Now she was wielding a weapon, a dark knitted cap masking her gray and white curls.

"The neighbors put wood chips in their yard."

"And…?"

Nonna made a sour face. "They're ugly and I don't like looking at them. Every time I sit on the porch in my rocking chair, it's all I can see." She lifted the flowers a few inches. "I going to plant these and give the yard some color. I sneak over and water them when I can."

Addie pinched the bridge of her nose, wondering how she was going to talk her stubborn Italian grandmother out of this one.

So far she was, like, zero for twenty on talking Nonna out of things she'd set her mind on, and she was extra crazy about gardening.

"You're gonna get the cops called on you," she warned.

"Not if I have a lookout…" Nonna eyed her in a way that meant she'd chosen her partner in crime.

Between the bridal shower at the fancy restaurant and the drinks that'd followed—lucky her, she was the DD and couldn't numb the sense of not belonging with alcohol—she was done with tonight.

Honestly, she'd mostly dropped by to get her yoga pants, because the rest of hers were dirty.

She was also hoping to sneak the dress she had on to Nonna, who was a miracle worker when it came to stains. She prayed OxiClean (something she was out of at home, big surprise) and a simple wash would make the fact that she'd climbed under a car earlier undetectable.

What with needing a favor and the determined set of her grandmother's jaw, Addie didn't have a lot of options. "Let me change real quick and grab my hat. If we get caught, I'm so telling everyone it was your idea."

Nonna Lucia beamed at her, obviously pleased with getting her way, even though it couldn't have come as a surprise, considering how often Addie caved to her. "Grab the extra flowers on the back porch, too, love. I was afraid I have to make two trips."

When Addie came back downstairs, T-shirt and her comfy, rediscovered overalls on and her ponytail threaded through her baseball cap, she heard voices. As she stepped into the entryway, she saw Nonna greet Tucker in her typical Italian fashion, one kiss to his cheek. Sometimes Addie got three or four.

When Nonna first moved in with them after Addie's paternal grandfather died, it took people in town a while to get used to it—that and her accent, which several people mistakenly assumed was

German—but now they all happily provided their cheeks, just like Tucker did.

His hair was longer than it'd been all those months ago when Shep announced his engagement, and he hadn't bothered slicking it into place. His face was scruffy, too.

When he'd stopped to help with their car trouble situation, she'd been extra self-conscious about being in a dress, too focused on herself to notice, but something was definitely up with him.

"Hey," she said.

"Why you no tell me he was moving back to town?" Nonna asked, aiming the question her way.

Addie looked at him, her spidey senses going into overdrive. "You're moving back?"

"I am. I saw my car was here and thought I'd come give you the news, but your grandma got it out of me first. She started scolding me for leaving in the first place and I caved."

"Caving in to her demands is going around." Addie placed her hand on her grandma's shoulder. "Nonna, maybe we can plant flowers another time?"

Right now, she wanted to find out what was going on with Tucker.

Nonna adamantly shook her head. "No. They out of town right now, so it's our only chance."

While Addie had tried to keep her words on the legal deniability side of the line, clearly her grandmother didn't practice the same caution.

"You're doing what now?" Tucker asked, one eyebrow arching as he glanced at Addison—she quickly feigned innocence.

"You're a lawyer now, right?" Nonna asked, and

he gave a noncommittal head-wobble before saying he was.

"Addison and I are going to go plant flowers in our neighbors' ugly yard—it's unbearable, all those bland woodchips and no color."

Addie pressed her lips together to hold back her laughter. "This is what I do for fun since you left. Break the law with my grandmother. Trespassing tonight, then grand larceny tomorrow." She turned to her grandma. "Did we plan on knocking over the liquor store this Friday or the next?"

Tucker chuckled, and happiness warmed her insides.

It was good to hear that familiar laugh, the same one that usually preceded hijinks of their own. "Well, I'm not sure you should be telling me all this. Although you seem to be dressed for it. You went from imposter in a dress to farmer in a flash."

She stuck her tongue out at him. "Very funny. And for the record, I tried not to confess what we were up to, but Nonna's never been the best at secrets."

Addie nudged her with her elbow, and her grandmother's mouth dropped.

"It's not secrets. All this is attorney-client privilege."

Tucker shook his head and let out a long exhale. "I'm afraid that only applies if you pay me."

Nonna shifted her flowers to one hip, dug two dollars out of her pocket, and thrust them at Tucker. "Here's your retainer."

Now Tucker's mouth was the one that dropped.

He gaped at Nonna as if he had no idea what

to say or do, so Addie retrieved the purse she'd left near the door, pulled out the wad of ones she'd received for change after drinking a Coke, and then tucked two into the waistband of his jeans. "There's mine, since I'd hate for you to bail out my grandma and leave me to rot."

"Seems like you both have an excess of dollar bills laying around."

"They're for when we hit the strip club," Addie said with a wide grin. "Naturally."

Nonna turned red and clucked her tongue. "Addison Diana Murphy."

"Relax, Nonna. He knows *I* don't go to the strip club, but man are the rumors gonna fly about you."

He laughed again, and her grandmother reverted to muttering Italian swear words as she scolded them both. In the most loving way, of course.

Addie readjusted the flowers in her hands, since the plastic kept bending weird. "Now, if you'll excuse us, we best get to plantin'. I'd ask you along, but I'm afraid it'd be harder for our lawyer to get us out of jail from the back of a cop car."

Tucker snagged her overalls where they crossed in the back as she started past him, reminding her of the downside to the shoulder straps—he'd used that move in football and soccer games before and it drove her crazy. "Maybe I could get my car keys so I don't have to walk home?"

"Oh. Right." She handed him the flowers and retrieved his keys from her purse. "Thanks again for savin' the evening, although I would've been perfectly happy to skip the bridal shower."

"How was the hoity-toity restaurant, by the

way? Did you scare off all the preppy gentlemen, or did you actually let a few of 'em hit on you before putting the fear of God in them?"

Nonna paused. "Oh, I'd like to hear the answer to this one, too. Although, aren't you dating the dentist?"

"You went on a date with Mr. Beasley?" Tucker asked, judgy-edged bafflement clear in his tone.

The face of the sixty-five-year-old grandfather type who'd filled one of her cavities flashed to mind. *"Ew. No."*

"There's a new dentist in town," Nonna happily provided. "Young. Handsome. Total eligible-bachelor type."

"Listen up, gossip girls, my dating life is neither of your business." That didn't sound right. "Businesses?" Nope, that wasn't it, either. "Whatever, you know what I mean."

Besides, in order for her to tell them, *she'd* have to know what was going on with the dentist, and she hadn't a clue.

"As for the restaurant, I will say the food was good, even if they were super chintzy when it came to serving size. And that's all I'll say."

Tucker held up his hands in retreat. "Fair enough, fair enough. Hey, so between all your criminal activities over the next few days, give me a call when you get the chance."

"Sure." It killed her to not pry out the truth right here and now, and she opened her mouth to fish for at least a clue, but Nonna spoke up first.

"I love you two, I do, but I'm an old woman who needs her beauty sleep."

Which was naturally why they were sneaking out to plant flowers at eleven at night.

Addison took back the pack of seedlings. "I'll call you soon so you can catch me up on your life and make some plans for after you break me out of the slammer."

"Sounds good," he said, and he even escorted them outside. Then he climbed into his car while she and her grandmother snuck across to the neighbors' yard and planted a mix of pansies and petunias.

As you do.

• • •

Tucker felt like a bit of a stalker waiting in his car, but people in town felt very strongly about their second amendment rights, and he wanted to make sure Addie and her grandmother returned home safely.

He doubted anyone would threaten them once they saw what they were actually doing, plus Addie was good at stretching the truth on the spot.

They'd had lots of practice, after all.

Like the time he'd seen one of Principal Pike's "casual Friday" Hawaiian shirts on the clothesline and had the bright idea to borrow it and make a scarecrow version to display during homecoming week.

When they'd been caught by the next-door neighbor, Addie spun an explanation about spotting a hole in the shirt, and how her mama was good at patching and they wanted it to be a surprise. The woman bought it hook, line, and sinker (in her defense, she had been new in town and therefore, not yet aware of their reputation), not even bothering to get their names before they'd turned tail and fled.

Man, the girl could talk her way out of almost any situation—sometimes he'd thought *she* would've made the better lawyer.

With that in mind, he wondered what he was still doing playing lookout. If anyone did threaten to call the cops, Addie could always hit up Easton for help. But what with his being on retainer, Tucker figured he might as well make sure tonight's hijinks stayed in the solely ridiculous category.

Plus, he'd landed her in trouble enough times to feel like he owed her.

While his logical side knew they'd had to grow up eventually, he'd missed the way she was always down for an adventure.

These days, he felt a lot less adventurous.

Even this thing with his job felt more like jumping off a cliff with no parachute.

And there it was. The other reason he was sitting here, delaying the inevitable.

He could still see the shock on the partners' faces as he turned in his two-week notice. Could feel it echoed in his chest, even as he'd tried to hide it.

They'd offered him more pay.

He'd wondered if he'd been stupid to turn it down.

Strike that past-tense version—he *still* wondered.

Still fought the urge to tug on that cord and see if the parachute would catch him before he hit the ground.

Between his parents' divorce, his mom moving in with a congressman before it was even finalized, and the foreclosure, Tucker had seen how the stress turned his father into a different man. After experiencing the awful instability, Tucker had sworn he'd do whatever it took not to have that threat of losing everything constantly hanging over him.

Yet here he was doing the exact opposite.

One of the reasons he hadn't told any of his friends about quitting his job was because that'd make it real. He'd just let go of his best chance at being secure, financially and career-wise, and… He tugged at the collar of his shirt, his heart beating double-time.

What the hell was I thinking?

That was easy. Every thought had circled back to the night in the houseboat.

Tucker had tried the city thing for two long, hard years. Tried being a lawyer and having the type of high-paying career Dad had always encouraged him to have. He'd made good money and hated every second of it.

The lake called to him. Small-town life called to him.

He'd missed his friends and the ability to go to Addie for advice. If anything, talking to her on the phone only made her—and the old life he'd longed to return to—feel further away.

While he'd done his best to keep up with the gang over the past few years, he hated that he'd become so unreliable for the people who'd always been there for him, no matter what.

All it took was one night playing poker and he

couldn't stop thinking about returning home, where he belonged.

Life was too short to be miserable.

It was also too short to move back, screw everything up, and live with regrets.

Which was why he would give himself one more minute to think of Addie's legs in that dress, and then he'd shift back into friendly territory and her in those baggy overalls.

Where his thoughts were definitely going to stay.

CHAPTER FOUR

"Addison will know."

Her spine straightened as she heard her name coming from the lips of the biggest gossip in town. She wondered what she was supposed to know, since usually she tried to avoid knowing things—knowing things landed you smack-dab in the middle of drama.

Not to mention she was kind of busy prepping for the soccer match she'd be coaching momentarily, one of the highlights of her week.

Lottie and her group of other baby boomers and middle-aged mothers left the fold-out chairs they'd set up on the grassy sidelines of the soccer field, and as they approached, Addie wondered if playing possum would work. Just flop to the ground, stick out her tongue, and hope the group of women would give up.

Experience told her Lottie didn't care about an inconsequential thing like whether or not someone was dead or alive when it came to gleaning gossip.

So Addie plastered on a smile as she turned to face the question-firing squad, otherwise known as the Craft Cats, since they liked to scrapbook, quilt, and do a variety of other crafts as they plucked items from the grapevine. They also had a fondness for felines. Or maybe just for wearing cat-themed clothes.

Lottie peered down her sunglasses at Addie.

"What did Tucker do to get fired from his big fancy lawyer job?"

"Fired? I doubt he got fired."

"You don't *know*?" she asked, all incredulous-like, and the need to defend herself rose, which was absurd. Regardless of what the Craft Cats thought, it was okay not to know everyone's business.

Addie tucked a soccer ball under her arm. "He just got into town." *Like day before yesterday, dudes*

Lottie pursed her lips, disappointment bleeding into her features. "Hmm. I thought you two were close."

The thing about this particular group of ladies was the way they could lob implications and casually insult you, their sugary-sweet smiles never leaving their lips.

Of course they probably had no clue how badly those words would sting, and they shouldn't. She and Tucker might not be as close as they used to be—and no, he hadn't told her he was moving back—but he'd let her borrow his car, no questions asked, come over to give her the news about the move, and promised to represent her and her grandma if they got busted.

That was what counted. They were still friends, the kind that remained unshaken by time apart.

"Close enough that when you two put a baseball through the window of my craft store, you then tried to tape it up, like I wouldn't notice. Thick as thieves, and equally as mischievous."

And this was why Addie occasionally entertained the idea of moving away.

Sure, she'd miss her family and the community,

nosy or not. But they could recite every bad thing she'd done since birth.

Yes, she and Tucker had tried to tape together the *cracked* window that the baseball didn't go through but simply slammed into. In their defense, they'd been in fourth grade and Lottie was one of the scariest ladies in town. Addie still had a scar on her palm from when the pane had given way and sliced her skin.

That was when the crack had turned into total glass annihilation.

When the blood pooled in her palm and dripped onto the ground, Tucker took off his shirt and wrapped her hand in it. Then she'd been embarrassed on two fronts—he'd been shirtless, and he'd had to take care of her, and she was perfectly capable of taking care of herself!

Lottie had shown up about then. She'd *tsk*ed and made a comment about manners unbecoming of a lady, but failed to remark on Tucker's behavior, because "boys will be boys."

Their parents were called, and they'd had to do Lottie's yard work all summer to pay for the window. The labor was nothing.

The constant remarks about how she couldn't believe Priscilla Murphy let her daughter run around with such a ragtag group of boys had been the real torture.

"Do you at least know what he plans to do?" Virginia, one of the town councilmembers, asked. "Is he setting up a law firm here? If so, he needs to meet with the board. Certain permits are required, and I hate to be the bearer of bad news, but there aren't any open office spots right now."

Virginia was married to one of the two lawyers in town, so obviously she didn't want Tucker to open an office and put a dent in her husband's business.

The lawyer who'd moved into town about three or four months ago had already done significant damage, in spite of his rep as an asshole who treated you like crap while he took your money. He won a lot of cases, so some people thought it was almost worth dealing with his shitty temperament. He had clients throughout the county, too, which meant out-of-towners coming in and spending money in Uncertainty's shops.

"Or is it just temporary, until he finds another job and heads off to the city again?" Nellie Mae asked.

With the sharks circling, you would've thought Addie had cut her hand again. Apparently they smelled blood anyway.

This week they wanted information about Tucker; last week they'd wanted to know what had happened with the nice new dentist. (One date three weekends ago that everyone somehow managed to crash, what with it being at Mulberry & Maine, the one linen-tablecloth restaurant in town, followed by radio silence. Not that she'd given them that information. Regardless of how many times she'd made it clear she was never going to change, they'd never let up with the "unladylike" comments, and she hadn't wanted to hear "I told you so.")

The sounds of van doors sliding open and girls shrieking as they ran toward the field filtered through—saved by a group of rambunctious, easily distracted eight-year-old girls. "I'm afraid I don't have time for gossip." Addie bounced the ball on her knee and caught it. "I have a game to coach."

"Doesn't the dentist's niece play on your team?" Lottie asked, as if she didn't already know.

Addie backpedaled, trying not to think about the dentist's possible attendance, because she didn't know how she felt about him besides slightly rejected. "Yes, I would love if you all cheered extra loud for us! Thanks for offering!"

Her team barreled into her as soon as she turned around, and as they enthusiastically hugged her, she remembered why her daydreams of moving away were only that.

There was too much here she'd miss, and she couldn't imagine living anywhere else, her history of being an unladylike ruffian be damned.

• • •

Addie was turning out to be ridiculously difficult to pin down.

Whoa. Maybe let's not put it that way. No pinning down. No…just no.

It was like ever since he'd seen her underneath the hood of that car, his thoughts were no longer safe.

Since she'd refused to give the tall bridesmaid his number, he'd have to ask Shep to hook him up. Then he could work on ending his recent drought and everything would return to normal. Or at least his new normal.

He'd spent most of yesterday moving into the houseboat, and by the time Sunday afternoon came around, he went in search of food that didn't come from a box or can. He'd run into Addie's mom at the diner, and after exchanging pleasantries, Mrs. Murphy informed him Addie's soccer game had just started, so he'd driven to the field.

He hadn't known that Uncertainty ran adult soccer leagues, and when he arrived, he saw that they didn't.

Parents and several of the who's who in town sat on blankets and lawn chairs, watching the kids running around the field. It took him a few minutes to find Addie's brown ponytail in the crowd.

He smugly put on his battered Saints cap, bailed out of his truck, and made his way to the less cramped end of the sidelines.

Addie gathered her team in for a huddle and gestured wildly with her arms, the same way she used to give him and the guys instructions on the sidelines. They'd all fought to let her play on the boys' teams growing up, and it'd worked up until high school when the town and school had drawn the line.

Tucker never had any doubts whatsoever about her athletic ability, whether it be football, baseball, soccer, or basketball. He knew she'd be an asset to whatever team she played for, and while he'd never admit it to her face—he happened to like breathing, non-broken limbs, and not having her pissed at him—that was around the time he'd started to worry she might get hurt.

Simply because while he and the guys had shot up and begun to fill out, she'd remained scrawny. Then he and the boys would've been obligated to retaliate, and it would've gotten ugly, no doubt about it.

She absolutely *hated* when they treated her like a girl, something he was probably the guiltiest of growing up. Since so many people talked down to her, forever telling her she should be more like her sister, or act more like a girl, or be more of some stupid shit or the other, he'd always felt compelled to defend and protect her.

Even as she proved time and time again that she didn't need it.

And thank God she'd never listened to those people, because if she had, he'd be missing half of his best childhood memories.

The soccer game burst into action, kids running everywhere—including toward the opposite side of the field where the ball went. Parents yelled and cheered and Addie hugged a clipboard to her chest as she leaned one way and then the other, as if that'd help her team do the same.

The setting sun lit up the strands that'd escaped her ponytail and highlighted her makeup-free face. She had on a team shirt and soccer shorts, and he couldn't help taking a quick glance at her legs, toned from all her years of sports.

Just a matter of fact, kind of like how she'd commented about him being more "jacked" at the houseboat. In his case, he'd been using exercise in an attempt to quash the restless sensation that wouldn't leave him alone.

Although clearly that hadn't worked.

Addie bent to talk to one of her players, and while he noticed the curve of her butt more than he should've, the guy standing a few yards behind her unashamedly gawked at it.

A burning sensation he didn't want to examine too closely bit at his gut. She was coaching a kids' soccer game. Dude needed to keep his eyes to himself.

Hypocritical? For sure, but he didn't give a shit.

She'd always attracted assholes who couldn't handle her, and this prick fit that category, he could just tell. His stupid ass smirk also made it clear he was the type who dripped false charm and used it on every lady in his path.

Tucker moved closer, putting himself between Addie and the guy's line of sight, barely resisting the urge to glare at him.

Addie did a double take when she glanced his way, and she flashed him a quick smile and waved before returning her focus to the game.

Take that, chump. She waved at me.

Unfortunately, the dude didn't seem deterred. He just shifted left so he could continue ogling Addie as she coached the rest of the game.

She really was an amazing coach, one they could've used when they were kids—good thing she'd just jumped in and took over the position anyway.

Her team won by two, and since his attention was on the celebration in the center of the field, he didn't notice Uncertainty's gossip queen approaching until she was right on him.

"Tucker Crawford," Lottie said, practically rubbing her hands together. "I heard you were back."

"Looks like some things never change—word travels as fast as ever."

"Even faster with wifi hot spots and everyone and their smartphones." It sounded more like a threat than a fact. "So that big-city law firm didn't work out?"

"Nope." Remaining vague meant more digging, but Lottie was one of the main women who'd blathered nonstop about his parents when they were going through their divorce. She'd also implied that Mom had moved on *before* the split, and the women had turned on his mom just like that.

The last thing he would do was give Lottie any morsels to stretch and spread. He planned on keeping mum to everyone except his closest friends till he got his shit together.

Until then, let the town talk. He didn't care.

Tucker noticed the guy who'd been checking out Addie the entire time had stayed on the sidelines, his gaze still following her too closely. For once the fact that Lottie stuck her nose in everyone's business might actually come in handy. "Who's the new guy?"

"You are now," Lottie said, and he shot her a look. "That's the new dentist, David Nelson. Moved into town a couple months ago with his brother and fixed up the old practice. Nice guy."

The information tickled something in his memory, and after a couple of seconds, he put together why. Addie's grandma had mentioned "the dentist."

"His niece is on the team, and since her father is recently widowed, he helps out. Oh, and he and

Addison went on a date a few weeks back."

Of course they did.

While he might be too late to warn her the dude was a tool *before* she went out with him, he'd definitely be keeping a close eye on him.

Seriously, she had the worst taste in guys. Since the dentist was apparently so damn nice, it made it a bit harder to play dirty—not that he was going to do that or there was any reason to.

Yet.

The expression Lottie aimed his way held a hint of glee, making him worry his feelings were on display. "So, are you plannin' to open a law firm here or just look for jobs nearby? Exactly how long do you plan on being in town?"

"Long enough," he said, and Lottie opened her mouth, but then Addie showed up next to him.

"Hey, I really need to talk to you. Right before the game, Lottie was pointing out how close we are, so I know she'll understand if I steal you away."

Addie clamped on to his arm and tugged him away, and he happily went.

"You saved me."

"Someone's gotta do it. Unfortunately, you weren't around when I needed savin' from her earlier. She had her lackeys with her, too." Addie gave a mock shudder.

He placed a hand on her shoulder and gave it a light squeeze. "Sorry about that. I'm tryin' to fix it, I swear."

The corner of her mouth kicked up, but before she could say anything, the dentist came over, hand in hand with his niece—anyway, Tucker assumed.

"Thanks again, Addison."

Addison. Tucker hated the way he used her name, way too intimate.

And last he knew, she never went by her full name. Her mother and the older ladies in town were the only ones who used it, and they wielded it almost like a weapon to remind her that she was a girl.

"Of course. Great game, Sara. That fake you pulled off before scoring that final goal was amazing." Addie held out her hand for a high five and Sara slapped it, a toothy grin spreading across her face.

When the dentist drifted closer to Addie, Tucker planted his hand on her lower back. He'd done it on impulse, and Addie glanced at him.

"Oh, I'm forgettin' my manners. Tucker, David, the new dentist. David, Tucker Crawford. He and I went to high school together, and he just moved back into town, although if any of the gossips ask, I don't know for how long, and even if I did, they'd have to pry it from me."

David laughed, and Tucker wanted to, but he was too busy being annoyed at the way the dentist was still looking at his Addie. It was all lust-fueled fake charm, and it reminded him of the guy she'd dated senior year. The one who'd broken her heart.

It was one of the few times he'd ever seen her cry, and he'd felt totally helpless.

Forget being above playing dirty.

People needed to learn that the real world could be tough, small town or not. Especially if that person was trying to take advantage of his best friend.

"I'm sticking around for a while," Tucker said, nice and firm, for both their sakes.

Sara tugged on her uncle's arm—she could tug a little harder in Tucker's opinion—and at long last, he started away from them. But not before shooting Addie one more smile and saying, "I'll call you so we can set up a time for Saturday night."

Addie's cheeks colored, more embarrassment than attraction, he hoped, but he couldn't tell.

He used to be able to read her better, and he hated that he'd lost the key somewhere along the way.

Finally, most everyone had cleared the field, the fold-up chairs and blankets gone from the sidelines. Tucker helped Addie gather the supplies and put them in the back of her truck.

She glanced up at him, shook her head, and then tapped the bill of his hat. "Seriously, that thing needs to be put out of its misery."

"I'll give it up just as soon as you give up your Falcons sweatshirt."

"You'll have to pry it from my cold, dead fingers. I'd put it on just to spite you if it wasn't so freaking hot this afternoon."

He sort of wished she would.

The bulky hoodie helped her stay in the ambiguous category she belonged in. Probably wouldn't cover those legs, though.

Stop thinking about her legs.

He pulled a soccer ball out of the bag and bounced it on his knee. "Have time for a quick game?" He bounced it on his knee again, and she swiped it out of the air.

That challenging gleam lit her eyes, the familiar one that meant they were about to have a whole lot of fun. "Against the guy who's sat in an office the past few years getting soft and out of shape? Hell, yeah."

Maybe he hadn't lost the key after all.

CHAPTER FIVE

"This is so, so much cheatin'!" Addie kicked her feet, but since Tucker had lifted her off the ground, it didn't propel her toward the goal, and the ball was out of reach as well.

"You called me soft," he said, kicking at the ball and nearly dropping her.

She clung on to the forearm clamped around her midsection, and between the muscles there and the firm planes of his chest pressing against her back, there was no softness to be found.

"Okay, so you're not soft, just a giant cheater." She elbowed him in the gut, satisfied at the grunt he let out.

His arm loosened a mere fraction, enough for her to duck out of his grip and kick the ball. She raced for the goal, her heartbeats right on top of each other, and went to kick it home.

Dang Tucker got in the way—he was even faster than she remembered—and they devolved into a shoving and tripping match that would have any ref calling them for fouls, and possibly even tossing them out for misconduct.

Using every ounce of strength she had, she shoved him again and kicked the ball. He dove to block, and she dove on top of him to block *his* block. They hit the grass hard, a pile of tangled limbs.

She groaned. "This didn't hurt as much when we were kids."

"Who's soft now?" he asked, but his ragged breaths made it clear he was as tired as she was.

She noticed the ball had landed just short of the goal line and, not one to lose, she launched herself over Tucker's prone form and bumped it with her fist.

Tucker wrapped his hand around her upper arm, but he was too late.

The ball rolled over the white line and she let out a whoop of victory.

Now that she'd scored, her exhaustion hit her all at once, and she let her body go limp.

For two whole seconds before realizing she was straddling Tucker's chest and his face was buried between her boobs.

Face flaming, she quickly rolled off him, glad the setting sun left them in semi-darkness. She waited to see if he'd comment—hoping he wouldn't.

Even though he'd been the first guy close to her boobs in a very, very long time.

Let's not go down another embarrassing path just to get away from this one.

Besides, she had date number two with the dentist, which she supposed meant she should start referring to him by name, and fingers crossed, maybe her dry spell would end. *Oh holy crap, it's been so long, I think I've forgotten how to even be intimate with a man.*

Not that she'd ever really rocked at relationships and everything they entailed.

Her awkwardness surged forward on dates, all the unsolicited advice she'd received through the years choosing then to mess with her head.

She wasn't a total novice, though. Just out of practice.

After what seemed like a blink of an eye *and* forever, Tucker shifted to his side and propped his head on his fist. "I'd like to challenge you to a rematch, but I think I need a week or so to recover."

"How handy for me. I just so happen to be here every week."

"Because you coach soccer. How didn't I know that?"

"I guess it doesn't come up a lot in conversation, 'specially since we haven't had much chance for that lately. I love it, though."

"You're good at it."

"Thanks." She rolled onto her side to face him. "So, you're back in town, for quote, *a while.* Care to give me more details? I promise to keep them close to the chest"—a weird beat passed as she remembered how close he'd recently been to her chest and she quickly plowed on with the rest of her sentence—"I mean, I won't reveal them to anyone. Even if Lottie employs waterboarding. I've got a cyanide capsule in a false tooth and everything."

"Wow. That's a lot of dedication to information she'll just pry out of someone else."

Addie shrugged. "I'd rather go out honorably than rat out my friends."

Tucker sat up and raked a hand through his hair, sending a couple of the waves off in different directions. "It'll be longer than a while, actually. I needed a break from the lawyer thing, and I'm not plannin' on going back."

"Rumor has it you were fired." She doubted it

was true but withheld saying so in case it ended up being accurate.

He laughed, the sound on the mirthless side. "I'm sure they think that. Screwup Crawford couldn't make it in the big city." He ran his fingers along his jaw. "Maybe they were right about that, but I wasn't fired. I quit. The crazy hours and the fact that my job consumed my entire life just didn't seem worth it anymore."

Addie pushed to a seated position and scratched the spot on her leg the grass kept tickling. "I could see that. Honestly, it always was hard for me to picture you behind a desk."

"Trust me, I made it work."

Sputtered laughter escaped her lips. "Humility was never one of your crosses to bear."

His grin widened and then faded a little as his blue eyes met hers. "I also hated that my job made me a liar so often."

She tucked up a knee and looped her arms over it. "Probably a might shortsighted on your part," she teased, "considering all those liar/lawyer jokes."

Tucker pinched her side, and a strange tug pulled in her gut, throwing her off for a second.

A fraction of a second, really.

"I mean how it made me a liar when I told you I could make it home for things," he clarified. "Or that I'd call."

"I get it," she said, shrugging it off, the way she'd tried to when it'd happened and disappointment set in.

"You shouldn't *have* to get it."

The two years they'd spent apart melted away,

and just like that, things realigned. It was as if something she hadn't even realized was broken was fixed.

The rest of the guys would drop whatever they were doing if she needed help, but it never went as smoothly as when she turned to Tucker and he somehow knew exactly what to say. Or what to do to take her mind off everything.

Back in high school, she'd often been left behind in the name of pursuing girls, and while Tucker had done plenty of that—and a fair amount pursued him, too—he'd always made sure she wasn't stranded after a ball game or at a party.

Still, she'd missed out on a few big things like senior prom. Her boys had dates, and thanks to always hanging out with them, she hadn't made other friends and had recently broken up with her boyfriend at the time.

Occasionally she regretted missing out on rites of passage, dress-wearing and heels, notwithstanding.

But that was neither here nor there.

A truck with a growly engine approached, and she recognized the black Dodge Ram with its massive grill, roll bar, and lights. Ford was ridiculously proud of his "badass truck," but considering he was a firefighter who pulled double duty on the Talladega Search and Rescue team, it was also a necessity.

Where most people ran from trouble, he ran toward it.

Ford opened the door and stood on the frame. "There you guys are. Remember how we're supposed to meet Shep and his fiancée at the Old

Firehouse ten minutes ago to watch the game?"

"Oh, shit." Addie looked for her phone so she could check the time, but it was tucked into her duffel bag in her truck. Once Tucker had issued the soccer challenge, she'd forgotten about everything else.

The light bulb over Tucker's head remained unlit. "We had plans to watch the game with them?"

"Well, the rest of us did. You would've gotten an invite had we known you were moving back."

"Good, because watching football without you guys isn't nearly as fun." He hopped to his feet and extended a hand.

Addie finger-combed her ponytail, trying to dislodge as much grass as she could. "Crap, do I look okay?"

It popped out before she'd thought better of it. Years of being told she needed to look and act more like a girl if she ever wanted to snag a man, and the brainwashing had chosen now of all times to kick in.

"Never mind. We're just going to the bar, duh."

She wasn't sure what to make of Tucker's crooked grin. "You look great," he said, and it warmed her from the inside out, even though she told herself she'd asked, and he'd simply answered a question. The "you look like you," he added left her wondering what exactly that meant.

Of course she looked like herself.

When she caught her reflection in the window of Ford's truck, she decided that for all Tucker's talk about not liking having to lie, he was a big fat liar. The *last* word she'd use to describe the girl in the reflection with the grass-stained clothes and lopsided ponytail was "great."

Not that she cared.

She used to not care.

She'd always been comfortable with who she was, but lately she didn't feel feminine enough, or attractive enough, or a whole mess of other things she didn't want to examine.

And she couldn't help noticing that while she looked like a dirty mess, Tucker looked sporty and sexily disheveled.

Guys took so little effort, which was supremely unfair.

Lately she'd had to deal with the possibility of seeing the dentist everywhere, which made her feel even more self-conscious. She wasn't even sure how she felt about David besides the general hallelujah, a single man her age actually moved into Uncertainty, and this might be her only chance to date in who knows how long.

No pressure or anything.

It'd sure be nice to fill my life with more than long days at work where my boss slowly drives me insane, followed by quiet nights spent mostly alone, only to get up and head to work again.

The plastic of the bench seat gripped her thighs as she scooted to the middle, Ford on one side, Tucker on the other. She used to complain about always having to sit bitch, but at one point, they grew taller and filled out, and then she was the only one who fit in the middle, so she dealt with it.

"Dude, it smells like ass in here," Tucker said.

"Piece of ass, actually," Ford replied. "You probably don't recognize it, because of your lack of game. I can give you some tips if you'd like."

"Like I need tips from a guy who thought it'd be romantic to take the hottest girl in school hunting for nightcrawlers."

Ford shifted the truck into reverse. "That was just the excuse to get Daisy Price out under the stars. Course, I was goin' fishin' the next day, so I call it a fine bit of multitasking."

Back in the day, Addie had to hear how hot Daisy Price was so often that the name still made her eye twitch.

They'd all made stupid bets about who'd get her to go out with him first and then attempted to sabotage one another.

"And I got to second base before the can of dirt fell over and the worms wiggled out and into her shorts," Ford continued. "I also got to fish 'em out while she was screaming my name—see, that's what women do when they're satisfied."

"Oh, I know." Tucker grabbed the bar over the window. "Your mom's quite the screamer."

Ford knocked into her as he slugged Tucker's shoulder, and Tucker laughed and backhanded him while she shielded herself from friendly fire.

"And the award for maturity goes to Crawford and his *your mom* jokes," she said, rolling her eyes, although she found comfort in the automatic back and forth, untouched by time apart.

As they turned down Main Street, still exchanging verbal jabs, an overwhelming sense of nostalgia hit her.

Add Shep and Easton crammed in the back or driving behind them in Shep's truck, and it was high school all over again.

The guys had liked her for her back then, and they liked her for her now.

So while she was a pinch worried that Lexi would take one glimpse of her tonight and regret her decision to let her be a groomsman, she could only imagine the odd looks she'd get from Ford and Tucker if she requested a fifteen-minute stop at her house to freshen up.

Besides, the ship to make a good impression on Lexi had sailed already.

• • •

The Old Firehouse was exactly what it sounded like—a bar built from the old redbrick firehouse. There was a shiny pole that no one ever slid down, since they'd sealed off second floor access, but drunk chicks occasionally "jokingly" danced on, and they had cold beer and amazing wings and all things fried and artery destroying.

They also had two flat-screen TVs, which meant the game was visible from about everywhere, unless you arrived super late and got stuck in the far corner. With a cop and a firefighter in their crew, people were extra accommodating, so that hadn't happened in ages.

Being on the up and up of the legal side these days had its benefits.

Addie was three beers in when Lexi sidled up to her. There was a wild gleam in her eye that automatically set her nerves on edge.

"This is a list for how to plan a wedding in six

months." Lexi slid it toward her.

Addie glanced at the lengthy checklist, with its wedding bells decoration and hot pink swirly print. "It's nice."

"We're only two months out, and I still have four months of stuff to do. When we first became engaged, I mentioned hiring a wedding planner, and Will's mother acted like I'd demanded a throne of diamonds. 'Oh, honey,' she says to me, 'here we don't throw money away on weddin' planners. We save that so we don't start our new lives in a heap of debt, which also makes the marriages run more smoothly.'"

Honestly, it was a damn good impression of Shep's mother. Super sweet, albeit slightly judgmental, and 100 percent her way or the highway.

"Then she rattled off names in a whir. So and so always does the cakes, and another person caters, and apparently someone's son recently became a DJ, and of course we'd hire him, wouldn't we?"

"Josie's," Addie said. "And he's not bad. You just need to be super detailed with the playlist or he'll go rogue, and suddenly you've got 'Smells Like Teen Spirit' playing at the nursing home's summer bash, and half the attendees are having heart attacks—to be fair, only one of them was a literal heart attack, and it was mild and most likely not the music's fault. Allegedly."

"Oh, jeez." Lexi tapped her pen to her list. "She kept on going and going, Energizer-Bunny-style, and I just nodded, because she already thinks I'm too high maintenance. But I didn't write anything down and I'm scared to ask her again, and I'm starting to freak out."

Addie squinted at the list as if that'd help her decipher the madness.

Then the Falcons scored, and she jumped up to high-five the guys over the table—save Tucker, since he was cheering for the other team out of stubbornness.

He got a "Suck it, Crawford!" She grinned at Shep. "I told you our new tight end was hitting his stride."

"It's about time," Shep said, reaching for another wing.

"I need help." Lexi's voice sounded small in the noisy bar.

Addie turned, trying to piece her words together with what they'd been talking about before the touchdown.

Then it hit her. Surely she didn't mean…?

The blonde blinked big, flawlessly lined eyes that perfectly complemented the vintage floral dress she'd worn. She walked in five-inch heels like they were sneakers and somehow never managed to get wing sauce all over her fingers and face, whereas Addie's lips were burning from the fiery sauce, and she was sure her fingers would be orange for days.

This was why she knew she'd never truly impress Lexi, no matter how hard she tried.

"I need help planning this wedding," Lexi repeated.

"Oh, you've come to the wrong girl." As much as she liked Lexi, mostly because she clearly adored Shep and had been more accepting than most of her friends' girlfriends, Addie held no pretenses that she could be the wedding-planning friend a bride needed. Wasn't that what a maid of honor was for?

Before she could ask, Lexi sighed and hung her head. "I know."

Well, that was…comforting?

She jerked up her chin, eyes wide as if she'd realized how that came out. "I mean, I know it's not your thing. But Will loves this town, and I've come to love it and the people, too, enough to make it my future home. I don't want to offend someone by accidentally not including them, and while I've met most everyone, there are things I'm still unfamiliar with, and there's so much to do. And my friends and family live forty minutes away and are so busy with their lives. I'm not saying you're not busy, I'm just saying you're…"

"Here," Addie filled in.

She doubted Lexi would be asking any of the other groomsmen, and as she took them in, their fingers also covered in orange wing sauce, eyes glued to the TV, she wondered how she'd managed to be enough of a guy that no one considered her a girl, but not enough of one to get out of wedding planning.

The fact that Lexi was so nice, combined with rocking that impression of Mrs. Shepherd and the Energizer-Bunny joke, made it impossible to flat-out say no.

"Look, I can try to help and point you to the right people to talk to, but again, this is way out of my comfort zone."

"It's not so bad. It's mostly just legwork."

Addie glanced up and met Shep's gaze. He

mouthed "thank you" and she wasn't sure if he was in on it or simply thanking her for chatting with Lexi and trying to make her feel accepted.

She thought about the day she'd wrecked Dad's new four-wheeler into a fence post. Shep had snuck it into his father's shop and quickly fixed the dent so that no one besides the five of them would ever know.

She'd argue that Shep initiated the race that'd made her take the corner that fast, but she'd been at the wheel, unable to back down from a challenge as usual. It accounted for about 80 percent of why she'd landed herself in trouble. The guys sure used it to their advantage, just like she'd used the fact that Ford couldn't resist a bet to hers.

Speaking of… "Hey, McGuire? Care to make a wager on the outcome?"

"You already owe me for last week's game," Ford said.

Yeah, yeah. She'd called one game wrong in a long string of getting it mostly right.

The two of them had always had a competitive thing, and while they'd both been studying anatomy for their respective careers, they'd had a bet going about who could get a better grade. It'd made them work harder, and when they both earned A's, they'd celebrated. "Double or nothing?"

They negotiated the terms and she ordered another beer. Then she turned to Lexi, who still had stress hanging heavy in her features. "All right, I'll help. What do you need me to do?"

• • •

Tucker finished explaining to Easton, Shep, and Ford about how he'd quit his job. He told them he wasn't exactly sure what he was going to do yet, but he was done with city life, so the plan was to stay in Uncertainty.

"We could always use someone with a firm grasp of the law at the station," Easton said. "I know most of the guys who run the courthouse in Auburn, too. Just say the word and I'll poke around and see if I can't get you a job."

"You could work at the school," Shep said. "They need people. *I'm* on the school board, for hell's sake."

Tucker laughed. If you'd told him that one of the guys who'd frequently landed him in detention would be on the school board one day, he never would've believed it.

He glanced at Ford. For all his joking and light-hearted demeanor, when shit went bad, you wanted him by your side.

In addition to responding to medical emergency calls and fires, he trained the K-9 units. Not only for the local search and rescue team, who spent a lot of time rescuing hikers and hunters and occasionally went down south when hurricanes hit, but also most of Alabama's search and rescue teams. Which was pretty different from his original goal of becoming a professional stuntman in the movies.

All the same risks and then some, way less glory.

At one point, Tucker thought all it would take to be happy was to make a ton of money. Ever since he could remember, way before the divorce, his parents had constantly fought about money. Which was why he'd sworn he wouldn't settle down until he'd saved enough for a down payment on a house and had a decent chunk of change in a 401K.

He wanted something to live on for at least a year if life threw him a curve ball he couldn't hit.

But he hadn't saved nearly that amount, and now he'd undone what little progress he'd made on his financial goals.

His worries tightened his chest, along with the pressure to choose the right career and quickly.

One idea wouldn't leave him alone, and he figured it'd only take a few weeks to get it out of his system, even if it didn't end up being a solid lead. "I appreciate it, boys, but I've got somethin' else in the works. I just wanna see if it's gonna shake out before I go announcin' it to everyone."

He needed to figure out if it could be profitable before the town jumped in and told him why it wouldn't be and what he should be doing with his life instead.

"Dude, we got your back," Easton said. "Whatever you need, let us know."

The pressure in his chest eased a fraction.

"Tucker Crawford?" Someone hugged him over the back of the seat before he could crane his neck and get a good look at her.

Delilah, one of their former classmates and his girlfriend for most of senior year.

The irritation twisting Addie's features led him to believe her and Delilah's relationship was about the same as it had been back then.

Shortly before graduation, Delilah demanded he choose, her or Addie. It'd been a no-brainer.

While she'd pitched a giant hissy and screeched he was *the worst* during their dramatic hallway breakup, the kiss she dropped on his cheek now indicated he'd been forgiven.

Delilah's gaze flicked across the table. "Oh, hey, Addison. I admire how you always just wear whatever. It must be so nice not to worry about makeup, too. I'm not sure I could do that—but you do know that you have grass in your hair, right?"

Tucker opened his mouth to happily take the blame, but Lexi beat him to the punch. "You know, sometimes I think it's sad that no matter how much makeup people put on, it doesn't make their soul any prettier. Then again, it's always nice to spot those people right away."

Delilah reared back and did that sassy head-wobble thing. "Who the hell are you?"

"She's with me," Shep said, aiming a wink at Lexi. "She's my fiancée."

Delilah heaved a sigh. "Looks like this group hasn't changed a bit."

"That's what makes it so great," Addie said. "Now if you'll excuse us, we're watching the game, and your overly coiffed hair's getting in the way."

Tucker wanted to catch Addie's eye and make sure she was as okay as she put on—she'd always brushed off the slams on her lack of "girliness," but sometimes he thought they got to her the tiniest bit.

She quickly returned her attention to the paper in front of her and Lexi, though, and they continued whatever they'd been discussing before the interruption.

He'd already liked Shep's fiancée, but that

exchange solidified it.

She was one of them now.

As he looked around the table, Tucker realized how much he needed these guys. This here, being back with his friends—his family, really—was worth the stress over quitting his job and heading toward the unknown.

So when Addie jumped up to rub her team winning in his face, going so far as to celebrate with a booty shake, he ignored the hint of heat in his veins.

First her legs, now her ass. But seriously, had it always been that curvy?

Today on the field, he'd been briefly introduced to her other curves, too. She definitely wasn't on the scrawny side anymore.

Shut it down, Crawford.

If he didn't control his stray thoughts where Addie was concerned, it'd complicate things. She'd said the great thing about them was their group hadn't changed, and he agreed. He'd never risk screwing that up.

CHAPTER SIX

Tucker threw open the doors to the old shed, coughing and waving at the cloud of dust. He used to spend hours out here with his grandpa, who'd left the place and its contents to him in his will, along with the untamed two and a half acres of land it sat on.

Tucker worried Dad would be upset *he* hadn't inherited it, but Dad had told him there was nothing but junk in the shed anyway.

For years, Tucker hadn't thought much about the summers he'd spent working with his hands. But late one night, about two months back, he'd been gazing out over the city and missing home. He'd thought about those teenage years in this shed, doing the type of tiring labor that left you pleasantly exhausted by the end of the night.

Grandpa had built and restored boats as a side hobby that occasionally made money, and the one left in the shed was one he'd bought for himself, the idea that he and Tucker would fix it up that last summer before he left for college.

Only he'd passed away before they'd gotten the chance.

Right then, Tucker had resolved to fix up the dilapidated boat.

He hadn't realized how many years it would take him to get to it, and he'd definitely never thought of doing it as a sort of test run business idea.

He wasn't sure if it was a plausible career. But the other morning, as he'd been watching all the types of ships gliding over the glittering surface of Lake Jocassee, a plan had formulated.

There were tons of old boats in need of repair, and he had the skill set and tools. Anyway, he hoped he still did.

He wished Grandpa were around to give him advice. To tell him when he hadn't shaved down the wood enough or to stand across from him and admire his handiwork, even as Tucker wondered why he didn't jump in so they could get done sooner. Why he made him redo sections he'd deemed "good enough."

Now he appreciated that his grandfather had put in the time to teach him to do it himself, and to do it well.

Tucker surveyed the tools, noted which ones needed upgrading and which boat repairs to start with, and made a quick run into town. He asked Easton if he could borrow his truck, which was tricked out for fun, mud-bogging reasons, as well as the fact that he worked on the search and rescue team with Ford when needed. His friend let him borrow it, no questions asked, and as he drove the load of lumber, tools, and other supplies back down the bumpy road, he knew he'd made the right choice.

As nice as his Prius had been in the city, it was no match for these dirt back roads with their deep ruts and grooves. Not like he could've loaded the lumber into his car's trunk anyway.

I'm definitely gonna need to upgrade to a truck.

Which of course cost money, and his heart beat faster as he stressed over how much start-up cash a new business required.

Shoving that away to be worried over later, he unloaded the wood and pulled out the saw. Then he got to work, his thoughts on the day he'd be able to take the refurbished boat out on the lake.

He knew who he wanted to be in the boat with him for that first ride, too.

As friends, of course.

Then he could tell Addie his plan, and she'd give it to him straight and hopefully help him figure out how to do it. Since her fear of alligators was one of the few semigirly things about her, persuading her to go out on the water with him would be the hardest part.

Despite his spouted statistics and the many reassurances about the boat's safety features, it took years to convince her how fun the lake could be. He'd been *this close* to getting her to admit that fishing wasn't "totally boring" like she'd always claimed—mostly because she refused to admit to her fear of alligators—when he'd screwed it up.

His seventeen-year-old brain clearly hadn't been firing on all cylinders when he'd decided it would be funny to show her *Lake Placid*, an older horror movie about a giant gator.

After that, it took bribery and just about carrying her on board kicking and screaming to get her to go way out to the center of the lake.

His brain snagged on the kicking and screaming image too long.

How fun it'd be to throw her over his shoulder

and—and then put her down nicely in the boat. Yeah, that was it. Friends giving each other a hard time.

Just friends.

• • •

Tucker cut across the town square, glancing around for the familiar brown ponytail.

He'd put in a solid three days on the boat, and as he'd been forcing his stiff muscles to power through this afternoon, it felt like his arms were a hair from giving out. Now they were in the limp noodle range.

Addie had teased him about being out of shape after sitting behind a desk for so long, and while his gym sessions had kept him fit, he was feeling the burn.

There was just something different about manual labor, gym or not.

He'd been wanting an excuse to stop while telling himself he couldn't start his own business and make it successful by taking half a day off partway through the week when his phone had rung.

"So, you know how you're a bum now?" Addie had asked the second he'd picked up.

Glad for a legitimate reason to take a break, he'd dropped his tools and leaned against the wall of the shed. "Really? A bum?"

Her laugh had carried over the line and made him smile. "It's my day off, but Lexi roped me into helping her plan the wedding—"

"She asked you to help with wedding stuff?" It was too funny, picturing her picking out dresses and flowers—hell, he bet if any guy tried to buy her flowers, she'd hurl them at his head while yelling something like, *How dare you treat me like a girl!*

"Okay, Mr. Incredulous, I had the same reaction, but apparently, much like Obi-Wan Kenobi, I'm someone's only hope. And it'd help me not be so bored if you came along for the ride."

Damn, how could he resist such a solid *Star Wars* reference?

Not that he wouldn't make her work a little harder for it. "What's in it for me?"

She made an offended noise. "You get to hang out with yours truly, and we might actually get a chance to catch up without being interrupted every five minutes—well, since we'll be in town, that's not entirely true, but you get what I'm sayin'. Plus, we can give the rumor mill a push and scare all the older people that we're together again and most likely plannin' shenanigans. They'll bar up the windows, bring their pies in off the sills."

"So we're bears?"

She growled, the weakest-sounding bear ever, then snort-laughed. "Pretend I didn't do that."

"Not sure I can unhear it." He'd glanced down at himself, thinking he could use a shower. You know, for shenanigans reasons.

Not because he cared about being sweaty and covered in sawdust in front of Addie.

He'd told her he'd meet her in thirty, and he even wore the beat-up Saints hat she loathed to keep himself in line.

Maybe that would also keep her in line, which was a moot point, because she didn't seem to be having any trouble.

The shops lining the streets appeared very much the same. A few had new paint and new names, but not much had changed. Not much ever did here, and after years of too much change, too much traffic, and too many people, he took a moment to enjoy the slower pace and nostalgic timelessness.

Then he spotted Addie. She'd paired a simple T-shirt with frayed, cut-off shorts that displayed a whole lot of leg, and he quickly jerked his gaze back to the unchanged buildings.

Now if he could only keep his feelings for one of his best friends from changing, that'd be great. Apparently it was going to take extra effort.

"How do you feel about the fact that I'm only here because I had literally nothing else to do?" he joked as she approached.

"Relieved," she said, without a hint of teasing. "I thought maybe Nonna Lucia would wanna help, but she informed me she has a social life and then added that I needed to get one, too."

"Real subtle, your grandma."

"Right?" Addie pulled a folded paper out of the back pocket of the shorts that he absolutely wasn't looking at. "Okay, so first up, I need to figure out how many strings of lights and yards of tulle we need to decorate the gazebo." She looked from the list to the gazebo and then back to the list. "I'm assuming yards means tulle is a fabric?"

He shrugged. "Sounds right to me," he said, although he was totally out of his league, a feeling he could see reflected in Addie's expression.

She twisted the end of her ponytail around her

finger. "So, uh, that means, like…draping?"

"Well, when we decorated with tulle at the law firm…" He moved closer to peek at the list, but further details didn't magically show up. "I guess we draw a diagram with the dimensions?"

"Seems as good a place to start as any. And since I figured your sissy car wouldn't have room for things like a tape measure and tools, I brought mine."

"One, leave my car alone, and two, it just so happens I do have one in there." Partly due to his recent habit of measuring supplies, and since he thought he might pick up more while he was in town. "A few more months, though, and I would've fully completed my city boy transformation."

"Sounds like you got out in the nick of time," she said with a laugh, and then they walked up the steps of the gazebo and got to measuring.

"How are things with your job, by the way? Still bumpy, or has it smoothed out?" Every time he brought up work over the phone, she either said she didn't want to talk about it or she ranted about her boss.

"Bumpy with a side of *grr*. Moody Overlord wants everything done his way, even though it's the old-school way. Modern medicine has grown leaps and bounds since he got his degree, but any attempts to drag him into the present result in a power struggle, and in the end, I work for him. Unfortunately." She hooked the tape measure on one of the side sections and extended it to him so he could take it to the other end. "What about you? Any idea what you're gonna do now?"

"I've got something in the works."

"And that something is…?"

"You'll be the first to know when I decide if it's actually something." If anyone knew what it was like to be unhappy at a job but to grit your teeth and power through it anyway, it was him. Until recently. "How often do you go home hating your job?"

She shrugged. "I don't hate the job. I just wish I had a different boss. Mr. Watkins is condescending and hard to please, and he never thinks anyone does anything as well as he does. The other day he walked into the room where I was working on a patient, instructed me to step aside, then told the guy 'sometimes women just aren't strong enough to manipulate the muscles the way they need to.' I was so tempted to tell him that I'd happily manipulate his muscles. Since his head is figuratively up his ass, I might as well help him with the literally."

Tucker chuckled. "I'm surprised you held back."

"I like eating, not having to live with my parents, and paying the bills. I mean, I don't so much like paying them, but you get what I'm sayin'. It means a lot of counting to ten while I control my temper, and you know that's never been my strong point."

"I'd say *boy, do I know,* but then you might lose your temper."

She let go of the tape measure and it came reeling back and snapped his finger. Case in point.

"We'll just call that Exhibit A." He gave her the measurements to jot down and then moved to the next section of the gazebo, taking the end of the tape so she'd get *her* finger snapped if he let go. "Wasn't the goal always to become a sports therapist for a team?"

"Yeah, but then my grandma had pulmonary emboli in her lungs, and right after she stopped having to constantly go in to get her blood checked, she fell and broke her hip. It was like every time I went to search for a job, I got proof that even a thirty- to forty-minute commute to Auburn might be too far."

"She's stable now, yeah?"

"Well, yeah. But once in a while her combo of meds hits her wrong."

"She has your parents, and I can check in on her, too. I know Ford and the rest of the guys would say the same. You can't hold off doing what you want forever. I quit my shitty job, and besides the total lack of stability, I feel great!" He added a laugh to show he was mostly joking, and she joined in.

"It's the middle of the season, and—"

"So? Put out some feelers. It doesn't hurt to see."

She sighed. "You're right. Working for the overlord was always supposed to be temporary. I do like the clients, though, so if I don't get another job, I'll focus on that."

"Look at you. All sunshiny and shit."

She rolled her eyes. He wanted her to find something she loved with people who realized how great she was, and she'd be amazing at working with a team.

His eyebrows drew together as he realized he'd just pushed her to get a job that would make her less accessible. But it was only a half hour or so drive each way, one they'd all made in college, and they'd managed to squeeze in time. On top of studying, no less.

She'd still be living here, and she'd be happier. Win, win.

"Tucker Crawford, just the person I was looking for!" Out of the corner of his eye, he spotted Nellie Mae striding toward him, and were those dollar bills in her hand?

Instinctively every muscle tensed, then ached, thanks to the stiffness he was starting to believe would never go away.

Faye Dunville was right on her heels, a large, leashed pig reluctantly following her with each tug. "Oh, no you don't. He needs to hear my side of the story, too."

"Her pig ate half the food in my garden," Nellie Mae blurted out.

"I told her she needed to fix her fence, but she didn't listen. I can't help that my animal does what animals do."

"You're responsible for what your pig does! And if you're not, I can't be responsible for what I do to your pig."

Faye gasped, her free hand going to her chest. "You wouldn't dare!"

"Oh, I would."

They both directed their full attention to Tucker, and he glanced at Addie, who, instead of helping, had the gall to look amused.

If he didn't know better, he'd think someone had dropped him in the middle of an overly dramatic play.

"Y'all know I'm not a judge, right?" Tucker asked, not sure why they'd brought their feud to him.

"I want to sue her pig for damages lost," Nellie

Mae said. "I've kept records of it—pictures and dates—so I know I have a strong case."

The image of a pig sitting on the witness stand popped into his head and then a snort-laugh escaped.

That sent Addie laughing, and then they were both getting the type of glares they used to get when running down the sidewalks of town too fast. And only a few of those times had been because they were fleeing the scene of a crime.

Okay, maybe more than a few.

Faye crossed her arms and glared at him, and he clamped his lips. "And I wanna restrainin' order that keeps Nellie Mae from comin' within a hundred yards of my house."

"My house is within a hundred yards of her house."

Well, he'd decided he was sick of wading through evidence of people's guilt and trying to find loopholes to get them off anyway, and this was definitely a change from the norm.

Small-town life might be less quiet than he'd remembered, but he could honestly say that one day was never quite like the next.

Not that he planned on getting involved. Not in the legal drama or any other form of drama.

"Ladies," he started, "haven't you heard the rumors 'bout me gettin' fired from my law firm?"

"We'll have to make do with you anyway, seeing's how we don't exactly have a surplus of good lawyers round here," Nellie Mae responded, sending Addie into another fit of giggles that earned her an admonishing glare. "And I realize that suing the pig is probably a far stretch, but Faye and I've been neighbors goin' on forty years, and until this hog came along, we used to live in harmony. But if he keeps on eating *my* food, I should get to eat *him*."

Faye gasped, then dropped down to cover the pig's ears.

"Well, that escalated quickly," Addie mumbled.

He widened his eyes at her—he needed to de-escalate the situation, not laugh and make it worse. She gave him a what-can-you-do shrug.

He did his best to telepathically plead for help, and Addie finally stepped up next to him and flashed the women a big smile. "Now, ladies, I know you guys care about each other—"

"*Guys?* Not all of us like to be called guys, missy."

Addie's smile turned plastic and a smidge forced. "Oh, yeah? Not all of us like—"

"I think what Addie's saying," he loudly cut in, "is that we'd both hate to see your friendship ruined over something like this. I'm not currently taking cases, and—"

"Lucia told us that she has you on retainer, and in fact, she's the one who told us if we needed any legal help, we should find you. Which reminds me, here's your retainer." Nellie Mae extended two crumpled bills. "She said you were much better than those other two schmucks we have."

Faye quickly pulled out two dollar bills, batted away Nellie Mae's hand, and waved her money at Tucker. "No, take mine. I have a much stronger case."

Of course Addie's grandmother had gone and

told them he'd help with their legal issues, although the compliment about being better than the others was nice, he supposed.

Addie gave another one of those absolving shrugs.

"The business I'm conducting for Lucia Murphy isn't anything that would require going to court."

"You mean you sure hope it doesn't lead to that," Addie muttered and then zipped her lips when he darted a glare at her.

He returned his attention to the fired-up women, who were still shoving each other's arms down in an attempt to get him to take their money first. "How about we call in Deputy Reeves and see if among all of us, we can't come up with a good solution?"

They grumbled about it but reluctantly agreed, and he made them go sit on park benches on opposite sides of the town square.

Tucker took off his hat, ran a hand through his hair, and then settled it back on his head. "Somehow when I was daydreaming about moving back to my calm, carefree town, where everyone knew everyone, I repressed these type of ridiculous situations and how often they happen."

Addie clapped him on the back. "Welcome back to Uncertainty, Tucker Crawford. Where the only certainty is that some inane thing will get blown out of proportion and send people into a tizzy. But hey, at least we go the unique route. How many pig cases did you solve in Birmingham?"

"You'd be surprised."

Her forehead crinkled before smoothing with the realization he'd been pulling her leg. She went for her usual retribution, going to smack his arm. Only he was ready for it and caught her wrist, and when her lips parted in surprise, a swirling, zinging sensation shot through his gut.

"How long is this gonna take?" Nellie Mae called from her bench with a huff. "I have things to do."

"If you'll excuse me," Tucker said, slowly letting go of Addie's wrist and trying not to think about how soft her skin felt beneath his fingertips or the strange urge he had to pull her closer. "Looks like I have some funny business to attend to. What are the odds Easton won't just laugh and leave me out to dry?"

Addie stuck her hands in her back pockets, and of course it made her shirt stretch tighter across her breasts, another part of her body he shouldn't be noticing. "He deals with those bickering two all the time, so he'll be good backup, if a little slow to show. Now you're gettin' a taste of my life here— usually I'm asked health questions I'm nowhere near qualified to answer, so this should give me a nice break."

"Hey, Addison," Faye called. "While we're waitin', could you be a dear and come look at my hip? It's been acting strange lately."

"Then again, maybe not."

Tucker gestured her ahead of him, realizing too late that it put him in the perfect position to watch her backside and those long legs cutting across the distance. More and more, it felt like he was seeing her for the first time, yet he still had all the good memories attached, too, which made it hard to feel neutral or suppress feelings he shouldn't be having.

Couldn't be having.

The flicker of attraction remained in the background, though, so evidently he was going to need to find a more effective method than mentally telling himself to knock it off.

• • •

Addie's phone rang while she was seated on her couch with her laptop, scrolling through job positions online. When she saw her sister's name, she debated a moment on whether or not to answer. Then she felt guilty and quickly accepted the call. "Hey, what's up?"

She braced herself, waiting for Alexandria to tell her that she'd found a stain on her dress, even though after Nonna had worked her magic, Addie couldn't see a single speck of dirt.

Maybe the lace had frayed?

"I talked to Mom earlier, and she says you're dating a dentist now. I'm glad, because honestly, I was starting to worry about you."

"No reason to worry about me." Addie didn't know what else to say to that. If she asked why she was concerned, her sister would probably list off so many items that her phone's low battery would cut off the conversation before she finished.

"I do, though. You're always with your group of guys, and no one's going to approach you because of them. You realize that, don't you?"

"How do you know the dentist didn't approach me while I was with my friends?"

Alexandria sighed this my-sister-is-so-clueless

sigh. "I just know. But please, enlighten me if I'm wrong."

The temptation to lie was strong, but Alexandria always managed to see through even a hint of falseness, and becoming a mom had only heightened her ability. "Fine. I coach his niece, and then one day when I was running errands, we got to talking, and he asked me out."

"Has he seen you in something other than your workout gear?"

"I wore jeans on our date. Dressy ones, too," she quickly said before Alexandria could tell her jeans weren't good enough, not when you needed to convince guys you weren't as masculine as they were—yeah, she'd literally said that before, after Addie was upset and wondering why her college boyfriend broke up with her without a word of explanation.

Now she was thinking she'd chosen wrong when she'd answered the phone.

"Well, that's somethin', at least. Come on, I need more details. Lately my life revolves around the kids' appointments and waiting for Eli to come home so I can have some actual adult conversation—I'm practically starved for it." Her voice lowered. "Have you slept with him yet? And how was it? Did he... *drill you good*?"

"Oh my gosh, we've only been on one date." A small glimmer of hope rose—maybe it could actually go somewhere. "But we're goin' on another this weekend."

"It's been a while since you've gone on two dates with a guy."

"Thanks, *Alex*. I'm well aware."

"You're very welcome, *Addison*. Just thought I'd remind you that it wasn't somethin' to turn your nose up at."

She loved her sister like crazy, but sometimes she also made her crazy. If it didn't come from a place of love, Addie would've simply hung up on her. Instead she defiantly turned up her nose—it was nice that her sister couldn't see her right now.

Fewer repercussions that way.

"The reason I also bring up that it's been a while is because that means you've been hanging with your boys a lot, and I'm sure you're used to how things are between you and them, and…well, what I'm saying is, you're different with the guys."

"Actually," Addie said, "I'm different with you. With pretty much everyone except them."

With the guys, she never had to censor who she was, and she loved having a safe place to completely be herself.

"Don't worry," she added. "I'm used to being an edited version of myself around other people."

"Good, good," Alexandria said, again not one for sugarcoating. "Okay, I know you're gonna want to reject this idea before I even finish, but please, Addie, just once in your life, listen to me. I know quite a bit about dating and landing a man."

"Maybe I don't want to land one."

Even before her sister met Eli, she'd always had steady boyfriends, the kind who adored her. Addie didn't want to feel like she had to "land" a man and do whatever it took to make him stay, but she could get on board with a little adoration.

"You wanna die alone?"

"Oh, for sure." Addie set her laptop aside, since it was getting too warm and she clearly wasn't going to get back to her job search anytime soon.

Alexandria sighed again. "I want you to go and buy some sexy lingerie. Wear it underneath your clothes on your date."

"I'm not sleeping with him on date two."

She didn't think.

Depended how well it went.

No, it was too soon.

Shoot, she didn't know.

Like her sister pointed out, it'd been a while since she'd gone on a second date. Still, she usually dated for a while before she was ready to add sex to the mix, and she needed to be sure before she crossed that line.

"It doesn't matter whether you sleep with him at the end of the date or not. It'll make *you* feel sexy. You're all about not impressing anyone, right?"

In spite of it feeling like a trap, Addie said, "Sure."

"Do it for you, then. When you feel sexy, it'll show through. You'll automatically be sexier, to yourself and to him."

Addie spun the idea over in her head.

It'd been a long time since she'd felt sexy.

Honestly, she wasn't sure she'd ever felt truly sexy. Comfy always seemed to take precedence, and while she was confident in a lot of areas, the bedroom wasn't one of them.

While there was a general attraction to the dentist she hoped would grow stronger in time, part of her thought maybe she just didn't feel sparks anymore. Like, maybe she'd grown immune to them.

But then…

Nope.

She wasn't going to think about the way she'd gotten that fresh-from-the-roller-coaster feeling when Tucker caught her wrist earlier today. That was…well, there was a logical explanation, and she'd figure it out later.

If anything, it was more reason to focus on the dentist—*on David*. She was so sexually deprived, she was imagining things.

"Promise me," Alexandria said. "I'll just call you every few hours until you agree. You know I will."

With Eli working so many late nights lately, Alexandria had way too much free time to worry about Addie's social life. She had a feeling her sister would even load her kids in the car and drive down this weekend if she thought Addie needed a push.

"Fine." It wasn't a totally horrible idea, she supposed.

And she didn't want to die alone, although there were like one hundred levels between landing a guy and that. Right now, she'd settle for not feeling the loneliness her empty house occasionally echoed back at her.

What she truly wanted was a guy who wanted her. Who couldn't wait to see her.

Possibly she could even try the cuddling thing and see if it was all it was cracked up to be.

After all, Shep was getting married. Once he'd met Lexi, things moved pretty fast, and it was only a matter of time before the rest of the guys found girlfriends of their own.

Then where would she be? Perpetually third wheeling it?

"Fine as in you promise?"

"I promise," Addie said. "In fact, I'm going online right now and I'm going to rush order some sexy underwear."

"Ooh, which site? I'll help you look."

At first Addie thought it might be weird, but she was utterly clueless about lingerie, so she went ahead and let her sister take the wheel.

And about thirty minutes and an outrageous amount of money later, several matching sets of underwear and one bustier that she feared she'd feel too ridiculous to ever actually squeeze herself into were on their way to her house.

CHAPTER SEVEN

Thursday night football meant the Old Firehouse was packed, and Addie couldn't stop watching the door every time it opened, hoping the next person who walked through would be Tucker.

They'd been interrupted by the dueling neighbors yesterday, and while Easton had come to the town square and done his best to help defuse the situation, threats of legal action were still being flung around as Tucker took Faye and her pig one way, and Easton took Nellie Mae the other.

I should just text him and tell him to get over here.

Only she was meeting Lexi, and she had no idea how long their planning session was going to run. When it came to all things wedding related, she wasn't sure of pretty much anything besides how happy Lexi made Shep.

Which was what she held on to when she wanted to crumple the confusing list and throw it in along with the towel.

As if her thoughts had summoned them, the betrothed couple strolled in. Shep had Lexi tucked under his arm, and Addie wasn't sure how he wasn't tripping over tables and chairs, because he never broke eye contact with his fiancée as he led her to the table.

"I'll be over at the bar watching the game if you need anything," he said, and Addie nearly begged him to take her with him.

Then he gathered Lexi to him and kissed her, really giving it his all.

Admittedly, a few times while being exposed to way too much of their PDA, a thread of longing had risen up in Addie, making her wish she had someone who'd kiss her that recklessly. Someone who didn't care who was watching, because the need to touch and taste each other was too strong.

The yearning that'd been growing more frequent as of late drifted to the surface now, and she told herself she had her group of guys, no matter what.

Which she did, and they'd be there if she needed them, but it wasn't the same. Even if she'd accidentally thought about Tucker too many times today. Not just that moment in the gazebo when his strong fingers had been wrapped around her wrist but about how she laughed harder with him than anyone else.

"Is Tucker coming to watch the game?" she asked Shep when he came up for air.

"Not sure. Did you text him?"

If she asked Shep to text, he would wonder why she couldn't do it herself, and the great thing about their group was that things had never been weird between any of them.

Well, besides the week or so back in high school when Shep's status had changed and they hadn't known how exactly to fit him into the group anymore.

It was so long ago that it'd been forever since she'd even thought about that, and it all worked out for the best, thank goodness.

Lexi took the stool across the table from Addie

and then glanced back. "Will, honey, can you have the bartender send over a glass of rosé?"

"No shit, they actually serve rosé here?"

Lexi gave her an aren't-you-precious look, but since Addie knew she didn't mean anything derogatory by it—and since she'd spoken up against Delilah without needing to hear any of the details about how rude she was in high school—she let it slide right off her.

"Did you want something else?" Lexi wrinkled her nose as she eyed the puddle of foam left in Addie's glass. "Another beer?"

"Sure."

Shep nodded, already understanding, and Addie resisted wrapping herself around his ankle and forcing him to drag her closer to the bar where the action was. She extended the beat-up paper with its rough sketch of the gazebo and measurements.

"We got interrupted by a case of pig versus garden, but I managed to get the dimensions down."

Lexi arched her eyebrows, high enough they momentarily disappeared into the platinum blond. "Pig versus garden? Do I even wanna know?"

"Probably not. And I have to warn you there's a gag order in effect, so if the pig tries to talk to you, you just call Easton or Tucker."

Lexi laughed. "And see, here I thought I was getting out of the city and moving to somewhere safe. Somewhere where pigs and gardens could get along."

Addie snickered, Lexi's unexpected humor easing some of the tension in her shoulders—she kept on surprising her.

The paper crinkled when Lexi lifted it. She frowned at it, lips pursed. "Uh, what does this mean?"

"Oh, I thought you'd know. I'm not sure how you want to drape the tulle, or if you were, like, wrapping it, or…"

Using the side of her palm, Lexi smoothed out the paper, the ink smearing slightly and leaving streaks on her skin. "I'm not sure. I don't really know what I'm doing."

"That makes two of us. I'm more the girl to call if you wanna know who to put on your fantasy football team or where to buy the best yoga pants. I can also go on all day about what makes the perfect hoodie—a mixture of fabric that's thick and snuggly without being bulky and constricting. I prefer a zip-up for traveling and a pullover for watching TV at home or for doubling as pj's on cold nights." Addie's gaze ran over Lexi's red dress and matching heels. "Have you ever even worn a hoodie?"

She laughed. "Of course. I'm not always dressed up. I just feel naked if I go out without my dressy clothes and makeup."

Shep materialized, a glass of pink wine in hand. "Did someone say *naked*?"

She giggled as he set down her drink and kissed her cheek. "You seriously must have a sixth sense for when I say something improper."

"And I highly encourage you to set it off as much as possible." Shep slid a beer bottle across the table, and Addie caught it, the condensation wetting her palm. He tipped his beer at her, and after she reciprocated, they both drank.

Then cheers erupted and they lost him, his attention drifting over his shoulder.

Addie braced her forearms on the table and peeked around the mess of bodies so she could catch the replay. Neither team was one she cared much about, besides seeing how they might measure up to her beloved Falcons.

Still, any day with football on TV was a win in her book.

Lexi encouraged Shep to return to the bar to watch, since they were in the middle of "boring wedding planning" and apparently saying "no kidding" about the boringness wasn't the right thing.

Oops.

"What about poker?" Lexi asked once they were alone again, the din of the game and celebration back to a normal, background-level decibel.

"At the wedding? That'd seriously rock."

She frowned, and Addie felt like she'd failed a pop quiz.

Lexi twisted the stem of her wineglass between her fingers. "You were saying you were the girl to call to learn about football." She took a demure sip of her drink. "I meant could you teach me how to play poker?"

"Oh. *Oh!* For sure."

The concern faded as a smile curved her red lips, somehow unsmudged despite the kissing and drinking. "Will just talks about your games so much, and I'd like to try my hand at it. I don't think I could get my mother on board for poker at the reception, though. Pretty sure she'd have a heart attack if I even mentioned it. She thinks I'm crazy to be getting married here and moving here, and basically, she just thinks I'm plumb crazy. Which, when it comes to that sexy man over there…" Her gaze drifted to Shep and a dreamy quality entered her features. "I am."

"It's nice to see, actually. And the townspeople will love you forever for having the wedding here and letting them be part of it." Addie picked up one of the stray coasters and spun it to give her fingers something to do. "And I'm sorry about saying that wedding planning is boring. It just…"

"Is," she supplied. "I mean for me, it's overwhelming, but like I said when I asked for your help, I know it's not your thing."

"I seriously don't mind helping. But admittedly teaching you poker is something I'm way more qualified for."

It also gave Lexi more bonus points. Clearly she was embracing small-town life and trying to fit into the group, and hopefully that meant things wouldn't have to change too terribly much after they were married.

It also gave her an excuse to text Tucker and ask him to bring a deck of cards if he happened to swing by the bar to catch some of the game.

While Addie waited for his response, she and Lexi made yet another to-do list from the master to-do list. Addie took the items she thought she could handle, or at least could find townspeople willing to help make them happen.

In a lot of ways, discussing everything that needed done and how they'd go about handling them highlighted their differences, but along the way, they also connected.

Which was probably why, when Tucker showed up and tossed a deck of cards across the room to Addie, Lexi felt comfortable enough to ask if she thought Tucker would be interested in Brittany. Evidently the meticulous brunette couldn't stop talking about the way he'd swooped in and offered his car, and how sexy he was.

What Addie wanted to say as she pulled the deck of cards out of the well-worn box was *I'm not sure she's his type*. But his type had always been pretty Southern belles, ones who didn't understand or care for Addie.

So honestly, the bridesmaid was right up his alley, and now she was remembering that during the whole car-breakdown debacle, he'd requested she put in a good word.

"Yeah, he'd probably be interested," Addie said, and why did that make a pit form in her stomach?

It had to be because she'd been thinking about what would happen if all her friends coupled off and she got left behind.

But she forced herself to push that worry aside and say, "I'm sure he'd give her a call if you gave him her number."

More gut sinking immediately followed, which was stupid.

Well, not exactly stupid. They'd been apart for two years and it sucked. With him in a different city, and communication between them slowing to a trickle, there'd been a few times when she wondered if she was forgettable.

Replaceable, even.

Mostly just on dark days when she'd been missing Tucker more than usual or when she'd felt especially lonely.

Part of the fault belonged to her, too. The roads went both ways, and she could've made more of an effort. So she resolved to do better, even if he got a girlfriend.

She'd also try to ignore the jealousy—jealousy she'd feel for anyone who took away any of her time with him.

She met his gaze, and he winked at her, a smug, semimocking grin on his lips that made it clear he was teasing her about her current wedding-planning situation.

It also made her heart stutter the tiniest bit.

Underneath the table, she thumbed out a text.

ADDIE: *FYI, I'm going to drag you with me to at least half these tasks, so wipe that smug look off your face.*

TUCKER: *Why don't you come wipe it off for me?*

A swirl went through her stomach. Because of the challenge—she loved a good challenge.

ADDIE: *Oh, I'm coming for you. But it'll be when you least expect it. Be afraid. Very afraid.*

TUCKER: *Unlike most guys, I'm not afraid of you.*

Her mouth dropped. He did *not* just go there.

She glanced up in time to see his shoulders shaking in silent laughter, and she summoned the dirtiest look she could and aimed it his way.

He dragged his finger around his collar in an exaggerated *yeesh* gesture, clearly thinking he was hilarious.

"Addie?"

She jerked her attention back to Lexi. "Sorry. Where were we?" She shuffled the cards and threw herself into explaining the ins and outs of poker. They went over the general rules, lingo, the hands and what beat what, and how the betting worked. It was way easier than discussing wedding decorations.

Not to mention more fun.

Later, when the guys came over, Lexi gave Tucker Brittany's number, and as Addie watched him enter the digits into his phone, she became more and more determined to do whatever it took to make sure her date with David went well on Saturday.

If she didn't feel some sparks, she was going to take things into her own hands and freaking *make* some.

CHAPTER EIGHT

One lesson and a mini refresher over the phone wasn't exactly a lot, but when it came to poker, Addie decided the best way to truly learn involved jumping right in.

As planned, she and Lexi met at the houseboat a few minutes early—Lexi wanted to surprise Shep by showing up at poker night, not just to spend time with him but to play.

Despite Addie's warnings about the banks being on the marshy side, Lexi had on tall wedge shoes. She'd opted for dressy white capris instead of a skirt, ones that probably wouldn't remain white, but Addie kept that tidbit to herself.

Especially since she'd worn her dressiest jeans and a purple shirt that had more polyester than cotton, which was dressy as far as she was concerned. Factor in the draped neckline and the lacy black push-up bra that left the girls right under her chin, and…well, she felt super overdressed for poker.

But she had a date later tonight—exact time yet to be determined—and as promised, her underwear was on the super-sexy side. Also a lick tight, and the panties were riding up her ass a little, as they didn't have enough fabric to fully cover both cheeks.

"That top looks amazing on you," Lexi said, and Addie tried to take it as a good sign that Lexi liked it, but it also made her worry the guys would wonder what in the world she was trying to pull.

She didn't rightly know; she just thought she'd add some fuel to help with sparkage.

But now one side of her shirt kept slipping off her shoulder, and she felt exposed and stupid, and what the hell was she thinking? "Are we going to go in?"

"What? Oh. Yeah." Addie crossed the plank and knocked on the door to the cabin before spinning to face Lexi. "You ready for your poker-playing debut?"

"I'm more nervous than I thought I'd be."

"You'll do great."

Me, that's a different story.

Tucker swung open the door and greeted them with that great smile of his, the one that brought out his strong jawline, and without having to shave every day, a delicious amount of scruff dusted his jaw.

Wait. Delicious? Calm it down, brain.

"Come on in," Tucker said, leading them toward the small living room area. He gestured to the couch. "Go on and make yourself at home, Lexi. There are drinks in the fridge, and I set out some chips. The guys should be here soon."

Before Addie could get the "hey" on the tip of her tongue out, something barreled into her legs. She let out an unpreventable squeal when she spotted the culprit—a bouncy white Labrador puppy. "Oh. My. Gosh."

"I...did a thing," Tucker said.

Addie scooped up the puppy and laughed as he went to licking her cheek. "He's so cute! He looks like Casper the Second."

Growing up, Tucker used to have a white lab named Casper that had followed them around most everywhere they went. The only time she'd ever seen Tucker choked up was when the dog had to be put to sleep after a long, full life, and it was one of the few times she'd let herself cry in front of him.

A mix of sorrow and sentimentality met the happiness holding the puppy brought her, and it was a lot of emotions to process at once.

Tucker scratched the top of the dog's head. "That's why when Ford called me yesterday and said they'd rescued a white Lab and her puppies from a home where they'd been neglected and asked if I wanted one, I jumped at the chance. Remembering how much work puppies are set in afterward."

"That's the beauty of spontaneous decisions," she said with a laugh.

The rumble of engines broke through, followed by deep voices that sounded like the bass line of a song until the guys got closer and the words became more discernible.

The second Shep stepped inside, Lexi jumped off the couch and threw her arms around his neck. "Surprise," she said. "I came for poker!"

The other guys walked past with muttered hellos and head nods, relatively unfazed by the new addition, heading right toward the food and drinks as usual.

Addie turned back to Tucker, her fingers rubbing one of the puppy's fuzzy ears. "Have you named him yet?"

She dodged the puppy's tongue as he shifted in

her arms, climbing higher to lick at her jaw. After a few seconds, she gave up and let him lick away.

Tucker was staring at her, eyes wide, mouth slightly ajar. "You, um…" He swallowed, his Adam's apple bobbing up and down. "Your shirt."

She dropped her gaze to see the wiggly puppy had pushed down her shirt, revealing a generous portion of one half of her bra, and thanks to its hoisting powers, a whole lot of cleavage.

Heat crept up her neck and into her face and she thrust the puppy into Tucker's hands, then quickly went to work adjusting her shirt.

This was why she didn't wear stupid dressy shirts with drapey necklines. She did far too many things that could result in a wardrobe malfunction.

Then again, not even her beloved clothes were totally safe—back in high school, she'd once stripped off her hoodie in front of Tucker, only for her T-shirt to come along for the ride.

She'd barely been able to look at him for days.

For some reason, this felt far worse—most likely because it was happening now, and she'd worn the demi-bra that left so much of her exposed, and maybe the fact that it was lacy and pretty made it better, but *oh, holy crap* her cheeks still blazed and the temperature turned stifling.

After a moment or two contemplating fleeing the scene, she dared a glance at Tucker. He'd put the puppy on his dog bed and he flopped down and tucked his nose in the blanket, tired after doing all that assisted flashing.

Tucker seemed to be avoiding eye contact as he asked if he could get her a beer, and she avoided it as she took it from him.

It gave her some small semblance of comfort that since everyone else had already been settling in at the table, he'd been the only one to see it, but considering the awkwardness in the air, dressing up had done the opposite of what she'd been going for.

Not that Tucker was the target of her lacy push-up bra, but what if she just couldn't pull off being sexy? What if she made things awkward with David and scared him away?

Then there'd be no sparks and no relationship and dying alone.

Great. Now my sister's in my head.

"I'm eager to see my girl in action," Shep said, rubbing his hands together. "Let's get this game going."

Addie started to take her usual seat, but Lexi patted the one next to her—Tucker's unofficial spot. "I want you next to me in case I need a teensy bit of extra tutoring. Is that okay with everyone?"

A beat of silence, and then the guys sorta half-heartedly agreed. Not uncommon when a new person sat in on their poker games, although when she'd brought her former boyfriends, they were more vocal about their disdain, especially if Addie had to remind the guy which hands beat which.

And when one of her boyfriends was actually good at poker, they were even more annoyed.

Looks like we've all grown up a bit. Maybe. Not enough to just acknowledge the boob flash had been weird.

Not that she wanted Tucker to say anything about it. Like, ever.

"You okay, Murph?" Ford asked. "You look all flushed."

"I'm fine," she quickly said.

Ford leaned across the table to feel her forehead.

"Dude," Easton said, slapping his arm away. "That's such a mom move."

"No, it's a paramedic move to make sure she's not going to pass out halfway through the game. I've already had to carry too many people out of their houses today for heat exhaustion, and my arms can't take one more body."

She tilted her head. "Well, at least it's not because you actually care about me."

"I care." He dropped back in his seat and jammed a ridiculous number of chips in his mouth before talking through the crunch. "That our game doesn't get interrupted. Now, drink some water already."

"Yes, Mom," she said, making a big show of reaching for a water bottle and glugging half of it.

Then, in an attempt to get things back to feeling like a normal poker night where she hadn't flashed her best friend, she asked Tucker and Easton if they'd made any headway in the Pig Versus Garden Case.

And okay, maybe she looked at Easton as she asked, but she could sorta see Tucker in her peripheral.

"Crawford saved the day with that," Easton said. "I've been breaking up fights between those two ever since Faye got that damn pig, so if this actually works, I'm gonna owe him more than the two dollars both ladies kept tryin' to pay him."

Tucker shook his head, and she snuck a tiny glance at him. She couldn't fully meet his eyes, but it was mostly normal.

Phew.

"What'd you do?" she asked.

"I drew up a binding legal agreement with concessions on each side. Fair rules about boundaries and fences. Fines they pay to each other if they break 'em, and with any luck, peace and their friendship will be restored, and the pig won't end up on anyone's dinner table unless Faye agrees to it."

Which she never would, even though the pig had started off with that fate. Somewhere along the way, it'd become a pet.

The trash talk got going as they threw in money and converted it to plastic chips, and Ford took charge of the cards, shuffling them thoroughly before dealing.

Lexi asked how often they played poker, which led to talking about their history, from back in the day when they used to play Whiskey Poker—one communal hand, which meant a bigger chance of super-high hands—to when they'd switched to Texas Hold'em to be more "legit."

Tucker nudged her from the left side—still felt weird for him to be there instead of to her right. "Remember that night when the wins and losses were so even that we kept on playing till we basically passed out?" He pulled the top card off the deck and added the turn to the other three.

Addie fought to keep her face neutral when the three of diamonds gave her two pair. "Of course I remember. We woke up to your parents and mine over us."

"Oh yeah," Tucker said. "Because we hadn't cleared sleeping over in the houseboat, and their first assumption when they woke up and found we weren't in our beds was that we must've died."

Usually she'd let her parents know when she planned on staying the night, and while there was occasionally some blowback about her needing to spend more time at home, they were mostly cool with it.

That night they'd gotten caught up in the game-that-wouldn't-end, and she only vaguely recalled stumbling to the double bed where she and Tucker had crashed out.

"It's your turn," Addie said to Lexi when she didn't make a move.

"Right." Lexi met the bet, and the crinkles between her eyebrows made it clear she was thinking hard, only she was staring at Addie instead of the cards. "It was just you and all these guys?"

"Once in a while, we held some mild parties with a few more people, but as soon as everyone else cleared out and the poker games turned serious, it was always the five of us."

"I…" Lexi shook her head. "Never mind."

Addie's muscles tensed. "Go ahead and say whatever you're thinking. I've probably heard it before."

How she should act like a girl; how she'd never get a date hanging around the guys; how it made other girls unable to trust her—she had never understood that one, but it seemed to be true enough.

"Well, if a girl in my high school stayed overnight

with four guys... It wouldn't be very good for her reputation. Everyone would assume... You know. One girl, several guys, all-night parties."

For the second time that night, heat settled into Addie's cheeks. "Funny enough, I never heard rumors like that. But you know that song about not giving a damn about my bad reputation? It was pretty much my theme song."

"Most people knew us well enough they didn't say stuff like that, though." Ford flattened his cards to his chest and shifted in his seat to more fully face Lexi. "See, Murph hasn't been a girl in years."

Addie's mouth dropped open. "Hey! I'm still a girl!"

Ford shrugged a shoulder. "Eh." Shep and Easton gave about the same response, and Tucker remained stone-faced at her side, not contradicting it, which was basically the same as agreeing in this circle of friends—they'd never been shy about disagreeing or throwing in their two cents.

No wonder it took David so long to ask me on a second date. I'm not even a girl.

She checked her phone to see if he'd texted yet. He'd told her he was slammed these days, and that it might be late before they could get together. Still, when she didn't have any new messages, her ego took another nosedive.

I'm dealing with a lace and satin wedgie for nothing.

What was I thinking, trying to be something I'm not?

She tried to keep her spirits up as they played the next hand, but with every minute the dentist didn't text or call, they dipped that much lower.

Lexi's shoulder bumped Addie's as she leaned closer and whispered, "I forgot which is better, a flush or a straight?" She flashed Addie her cards as she asked, and a grumble went around the table before the guys could help it.

"It's okay, babe." Shep grabbed her hand, kissed it, then swept his gaze around the table. *"Right?"*

"Sure," Easton said. "As long as Murph's disqualified from winning this round."

"Sounds like someone's scared." Since she didn't have anything anyway, Addie folded, and when she noticed Easton's anxious tell of curving his hand around the bill of his hat, she nudged Lexi under the table.

Lexi raised, and after he matched what she'd thrown in, they laid down their cards. The high-pitched squeal that came from Lexi when she won made Addie flinch, but it also made her smile.

The girl was so dang happy about winning a hand.

Then she surprised Addie with a tackle hug, and if Tucker hadn't shot out his arm, her chair would've toppled over and she probably would've experienced her second wardrobe malfunction of the night.

As it was, everyone was examining them a hair too closely, eyes glazing over, the kind of look dudes gave when two girls were squished together.

"Really, guys?" Addie scolded as Lexi retreated to her own chair, and the girl's eyebrows drew together.

"What?" Clearly she hadn't hung around guys in the "just friends" setting, or she'd know that anytime girls so much as hugged, most hot-blooded males got images of experimenting females who couldn't keep their hands off each other.

Glad to know she qualified as a girl in *that* type of situation.

"Never mind," Shep said. Then he cleared his throat and the guys straightened in their seats and refocused on the center of the table as the cards were shuffled and re-dealt.

At the end of the next round, Shep prematurely folded and gave the pot to his fiancée, even though she was clearly bluffing.

She bounced in her seat, a satisfied smile on her face. "That was way more fun than I expected it to be. Winning probably helped." She squeezed Addie's hand. "Thanks again for teaching me so I could come play tonight."

"Happy to help," Addie said, and more than that, it was true.

"Admittedly, when Will first introduced me to you, I didn't understand how one of his closest friends was a girl."

"Apparently I'm not a girl." Addie fired a glare over the table at Ford.

"But you're very pretty, regardless of your preferred hobbies. I'm surprised that none of you ever dated."

Everyone froze, panic slowly bleeding from face to face. Their expressions were so gonna get them busted, just like their smug ones always had after they'd pulled off a prank.

Addie had taken a swig of beer but couldn't seem to swallow, and Shep squirmed in his seat. Then he cleared his throat and they were done for.

Lexie turned to him, her forehead all scrunched up. "Will?"

"Well, technically, at one time, Addie and I…" He left that hanging, as if not mentioning the fact that he and Addie had been boyfriend and girlfriend a lifetime ago would undo it.

Lexie's shoulders tightened, and her fingers wrapped around her glass, the cheery pink of her nails at odds with the violent squeeze. "Are you telling me that one of my bridesmaids is your ex-girlfriend?"

"Groomsmen," Addie ever so helpfully added without thinking. Her blood pressure skyrocketed as she worked to fix it. "What we did could hardly even be called dating. I mean, it was the beginning of high school, and neither of us could even drive yet."

"How. Long?" Lexi asked, her voice a few degrees icier than usual.

"It was also during football season, which hardly counts because we rarely saw each other," Shep said, digging their grave a little deeper.

Addie grabbed a shovel and got to digging, too. "Right. He was the new guy in town, so I didn't really know him that well before we went on a date to the movies, and it was our one and only official date. Then I introduced him to the guys, who naturally thought he was awesome, and we ended up doing all group things."

"Then Shep couldn't handle that she was the dude in the relationship, which made him all insecure and shit," Easton said, and sniggers went around the table.

They were yucking it up, but Lexi still looked legitimately upset, all of their connecting coming undone.

Addie's stomach bottomed out, desperation filling the suddenly empty space, and she grasped for a way to fix it. "It was more that we realized it'd been a while since we'd held hands or kis—" At the wild gleam that entered Lexi's eye, Addie decided to forgo mentioning their kissing and quickly revised it to, "Hugged. Along the way we'd become friends instead, and we found we preferred that to dating. We work really well as friends, and in a lot of ways he's more of a brother than anything."

Shep grabbed his fiancée's hand, his eyes imploring hers. "Honestly, babe. The main reason I even asked her out when I first moved into town was because we had so much in common. Like football and cars, and like I've always told you, she's just one of the guys."

"He didn't know any better," Tucker said. "He'd never played T-ball with her. I still have flashbacks of the day she got so mad at me that she picked up the nearby bat and chucked it at my head."

He raised a hand to the side of his face, like he might need to block her now, and he wasn't totally off base.

"I only threatened you with it, you big baby, and that was because you told me I should play right field, where the ball never goes, just so that you could catch a pop fly for once. Not my fault you were too damn slow."

"See," Tucker said, gesturing to her. "He didn't know that she'd just as easily maim you as kiss you."

Addie scowled, and while Lexi had seemed to be thawing the tiniest bit, the "kiss you" part made her withdraw her hand from Shep's.

"Awful kissing, really," Shep said, panic flooding his features. "Awkward enough we stopped a good month before we officially broke up and transitioned to being friends, which, again, fit us so much better."

A twinge went through Addie's chest, his words hurting more than she wished they did, in spite of knowing he'd said them to get them both out of this tense situation.

Chair legs scraped the floor as Lexi pushed away from the table. "I just…" Tears bordered her eyes. "I need to go."

She headed toward the door, and Shep nearly knocked over the table when he jumped up to go after her.

And Addie just sat there, an awful pit in her gut as she kissed the idea of actually being friends with Shep's fiancée goodbye.

CHAPTER NINE

Tucker finished throwing the bottles in the recycling and waited for his rambunctious puppy to finish doing his business. Then he scooped up the furball and thought way too much about how his dog had pulled down Addie's shirt and caused an accidental peep show.

Tucker's heart thumped hard in his chest as he replayed the flash of her sexy black bra and how she'd nearly been spilling out of it.

He couldn't stop thinking about it. Or the way she'd blushed.

As he'd been trying to reiterate Shep's point about Addie being just one of the guys, he'd told himself he needed to go back to that way of thinking.

But she was more than that—one of his very best friends, for one—and right now she was hurting.

His footsteps echoed through the quiet as he crossed the wooden deck to where Addie sat, legs dangling over the side. He lowered himself next to her. "Hey."

She glanced at him.

Shep had taken off after his girl, and Easton and Ford said they had to get up early so they took off, too.

Obviously none of them knew how to undo what'd happened. Why the hell hadn't Shep warned Lexi that he'd dated Addie?

Then again, it'd been eons ago, and Tucker knew as well as anyone that being friends with her brought plenty of complications to relationships.

"I'm fine," she said, a little too quickly, her words short and pinched. "It's just that she and I sorta bonded, which doesn't happen very often when it comes to you guys' girlfriends, and—" Her voice cracked, and her tough facade crumbled along with it. "Oh shit, now I'm gonna cry and die twice."

Tucker cautiously wrapped his arm around her shoulders, and when she didn't shove him off, the way she'd done a few times back in the day when he'd dared to console her, he curled her closer. "Don't worry. I'll take it to the grave."

"I'm not sure I can chance that. I might have to push you off the back of the boat now."

"Sure. If I didn't know how to swim, that'd be a fail-safe plan."

"Maybe the gators will get to you first," she quipped, only then she tucked her feet up, like she'd remembered there might be a few of the toothy beasts slumbering in the water, despite the fact that they rarely saw any on this side of the shore.

She swiped a tear off her cheek and sniffed.

"I hate feeling weak. Hate feeling like a *girl*. Even though I'm apparently not one."

"You're not weak. I've seen grown men cry in my office, so I don't think it's a girl or guy thing."

"I notice you didn't admit to crying yourself."

He puffed out his chest. "Well, that's because I'm far too macho."

The last few times he'd gotten choked up had been over his dog having to be put down, his grandfather passing away, and—even though he'd done his damnedest to hide it—the day he'd said goodbye to his friends before leaving town.

The girl at his side was there for all those instances, but his conflicting feelings for her made it hard to admit to ever being anything but strong.

Like not saying it aloud would make her forget bike wrecks and scraped knees that'd brought tears, the times in his life he hadn't stood up for other people when he should've, or any other time he'd been less than strong.

Just do it, Crawford. Find a way to make her feel better, the way she always did for you.

"There were cases, ones where I was fighting for a worthy cause or for someone who truly deserved a break, and it didn't matter how much research I put in or how hard I fought, I'd still lose 'em. That made me feel weak and helpless." Those cases were why he'd originally chosen law, but they'd been so few and far between. "So did the cases where we had to defend people knowing full well they were guilty."

He gazed out over the lake, unable to look at her as he admitted the next part.

"I missed home and all you guys, but I quit over more than that, and more than the long hours." His fingers drifted down her arm, and her face tipped up, but he kept his eyes on the rippling reflection of the moon in the inky black water. "One guy walked on a stupid technicality because of something I'd found in the police report—some procedure the cop didn't follow. Everyone at the firm was celebrating, and I was sick over it. The guy deserved to go to jail, and no amount of money seemed worth ignoring that fact. It was the final straw."

Addie covered the hand he had on her arm with hers. "Most people wouldn't have been able to walk away from the money."

"I don't know about that. Half the time I still think I was an idiot to quit like that with no backup."

"If it makes you feel any better, I'm glad you're here."

He met her big brown eyes and smiled. "It does."

"I'm sorry you were so unhappy. I should've checked in more."

"I should've told you that I was struggling with my job. But that's neither here nor there. Now I'm on a different path, and all's I'm saying is, it's not weak to care about things. You're not a robot."

He renewed the drag of his fingers on her arm, and her chin lifted another inch or so, some of the sorrow fading from her features.

He tried not to think about how close her lips were to his, how he felt each one of his heartbeats, and how having her tucked against him made his entire body hum.

Despite knowing better, he couldn't help the words that slipped out or that his eyes dipped when he said them. "It also hasn't escaped my notice that you're a girl."

One corner of her mouth kicked up, even as pink spread across her cheeks. "I guess I can thank your puppy for that."

"I certainly plan on thanking him."

Addie half laughed, half groaned and dropped her head on his shoulder. After a long moment, she leaned back, his arm falling from her shoulders, and braced against her palms.

He didn't know how to interpret that, and he hated that he was now analyzing this easy thing between them.

The full moon lit her features, highlighting just how pretty she was. Growing up with her had left him so used to how she looked that he'd somehow forgotten.

Or maybe he hadn't ever truly noticed, which was just stupid on his part.

She worried her bottom lip with her teeth. "I'm afraid that Lexi is gonna kick me out of the wedding party, and not that I was dyin' to wear a dress, per se, but I'd come to terms with it, and what if she doesn't let me go to the wedding now?"

"I'm sure she just needs time to process," Tucker said. "I was trying to help in there, but I'm not sure it worked."

She shrugged.

"It couldn't have been easy being the only girl in our group sometimes."

"Actually, that was the easy part. Navigating it as an adult with all the added complications is what's hard."

One side of her shirt slipped down a few inches, and he told himself not to stare at her exposed black bra strap. Right now he was understanding added complications all too well.

"What about for you?" she asked. "Was it hard growing up with a girl as a friend?"

He gave her shoulder a shove to keep things going down the normal path. "Only when she tried to throw a bat at my head so I wouldn't have a chance at catching the ball."

"I did have a bit of a temper," she said with a laugh.

"*Did?* Past tense?"

She jabbed a finger at him. "You know what?"

Before she could finish, her phone rang. She whipped it out of her pocket, and a storm of emotions flickered across her face.

"I hoped it'd be Shep, calling to say he'd smoothed things over with Lexi, but it's David."

"David?"

"The dentist—you met him at the soccer game, remember? We were supposed to go out tonight, but something must've come up." Addie answered the phone and then said, "No, it's not too late to call." Pause. "Oh. Come over right now?"

She glanced at Tucker and then pushed to her feet. He curled his fingers around the deck railing so he wouldn't do something crazy like grab her phone and toss it in the water.

Yep, he was definitely losing it.

As much as he wanted to hear what they were saying, he also didn't want to know. Because he remembered the smarmy dentist all too well.

He pulled out his own phone to check the time, frowning when he saw it was nearly ten o'clock. A call this late was booty call territory, for sure.

She had to realize that.

Maybe that was their arrangement, and the thought of that sent a toxic burning through his gut.

Not jealousy, his brain tried to claim.

And even if it was, only because they'd finally had time to talk, and he didn't want her to leave yet. The more he thought about it, though, the more heat pulsed in his veins.

The guy thought he could stand her up and then call her at ten o'clock and have the end part of the date?

She stepped back out on the deck. "Hey, I'm gonna take off."

"To hang out with the dentist?" he asked, unable to hold it back.

She sighed, so she'd clearly caught the sharpness in his tone—it'd just sort of slipped out.

"Getting his dental practice up and running has taken a lot of time, and he helps his brother out with his niece a lot as well. They took her to a carnival in Montgomery today, and they got caught up for longer than expected, so he got into town a few minutes ago."

"And he barely got cell service? That's odd. Usually signal's better *outside* of Uncertainty."

She spun around in a huff and charged back into the houseboat, so he quickly pushed to his feet and followed her inside the cabin.

For some reason, she started angrily throwing all the beer bottles away, each clank of glass accentuating how pissed she was, but since she wasn't charging out the front door, he didn't bother stopping her.

She shoved the mostly empty bags of chips into a cupboard they didn't belong in, then turned to face him and crossed her arms.

"Okay, so he's obviously not perfect, but he's the only guy who's asked me out in a while, and I'm fairly sure he at least thinks of me as a girl." Her eyebrows scrunched together. "And I realize that makes it sound like my standards are super low, but…" She threw up her hands. "I don't know why I'm even bothering to explain any of this to you. It's none of your business."

He debated letting it go, but he couldn't seem to.

He moved closer and leaned a hip against the counter. "Addie, the guy's a player. I could tell when I met him, and the fact that he didn't bother calling to let you know he'd be late but now wants you to come running over at ten o'clock confirms it. Even if he's not a player, he's an inconsiderate asshole."

"Oh, big surprise, you don't like him." She advanced on him, an accusatory finger pointed at his chest. "You always rag on who I date—all you guys do."

True. But in their defense, the dudes she dated were never good enough, never truly appreciated how fucking cool she was, and they threw off numbers at poker night.

They were almost too easy to scare away, too. *I bet the guys and I could scare off the dentist, no problem.*

We'll all just take turns stopping by to warn him he'd better take good care of our Addie, and that'll be that.

"Meanwhile," she said, swinging her arms around for emphasis, "y'all go around dating airheaded Barbie dolls more often than not, and do I say anything about it?"

"You *constantly* say stuff about it. You ask us why we can't find girls with substance, or you throw out that Barbie insult or refer to them as vapid beauty queens. I can't think of a single girl I've dated who you liked. Same goes for Shep, Easton, and Ford, so don't act like this is something new."

"Whatever. That girl you dated in law school wasn't too bad, and I really like Lexi, and look at how well that's turned out."

"Well, admittedly, one of your boyfriends was actually pretty cool."

"Who?" she asked, and when he raised his eyebrows and gestured to the seat Shep had previously occupied, she scowled at him. "That doesn't even count. It was freshman year, and considering what's happened tonight because of it, I can't believe you'd bring it up."

She tried to nudge him out of her way, but in these tight quarters, there was no out-of-the-way, so her body brushed his as she moved toward the door.

Heat flared as the curves he'd gotten an eyeful of pressed against his chest, and he whipped up his arm and braced his hand on the opposite wall, barring her way. "I was just makin' a point. I know how to tell when a guy's a jerk or not."

"I guess you better find a mirror, then, so you can see a firsthand example," she said, and then she ducked under his arm.

He exhaled and scrubbed a hand over his face. She was driving him crazy.

One minute they were having an amazing talk, and the next they were in a huge argument.

This was what he got for letting his thoughts stray so far from where they needed to remain.

She's just one of the guys, she's just one of the guys, she's just…bending over to put her shoes on and flashing more cleavage.

He took a step toward her as she straightened, and he must have had a scary gleam in his eye because she took a step back.

Which only made him want to stalk forward, grab her, and kiss the hell out of her.

He wanted to see if that fiery passion transferred over.

Yep, that was the real problem.

While he didn't want some jerk to use her or hurt her, he also couldn't stop thinking about her lips and how badly he wanted a taste of them. Suddenly he was jealous of one of his oldest friends.

Tucker wished that instead of Shep, *he'd* been the one to kiss Addie a few times.

Only that would've ruined everything between them, and it had the potential to do so now.

He wasn't in any position to have a relationship, and if it screwed up their friendship, he'd never forgive himself. No one else was like Addie, and after not having nearly enough of her in his life the past few years, he knew exactly how empty life felt without her.

A good friend would be okay with her dating whoever she wanted, and perhaps even tell her to go have fun getting lucky.

The burning in his gut returned, and while the second part wouldn't be happening, he smothered his ego and the desire making a mess of his insides and opened the door for her. "I'm sorry, Addes. It's your business, and I probably shouldn't have said anything."

"You're right, you shouldn't have, no *probably* about it."

"I'll let it drop *after* I say one more thing." He leaned closer, close enough to take in the smattering of freckles across her nose that drew you right to her big brown eyes. "You deserve better."

She flinched, and he scolded himself for not leaving it at the apology.

She wrapped her arms around herself, and thanks to his big mouth, he knew she wouldn't be accepting a consoling hug from him anymore tonight. "That's for me to decide."

He nodded and forced words through his clenched jaw. "You're right."

Even if I hate it.

Surprise flickered through her features. "Holy shit, I don't think you've ever admitted I was right during one of our arguments before."

"Not making it any easier."

She gave a shrug that conveyed she thought he deserved to suffer at least a while longer. Little did she know how much he was suffering.

She toed a groove in the wooden floor, her gaze focused on the motion. "I'm not sure how things got so… Yeah."

"Yeah," he said, biting his tongue on everything else he wanted to say, which was anything that would keep her here with him longer. Then he shifted into strictly friends mode, walked her to her truck, wished her good night…

And experienced that very same sense of help-lessness they'd talked about earlier as he watched her drive away.

CHAPTER TEN

First thing Monday morning, after grabbing her usual cup of coffee on her way to work, Addie spotted Shep a few yards down the sidewalk, probably headed toward the school, and quickened her pace to catch up with him. "Hey."

He glanced at her, and panic bound her lungs at the resigned look on his face. "Hey," he said, but what she heard was that he couldn't hang out with her anymore and she was disinvited to the wedding.

The image of Lexi and her bridesmaids coming after her with pitchforks even flashed through her mind, unlikely as it may be.

Addie swallowed past the lump in her throat. "She's still mad."

"Not mad exactly. She's…" His sigh weighed about a hundred pounds. "Emotions are just high and planning a wedding is stressful, and…hopefully after the ceremony and reception are over and done with, we can get back to being us."

With that, he continued down the path that led them both to their jobs, and she stayed by his side, the silence heavier than their usual companionable type.

While Addie had been focusing on all the happy parts of a relationship she was missing as of late, it made her wonder if people truly did get back to just being them. Or did the pressures of life make it so there was always something in the way?

Her parents were happily married, but she'd also seen the toll caring for Nonna Lucia took on them. As easy as she could be most days, she could also be high maintenance and ornery as a polecat, and once her mind was made up, that was it—a la, planting flowers in the neighbor's yard.

Alexandria and Eli appeared to be the perfect couple, and while Addie knew they still loved each other, between a few years of babies and his nonstop work schedule, she'd also witnessed plenty of fights where they blamed each other for why things weren't as good as they used to be.

Shep and Lexi were ridiculously cute and in love, and yet the tension wafted off him in waves.

Extra stressors, like two sets of families in the mix, bills, how exactly to raise the kids, health insurance, mortgage payments, and a whole slew of other stuff added up so quickly.

The mere idea of balancing all that with someone else made Addie's skin tighten, and suddenly a touch of the shine got worn off the idea of settling down.

Part of that might also be because her date on Saturday night hadn't exactly turned out the way she wanted to—*thanks for that, Crawford*.

Without bothering with conversation, David had started a movie and opened a bottle of uppity wine that was supposedly super fancy and expensive but tasted like where she assumed that sour-grapes saying came from.

A few minutes in, his hands began roaming, and all she could think was that she *was* his booty call, when hello, maybe it was her sexy underwear putting out the vibe.

Again, thanks, Tucker Crawford.

And another thanks to him that when David wrapped his arm around her shoulders, instead of feeling a flicker of interest, she thought of how much better she'd felt with Tucker's strong arm around her as he'd talked her down.

She couldn't stop replaying the way he'd stalked toward her in the cabin of the houseboat, his eyes darker than she'd ever seen them. Tingles had broken out across her entire body, which had clearly gotten the wrong signal.

Then he'd delivered that last line, the one that'd kept replaying in her head: *You deserve better.*

Her heart had squeezed when he'd said it. In a way it was nice, and yet it'd still hurt like hell.

With her thoughts so messed up, she could only get halfway through the movie before making an excuse about being too tired and heading home—thank goodness she could only choke down two sips of that awful wine so she was able to drive.

And that's enough thinking about my messy love life.

She refocused on Shep, who'd kept striding in a bit of a daze, and what she could do to help. "I'm sorry things are so stressful right now. I'll bow out of the wedding if I need to."

He came to a full stop, the distraction in his features fading as he turned to face her. "You're in the wedding, Addie. It's my fault that I never told her you and I had dated, not yours. Since she'd already had trouble believing we were such close friends, I just didn't want to get into it, so I purposely glazed over the whole thing." He ran a hand through his hair. "It was more than a decade ago, for hell's sake."

"Right. It was nothing."

He cocked his head. "I wouldn't say that. I moved into this town, pissed that it was so small and that my parents had relocated us, and you made the transition so much easier. Then you introduced me to the guys, and my life got better than it'd ever been. Most people don't have friendships like that, ones that withstand high school and college and marri—well, guess we'll see about the marriage."

The words slammed into her chest, radiating pain, and she understood Tucker's frustration over losing cases no matter what he did, because this felt like a case she couldn't win, regardless of how much she argued.

"I feel so lucky to have you guys, too," she said. "You've always had my back, and words can't express how much I appreciate that. But I don't wanna get in the way. I like Lexi. You two make each other happy—I've never seen you so happy."

If she needed to step aside to keep that going, she could do it.

Shep reached out like he was going to grip her shoulder, something he'd done hundreds of times, but then he glanced around and seemed to realize this interaction could be reported to his bride-to-be and dropped his hand. "She's coming into town later today so we can get the cake squared away."

AKA, don't go near Maisy's Bakery this afternoon.

He probably didn't mean it that way, but she

made a mental note anyhow. The last thing she wanted was to make a scene and become the talk of the town.

Maybe I should go buy a cupcake now. I suddenly feel the need for one. Plus, like, a dozen doughnuts.

"Hey, I can see your shoulders slumping, and I know this girl who'd kick your ass if we were playing ball and I tried to pull that defeatist attitude." Shep chucked her chin, and she had to work for it but managed to prop a smile on her lips. "I'll talk to her. It'll be okay."

As much as she appreciated his trying to make her feel better, Addie had played poker enough with him to know that he wasn't 100 percent sure about putting money on that bet.

Which reminded her...

She dug into her bag and pulled out the envelope of cash from the other night's poker game. "Lexi should at least get her winnings."

"I'm sure she'd tell you not to worry about it."

"But I want her to have it, and I wrote her a note, and maybe it's lame, but can you just give it to her anyway? Please?"

"Of course." He took the envelope but seemed to be looking more through it than at it. "Sometimes I think we should just elope. Forget cakes and decorations and the money and tryin' to keep two families happy. It's all getting in the way of *us*."

Weddings were always talked about as these joyous occasions, and while Addie had seen Lexi's anxiety-inducing to-do list, she clearly had no clue what all planning a ceremony and reception entailed.

So she resolved to keep working on the items she could. She'd take her gazebo measurements and find someone who knew about decorating with tulle, and even if Lexi didn't want her *in* the wedding, she could ensure the gazebo looked like the best damn altar either side of the Mississippi.

• • •

The end of the leash zipped right out of Tucker's hand as he caught sight of Addie up on a giant ladder Wednesday afternoon, yards of gauzy white fabric in hand, a string of lights draped over her like rope on a mountain climber. His puppy ran for her, and when he jumped up on the legs of the ladder, Tucker lunged forward to steady it.

"Sorry," he called as Addie dropped the fabric and gripped on to the nearest support beam. "He's stronger than he looks. Come 'ere, boy."

He made kissy noises that the puppy ignored in favor of circling the floor of the gazebo, sliding around like it was an ice skating rink. Tucker dove for the leash but accidentally bumped the ladder and sent it wobbling again, so he decided to let his dog run wild until Addie was safely on the ground.

"You really should have a spotting partner to hold this steady," he joked.

The metal creaked as Addie descended the ladder, and since he'd gripped both legs to brace it, her ass was suddenly in front of his face and he no longer remembered what he'd been saying. Yoga pants today, and they didn't leave a whole lot to the imagination.

Though he still let his run wild.

"Before you two showed up, my ladder was doin' just fine." As soon as her feet hit the ground, she spun to face him, and he knew he should drop his hands and step back.

Instead he inhaled her fruity shampoo and took a moment to soak in having her caged in his arms.

"What on earth are you doing up there anyway? Did someone hear you were helping with wedding planning and make you the official town decorator?" He lowered his eyebrows. "And what festival have I forgotten about?"

He started running through them in his mind. He'd missed the barbecue festival—his favorite of the festivals, although he now stayed far away from the deviled eggs.

The scarecrow one wouldn't be for another month.

Football fest happened during homecoming week, and again if the high school and/or Auburn made playoffs, and then the Bama holdouts would come out and things would get rowdy.

And Winter Festival was even further away, although that was what the fluffy white fabric and lights brought to mind. Since they only had a smattering of snowflakes once in a blue moon, they had to manufacture their own.

"That's what tulle looks like, in case you were wonderin', and this is supposed to be a test run for the wedding I might no longer be a part of." Addie hiked the string of lights higher on her shoulder. "And if you tell people I'm the town decorator, I'll have no choice but to punch you in the face or kick you in the balls."

She raised an eyebrow and hitched her knee a few inches.

"Dealer's choice."

His blood heated even as the now-threatened body part shriveled at the thought. He tried to focus on what else she'd said. "Things still rough with Lexi?"

She shrugged. "I haven't spoken to her since poker night. I talked to Shep on Monday and gave him her winnings, along with this stupid note, but she hasn't called. Now I'm trying to figure out how much tulle she needs as some sort of twisted peace offering. I think I'd rather go the pipe-smoking route, but this is about her, so…" Her hand came over the center of his chest, and his heart kicked up its speed in response. "Um, Tucker? Are you gonna let me leave the ladder anytime soon?"

"And give you room to follow through on your threats? No way."

He'd tried to get some space from her over the past few days. He'd worked nonstop on his boat and had even texted Brittany to prove he wasn't hung up on Addie and absolutely did not care about how her date with the dentist went.

He'd foolishly hoped a little distance would snuff out the spark of desire that'd ignited Saturday night, but there it was again.

Igniting, spreading. Until his whole body blazed with its warmth.

A bark broke the spell, and then the cloudy fabric at their feet went flying as his puppy clamped on to it and bounded down the steps of the gazebo.

"Oh, shit," Addie yelled, stumbling after him and

grasping for the edges of the material. "I told Lottie I just needed to borrow some tulle for a little while and promised I'd bring it back good as new. She's gonna sic the Craft Cats on me."

That news jolted Tucker into motion, and the two of them ran after the puppy, desperately trying to catch him before he managed to completely destroy the flimsy cloth.

Over the trail, slightly muddy from the recent rain. Across the grass. Underneath the benches— well, the puppy went under, they went over, and even with them circling around, it took forever to corner him.

Addie finally snagged one end, only when she tugged, his dog sank his teeth into it, ecstatic to play tug-of-war, the way he and Tucker did with his rope toy.

"Don't rip it, don't rip it," Addie said, letting him have some slack but keeping her grip on the fabric.

Tucker approached the dog the way a cop might approach an armed-and-dangerous subject. He snapped his fingers. "Come 'ere, boy. I'll give you a treat."

With a growl, the puppy tugged, slowly backing under the bench, and Tucker dove, his sights set on the end of the leash.

Finally, his fingers wrapped around the rope, and he reeled in his puppy, who was so happy from their game that he licked his face.

Tucker grimaced at Addie, who was holding the mangled ball that didn't look quite as white as it had a few minutes ago. He gathered his dog to his chest and straightened. "How bad is it?"

"Um, it's kinda green, and there's a significant amount of mud. Maybe if I can slip it to my grandm—"

"Was that the fabric I lent you?" Lottie strode across the town square, nostrils flaring.

Damn her fabric shop for having that window facing the park. Not to mention her sixth sense that alerted her to everything happening in town.

"I should've known better. I told myself that you'd grown up, but add in this Crawford boy"—she swung an arm his way—"and there you go rollin' in the mud again."

His eyes met Addie's over Lottie's head, and then he had to fight back his laughter. He didn't remember rolling in the mud with her.

He wasn't totally opposed to the idea, though. "Sorry, Lottie. It's my fault, and I'll pay for the fabric. My puppy just got overexcited."

He pointed the puppy at her, hoping the big eyes would soften her heart.

Lottie sighed but reached out a hand to pat his head. "What's his name?"

Tucker had been working on it, and had even tried out a few monikers, but nothing fit.

As he glanced from the dog to Addie, it came to him—a bolt of inspiration, one might say. "His name is Flash."

"Oh, is that because he's so fast?"

Gaze locked on to Addie's, he said, "Sure. *One* of the reasons anyway."

She shook her head and lost her battle to hold back her smile, just like he lost his battle to prevent his brain from replaying the flashing incident.

Curiosity over what bra she had on today hijacked his thoughts, dragging them right into the gutter, a place he was perfectly happy to live for a while.

"Fine," Lottie said. "*He's* forgiven, but you owe me."

Tucker juggled Flash to his other side so he could pull out his wallet. "How much?"

"Not money. My daughter's getting divorced and she needs a good lawyer."

"Oh, uh, that's not really my thing. Even when I was practicing law, I didn't deal with divorces."

Lottie crossed her arms, and the canary-eating grin she flashed made him feel like he'd fallen into some sort of intricate trap. "Well, Tucker Crawford. Unless you can get me twenty yards of white tulle by the time I close up shop tonight, you'd better make it your thing."

• • •

After getting Tucker's phone number so her daughter could call him for legal counsel and one last disdainful look at Addie's muddy clothes, Lottie carried her grass-stained wad of fabric back to her craft store.

The whole thing made Addie feel like a kid who'd been reprimanded, but at the same time, it'd been the highlight of the past few days.

She wasn't sure if that was sad or not, but there it was anyway.

She scratched the top of the puppy's head. "Flash, huh?"

Tucker didn't even bother acting ashamed. "What can I say? It just fits."

As if she needed a reminder of that embarrassing flashing incident. Which was why she was back to her plain T-shirt and yoga pants wardrobe.

Her job meant helping people repair and retrain their muscles, and often included a lot of bending and demonstrating stretches. Her sports bra kept the girls plastered in place and her panties fully covered her butt. Maybe she didn't feel super sexy, but she did feel less exposed, not to mention more comfortable.

Tucker let Flash down to walk but kept tight hold of the leash as they headed toward the gazebo. "So, how'd the date with the dentist go? Or should I say late-night escapade?"

Her jaw dropped. "*Dude*. Not cool. Are you trying to start another fight?"

"I was trying to be the supportive friend who asks about your date," he said.

She shot him a skeptical look, and he shrugged.

"Fine. I was stirring up trouble. Seems to be a habit I can't break when it comes to you, a sentiment Lottie obviously shares."

The joke at the end softened it, but things had felt off the past few days, and it was more than the unknown heaviness with Lexi. Addie had gone to text Tucker more than once and then hesitated because of their last heated interaction.

While they hadn't argued a lot growing up—save football—when they did, gunpowder met flame rather quickly. "I just don't want to fight."

"Me neither," he said, shoving his free hand into his pocket.

More and more, her thoughts drifted into territory they shouldn't where Tucker was concerned. Even now she was fighting against noticing the way the muscles in his arms stood out, and her pulse quickened as she remembered the moment when he'd wrapped one around her and curled her to his firm chest.

It'd been so comfortable there.

But then that gunpowder had gone off and *poof*, the sense of security and happy vibes disappeared.

It was a good reality check. Allowing attraction and neglected hormones to filter into the mix sent tensions that much higher. Fights snowballed easier; they had more devastating effects.

After what Shep had said about the stress between him and Lexi, Addie had been thinking a lot about the complications relationships brought and how much hard work went into keeping one strong. If she crossed lines with Tucker, they'd never again just be the kids who grew up together.

With Shep it was different, because they'd only shared a handful of kisses practically a lifetime ago. Horrible kisses, evidently. Not that they'd blown her away, but she was starting to get a complex about her wooing and kissing skills.

But the fact of the matter was, she and Shep had been different people back then, so unsure of who they were and their place in the world.

If she gave in to temptation, wrapped her arms around Tucker's waist, and pressed her lips to his now, things would never be the same, whether he rejected her or kissed her back.

If he rejects me, I don't know if I could face him

again, and with things surrounding the wedding so rough right now, I really need him on my team.

He pressed his hand to her lower back, and she nearly forgot she'd just resolved not to feel anything beyond friendly feelings for him. "While I don't wanna fight, I think we could pull off a conversation."

She tried to smile, but her vulnerabilities got the best of her. "Our friendship is important to me, Tuck. When you moved away, it sucked, and I don't want to lose you again."

He reached up and cupped her cheek. "You won't."

Swallowing became impossible, and her lungs stopped taking in oxygen.

She opened her mouth, planning on saying something about wanting things to stay the same, and how she *needed* them to stay them—Addie and Tucker, troublesome twosome and best of friends— granted she could get her voice to cooperate.

He'd probably have no clue what she was talking about, but she had to put it out there. Just for her peace of mind.

"Addison! Tucker!"

She winced at the sound of her mom's voice. Normally she'd be fine with it; right now she was dealing with a storm of confusing emotions that weren't listening to reason.

She quickly took a step back and worked to plaster on a smile, and still she worried Mom would take one look at her and ask what was going on.

Not only did she not want anyone to witness her in this raw emotional state, she also refused to be one more thing Mom worried about, and she knew her family already worried she'd end up alone.

"Afternoon, Mrs. Murphy," Tucker said, and he sounded totally unaffected and normal, which made her question everything all over again.

"Why, butter my butt and call me a biscuit, it actually is you!" Mom wrapped him in a hug. "It's so good to see you! Why haven't you been by for Sunday dinner?" Before Tucker could answer, she said, "How's this Sunday? We can watch the game afterward, just like old times."

"Are you sure a Saints fan will be welcome in a Falcons household this Sunday?"

"No," Addie said.

"Addison! We try to be acceptin' of all people, even if they have questionable taste in football teams. Unless they go on and on about that Crimson Tide nonsense—I've gotta draw the line somewhere." Mom petted Flash, cooing something about him being "cute as a button," then returned her attention to Tucker. "Shall I set you a place?"

Tucker raised an eyebrow, silently asking if Addie would be okay with it.

Why wouldn't she be? Just because she was having trouble keeping her hormones in check didn't mean she should deprive her family of Tucker's hard-to-ignore presence.

She nodded, and he asked, "Are you makin' pie?"

Mom beamed at him. He'd stroked her point of pride. Fully intentional, no doubt. "Course I am!"

"Then I'm there." Ever the charmer, Tucker added, "For the record, I'd be there, pie or not."

"Lucky for you, you never have to choose one

over the other." Mom turned to Addie. "Would you mind picking up Nonna from her doctor's appointment? I already dropped her off, but I need to do the grocery shopping, and it's probably gonna take me a while."

"No problem."

Mom patted her cheek. "Thank you, sugar. Oh, and can you also water the neighbors' flowers while you're at the house? She's fixin' to catch heat stroke runnin' back and forth to water the plants without them noticing—yesterday she came back limping after rolling her ankle in the dark."

"I didn't realize you knew about the plants. Do the neighbors know yet?"

"Not sure. They haven't dug 'em up or called the cops, at least."

"If they do, call Tucker." Addie jerked a thumb at him. "Nonna's got him on retainer."

"Speaking of which, I wouldn't be opposed to her maybe not mentioning that to people anymore," he said. "Suddenly I'm the entire town's lawyer, and I'm not even really practicing law right now."

Addie clapped him on the back. "Good luck with that, Crawford. I think I can speak for Mom and say we know better than to try to talk Nonna out of things."

Flash pawed at her ankles, either needy or bored, and Addie scooped him up. Even though her T-shirt didn't have anywhere to go, she still checked that it'd stayed put.

"Okay, I best get goin'." Instead of moving, Mom smiled at them, and that prickling sense of foreboding crept across Addie's skin. "It's so good to see you two together again. Addie's been real lonely since you left, Tucker, and I'm so glad you're back."

Since she'd just admitted that his moving away had sucked, Addie supposed it wasn't absolutely horrible, although "real lonely" also sounded like "desperate and crying into her ice cream."

Which she'd only done once, for the record, and she'd been PMS-ing hard and had unknowingly picked one of those movies where someone tragically dies at the end.

It was the most extenuating of circumstances, and she'd never been so glad to be all alone in her life.

Mom chirped a goodbye and, her mind assumedly preoccupied with which pie to bake on Sunday, headed toward the grocery store.

In dire need of a subject change, Addie said, "Joke's on you. My grandma's supposed to be eating healthier, so that pie you're preemptively drooling over is gonna be a low-fat, low-sugar version. We all pretend it's as good—even Nonna does, although she sometimes sneaks in sugar while Mom's not looking. Then there's the mashed potatoes. My mom's taken to making them with cauliflower instead of spuds, and spoiler alert: they taste like disappointment, even smothered in gravy."

Tucker cracked a smile. "Compared to the prepackaged pasta meals I've been making as of late, it'll still be a step up, I'm sure."

His expression changed, too much concern in the set of his features, and he was undoubtedly thinking about how lonely her mom told him she'd been.

Since she couldn't handle pity or anything

resembling it, she thrust the wiggly puppy in her arms at him. "I'd better go pick up my grandma."

"Addie…"

She shook her head and gave him her most serious, don't-say-it glare. "If you even think of saying somethin' sappy or utter the word 'lonely,' I'll be forced to slug you, and then *you'll* be the one who gets pity-filled looks—not from me, of course, but I'm sure someone will come over and give you an ice pack."

He held Flash in front of his face like a shield. "Please, not in front of the puppy."

She grabbed his wrist and lowered the dog enough that she could see Tucker's blue eyes. "I'm serious. My mom was exaggerating. You know how obsessed with coupling this town is—they refuse to believe anyone could be happy single and living alone. I like my life."

Mostly liked it most of the time, anyway. No comment on the occasional loneliness, or how she'd recently tried to make it work with a guy who still hadn't inspired any sparks.

Obviously she needed new spark plugs or to fix her faulty wiring because she was misfiring, feeling things for the wrong guy, and that could mess up everything, and *ugh*.

She could really use a ball to kick or throw right now. Maybe even someone to tackle, but not the guy nearest her—that was a bad idea all around.

"What about your job?" Tucker asked.

"I'm workin' on it."

For someone who'd felt all kinds of motivated and on top of things earlier today, she felt distinctly not on top of them now. With Tucker back and the rest of the guys here, things would be just like old times, and those occasional bouts of loneliness would be a blip in the rearview mirror.

No reason to panic or start worrying she might be what got left behind.

Even if Shep's fiancée no longer liked her and that meant seeing less of him. The weirdo attraction vibes between her and Tucker were messing with their carefree relationship, and the more she thought about it, the surer she was that they were one-sided.

Tucker liked cheerleaders and beauty queens. Tall, skinny girls who wore sexy underwear more often than not.

Girls like Brittany.

Jealousy rushed in, and seriously, what the hell?

Twenty-eight years of being fairly detached and free of mushy feelings, and every single emotion decided to come at her at once?

So not cool.

It made her feel like a girl, and she didn't like it.

She could pinpoint the moment it'd happened, too.

I never should've put on that damn pink dress.

CHAPTER ELEVEN

"Are you a lesbian?"

Addie nearly choked on her water.

Her grandmother's face remained dead serious, narrowed eyes intently studying her.

The other night, Alexandria had called Addie to find out how her date with the dentist went, and she'd relayed that in spite of wearing sexy underwear, she still wasn't sure they had any chemistry.

Evidently her sister thought she'd said, *Please tell Mom and Nonna that I'm planning on sabotaging things with him so they can give me the Spanish Inquisition treatment when I next see them.*

While the three of them worked on preparing dinner in the kitchen, her mom and grandmother had fired off question after question. Then she and Nonna had been caught doing their distract-Mom-while-the-other-person-adds-sugar-and/or-butter scheme, and they'd been banished to the living room, where her grandmother continued to press for more information on where she and the dentist stood.

Addie had said, "Honestly, I'm not rightly sure. But I can't force myself to be more attracted to him," which led to the question that still hung in the air.

Addie glanced at her parents—first at her dad, parked in front of the TV in the living room, then through the archway leading to the kitchen, where Mom moved among the fridge, counter, and stove, busy with dinner preparations.

"It's okay if you are," Nonna said, taking her hand and patting it. "You never had very long romantic-type relationships with boys, and while *sì*, some folks in this town are closed-minded, I sure they be more accepting than you might expect. And who cares what they think anyway? I just want you to find someone who make you happy."

"As lovely as that sentiment is, and as much as I agree about not caring what people think, I'm not a lesbian, Nonna." Sure, she'd initially resisted the idea of going solo for the rest of her life, but she decided it would be easier if she simply embraced her fate. "I'm a spinster."

Her grandmother gasped. "No, *cuore mio*! This can't be!" Her spirited response gained the attention of both of Addie's parents.

Mom poked her head inside the room. "Everything okay in there?"

"We're fine," Addie said in a false singsong voice.

"This is no fine, missy." Nonna huffed as she crossed her arms. "Why don't you at least try to find nice girl who make you happy? Just see."

If only that wouldn't be as difficult as forcing sparks with the dentist, she'd seriously consider it. "I'm fine with being a spinster. It means I get to do what I want, when I want. No one else getting in the way."

Nonna adamantly shook her head.

The doorbell rang, saving her from enduring further grief on the subject of her dating life—albeit temporarily, knowing her grandmother.

Addie excused herself to answer, and her muscles did a clashing mix of sagging with relief and tightening with desire as she took in Tucker and the way the dark-gray button-down shirt somehow brought out the blue in his eyes *and* made him look like he'd recently been chopping lumber.

One errant wave stuck out from his gelled-down hair, and he hadn't shaved, something she shouldn't be so excited about, considering it only made her conflicting feelings that much stronger.

At one time, Mom had insisted they dress up for Sunday dinners. After battling Dad, Nonna, and Addie for an uncomfortable couple of months, Mom finally gave in but insisted Addie at least wear jeans and shoes that didn't need to be tied. She'd chosen Rocket Dogs that slipped on, a form of mutiny Mom only hadn't commented on yet due to the dentist discussion.

"Come on in," Addie said, stepping aside.

Tucker brushed past her, and she got a whiff of something woodsy and abundantly male, and while she'd already known, it confirmed that she was 100 percent into dudes.

Now if she could just find one at least 70 or so percent into her, maybe the spinster future her grandmother feared wouldn't be her fate.

"Dinner's almost ready," Mom yelled from the kitchen. "Go ahead and make yourself comfortable. Addie, can you offer him a drink?"

"No," she said. "But he can get his own drink."

Mom's sigh carried all the way into the living room. Sounded like she was still upset, either about

Addie refusing to divulge more details about her dating life or her and Nonna's kitchen shenanigans.

Possibly both.

"I might need a lawyer," she whispered to Tucker and, instead of laughing, worry bled into his expression.

"What happened?" he asked. "How bad of trouble are you in?"

"It was, uh, supposed to be a joke, but I like how you jumped to my being in trouble, as if it was the only option."

His muscles relaxed a fraction, his lazy smile spreading across his face. "Well, I know you."

"Hey! You were responsible for at least half our pranks. How you and Easton ended up on the right side of the law is beyond me."

"Just covering our asses. And yours, because we're cool like that." She swore his eyes dipped to her backside for a second before they met hers. "So, you don't really need a lawyer?"

"Nonna and I got caught sneaking butter and sugar into the food. In my defense, my grandmother was gonna do it with or without me, so it was either help and make sure she didn't go too crazy or end up in a sugar coma later." She sighed. "But now I feel guilty."

Tucker leaned in, his hand going to her hip, his voice dipping low. "Okay, first rule: never admit guilt—not feeling it, not thinking you might be guilty. From here on out, 'guilt' is a bad word."

Addie smiled even as her heart hammered harder in her chest, her body reading the signal of his hand on her hip all wrong. "What if there's a plea deal? Maybe I should take it."

"We'll cross that bridge when we get to it. Now, did you leave anything at the scene of the crime that we need to take care of?"

"My prints are on the lid of the sugar canister. And the measuring cup."

He shook his head. "There goes my hearsay defense. We might need to call an inside man, but don't worry, I'll take care of it."

He dragged his thumb across her hip bone, a motion he probably didn't realize he was doing, and her blood rushed to that spot, leaving her slightly light-headed.

Hadn't she decided that crossing lines would mess up their friendship?

"There's my handsome lawyer!" Nonna walked over and placed one kiss on each of Tucker's cheeks.

And for a brief moment, Addie was jealous of her grandmother.

I'm a quarter Italian. Maybe that means I can get away with one little kiss on his cheek?

Just a quick one.

Since that wouldn't be a horrible idea or anything, one that would make him think I'd gone crazy.

"I been talking you up to my friends, drumming up enough business so you stay here where you belong." Nonna beamed at him and squeezed both his hands in hers. "No need to thank me. Just promise I always be your number one client."

Tucker opened his mouth, then looked to Addie, presumably for help, but he was on his own. "I…I'm working on another job, so while you'll always be my number one client, I might not have time for many others."

"And what exactly is this mysterious job?" Addie asked, thinking maybe with the pressure of extra witnesses, he'd come clean.

"Tell you what. If your Falcons beat my Saints, I'll tell you. After watching the Falcons get their ass"—Tucker glanced at Nonna—"butts handed to them last game, let's just say I feel secure my secret will stay with me for a while."

Addie shook her head. "Low blow bringing up that last loss. And pretty big talk for a guy whose team has only won one game this season."

"They were working things out, but they've got it figured out now."

"*Pfft*. Yeah, until this afternoon when they play a good team."

"For someone so cocky, I noticed you haven't asked for the other side of the bet—for what I get if your team loses…"

Addie crossed her arms and put on her best game face. "Let's hear it, then."

• • •

Tucker's rapid pulse hammered through his head. He'd gotten caught up talking trash without an endgame in mind, and when Addie challengingly asked for his terms, all he could think was *If I win, I get to kiss you.*

Now he needed something else.

"We spend your next day off fishing." He waited for the inevitable slamming of fishing, and how she'd say that she needed more action—*better not think too much about that last part.* "I get to pick the spot."

She wrinkled her nose.

"What? Are you scared?" he asked, knowing that'd have her agreeing in no time.

"No. My team's winning this game tonight; you can bet your ass on that."

Both her mother and grandmother *tsk*ed over her swearing.

He had her right where he wanted her, so he confidently extended his hand, pushing her closer to the edge. "Do we have a bet?"

A beat of hesitation, and then she grabbed his hand and gave it one firm shake. He wanted to pull her to him and throw her off a bit, but her grandma was still standing there next to her, giving him an odd look that made the hair on the back of his neck stand up.

The woman was probably planning some kind of heist, and then he'd be smack-dab in the middle of a drawn-out legal trial on her behalf, since clearly he was never getting out of being her lawyer.

Mrs. Murphy called them to the table for dinner, and Tucker reluctantly dropped Addie's hand.

They passed around the platters of food, and when he covered his mashed "potatoes" in gravy, Addie reached over and tipped the back end of the gravy boat higher, making more spill out onto the pureed cauliflower.

"Trust me," she whispered. Then she doused everything on her plate in gravy.

While the rest of her family was distracted with eating, he asked if she'd heard anything from Lexi.

Her face dropped, and he wished he hadn't

brought it up—from now on, he'd ask Shep instead. "I tried calling. She didn't answer, so I texted her a picture of the tulle-wrapped beam of the gazebo, along with the yardage, and still nothing."

He'd just shoved a big bite of the cauliflower masquerading as potatoes in his mouth when Lucia asked, "Tucker, do you happen to know any nice single girls? I trying to set Addie up on a date."

As hard as he worked to convince himself to swallow the faux potatoes, his tongue had other ideas, and his reactionary inhale at her question made them hit the back of his throat.

He covered his cough the best he could and then washed down the food with water. "You wanna set Addie up with a girl?"

Pink had crept into Addie's face, and she shook her head, her eyes rolling to the heavens as if she needed help from above. "Nonna, I told you that I'm not into girls."

"You won't know till you try, and this makes perfect sense. You played softball and soccer. And you would have played football in high school if they let you."

Addie's fork clattered against her plate. "It takes more than liking sports to decide you also want to date girls."

"I thought she was dating the dentist," Tucker said, and that corresponding bite in his gut that happened whenever he thought about her with the guy dug in its teeth.

"She's fixin' to mess that up before it's even started," Mrs. Murphy said.

"Gee, thanks, Mom."

"It's only been two dates. One at Mulberry & Main, and one at his house, and Lottie said you left pretty early."

"Oh my gosh, you get gossip about your own daughter from Lottie?"

Mrs. Murphy threw up her hands. "You never tell me what's going on. I have to resort to crumbs from someone else."

Addie dropped her head in her hands.

Admittedly, he wanted a straight answer about the dentist. Not that he wasn't open to hearing more about her going out with another girl, but only in the imaginary-scenario-type way.

Reality was a different story, and he found that when he thought of it that way, he didn't want her with anyone else. But he didn't know if thinking of her with him was realistic, either.

Especially right now, with his life such a big question mark.

Actually, he knew it *wasn't* realistic because of that, along with the state of his finances. Even if he was ready to get serious—which he wasn't—he didn't have $40,000 sitting in the bank, and his 401K was in an even sorrier state.

Which meant entertaining thoughts of anything less than casual was out of the question, and he couldn't cross lines with his best friend for casual.

A rock formed in his gut—he was so far from so many of his goals, and while he didn't like the cold dose of reality, he'd needed the reminder.

"Tucker, you've known her forever," Mrs. Murphy said. "Maybe you can talk some sense into her."

He'd already tried—although his goal was to convince her the dentist was no good for her—and it hadn't gone so well.

This whole situation would almost be funny if Addie didn't look so distressed. Needing to help however he could, he reached under the table, curled his hand around her knee, and gave it a reassuring squeeze.

While his intentions had been innocent, the instant she peered up at him and licked her lips, his blood heated, pumping faster and faster. His self-control wavered, and he wanted to give in to the urge to drag his hand higher on her thigh.

To see if it'd affect her the way just thinking about it affected him.

"So?" Her grandmother leaned forward, the sleeve of her shirt dangerously close to dipping in the gravy. "Are you open to going out with a nice girl—for comparison's sake—or are you going to give the dentist another shot?"

•••

Underneath the table, Tucker's hand curled tighter around her knee. One glorious beat and then he let go, the warmth of his palm gone, yet the ghost of it remained imprinted on her skin.

Reading more into it was dangerous—Tucker had always sensed when she needed reassurance, and occasionally even crossed into slightly protective territory, to the point it'd sometimes irritated her because she could take care of herself. Despite thinking it might be nice to have help now and then.

But she couldn't think about any of that right now, because too many eyes were on her. She cleared her throat and lifted her chin. "I plead the Fifth. Tucker, tell them what that means."

"It means she's stubborn as hell, and she thinks we're all being too nosy."

She arched an eyebrow. *"We're?"*

"Didn't I recently get in trouble for putting in my two cents about the dentist? I believe I was told to mind my business."

"Good point, counselor. Thanks for reminding me. Yes, all y'all are too nosy."

Not one to be deterred, Nonna Lucia leaned closer to Tucker. "I would like to hear your thoughts on the dentist."

"I don't like him," Tucker said, unabashed, no time to think about it.

"You don't even know him." Addie wasn't sure why she was defending the guy. David hadn't called since attempting to feel her up on his couch, and the one afternoon he'd dropped off and picked up his niece from soccer practice, he hadn't bothered getting out of his vehicle to say hello.

Something she'd been secretly glad about, since she didn't know what she'd say to him after the way their date ended anyway.

"I know enough," Tucker said.

Nonna steepled her hands and rested her chin on them. "Well if Tucker no like him, I no think I like him anymore, either. Yesterday in the coffee shop, I heard him going on and on about how busy he is helping take care of his niece, since his brother is single father. The ladies were all sighing over it, but he certainly milks that cow like a dairy farmer in danger of going out of business."

Addie blinked at her grandmother. "What does that even mean?"

"It means he's a con artist," Tucker helpfully provided.

Addie looked to her parents to see if they'd help. Mom turned her attention to the gravy boat, twisting it point two inches so it'd line up with the design on the tablecloth. Dad had undoubtedly checked out of the conversation minutes ago, his thoughts centering around shoveling down his food as quickly as possible so he could get back to the TV.

"Hey, lawyer." Addie poked him in the side, satisfaction pinging through her when he jerked. "Why don't you plead the Fifth, too? Or go with that anything-you-say-can-*and-will-be*-held-against-you."

"Sorry. I forgot that I'm not allowed to say anything about Addie's dating life. We're tryin' not to get in fights."

"Exactly. Now, if the rest of you would follow his example, that'd be great."

Nonna pursed her lips and then glanced at Tucker. "We have a private meeting about this later. Don't worry. We figure out what to do."

"Then I guess I'll stop minding *my own business*," Addie said, "and go over to the neighbors and tell them that you planted those flowers in their yard."

"You wouldn't dare."

Addie scooted her chair out like she meant to go this very moment.

"Don't worry," Tucker said, hooking his ankle

around her chair and tugging it back to the table with a noisy drag. "I'll block her—she's not going anywhere."

She stuck her tongue out at him. "Suck-up."

"Troublemaker."

Before she could think of another retort, he reached over the table to bump fists with her grandmother.

"This is what it's come down to?" she asked. "You and my nonna ganging up on me?"

"Unless you're ready to talk?"

"Like you're ready to talk about your mysterious new job?"

He leaned in. "Are you trying to get out of our bet?"

She leaned right back. "Bring it."

The air shifted, and then she was noticing things she shouldn't be noticing all over again—that damn strong jawline, the way draping his arm over the back of her chair tightened his shirt and showed off his firm pecs, his lips and how they were only mere inches from hers.

Jeez, here she was, about to kiss her best friend in front of her family two seconds after they'd grilled her about her dating life.

At least it would give them something else to talk about.

If it wouldn't mess everything up, she might do it just to prove they didn't know her as well as they thought.

"Game time," Dad said, tossing his napkin onto the table. Everyone pushed away, their plates mostly cleared save the mashed cauliflower—Addie had forced down as much as she could to make Mom happy.

Only when she went to round the table toward the living room, Tucker turned and blocked the archway. She opened her mouth, planning to trash-talk his team a bit more before the game officially started.

The words died on her tongue as he reached over her shoulder and gripped the end of her ponytail. He'd teasingly tugged on it several times through the years, but this time was different.

Slower. More eye contact.

It also sent tingles dancing across her scalp.

A few oxygen-free seconds passed as they remained frozen in place.

"You guys coming?" Dad called out, and Tucker dropped his arm, almost as if someone else had momentarily inhabited his body and he'd just woken up wondering where he was and how he'd gotten there.

He gave her a sheepish smile as he stepped aside and gestured her into the living room ahead of him.

And suddenly, she thought maybe she didn't know anything at all.

CHAPTER TWELVE

Who'd be calling her right now, during one of the biggest games of the season?

Lexi's name flashed onscreen and Addie's plan to log the call so she could ignore it until after the game instantly changed.

"Hello?" The commotion on TV snagged her attention. "No, no, no! Why's he throwing it to him when Jones is wide open?"

"Interception," Tucker yelled, jumping to his feet and doing an in-your-face-type dance she'd call immature if she hadn't done a similar one a couple of plays ago when the Falcons scored.

"Addie?"

She jerked her focus to the person on the other line, stepping out of the room even though everything inside her revolted. With football on, she'd inevitably get caught up in it, and this was important. "Hey, Lexi."

"I appreciate you sending that information about the tulle. I'm, uh, not sure if that's how we'll drape it. My mother wants it more like curtains, but that should give us a basic estimate of how much we need. And now I'm rambling…"

Addie sucked in a breath and held it. She usually rambled when she didn't want to spit out whatever she needed to say, and she assumed Lexi was doing the same.

She'd also known those pictures she'd sent of the

decorated gazebo column were rough, but it was her first experience decorating anything besides a Christmas tree, and Mom and Nonna always rearranged the ornaments she put on anyhow.

"Will has assured me over and over that nothing really happened between you two, and I want to believe him, and it's not that I don't think he's not telling the truth, but you could see how I feel weird about one of his exes being in my wedding. It was already weird enough with you being a groomsman."

Every one of Addie's organs turned to stone.

She didn't realize how much she cared about being part of the wedding until she was sure that she wouldn't be.

"I understand," she started. "As much as I can, anyway, since it's not a situation I've ever been in. It's your wedding, so of course it's up to you. Just… please let me come to the ceremony. I'll sit near the back and then wish him well superfast and leave, I promise."

Lexi's heavy sigh came over the line.

Addie paced across the archway, and Tucker caught her eye. Then he was off the couch and walking over, and if he asked if she was okay, she'd probably burst into tears.

"I think it's harder to know what to do because I like you, Addie, I do," Lexi said. "If I told any of my bridesmaids about this, they'd think I was crazy for even *considering* keeping you in the wedding. I guess I just don't totally get your friendship with Will."

Hands curled around Addie's shoulders, and she leaned back against Tucker's chest. After he'd talked her down that night things with Lexi blew up, she'd decided accepting comfort from him wasn't weakness.

It made her feel stronger. Steadier.

"He's like my brother—all of the guys are. We know way too much about each other. We've never been a conventional bunch, but we've always been there for each other. I see how happy you make Shep, and I hope you know I'd never do anything to get in the way of that."

"Doesn't anyone call him Will?"

"You do. Will Shepherd is all yours, and you know him in ways no one else ever will. Shep is one of my closest friends, and I want him to be happy. And because of that, I'll help you with wedding stuff, even if I can't go."

Tucker tensed and whispered, "She's telling you that you can't go to the wedding? Shep will never agree to that."

Addie put a finger to her lips so he wouldn't get upset and ruin the leeway she hoped she was making, then she grabbed Tucker's hand and squeezed it, needing the extra lifeline.

"Of course you can come to the ceremony—I'd never keep you from the wedding. Can we…wait on the other thing?"

A knot formed in Addie's gut, and she swallowed and put as much conviction as she could into her voice. "Sure. Did you want to meet up sometime this week to deal with planning stuff?"

"I'll text you."

Addie couldn't help thinking that meant *no* without having to actually say no. Unable to do much else, she told Lexi goodbye, and after she'd disconnected the call, she spun and placed her hands on Tucker's chest. "Well, I'm going to the wedding. Not sure if I'll be *in* it, but whatever."

He frowned.

"Seriously, it's better this way. I'll wear a dress of my choosing and flats instead of heels, and it takes off some of the pressure."

Tucker took her hand and tugged her into the living room. They didn't sit on the couch but remained standing behind it.

"Ah, man, the Saints scored again?"

"Right after you stepped out." Tucker draped his arm around her shoulders. "Lexi probably doesn't get what a big deal it was for you to miss even a few minutes of that game."

"Probably not. But you missed a few minutes, too, and I do get what a big deal it is."

She wrapped him in a side hug, perfectly content to watch the rest of the game like this.

At least she *was* until Tucker's team scored again and he jostled her and went overboard celebrating.

"I think it's time for pie," Nonna said. "Maybe that'll turn this game around."

"I happen to like where this game is going," Tucker said.

Nonna gave him a dubious look. "Great. Now you can no be my coconspirator. How'd I forget you're Saints fan?"

"Does that mean I'm off the hook for being your lawyer?"

"Never," she said, shooting him a diabolical smile. "I get in far too much trouble to risk going without my very own attorney." She turned her smile on Addie. "You okay, sweetie?"

"I'm fine. But pie would tip the scales to better."

Nonna rolled her finger, and she recalled their plan and raised her voice. "With ice cream. I'm craving ice cream like whoa. Doesn't ice cream sound good, Tucker?"

"You ladies are gonna get me in trouble," Tucker muttered, and then he voiced his desire for ice cream, nice and loud, and Mom caved.

The pie and ice cream worked their magic, lifting Addie's mood considerably. But what truly turned the night around was the two Falcons touchdowns in the last seven minutes. The two-point conversion sealed their win, and Addie didn't hold back celebrating her own victory. "Time to spill your guts, Crawford."

He gave her a crooked grin. "I'll make good on my promise, but I need a few more days."

"What kind of bull-crap win is that?" She threw a whole lot of mocking into her tone. "Oh, I'll pay up when I'm good and ready, and you have to deal with it, regardless of how I clearly lost the bet."

"Come on, you know I'm good for it." He added eye-batting and prayer hands. "Just give me seven little days before you send your goons after me."

She put a fist on her hip. "You have five."

"Deal." He thanked her family for the food and company and then turned to Addie. "Now, why don't you walk me to my car like a gentleman?"

"I swear. You and the gang are always telling me I'm a dude, and now Nonna wants to set me up with girls. I'm about to get a complex." She shoved him in the direction of the door.

Their footsteps echoed against the porch, and she bounded down the stairs, two at a time, freezing when she noticed the big truck in their driveway.

"I also wanted to show you my truck so you'd stop mocking me," Tucker said.

"That was overly optimistic on your part." She laughed at his flabbergasted expression, but her laughter died as he put his hand on the small of her back and nudged her toward the vehicle. "Does this have something to do with your new job?"

He clucked his tongue at her. "Patience is a virtue, Addison Murphy."

Using her full name like that? "Them's fightin' words." Anyway, they should be. For some reason, her traitorous heart liked the way it'd sounded coming from his lips, something she so couldn't focus on right now. "And you know patience isn't a virtue I have."

"Oh, I know." He opened the door to the truck, showing off the interior before leaning against the side. "So? What do you think?"

"It's real fancy. In other words, a good truck for a city boy."

He jabbed a finger to her ribs, making her let loose a squeal. He covered a yawn with his hand. "Man, I feel like I'm about to pass out."

"Yeah, that pie and ice cream was the hard stuff—I should've warned you."

He rolled his eyes. Then, without warning, he grabbed hold of her hips and swiveled her in the other direction.

"Look." His arm stretched past her head; his

finger pointed to the sky. "See it?"

The falling star flickered out in an instant, but she'd caught the tail end.

"Make a wish," he whispered, and she closed her eyes and made a wish about being in a wedding.

And while she was making unlikely wishes, she also made one that involved the guy standing behind her.

CHAPTER THIRTEEN

Addie crammed into the huddle with the rest of the guys. It was uncommon to have a huddle pre–choosing teams and with only half the players, but Shep had motioned them in, and they'd formed a tight circle.

Always aware now, Addie had made sure Tucker was between her and Shep—she doubted his fiancée would thaw while Addie had her arm around Shep's shoulders.

"Okay, so full disclosure," today's ringleader said. "I have ulterior motives for calling for this football game."

"If you're trying to impress your fiancée, maybe you should've brought in some guys who don't know how to play," Ford said, because he never could help himself.

"You're gonna be on the opposite team, and I'm gonna make you regret those words."

Ford grinned, *glee* the best way to describe his expression. He basically ran on challenges, the crazier the better.

"Anyway, I had this idea that if Lexi saw Murph in her natural habitat, it'd ease her worries."

Addie scrunched up her forehead, confusion stepping to the forefront. "Not following."

"Football. Doing the sports thing."

He gestured at the field like that explained it all.

"You think tackling me will help her forget that

we used to date?"

"No, I'm not going anywhere near that landmine. Tuck'll cover you. You two don't have a problem tackling each other, do you?"

Addie glanced at Tucker. Tackling? Nope.

Thinking about his hard body while it was underneath or on top of her...?

That was another story, one starting at the very moment, considering the wall of muscle heating her side, his fresh cut wood scent making her think of Sunday night when she'd leaned back against him.

When his hands had been gripping her hips and he'd whispered in her ear about making wishes.

"Leave Addie to me," Tucker said. "I'll take her down, no problem."

"Oh, really? Just like that? If you'll recall, the last time you talked trash to me, you ended up eating your words."

"Doesn't sound familiar," he said with a smirk.

With their mini powwow over, they gathered everyone else who'd shown up for their pickup game and split into two teams.

Addie, Ford, and Easton were on one side, along with Easton's cop buddy and partner, a skinny teenager who had no idea what he was getting into, and a couple of their former classmates.

The other team consisted of Shep, Tucker, one of Ford's firefighter friends, along with David's brother, whose name had slipped her mind.

Kind of like how her name and the fact that she existed had clearly slipped David's mind.

Not like I don't have enough complications to deal with.

Addie caught sight of Lexi as they lined up. She wasn't sure watching a football game would change her mind about the past or future. Hope called to her, though, so she tried to convince herself it would, and added a friendly wave for good measure.

The tight smile in return didn't exactly instill her with confidence and, considering there'd been no text or call and the wedding was in a month, it wasn't looking good.

No thinking about that.

Exhaling a long breath, she decided to channel her frustrations and worries into the game.

After this past month of bottling up her emotions, it'd be nice to unleash them in an arena she was comfortable with.

The ball was hiked, everyone sprang into motion, and Addie ran straight for Tucker. With the guys being significantly bigger, they never full-on tackled her, but they didn't take it easy, either.

Luckily speed was on her side.

A few plays later, she faked one way and cut another, gaining a few seconds on her defender. She snatched the perfect spiral out of the air, and with some nice coverage from Easton, ran the ball in for the first touchdown of the game.

Of course that only spurred the other team to play that much harder.

They made play after play, going back and forth. A nice pass to Tucker that resulted in a touchdown and the firefighter caught another.

And right when Addie was out of breath and second-guessing how good of shape she was in,

Tucker peeled off his shirt and shot it toward the sidelines.

You've gotta be kidding me.

She thought she'd been breathless already.

Every ounce of oxygen escaped as she raked her gaze over his shirtless torso, the sweat highlighting every perfect inch, from the corded arms, to the pecs, and holy crap, he had a six-pack.

Apparently lawyering burned a lot of calories.

His stripping set off a chain reaction among the guys—one she refrained from following, despite the sweltering sun—and all of a sudden they had an even bigger crowd gathering.

Women changed course, carrying their groceries or pushing their strollers toward the park. The moms who'd been sitting on the park benches, only lackadaisically paying attention to the game, turned for a better view.

Sure, there were a few guys in the spectator mix—damn it, was that David who'd come out of the dentist office with his staff?

Anyway, her point was they'd definitely snagged the female portion of the crowd's interest the second the shirts came off.

Tucker set up opposite her, and she worked to act unaffected.

He raised an eyebrow. "You okay?"

Her tongue stuck to the roof of her mouth, so she simply nodded.

Then he winked, and the play had been live for several seconds before she realized she needed to be moving instead of staring.

• • •

That firefighter prick had tackled Addie—Tucker understood that she was quick, racking up points, and they needed to stop her in order to win, but he didn't have to hit her so damn hard.

Tucker sprinted over, grabbed the guy's arm, and yanked him off her.

"What's wrong with you? This is supposed to be a fun game, not NFL-wannabe hour. The goal isn't to injure someone, you moron."

Addie pushed to her feet—slower than usual, too, which made his blood boil—and brushed the grass off her knees. "I'm fine, Crawford. He didn't hit me that hard."

He glared at the guy. "Do it again and I'll show you how hard I can hit."

The smack on his arm drew his attention back to Addie. "*Dude.* Take a chill pill."

"You got one?"

She tilted her head. "I don't know. Do you have a plastic bubble I could play in? 'Cause that sounds real fun."

"I get that Shep has some master plan, and this is supposed to be your natural habitat and shit, but these guys are a lot bigger than you. You know that, right?"

That set her off, fire flashing in her eyes as she advanced. "I know someone who's being a bigger jackass than anyone else right now. Spoiler alert: it's you."

Shep came over and put a hand on each of their

shoulders. "You two good here? The rest of us would like to play, so why don't you take out your aggression during the next down, mmm-kay?"

Addie glanced at Lexi, stiffened, and swiveled out of Shep's reach. "No touching, remember? I think this is making it worse."

Shep swore and ran a hand through his hair. Then he put on his carefree happy facade, blew a kiss at his fiancée, and jogged back to set up on defense.

Tucker stopped Addie with a hand on her arm. "You sure you're okay?"

"I'm fine." She hitched up her chin and flashed him a haughty smile. "And I'll be beyond fine in a minute when I score on you. Do try to keep up."

His blood heated, half challenge, half want.

He'd better stifle thoughts of Addie's body underneath his before everyone could see where his mind was headed.

Still, he needed to get to her faster next time. Her stubborn nature meant she'd take hit after hit without saying anything, and that rookie firefighter had barreled into her as if he had something to prove.

For a moment, Tucker wished to be on the other team so he could set her up to score on the guy. Then maybe his ego would take a side seat.

Or more likely he'd only hit harder the next time.

Easton cocked his arm to throw, and Tucker knew it was going to Ford or Addie. He ran toward his man—or woman, in this case.

She saw him coming, pivoted, and Easton launched the ball. She reached for it, brought it down, and ran.

Tucker caught up to her, and instead of tackling her, he scooped her into his arms, lifting her off her feet and stopping her forward progress.

"Seriously? You get mad over a tackle, when you're full-on picking me up?"

"It's called lift football. You haven't heard of it?" He slowly lowered her to the ground.

She spun, her chest bumping his, and the anger coating her features made it clear she didn't find it funny.

"You don't have to treat me differently than everyone else."

"Well, I'm gonna, so deal with it."

She spiked the ball at the ground hard enough that if they had a ref, he would've called her for unsportsmanlike conduct.

He was tempted to blow his mock whistle and call her out, but retaliation would most likely come in the form of her knee to his balls. While he could block it, that'd only piss her off more, and regardless of what she obviously thought, that wasn't his goal.

Easton gave a low whistle and clapped him on the back. "Waving a red flag at the bull. Interesting tactic."

He wondered if his friends could see through him. If they'd noticed the struggle to keep his feelings in check, especially today.

"In fact, I'm seeing a few interesting things this afternoon," Easton added, and the narrowed eyes made him suspect that at least one of his friends was onto him…

And not a fan.

He didn't need to hear it—he knew it'd throw off the group dynamic if he and Addie tried to cross into more.

After all, Shep and Addie had hardly been a thing, yet their breakup had still thrown things off for a while. This was a much bigger scale.

This was every one of his longest friendships, and every one of them intertwined. If something affected one of them, it affected them all.

He needed to remember that.

Besides, it didn't matter how he felt if she didn't feel the same.

When she'd been on the phone with Lexi during the football game, he could tell Addie was upset, and he'd wanted to help however he could. The way she'd leaned into him when he'd wrapped his hands around her shoulders, actually allowing him to comfort her, made him think that maybe she felt the connection between them, too.

Then she'd told Lexi that Shep was like her brother. That *all* the guys were, and they knew way too much about each other.

It was the reality check he needed if not totally wanted.

As he lined up across from her for what Shep announced would be the last play of the game, Tucker wanted to forget reality and get caught up in the dream for a moment.

Unfortunately for him, it looked more like she wanted to tackle him to the ground and rip him limb from limb.

He and Shep pulled out an old play from high school, one most people didn't see coming. Addie knew the plays as well as they did, though, and she launched herself at him a fraction of a second after the pigskin hit his hands.

They fell to the grass, a tangle of arms and legs, and he managed to hold on to the ball. She sat up, her legs on either side of him, her palms braced on the ground next to his head. The smug expression, view of her breasts, mere inches from his nose, and friction spread the want firing through his body and drove him right to the edge.

This woman aimed to kill him.

This probably wasn't the way she'd originally planned to do so, but several cases came down to intent, so in his opinion, that was all that mattered.

He tried to think of non-sexy things like football stats and pond scum as he sat up.

But his hand went rogue on him and dragged up her thigh, and then pond scum wasn't enough. He was growing harder by the second, and if she hadn't already felt it, she would momentarily.

"That's game!" Ford called. "Losers buy beer at the Firehouse!"

Addie rolled off him. Were her cheeks that pink before?

And was it from the exertion, or had she noticed his reaction to her being on top of him?

She pushed to her feet and extended a hand, and he let her pull him up—well, with help, because as he'd pointed out, he weighed a lot more than she did.

She let go but he held fast, curling his fingers around her wrist and tugging her to him.

"Addes."

She tipped her face up to his. "Yes?"

"You still mad?" he asked, even though her clipped tone implied it.

"Depends. Are you gonna admit that I can take care of myself?"

"I'll admit that you're amazing out here on the field, and that you talk trash with the best of them. Playing against you is always a challenge, and next time, I wanna be on your team so we can see how much ass we can kick together. Would it be so bad if, in spite of knowing all that, I took care of you a little anyway?"

Some kind of internal struggle played out, her features creasing and smoothing. "In my experience, relying on yourself and what you can control is the best way to avoid getting hurt."

"Did somebody hurt you?"

He'd kill them. First them, then the firefighter who'd hit her too hard—he'd just take out everyone.

He'd always felt semiprotective of her, but the impulse nearly consumed him now.

"Not on purpose."

He frowned.

"Are you two heading to the Old Firehouse, or what?" Ford asked.

While Easton might be onto him, Ford obviously didn't have a clue. Maybe he should recruit the guys' help.

Because that wouldn't be weird or ruin the dynamic in their group at all.

Addie pulled away, and he fought the urge to tug her back to him one more time.

Crossing lines might be complicated, but holding

back was causing complications right and left, too.

The only thing he knew for sure was it wasn't worth risking their friendship.

That thought didn't do much to cool the jealousy that flooded him when he saw the dentist making a beeline for Addie.

If he so much as laid a hand on her, Tucker would happily remove it for him.

• • •

Football with shirtless boys was obviously a bad idea, especially if one of those boys was giving confusing signals. He wanted to take care of her? Why? In, like, a sisterly way, or did he…?

No. She was projecting.

Was she projecting? This would be where having more experience with dating and flirting would come in handy.

Did somebody hurt you? he'd asked, his tone conveying that he would hunt them down and make them pay, which would be quite the feat, considering *he* was the reason she'd hesitated to get too close to anyone else since he'd left.

Regardless of not meaning to, his leaving had hurt her.

She knew telling him she'd felt slightly abandoned when he moved away wouldn't do any good now.

She understood he needed to take a high-paying job after law school, just like she understood life got busy.

Only she'd continued to call, her weekends

filled with a whole lot of nothing besides work and studying, and he'd done less and less of it.

Every time she lifted her phone to see if he'd texted or returned her call, only to find a less exciting message from someone else, disappointment crept in.

Until she'd *expected* him to ignore her.

Why, oh why were these old hurts drifting up now? Apparently once the tap opened, emotions all rushed at you at once.

Another point for shutting them down.

"Addison!"

Ugh, *now* David wanted to talk to her? Maybe she *should* let Nonna set her up with a girl and see if they were less confusing and frustrating.

Maybe girls would pick up the damn phone and call.

"That game looked rough," he said.

She shrugged. "Ah, not too bad. My clothes didn't get torn, and I'm not even bleeding."

Ultimately disturbed best described his reaction, and she clamped her lips so she wouldn't laugh at how horrified he was over an activity she used to engage in on a regular basis. "Well, I'm glad I caught you. I was wondering if you wanted to grab dinner tonight? I'd give you time to clean up, of course."

Right. Most people going on a date would care about whether or not their clothes were grass stained with a side of ground-in dirt.

But why now? Why last minute, after yet another week of radio silence?

Perhaps he wasn't stringing her along, and maybe he had valid excuses for only calling late at night.

She thought of Tucker telling her she deserved better, and she did. Honestly, so did David.

Her feelings for him weren't strong enough to justify dragging this out any longer, anyway.

"She's already got plans," Tucker said, stepping up next to her, and he was seriously testing her patience this afternoon.

She gave her overbearing friend a menacing smile with teeth. "This falls under things I can handle myself."

He crossed his arms and, with his gaze locked on hers, took all of one step back. "I'll just be here waiting for you so we can walk to the bar."

Addie glanced at the heavens for strength and then turned her attention to David. With Tucker mere feet away, she kept opening her mouth, then feeling self-conscious. She grabbed David by the elbow and walked a few yards away, giving them at least a semblance of privacy.

"I do have plans tonight. I also think that you and I... Maybe we'd be better off just tryin' to be friends."

After a couple of seconds of silence, he slowly nodded. "That'd probably be for the best. I'm so busy with my new practice and helping out with my niece..."

"Who I coach, which only adds more complications."

"Right. And I hesitated to tell you before, but I only recently ended a long-term relationship."

She wasn't sure why he was telling her now, but since she wanted their...whatever this was...to keep going amicably, she went with it. "Oh. That must've been hard."

"Yeah. Amazing girl. Beautiful, too. She was always dragging me to these fancy restaurants and clubs. I complained about having to get all dressed up, but secretly I loved it, because she always made it fun."

Addie couldn't help taking that as how she paled in comparison, both as a date and as a female.

It stabbed that insecurity about not being girlie enough she liked to pretend she didn't have. Ironic considering how angry she was at Tucker for treating her like a girl. "She sounds lovely."

"She was. We just clicked, you know?"

Oh shit, he was getting choked up, and everything in her screamed *abort, abort*.

"Thanks for being so cool," he said.

Then he shocked her by pulling her in for a hug, and she could feel Tucker closing in. All she needed was for him to hear that she was consoling the guy over losing his beautiful ex-girlfriend.

After deciding this wasn't a shoulder-punch-type sitch, she hesitantly patted him on the back. "Once you are ready to date again, drop a hint in front of Lottie, and she'll have the single ladies in town lining up."

He laughed. "Funny enough, she's the one who nudged me toward you."

Yeah. Downright hilarious.

The joke was on him. Or her.

Or maybe both of them.

"I'll catch you later, Addison." One last smile and then he turned and walked away, and she didn't know how to feel. The hint of sorrow came more from losing the possibility of a relationship than anything.

Relief rose up, along with the worry over how her mom and grandmother would take the news.

The skin on the back of her neck prickled as she sensed Tucker come up behind her. "Let me guess, he wants you to come over after you're done at the bar."

Her emotions flipped in an instant, screeching toward offense and anger. "None of your business," she said, whirling on her heel and heading for the bar.

How dare he come back to town to judge who she dated and how? To act like she needed to be taken care of when she'd taken care of herself—not to mention helped out with her family—for years.

Tucker reached over her to pull open the door to the bar, his firm chest bumping her back, and her irritation morphed to desire, which caused another wave of irritation.

She strode over to the group of guys and plopped down on an open stool, sweeping the pieces of hair that'd fallen out of her ponytail behind her ear and directing her question to no one in particular. "Is this part of my natural habitat?"

"Hell yeah," Shep said, raising a beer, and Easton and Ford echoed their agreement.

"Perfect. I was worried about adaptin' and survivin', so it's a relief that on the football field and in the bar, I can be me." She coated her words in sarcasm. "As long as my overbearing big brother behind me approves it, that is."

Tucker placed his hand on her upper back, his

thumb going to the base of her neck, and a shock of awareness zipped down her spine.

"Real funny, Murph." Her muscles tensed. Most of the guys called her "Murph" on a regular basis, including Tucker. Hell, half the town still did.

But there was something different in the way Tucker had thrown it at her just now. She *hated* it and the way it threw up a wall between them.

As opposed to the other night when he'd called her Addison, and heat had flooded her veins.

It's official. I'm losing it.

"Would you like me to bring you a beer?" Tucker asked. "For adapting and surviving purposes?"

She risked a peek over her shoulder and found his face closer than expected. Her heart beat so hard and fast she feared everyone in the bar would hear it. "That'd be great."

Instead of simply dropping his hand, he dragged it down a couple of inches, and as soon as the heat of his palm left her skin, she missed it.

Because she was going insane.

"The guys and I were just going to go for round two as well. We'll help you carry it all back." Shep tilted his head toward the bar, and after exchanging some confused glances, they all got the memo and jumped up.

Then Addie and Lexi were alone at the table.

"Not real subtle, my guys," Addie said, then worried that she shouldn't have called them hers.

Lexi laughed. "About as subtle as a gorilla wearing high heels in a bowling alley."

Addie snort-laughed, but since the vibe between them seemed chill once again, she didn't even care.

"That's quite an image. You have a lovely way with words, Lexi."

"Why thank you."

Not a hint of tightness remained in the smile Lexi gave her, and Addie dared to hope that Shep's crazy natural-habitat idea had actually worked.

Lexi twisted the stem of her wineglass between her fingers. "There's a chance I overacted to the news about you and Will."

Addie froze, afraid to agree or argue or so much as breathe in case it would change her mind again.

"Planning a wedding is stressful, and I felt a tad bamboozled, considering I might not've been super into the idea of a female groomsman in the first place."

"It's all good. I understand that it's a little unconventional—that *I'm* a little unconventional."

Lexi teared up, and then she lunged right over two bar stools and wrapped her in a hug.

Addie patted her arm. *Wow. Two surprise hugs within minutes of each other.*

Apparently hot mess is a better look for me than I thought.

She also wasn't sure she could handle hopping on this roller coaster again. "I don't know what's happening. Don't get me wrong, I'm kind of happy thinking this means we're cool now, but I'm also a bit confused."

"The note you wrote about your friendship with the guys helped, and I've been trying to be understanding…" Lexi glanced around, and Addie automatically followed suit, paranoia jumping into her swirling tornado of emotions. "But what truly sealed the deal was seeing the way you look at Tucker."

The air whooshed out of Addie's lungs. "Like I want to spike the ball at his face?"

Lexi nodded, quick enough to resemble a bobblehead doll. "You only get that mad at someone you're crazy about. After watching you and Tucker interact this afternoon, I can clearly see the difference between just friends and more than friends."

"Oh, no," Addie said, her blood pressure steadily rising. "I mean yes about Shep, and how he and I are just friends, but Tucker and I are—"

"Don't worry. I won't say anything." Lexi's gaze flickered to where the guys were biding their time at the bar. "I'm assuming he doesn't know?"

The tight, tangled ball lodged in Addie's chest where her heart should be unraveled, leaving a raw, aching spot in its place.

She wanted to deny it.

She'd been doing a fair job of denying it, even to herself, although deep down she knew things had shifted, maybe for good.

Which only brought a whole heap of fears crashing down on her. A cold sweat broke out across her body, her panic shifting into overdrive.

Admitting it aloud might bring some kind of blowback on her that she wouldn't be able to deal with.

But if it made Lexi feel better about having her in the wedding party…?

Addie carefully picked through her feelings and words, trying to dance around the many landmines.

"Tucker is one of the most important people in my life, and he has been for as long as I can remember. Our friendship means too much to me."

Lexi scrunched up her face. "I get that, but maybe—table this conversation for later. Will and Ford are coming back." Keeping her arm draped around Addie's shoulders, Lexi turned to greet the guys. "Yes, things are good between us again, and I'm happy to announce that Addie's still one of my bridesmaids."

This time, Addie didn't bother correcting her. When in wedding-obsessed Rome, right?

Then Lexi went and added words that sucked some of the air out of her celebratory sails. "And tomorrow, we get to go try on our dresses and do the fittings!"

CHAPTER FOURTEEN

After handing Addie's beer over to Ford for delivery, Tucker held Easton back at the bar with him. Things seemed to be good between the two women, and he hoped they were, but he suspected Easton had already sensed something was going on, and he needed some peace of mind.

"What's up?" Easton asked.

"What do you know about the dentist? And could you maybe use your access to certain records to do a background check? I can get in touch with one of my contacts, but—"

"Already done." Easton set his beer on the bar and leaned a hip against the polished wood. "I like to know who's moving into town, but admittedly, I put a rush on it when I saw the way he looked at Addie."

"You know she'd kill us just for having this conversation," Tucker said with a laugh. "For daring to try to protect her from anything."

"That's why I only planned on telling her if something bad came back."

"And he was clean?" Tucker didn't want her to be dating a psychopath, but he would've liked something he could point at to convince her he wasn't the good guy she thought he was.

"Clean."

"Damn."

"My turn for questions. What's goin' on with you and Addie?"

Tucker took a large swig of the water he'd ordered. Adding beer to the mess of thoughts rushing through his head screamed disaster, as nice as drowning them in alcohol might be.

Again he thought of the group dynamic, but Easton was too observant to buy any attempt to downplay it, and he needed to talk to someone.

The guy was a vault, too.

"Honestly, I don't rightly know. I drive into town and see a pair of sexy legs sticking out from underneath a truck, only to discover they belong to Addie. As soon as I realized it was her, I tried to shut down those thoughts, but it's more than the legs."

Or the flashing incident.

He swore and dragged a hand through his hair. "I can't stop thinking about her. The more time I spend around her, the stronger the urge to cross lines is."

Easton sighed. "That's what I was afraid of. Don't you remember when Ford and Shep went for that same coed freshman year, and it almost tore apart the group?"

He slowly nodded. "I remember." It was right after his parents' divorce, and like them, his friends were constantly bickering and wanting everyone to pick sides. Poker nights turned tense at the drop of a hat and resulted in heated arguments, and they'd canceled it altogether for a while.

It was a shitty couple of months.

"And after that mess, we all swore that we'd never let anything get between us ever again. Bros above hos and all that, and it goes without saying that Addie's on the bro side of that line."

"Does that make me the ho in this situation?"

"Hey, if the street corner fits…" Easton chuckled at his own joke and formed circles of water on the bar with the condensation from his bottle. "Haven't you ever heard the saying don't shit where you eat?"

Tucker assumed that was rhetorical—*of course* he'd heard the saying.

"Dude, we *just* got things back to normal," Easton said, not bothering to hide the fact that he didn't like the idea, and when it came to this kind of thing, he'd be the most sensible one in the group. "I swear to God, if you screw up poker night—"

"Believe me, I know it's a bad idea. Especially right now. We're dealing with all this extra wedding drama, and I'm currently unemployed and living on a houseboat, for hell's sake. She's one of my best friends, and has been ever since I can remember. I hardly have a childhood memory that doesn't include her."

He'd told himself every single one of those things while trying to talk himself out of crossing lines, and saying them out loud made them feel even more overwhelming. His gut sank, and pressure squeezed at his lungs.

Crossing lines with Addie could screw up everything. Among *all* of them. "The high potential for disaster is definitely there, and yet…"

We might be great together.

That "might" messed with his head but didn't faze the shaky self-control problem he'd been dealing with lately.

"Does she know?" Easton asked.

"No. I overheard her talking to Lexi about how

all of us are like her brothers, and then she makes that overprotective comment." He checked to make sure no one else was in earshot, and then leaned closer, because the entire town had big ears. "I'm not just friend zoned. I'm brother zoned. I'm Luke Fucking Skywalker."

Easton barked out a laugh, nearly choking on his swig of beer.

"It's not funny!"

"It's a little funny," Easton said.

Tucker sagged back onto a barstool and ran his fingers over his forehead. "It's also slowly driving me insane." He set his cool water glass on his thigh. "And I seriously want to kill the dentist. I manage to piss her off every time I mention the guy, but I can't stop. Jealousy like I've never felt before takes over, and it's like I can't be rational about it."

"The good news is, the dentist is no Han Solo, and he sure as shit can't handle her." Easton tipped his beer at Tucker. "I'm not sure you can, either."

"Believe me, I know."

But a big part of him wanted to try.

He'd have to strap in, but it'd be one helluva ride while it lasted.

The "while it lasted" made him hesitate once again, because what if they crashed? What would happen afterward?

Would he be the guy who came back to ruin decades of friendships because he was selfish?

Easton looked toward the table where the rest of their friends sat, smiled at whatever tall tale Ford was spinning that required huge arm motions, and then turned back to Tucker. "You know I love you like a brother—"

"Thanks for using those exact words, jackass," Tucker said, knowing he'd done it on purpose.

"Welcome, dickwad. All's I'm saying is that I'm not gonna stand here and tell you that you can't cross that line, and I'm sure as hell not telling you it's a good idea. I am going to say that if things get messed up and she gets hurt, you'll have to deal with me, Ford, and Shep, just like any other guy would."

"I'd expect nothing less. I'm glad you guys have her back, actually."

He meant it, too.

Knowing she had extra protection took an odd weight off the center of his chest. He wasn't sure if it pushed him more toward ignoring the way his body buzzed around her, or toward taking a big-ass risk, jumping in, and seeing what happened.

Easton nodded. "Good. Let's go join our friends, then."

Anxious energy coursed through Tucker as they headed across the bar, and two steps before they reached the table, Easton clapped him extra hard on the back, and whispered, "May the Force be with you."

Was that supposed to encourage or discourage?

He became that much more determined to take control of the situation, even though he still wasn't sure which way to steer it. Regardless, he needed to check off a to-do item, and he planned on killing two birds with one stone and taking Addie along for the ride.

"Addie and I have to go," he said, grabbing her hand and pulling her to her feet.

She gave him a scrunched, distrustful expression. It stung, but he supposed he deserved it.

"We made a bet, and since I lost, it's high time I paid up."

Lexi mouthed something at Addie that he didn't catch, and she shook her head.

Since he didn't know what that was all about, he finished making his general goodbye. "Anyway, ball was fun, and we'll see y'all later."

Tucker led Addie toward the door, and while she dragged her feet at first, she eventually gave in.

While his glass of water had kept him sober for the drive, he hoped the one beer she'd had would help her forget that she was mad at him.

He pulled open the passenger door of his truck and gestured her inside. She, of course, crossed her arms, going into stubborn-statue mode.

"You don't want me to make good on our bet?" he asked. "Let me guess, you *wanted* an excuse to send your goons after me."

"Personally, I think you deserve a little roughin' up."

"You roughed me up plenty on the field."

"Obviously not enough."

"Get in the truck." He stepped closer, pinning her against the open door. "Please, Addie."

"Don't you mean Murph?"

So she'd caught that jab. The woman made him so crazy sometimes.

Now.

When they'd first entered the bar.

On the field.

Every second of every damn day since he'd

returned to town.

They'd had their arguments in high school, but a different undercurrent flowed during their interactions now, and he couldn't help thinking that pressing her harder against the door and kissing her would be a good way to relieve the tension.

Only you're trying not to ruin everything, remember?

"I want *you* in that truck," he said. "I wanna show you something—only you. Addie, Murph, Addison. I'll call you whatever you want, just climb in and let me take you somewhere."

A bit of the anger leaked out of her posture. She huffed, making a big show of how much he'd put her out, and then turned to climb inside.

"By the way, I forgot to tell you somethin' earlier." He shouldn't follow through with the errant thought running in his head, but unable to help himself, he smacked her on the ass. "Good game."

Her mouth dropped, and he closed her door and rushed around to the other side so he could climb in before she bailed.

"If you think you're funny, you're not," she said.

He fired up the truck and headed down the road. "I thought you wanted me to treat you just like the rest of the guys."

"I didn't see you smack any of them on the butt after the game."

"That's what we were doing while we were waiting for you and Lexi to talk it out. Looked like it went well."

She glanced out the window, watching the graying skyline and trees blur past. "Yeah, I think so. You gotta wonder 'bout your mental state when you're *glad* you get to go try on dresses."

He thought of her sexy legs in that lacy pink dress, and "glad" didn't touch the way he felt about her wearing a dress.

Even in those formfitting yoga pants, he could hardly stop thinking about her legs and her ass, and man, she was sexy no matter what she wore. "I'm looking forward to seeing you in that dress."

She aimed a ridiculously cute dirty look his way.

"*But* if you need a rescue tomorrow afternoon, give me a call, and I'll drop everything to swoop in and save you."

"Why is it that I'm less annoyed by the thought of you savin' me from a dress shop than an overly aggressive dude hell-bent on proving how tough he is on the football field?"

"Because"—he reached over and flicked her ponytail—"you're a little weird."

The eye roll came out, but so did the crease by the side of her mouth that hinted at a smile.

They bumped down the rutted road, and Addie grasped the bar over the window—if she thought this was rough, she should've been with him when he high-centered the Prius.

A few minutes later, the headlights illuminated the north side of the shed.

Addie leaned forward and squinted out the window. "If I didn't know you so well, this would be the part where I'd realize way too late that we were in the middle of nowhere, and my fight-or-flight response would kick in as I deduced that you'd obviously brought me here to kill me."

"Sounds like you've been watching too many crime dramas." He cut the engine. "Guess this is the moment when I get to see just how much you trust me."

Without a moment of hesitation, she reached for the door handle, and for such a small gesture, the fact that she did trust him sent pure sunshine through his chest.

He bailed out and rounded the hood, and his countless mental reminders about not screwing up their friendship weren't enough to stop him from putting his hand on her lower back as they headed to the shed.

He really should decide one way or the other, because like all the drug counselors warned, if you didn't decide to say no, when presented with the temptation, you'd kiss the hell out of your best friend and get addicted.

Or some such.

"I reckon the rough roads are why you needed to buy a truck?" she asked.

"Yeah, the one time I drove the car you like to mock out here, I was pretty sure I'd never get back home. The alignment is still off thanks to getting high-centered a few times. I borrowed Easton's truck here and there, but I wanted to hold off dumping money into a vehicle until I was sure I could even pull off this crazy harebrained scheme I came up with."

"Curiouser and curiouser." She gestured to the shed doors. "May I?"

"Go for it."

She swung them open and stepped inside. The

dusty, stale scent remained in the air, although now cedar and paint mixed in, freshening up the place. "It's a boat."

She looked at him, her eyebrows ticking together.

"Are you a land-boat captain? 'Cause I gotta say, I'm not sure if those are in very high demand these days."

"Smart-ass."

He moved next to her, picked up her hand, and placed it on the boat.

"Feel this?" He dragged her fingers along the bow that'd been weatherworn and splintered a month ago. "Smooth, right?"

A smile crept across her lips, suspicion in the curve. "A little too smooth."

He realized she was teasing him, not so much speaking to the boat. Did that mean she was onto him? Maybe they did know too much about each other, but he liked that he knew so much about her.

That she ate her burgers from the outside in so that the last bite was perfect.

That she went overboard on her poker face, to the point sometimes she appeared to be having a stroke.

That she could pivot on the football field in ways he only dreamed of doing.

And that she was still scared of gators, even though she'd deny it for the sake of keeping up appearances. And possibly so he wouldn't make her watch another scary movie about them.

"So, why exactly am I feeling up a boat?"

He chuckled. "Because I spent hours sanding it, and wanted someone to appreciate it."

"Ooh, nice. So big and sleek, I want to pet it all day."

The joke would be a lot funnier if it wasn't turning him on.

Pond scum, pond scum, pond scum.

Her ass pressed against his crotch as she bent to run her hands over the line of the hull, and then the thought of pond scum wasn't enough.

She glanced over her shoulder, the dim lights of the shed reflected in her big brown eyes. "I'm still waitin' for you to unveil your new mystery profession."

Working on redirecting his thoughts, he inhaled through his nose and blew out through his mouth. "The hardest part about unveiling it is I'm not rightly sure how to define it. Do you remember how my grandpa had that side business fixing up boats? Sometimes he also bought old ones, restored them, and then sold them."

"Yeah. I was always so bored on those weekends and summer days you disappeared to work on boats with your grandpa. When he passed away, I was glad I hadn't let my selfish side keep you from spending time with him."

"Sometimes I resented how many hours it ate up, but I learned to love it, and after working in an office for two years, I found a new appreciation for it. It's something I enjoy, and you can hardly toss a football in this part of Alabama without hitting an old boat that needs serious repairs.

"I thought maybe I'd open up a workshop for all things boating, from accessories to renovations. Or I could do tours of the lake, or all of the above, or…"

He let out a long exhale. "This is why I haven't told anyone my plan yet. I can't quite pin down the best course of action. First things first, I needed to prove to myself I could do it."

"I'm guessing your dad wouldn't be very supportive?"

He curled her hand into his and lowered his lips until they rested on the back of her head, the scent of her shampoo helping calm his nerves. "I didn't tell him I was leaving the law firm until I was on my way back to Uncertainty, and he spent an hour trying to talk me out of it. I get that a lot of new businesses fail, and that it's not as lucrative as being an attorney. If I don't ever try, though, how will I know? And I can always go back to being a lawyer."

"I'm not sure you can ever get out of being one here, not with my grandma sending so many clients your way."

He smiled, then waited a beat, wanting her to say…he didn't know. Maybe that he hadn't lost his mind, and that this kind of life would be good enough for her, in case they crossed lines and things went well, and…

Wow. Now I'm getting way ahead of myself.

"Do you have the before pictures?" she asked.

He dug his cell out of his pocket, pulled up the pictures he'd taken the first day he'd opened the shed, and it wasn't exactly a hardship that he practically had to hug Addie to show her the images.

"Are you sure this is the same boat?"

"Unless fairies replaced it while I wasn't paying attention."

She took the phone from him to study the

pictures, then glanced from the screen to the boat, back to him. "It's very impressive, Tucker. I think you've got something here. I'll help however I can."

Several threads from the tight ball of nerves that'd been his constant companion since moving here unraveled, allowing enough room for hope to filter in.

Her words made it okay to let himself be optimistic about this new prospect.

She extended his phone to him and he wrapped his fingers around it and her hand, wanting to test the boundaries—hell, wanting to break them right down.

"You wouldn't wanna take a ride out on the lake with me, would you?" He dragged his hand up the silky-smooth skin of her arm. Her shallow breath spurred him on, only when he reached her shoulder, she spun to face him.

Her pupils had taken over the brown, and he couldn't tell if that meant she was feeling the tug between them or if she was scared.

"Tonight? It's all but dark."

Great. She was thinking about alligators.

Clearly, her thoughts were miles away from his.

Yep. Just call me Luke Skywalker. The pathetic, pre-Force version at that.

"I've got a light at the front." He jerked his chin toward where it sat. "But if you're scared…"

Her head whipped toward him. "I'm not falling for your pathetic attempt at reverse psychology, so don't even start."

"What? You think the gators can climb up the boat and hop on board? Even if they could, I'd fight 'em off for you. Remember how annoyed you are that I won't let anything happen to you?"

She did this saucy head-tilt, pursed-lip combo. "No, it's not the gators. I got over my fear of them long ago." Her gaze drifted to the boat again and she bit her lip. "Have you even tested it? What if we get out on the lake, only to find it doesn't float very well?"

Wow, her confidence in his skills was astounding.

Good thing he wouldn't let a tiny thing like that discourage him. "There's only one way to find out."

CHAPTER FIFTEEN

Plumb crazy, that's what this was.

She'd lost her mind because Tucker asked her to go for a ride in a beautiful boat he'd renovated.

At night.

With nothing but the moon and a mounted light that Addie had thought would be a lot brighter.

They pushed off from the shore, and she longingly eyed the solid ground as it drifted away, wondering what she'd gotten herself into.

For a boy, nonetheless.

It wasn't that she didn't like boats. It was that she didn't care for the murky water and entire ecosystem taking place underneath her feet.

Including gators—yeah, she was a liar, liar pants on fire when she'd denied that factored into her first *hell no* reaction.

Not that she'd admit that to Tucker. Everyone round these parts rambled on and on about how people weren't an alligator's first choice of a meal. That went to amphibians, birds, fish, and small mammals like rabbits and raccoons.

All fine and well, but she didn't want to be their *last* choice that they forced themselves to eat anyway, the way she did with Mom's fake cauliflower potatoes.

Even swimming holes people claimed were fine sent her internal alarm screeching, and she preferred pools with water so clear you could see to the bottom.

Not this swampy lake water surrounding them on every side, and definitely not at night when she couldn't see anything until they were right up on it.

Tucker thought she hated fishing. Much like an alligator making do with a human as a meal option, it wasn't her number one pick for how to spend time, but she also felt it was tempting fate.

Catch a fish and see if a gator doesn't come over and try to steal it while you're reaching into the water for it. So fun!

But she'd been drunk on the drag of his callused fingertips.

The firing sparks had reignited when he'd wrapped his hand around hers, and she couldn't tell if they'd been friendly touches or more, and both terrified her.

There was so much at stake, and he was one of her very best friends, and yet she swore that earlier today on the football field, right after she'd tackled him, that she'd felt…

You were straddling him. He probably couldn't help it.

She'd been so mad at him for treating her like she was fragile, but now that her temper had cooled, a different type of heat rushed through her body.

She glanced at him, so comfortable and confident behind the wheel of a boat he'd redone with his own two hands, the wind stirring his hair. Her heart skipped a couple of beats and desire pooled low in her stomach.

Yep. I've definitely lost my mind.

Keeping a hand tightly wrapped around the

top of the windshield, she tipped onto her toes and surveyed the spotlighted water.

"Havin' fun yet?" Tucker asked as he slowed the boat, the engine going from a high-pitched buzz to a soft chug.

"So much fun that I think we should go back to shore. The boat didn't sink, so yay, test run successfully completed."

"Ten minutes isn't enough to thoroughly test for leaks."

Her lungs squeezed, forgetting how to take in oxygen for a second or two. "How comforting."

He laughed, and she wanted to toss something at his head, regardless of the way the deep sound echoed through her chest.

He killed the engine, leaving only the sound of the lapping water, some noisy crickets, and the rapid hammering of her heart.

The boat rocked as Tucker stepped toward the back, bent down, and flipped open a side compartment. He pulled out two fishing poles and extended one to her.

"*Dude*," she said. "In case you don't remember, *I* won the bet. This is having your cake and eating it, too."

"And what's so wrong with that? Now we both win. Besides, if I won, I scored fishing on your day off, and this is only gonna be an hour or so. Hardly the same thing."

She shook her head. "This is what I get for trusting you."

"You're welcome for a great night under an amazing sky."

He gestured above them, and when she tilted her head, her breath literally puffed out of her.

She'd been too preoccupied to pay attention to the stars, which was a huge oversight on her part. They glittered like crazy in the sky, more visible away from the lights in town.

The boat swayed, catching her off guard, and she wobbled, but Tucker was right there to steady her, his hands gripping the sides of her waist.

"Sorry," he said. "I didn't realize you were stargazing. I was trying to show you your lure options."

She studied the fake worms and bug-like jigs in his hands. "Fishing lures or stars? Hmm. Hard decision."

"Once you put your pole in the water, you can go back to stargazing."

"Then what's the point of putting it in the water?"

"It makes you feel more productive, just trust me."

"Oh, I trusted you already too many times today, and it's landed me on a boat late at night, holding a pole and talking about lures."

Did he move closer or was that her imagination? "And you have somewhere better to be?"

She tipped her head to one side and then the other. "Somewhere better than being with you? I'm not sure that exists."

A hint of vulnerability crept in as soon as the words left her lips, leaving her chest too tight.

It could be taken as friends, or it could be taken in a flirty way. She wasn't even sure how she'd meant it, only that she was always happier with Tucker by her side.

Had been ever since she could remember.

"Right back at you," he said, reaching around her, grabbing the end of her fishing line and attaching a fake worm. His chest bumped her shoulder and every cell in her body stood on full alert.

Maybe Lexi was right; maybe she should tell Tucker how she felt.

Easy for Lexi to say. She's pretty and blond and rocks a dress and heels three ways till Sunday. Shep sure doesn't call her kisses awful.

Not that he waxed on and on about it, but Addie had witnessed enough of them that she could just tell, and now all she could think about was how awkward it'd be if she and Tucker kissed and it was awful.

What if I'm all about it, but he thinks I'm a bad kisser? That'll definitely mess with our friendship.

And my self-esteem.

And oh, holy shit, I can't risk it.

Tucker wiggled the worm in front of her face. "You're good to go." After releasing her baited hook, he turned to ready his pole, so Addie cast and then sat in one of the two mounted chairs.

A minute or so later, he cast and parked himself next to her.

Every time something moved in the water, she tensed and gripped her armrest, and when she noticed Tucker's amused grin, she spun her chair and nudged his knee with her foot. "Jackass."

"Scaredy-cat."

Addie resolved to stop reacting to anything that happened on the surface of the water. Outwardly anyway. Unless, you know, she actually saw eyes and nostrils pop up.

The problem was, way too many things out here glittered in the moonlight. While she usually loved lightning bugs, she kept seeing them as glowing gator eyes, and she swore some creature had surged through the water to eat those eyes.

Probably just a fish. And since they were snacking on bugs, that explained why they weren't taking the bait she left in the water while Tucker kept reeling and recasting.

So she wouldn't go thinking too much about what might be hiding underneath the surface of the lake, she searched for something to talk about. Something neutral that might also distract her from her confusing thoughts involving the annoyingly sexy guy at her side.

"How are things going with Lottie's daughter and her divorce? Did you get out of that yet? Or are you too scared of Lottie—which makes *you* the scaredy-cat."

Tucker ran his thumb over the handle of his fishing pole and it made that intriguing line in his forearm pop out. "Her daughter brought by the papers the other day. Maribel's enough older than us that I didn't remember her, but she's ridiculously nice. I was all set to simply check the box to get Lottie off my back, but Maribel's husband's lawyer had put a ton of these confusing wordy provisions in so she wouldn't know just how much she was signing away. If Lottie hadn't stepped in, she probably would've signed it. We worked out a rate, and I added enough addendums to make the guy's head spin. Still waiting to see what he comes back with."

Well, that certainly didn't help her forget her ever-growing attraction. "That's nice of you."

"Don't go spreading that around, or between you and your grandmother, I'll never get a moment's peace."

She grinned. "No promises."

He secured his pole in one of the circular holes on the side of the boat and moved to get something out of his box of fishing gear.

On his way back, he stopped midstride and shifted closer to the edge of the boat. "Did you see that?" he asked, pointing at the surface of the water.

She reluctantly stood and peered into the rippling darkness. "What is it?"

"A gator, I think. A big one."

She wrapped one hand around Tucker's biceps, afraid to look but more afraid to not know where it was coming from if it turned aggressive. "Where?"

"Right…" He jabbed her in the side as he yelled, "There!" and she jumped, and he cackled like crazy.

Addie shoved him. "You jerk!"

He caught himself on his palm, the boat wobbling with the movement. "Watch it. If I fall in, you'll have to come save me."

"No way, dude. You'd be on your own."

"You'd leave me to fight off the gator myself?"

"No reason for both of us to die because *you* insisted on coming out here in the middle of the night."

"Cold."

"Yep, that's me."

"No, that's just what you want people to think."
He took hold of her hand and ran his thumb over
her knuckles, and corresponding zips fired up her
arm and twisted through her core. "But you're a
softie, Addison Murphy."

"Say somethin' like that again, and I'm gonna
push you in for reals."

It came out too breathy to effectively scare him.
Not that she thought many of her threats scared him
anyway.

His low laugh danced across her nerve endings.
"Wouldn't you miss me too much?"

Obviously he was kidding, but her eyes met his
and her thoughts turned literal.

She'd already missed him for two years, and if
she ruined their friendship by pushing for more, it'd
almost be worse than missing him, because she'd
have to do it while living in the same town. "I really
would."

Using his grip on her hand, he drew her in for a
hug and she let herself relax into it.

As much as she could, anyway, considering her
whirring thoughts and racing heart.

The quiet crept in again, neither of them moving.
As if both of them were scared of what might happen if they said or did the wrong thing.

Or maybe she was alone in that. The more she
thought about the complications that would come
about if she told him her feelings for him were
growing stronger—and in a totally not platonic
way—the tighter the band around her chest became.

Fear took over, whispering how crossing lines
could ruin everything between them, and then she'd

lose him all over again, but for good this time.

It probably makes me a coward, but I can't risk it. Too much could go so very wrong.

Addie broke the hug, glanced at the water, and steered the conversation down a side street. "A few years ago, we went to visit some of my mom's Yankee cousins, and one morning while we were there, I woke up to a scream that made me shoot right out of bed. I seriously thought I was rushin' toward a crime scene. My cousin had gone to take a shower, but there was a spider in one corner. I grabbed a tissue and killed it. Then I told her at least you could smash a spider; if you stepped on an alligator, all he got was mad. She seriously looked at me like I was from the backwoods."

"You are from the backwoods." Tucker swung his arm, encompassing the lake and the shadowy trees along the shore. "Exhibit A."

"Well, counselor, I prefer to think of it as the front woods." She shivered as the breeze kicked up a notch, and Tucker rubbed his hands up and down her arms.

He noticed so much, and she couldn't help wondering if he could see right through her. If he already knew she'd been warring with her feelings for him.

"I'm guessing you didn't buy my claim that I was over my fear of gators?" she asked, since it was a less complicated question.

"Not for one second. I know all your tells." He touched the corner of her mouth with his thumb, and her self-control thrashed in the desire quickly flooding her system. "You get this twitch here."

"Do not."

"It just twitched again."

Now she was going to have to focus on what her mouth did during poker, and what his mouth did.

Wait. Scratch that.

No watching Tucker Crawford's mouth or thinking about what it'd feel like pressed against mine.

If he could see through her and he hadn't made a move, that must mean…

Her stomach sank. Where was the exit for this emotional roller coaster? Because she wasn't sure she could handle the ups and downs much longer without going insane.

Tucker glanced at his watch. "Guess my hour's about up. The fish aren't biting anyway, and it's getting late." He began reeling in his line, and Addie did the same. "Extra silver lining, my boat didn't sink."

"And neither of us ended up as alligator bait. Knock on wood."

She rapped her knuckles on the nearest surface.

As soon as they'd packed up everything, she said, "I like your idea about repairing and restoring boats, by the way. It suits you, and I think it'll make you money. What if it doesn't, though?" She sucked in a deep breath, fortifying herself for the answer. "Will you go back to Birmingham?"

He shook his head. "When I was sitting in my high-rise office late at night, surrounded by stacks and stacks of paperwork, I used to dream about being out here on the lake. Even when I went home to my apartment, it never felt like home. I'm done with city life." He flashed her a smile that she felt deep in her core. "Give me backwoods any day."

At least that was something she could cling to.

He ran his fingertips down her arm, the same way he'd done to convince her to come out on the lake with him, and she wondered what she was about to get talked into now. "You wanna drive back?"

Her inner child jumped up and gave a squee. "Does a hog like mud?"

Tucker folded her hand into his, and as he tugged her toward the front of the boat, she practically floated. "According to people in town, you and I like mud."

She raised an eyebrow. "Are you callin' me a hog?"

He positioned her in front of the steering wheel and placed her hands on the smooth, polished wood. "I'm calling *us* hogs."

"So much better," she said with a laugh. She glanced over her shoulder at him. "If you're a hog, I'm a hog."

"We have weird conversations."

"Don't act like you don't like them."

His chest bumped her back as he guided her hand to the throttle. His lips brushed her temple, and her body turned drunk-with-desire once again. "I count down the hours until we can have them."

A swirl went through her gut, her thoughts about whether or not she should attempt line-crossing switching sides on her.

He hadn't come out and said he felt the pull, but he wouldn't constantly be putting his hands on her if he didn't.

Would he?

CHAPTER SIXTEEN

Addie had been sending confusing signals all night.

Tucker would be sure they were on the verge of tipping the scales from friendship to more, but something held her back, which made him hold back.

He didn't want to push. Didn't want to ruin their easy hangouts and years of effortless friendship.

Yet he couldn't seem to help himself when it came to touching her. He wrapped his hand around the curve of her hip, splaying his fingers.

She sucked in a sharp breath. So definitely not unaffected, but he needed more than that to risk breaching the friendship boundary.

"That's the dock, right?" she asked.

Oops. If he didn't pay attention, his freshly finished boat would end up in need of fixing again, they'd be taking an impromptu swim, and Addie might never forgive him for wrecking them in occasionally gator-infested water.

Teasing her about them had made her move closer and grab hold of him, and he *might've* taken advantage of that fact. If it meant having her cling to him like that, he'd see alligators everywhere he looked from here on out.

"Yeah, so just ease off the accelerator, and then…" He reached over her and maneuvered them next to the dock.

He climbed out of the boat, secured it in place, and extended a hand.

Even after semi-allowing his help lately, he halfway expected her to slap it away. Instead she placed her palm in his and let him pull her onto the wooden dock.

A mere breath of space remained between their bodies, and when the breeze stirred her hair, the strawberry scent that'd imprinted itself on his brain and slowly driven him crazy wafted over him.

Her eyes met his, and she licked her lips.

Right as he'd decided that was a signal, and he was going to go for it, she took a step back.

She rubbed her neck and glanced at the boat, the crinkle in her forehead making it clear she was battling the thoughts going through that beautiful head of hers.

"Remember how I can read your tells?" He cupped her chin and gently tipped her face to his. "Talk."

She arched an eyebrow. "And if I refuse?"

At this point, he supposed it didn't matter, because he couldn't keep his mouth shut any longer.

He needed to know if something else—namely someone else—was in the way. "Tell me you're not holding back because of the dentist. I hoped watching you play football this afternoon with your burly group of friends would scare him off, even if that makes me an ass."

"You're definitely more ass-like than usual whenever it comes to him."

It probably didn't speak well to his mental state that he preferred her not pulling punches. It meant things between them were at least normal-ish. "I know."

"At least you acknowledge it."

He traced her jaw with his thumb, and when her hot exhale of breath skated over his wrist, longing seized hold of his body and refused to let go. "I don't want you seeing him anymore."

She swallowed. "Why would you care?"

"You know why. We've been dancin' around it for a while, but I doubt you've failed to notice that something's changin' between us."

Before taking her out on the boat, he'd worried he was the only affected one, but between the way her body had melted against his on the drive to the dock, the way she was curling her fingers around his wrist, and her dilating pupils, he was sure the electricity was traveling both ways.

"Don't act like you don't feel it," he said.

He slid his arm around her waist, tethering her to him, and the instant their bodies met, liquid hot need flowed through him.

"Part of me wishes I could pretend I didn't," he added. "That we could go back to how things used to be because it would be easier. Simple. Normal." He hadn't felt normal about her in weeks. Nothing felt right until he was with Addie again, and the thought of her with anyone else opened up a raging, possessive side of him he didn't know existed till now. "But there's no simple and normal between us anymore."

"That's what I'm worried about," she said, and her eyes fluttered shut as he dragged his thumb over her full bottom lip. "There are so many complications and variables, and I don't wanna create unnecessary drama." Her eyes opened and locked on to his. "I don't want to ruin things."

"One problem at a time, Addes. Right now we're discussin'"—he gritted his teeth—"the dentist."

"He and I are done. Pretty sure we were done the instant you returned to town."

Unable to wait another second, Tucker crashed his lips down on hers.

Relief and desire hit him at once, and he dove into the heady sensations.

He tugged on her ponytail, the way he'd done on countless occasions, but this time he used it to angle her head and deepen the kiss.

Her lips opened for him, her tongue tentatively touching his, and everything inside him roared. He pressed her closer and stroked his tongue over hers, tasting her moan as it vibrated through him.

The kiss was everything he'd fantasized it'd be and more.

And speaking of more, he couldn't seem to get his fill. Even plastered against him, she wasn't close enough.

He slid his hands lower on her back, and just before he gripped her ass and lifted her into his arms, he caught himself and—summoning all his self-control—forced himself to slow it down. To be cautious in his recklessness.

Torturous, but not nearly as torturous as it'd been to be around her these past few weeks without kissing her.

He broke the kiss but kept his hold on her.

She made a low *mmm* noise as she looked up at him through her lashes, a sexy move that had him wanting to kiss her all over again.

His thumb slipped underneath the hem of her shirt and skimmed across the smooth skin of her lower back. "You don't really expect me *not* to kiss you when you say something like that, do you?"

"Do you really think we can kiss and not screw up our friendship?"

She placed her hands on his chest, where his heart pounded out a rapid, erratic rhythm.

"Factor in the upcoming wedding I'm now in again, our tight group of friends, my family getting involved, the whole town getting involved—basically, a lot of involvement all around."

He wanted to tell her "of course" because they were Addie and Tucker, and they could take on anything.

Then he remembered Easton's reminder of how much it sucked when the group dynamic was thrown off, and the pressure of nonstop gossip, and how once the town got involved, even the strongest of couples could hardly take it.

Lead filled his lungs, replacing more and more of his oxygen.

Man, the things he'd heard about his own parents when people didn't realize he was around and listening. Not everyone was horrible, but several of the things he'd heard about Mom were.

She'd cried about it more than once, and it was one of the reasons she'd fled town as quickly as she did.

He didn't want Addie to be dragged through that—she was tough, but everyone had a breaking point, and words often sliced and scarred worse than anything else.

He hadn't had a long-term relationship in years, either, but every single one had included ugly fights. His life was in total upheaval right now, too.

He groaned, and she gave him a sympathetic smile.

"My thoughts exactly," she said.

"I get what you're saying, but I can't stop thinking about you, no matter how much I tell myself not to mess things up." His hands drifted down to her ass, not lifting like he wanted but copping a generous feel. "And, Addie, I *need* to kiss you. I don't think I can go without doing it again."

She trailed her fingers over his jaw and flattened her hand against the side of his face. Their lips met in the middle, and he lost the will to hold back—not that he had much of one in the first place.

He lifted her into his arms, anchoring her to him as he rolled his tongue over hers. She drove her fingers through his hair, her fingernails dragging across his scalp, and it felt so damn good he worried his knees would give out and he'd dump both of them in the water.

He walked them toward the truck, blindly reaching out for the hard metal surface, and as soon as he found purchase, he pressed her against it.

She dropped her forehead to his, her rapid breaths sawing in and out of her mouth. "Weren't we in the middle of discussing how this is a bad idea?"

"I don't recall that, no," he said, kissing her again.

She laughed against his lips, and then she pulled back and looked him in the eye.

He'd seen her in just about every state, but he'd never seen her like this. Lips swollen from kissing, lust swimming in her big brown eyes.

It turned him on all over again, until his veins contained more fire than blood.

"Maybe if we…take it slow?" she asked. "And constantly check in with each other? And we have to be honest about how we're feeling, no holding back."

"Sure, we can do that." His concerns about the gossip bobbed to the surface again. "And we should definitely keep it just between us right now. That'll help cut out a lot of that extra pressure and unnecessary drama."

She pursed her lips together, getting that deep-thinking crinkle again, and then she slowly nodded. "Right. And if it starts to get in the way of us…" She ran her hand down his cheek, and it calmed everything inside him even as it also stirred it up. "I need us to be us."

"God, me too."

"In the name of going slow, I think you better take me home."

A groan ripped from his throat as she slid down him in one torturous drag, and when she turned to open the truck door, he tugged her back to him and pressed his lips against her neck.

"I know, I know," he whispered. "I've just been thinking about kissing you for a while, and I worry if I let go, I might wake up."

She pinched him, and a sharp pain shot up his arm.

"Ouch."

"Not a dream," she said.

"I appreciate you using *me* to make sure."

She smiled over her shoulder at him. "Anytime."

This could work. They could go slow. Check in.

It'd be them but with kissing and hopefully, eventually sex, because he was rock hard from the amazing things she did with her tongue, and thinking of having her legs wrapped around him propelled him into the blue-balls-for-days stage.

He boosted her into the truck via a hand on her ass, rounded the hood, and readjusted himself the best he could as he settled behind the wheel. He glanced at her long legs in those yoga pants and *holy shit*, her nipples were hard and straining against her thin T-shirt.

"While we're taking it slow, maybe you can wear that ratty sweatshirt you love and help downplay those curves. Baggy sweats, too—didn't you used to wear those all the time? Or those fucking farmer overalls."

"Hey," she said, but she laughed. "You'd better wear your disgusting old ratty hat, then."

He reached behind the seat, grabbed hold of it, and tugged it on, pulling the brim nice and low.

"Maybe you should wear it on your lap," she said, her gaze homed in on his situation, which only brought it raging back.

"Not. Helping."

Her laugh turned borderline evil.

As they started the bumpy return drive to town, though, silence fell between them. It grew heavier and heavier, like they were both realizing the huge line they'd crossed.

He wanted to reassure her it'd be fine—they had fail-safes in place. *We'll figure it out. It'll all be okay.*

"Do you need to get your truck from the bar, or should I drop you at your house?"

"I actually walked to the field, so home. My home. Not my parents' home."

"I figured, although I was about to head there out of habit."

Funny enough, he only knew where it was because she was renting the old Sumpter place. Since Addie moved in shortly after he moved away, he hadn't been inside.

She lived just off Main Street, and he parked along the curb next to her mailbox. In the dark cab of the truck, they were at least semiprotected, but if they stepped out onto the streetlamp-lit sidewalk together, dozens of eyes could be on them in a matter of seconds.

"Check-in time," Addie said, twisting to face him. "Do things feel weird now that everything's sunk in? Are we okay?"

"Not weird." He glanced around, then leaned closer and brushed his lips over hers, satisfaction winding through him at her tiny whimper. "I'm better than okay. You?"

She nodded. "I'm okay. But this is going to be tricky."

Understatement, but he was too happy right now to care.

She reached for her door handle. "Good night, Crawford."

He wanted to do the gentlemanly thing and walk her to the door; he just knew that if he did, he'd forget about being a gentleman, pull her into his arms for another groping session, and kiss the hell out of her anyway.

Then someone in town would be wagging their tongue, and those complications would rush at them from all sides, and he refused to destroy this before it even had a chance.

So he playfully punched her shoulder and said, "Night, Murph."

CHAPTER SEVENTEEN

"Oh my." Addie stared at her reflection, taking in the strapless bridesmaid dress and how much of her cleavage was on display—the "sweetheart" neckline had sounded so innocent when Lexi first mentioned it, too.

Between having to coach a soccer game and the fact that the bridal shop was two towns over—and okay, Auburn was also playing that same evening— she'd missed the original dress-shopping excursion.

She didn't think it would matter much. To her, a dress was an uncomfortable dress, so it wasn't like she was qualified to give input. She'd simply texted her measurements to Lexi and told her she'd wear whatever.

In hindsight, not the best idea, but after everything that'd happened, it wasn't like she'd say she didn't want to wear the strapless number that landed a few inches above her knees.

Since so much of her bra was on display, she was also glad she'd worn one of the sexy ones her sister helped her pick out. She knew she'd be trying on a fancy dress, and well, it cost a shit-ton compared to her usual boring white bras, but the dark purple straps stuck out, clashing with the crimson fabric.

Yeah, *crimson*.

I wonder if Shep knows his wedding is gonna look like it was thrown by a bunch of Bama fans.

"You look amazing," Lexi said.

"I look…" *Half naked.*

She tugged at the top, not trusting it to stay in place. She'd already had one flashing incident, and if she flashed any of her other guy friends—or worse, the whole town—she'd have no choice but to flee and assume a new identity.

"I'm guessing you don't want my bra straps hanging out on the big day?" She flicked the strap. At least it wasn't a totally torturous undergarment, although not quite as comfortable as Alexandria let on.

Admittedly, it did make her feel a little bit sexy, and she could use that right now.

"You need a *strapless* bra for it," Brittany said. Naturally she'd come prepared wearing hers.

She'd also stripped in front of everyone in the general fitting area, showing off her willowy figure, while Addie had stepped into the dressing room to change and then seriously considered never coming out. "I'd recommend a thong, too, to avoid panty lines."

Right. Because what was missing from this whole experience was a tiny strip of fabric riding up her ass.

That way, when she inevitably tripped on her heels, she could expose her bottom half to the entire wedding party.

Hey, maybe *then* the townsfolk and her friends would acknowledge she was a girl!

At least Tucker knows.

A smile spread across her face as she thought about last night.

About his lips and his tongue and his hard body

pressed against hers, and how close she'd been to throwing out logic and what-ifs and telling him to take her back to his place.

If the thorough, fevered way he kissed was an indication, they'd have a very good time for a very long time...

The temperature in the room rose, and suddenly she was grateful for her half-naked state.

Until she caught her reflection again. How could she wear this in front of the whole town?

Sure, strapless and midthigh was respectable in theory, but she'd never displayed quite this much skin at once.

Addie tugged down the skirt but that only made the top dip down to display more of her bra. "How do your boobs stay up without straps?"

"Magic," Lexi said with a giggle—the bridal shop kept plying them with champagne, and even though it wasn't Addie's drink of choice, she took a healthy gulp from her glass.

"Hear me out. How 'bout instead of a dress, we wear yoga pants and matching T-shirts?" She punctuated her joke with a clap.

Brittany curled her lip, but Lexi laughed. "Will said you weren't a dress-and-heels-type girl."

"Thus the groomsman title."

"Come on. You look amazing." Lexi placed her hands on Addie's shoulders and spun her to face the mirror again. Then she tipped onto her toes, nearly knocking her off her feet, bare as they may be, and whispered, "I bet Tucker will think so, too."

"I think he'll laugh." All the guys would. "I'm not sure I can pull off sexy."

So much for the momentary boost her lacy underwear had bought her.

"Of course you can," Lexi said. "And trust me, he won't."

Now Addie didn't just have the potential to make a fool of herself in front of *a* guy.

She'd be making a fool of herself in front of Tucker, who usually dated Barbies and beauty queens.

Whereas she was the girl who'd eaten twenty-one deviled eggs in under a minute; the girl who'd gotten overly competitive and accidentally elbowed her first serious boyfriend in the nose when he tried to steal the ball from her on the soccer field.

She'd broken his nose and he'd been her first heartbreak.

Her sexual experience was best summed up as "few and far between," and even the during was nothing to brag about.

I need a How to Be Sexy for Dummies *crash course before I sleep with Tucker.*

If *I sleep with Tucker.*

Desire streaked through her as she relived more of the kissing, and the way his big body had pinned her to the truck as he ground against her.

Dang, I wanna sleep with him.

She couldn't stop thinking about it, even as she reminded herself they were going slow so they didn't accidentally ruin everything.

Addie glanced from Lexi to the three other bridesmaids. That "One of these things is not like the other" song played through her head, but if she managed to impress Tucker, she supposed she could suck it up and focus on that.

"You know we're not wearing ponytails to the wedding, right?" Brittany said.

Addie gave her a syrupy sweet smile. "You know what I do know? How to throw a killer right hook."

She was aware she shouldn't derive so much pleasure from the wide berth Brittany suddenly gave her, just like she fully realized she'd have to call in some favors if she was going to wrangle her hair into the complicated updo all the bridesmaids—and one of the groomsmen—were going to wear.

When the champagne made the rounds again, Addie filled her flute to the top.

By the time they stood for alterations, she was buzzed enough that Lexi talked her into borrowing one of her dresses and going with them to some ritzy club, as a practice-wearing-a-dress-and-heels-slash-bachelorette-party twofer kind of thing.

The rest of the evening went much like that, with her agreeing to crazy things that would normally make her run—she was as surprised as anyone when she found herself genuinely enjoying herself.

And when the bridesmaids asked if the other groomsmen were single, since apparently after flirting with Tucker through text messages, Brittany had already claimed him, Addie held it together.

By asking Lexi to take her onto the dance floor and teach her some sexy moves. If she had to compete with women like Brittany, she didn't have time to waste on things like common sense.

As they danced, Lexi also gave her flirting tips. Despite insisting she should practice, Addie forewent trying them out on guys in the club.

For embarrassment's sake, and out of respect for Tucker—although considering Brittany's claims, she'd be getting confirmation that went both ways ASAP.

When she received a message from Mom, Nonna Lucia, and Lottie, about how David had been seen around town with a woman rumored to be the beautiful ex-girlfriend Addie paled in comparison to, she took it in stride.

By ordering shots.

And at the end of the night, when the taxi driver asked where to drop her tipsy ass, she decided to run with the crazy, take advantage of the fact that she still had on not only Lexi's little black dress but also sexy purple underwear, and told him to drop her at the houseboat.

• • •

Banging accompanied things falling to the floor, and Tucker sat up in bed, listening for the intruder as he reached for the baseball bat he'd unearthed when he'd moved in.

It could be a critter, maybe a raccoon, but it sounded bigger than that, and he worried about Flash darting out and getting hurt.

Then a familiar strawberry scent hit him, turning his thoughts from attacking to…well, a different type of attacking.

Another bang as what he guessed was his box with boat parts clanged to the ground, and she muttered a loud "Ouch" followed by a stream of swearing.

Flash barked, and Addie's "whisper" cut through the room. "Flash, *shhh*. You're gonna get me found out, and it's supposed to be a surprise."

Tucker flipped on the light, grinning when she jumped. "Too late. You were found out the instant you stumbled in and your perfume hit my nose."

She blinked at him, and *holy shit* what was she wearing? It was one of those little black dresses, tight and sequined, and her brown hair spilled around her shoulders. Her cheeks were flushed, and she had the look of a woman in need of ravishing.

Whoa, thoughts. Let's take it down a notch.

He swallowed past a dry throat, trying to focus on something besides Addie's never-ending legs and how much he wanted to get his hands on them. "Whatcha doin'?"

"I went to a dance club," she slurred.

He didn't like the thought of her in some club, men constantly approaching and buying her drinks and staring at her in that sexy dress, and the thought of them touching her sent jealousy surging up to the forefront, even as he told himself to keep it in check.

"A dance club? That's rather far from your usual jaunts. Did you dance?"

"I did, and if there's not a video of it on YouTube, titled something like 'America's Worst Dancer,' it'll be a frickin' miracle."

"Oh, I doubt it was that bad."

In that dress, it didn't much matter how she moved.

His eyes dipped to her cleavage and the way her chest rose and fell, rose and fell.

She swiped the hair that'd fallen in her eyes

behind her ear, and was she purposely trying to kill him with the way she dragged her hand down her neck and over the swell of her breasts?

"Anyway, it was like a test run, although the bridesmaid's dress is a bit more revealing and doesn't have any straps, and how is my bra supposed to stay up without straps?"

Tucker assumed saying *who cares if it stays up?* wasn't the right answer.

His fingers twitched with the urge to test the bounds of her current straps—to tug them down and take a taste, just a tiny one.

"Then I got drunk, and when my taxi driver asked where to drop me, I told him here."

"You took a taxi while you were wasted and alone?"

She crossed her arms. "Don't get all huffy and overprotective. It was one of the Colburn boys from Loachapoka. Course, I wasn't really thinking 'bout how he might blab just as easily as Lottie."

He still didn't like the idea of her alone in a cab in her drunken state, but before he could renew his lecture, she ran her gaze over him, lust widening her eyes. "I thought *I* was mostly naked, but you're only wearing your boxer briefs."

They were feeling tighter by the second, too. "I wasn't exactly expectin' company."

Addie took a large step, wobbled, and braced her hand on the counter, and in a few more strides she was toe-to-toe with him.

"Hey," she said, a giggle following.

"Hey."

She rolled her head, flipping her hair, and if he

hadn't dodged in time, they both probably would've gotten a nosebleed.

What the hell's gotten into—

She ran a hand down his torso, her fingers pausing at the waistband of his underwear. He wrapped his fingers around her wrist, stopping the motion, in spite of his body's begging to let it go on.

Her tongue darted out to lick her lips and she slowly looked up at him.

Her eyes were lined in black, making them look bigger, and the smudged right one made him think she'd been resting her cheek against her fist on that side, the way she usually did when she rode in a car.

A smile spread across her red lips, and she shook her hair out of her eye. "Hey."

"We did that part already."

"Which part?" She moved closer, her chest bumping his as she slid her hands up his arms and linked them behind his neck. "Did I miss it?"

He gripped her hips and lowered his forehead to hers, taking a moment to soak in the warmth of her body and the way her silky hair brushed his bare skin.

He groaned. "Addes, I'm not taking advantage of you while you're drunk and lookin' for trouble."

She pouted her lips, something he swore he'd never seen her do before. "Is it because I can't pull off this dress? I told Lexi I thought I looked ridiculous, but she insisted, and to be honest, I was already a wee bit drunk, so it seemed like a good idea at the time. Plus, I'm tryin' to keep her happy so she's glad that I'm back in the wedding lineup."

"The dress looks amazing on you." His fingers

dug into her sides as he fought the temptation to tug her closer instead of holding her in place. "As for pulling it off, I definitely wanna help you do that."

A saucy smile curved her siren mouth, and she tested his willpower by toying with one of the straps of her dress.

Then she winked at him—or tried, anyway. It was twitchy and the other eye half closed, too.

He wasn't sure what kind of drinks they served in that club, but she'd obviously had more than enough of them.

Last night she'd made it clear that she wanted to go slow. Coming over like this landed in the mixed-signals category, but that was the thing with alcohol. It made a mess of logical thoughts and played a little too loose with inhibitions.

After taking a quick moment to glance at the ceiling and fortify his self-control, he quickly maneuvered her so she sat on the edge of the bed. "I'm gonna get you some water and aspirin before I put you to bed."

She slowly crossed one leg over the other, her skirt hiking so high he got a glimpse of lacy purple panties. "You mean *take* me to bed."

He straightened and scrubbed a hand over his face.

His body didn't get the memo about not taking her to bed, so he got to walk around his kitchen aroused and suddenly way too awake and aware of the beautiful woman in his bed.

His best friend.

Shit. This had disaster written all over it.

There was crossing boundaries and then there

was plowing through them with a tank, and now it was up to him to ignore the want that seared through his veins as he took in her sexy curves and those bare legs and take it slow.

After talking her into taking the pills, he nudged her back on the bed and pulled the covers over her.

Her fingers circled his wrist. "I know we barely kissed yesterday, and I don't wanna sound like one of those clingy chicks, but are you gonna keep kissing other girls? Gonna keep flirting with Brittany over text? I just need to know."

Oh. That helped explain some of whatever was going on. "I only texted her a few times. We haven't gone out on a date or kissed, and she texted me tonight—"

Addie shot up, eyes ablaze.

"But I told her I'd started seeing someone."

Because he hadn't wanted to mess things up with Addie, no matter how out of his league he felt, and he still worried he was going to screw it all up, especially right now.

He eased her back down. "No kissing other girls, I swear."

"You haven't kissed me tonight, either," she said, and the pout returned.

He tapped her lips, earning a scowl. "Because if I kiss you, and you start getting all handsy again, it'll be hard to stop."

"So?"

He grabbed her hand, halting its downward progress, and laced his fingers with hers. "*So*, you're drunk and we're taking it slow, remember?"

"What if I changed my mind?" she asked, and he

shook his head. She frowned. "Was it my moves? I knew I wasn't doing them right. Lexi told me guys were simple. A few hair flips and toying with your dress strap, add a wink, and *bam!*"

He bit back a grin, knowing it'd piss her off or hurt her feelings. "Not your moves."

He almost added that he'd be equally tempted by her ponytail, stripping off her sweatshirt, and a solid shoulder punch, but that might have the opposite effect of hitting the brakes.

Trying to reason with a drunk chick was as difficult as getting a defense attorney to admit his client was guilty.

She let out an epic sigh. "I'm in a freaking dress, and still I scare off guys. I already know I'm a two-date-maximum kind of girl. The girl you date before you decide you want, like, a girlie girl."

"You know better than anyone that I don't scare easily." He tucked her arm underneath the covers and stood, moving far enough away that she'd have a hard time reaching him, even if she broke free.

"You're literally pulling away, Tuck."

"That's because, as I said, I'm not taking advantage of your drunken state. But believe me, I want to."

She sighed again. "I guess that's at least something."

He leaned over and brushed her hair off her face. "Promise me something?"

Her eyes fluttered closed. "Hmm?"

"Anytime you get this drunk, you come to my houseboat instead of going home."

He would rather wrestle his willpower and know

she was safe with him than worry about her alone in this state any day.

She yawned, her eyelids remaining shut. "Fine. But remember, I can take care of myself."

He smiled and pressed a quick kiss to her lips. "Got it."

Back in the day, he would've climbed in bed next to her, the way he had dozens of times before, not thinking twice about it. If he curled up next to her now, it wouldn't be for extra warmth or minor cuddling, and he'd never be able to fall asleep.

Flash happily took the spot Tucker wanted, jumping on the bed and curling up next to her, and then he was jealous of his dog.

He carefully weaved around everything Addie had spilled on her way in and lay back on the couch. Every sigh, every moan, they all carried over to him, making it damn near impossible to fall asleep.

Eventually he managed to drift off, and no surprise, nearly every one of his dreams involved the woman who'd crashed into his house and taken over his bed.

CHAPTER EIGHTEEN

A wet, rough tongue woke up Addie, heavy panting accompanying it.

While she'd been desperate for a kiss last night, this wasn't exactly what she had in mind.

She feared opening her eyes would confirm the blips of memories flickering through her head had actually happened, but after another doggy kiss, she decided it was face reality or death by puppy breath.

Sunshine assaulted her eyes and she squinted as she pushed herself to sitting.

Flash barked like he'd been waiting years for her to wake up, and she scratched his head as she noted her surroundings.

The houseboat.

She glanced down. Sequined black dress.

Nope, not a dream.

She'd shown up at her best friend's house and propositioned him.

With a groan, she dropped her head in her hands, then peeked through her fingers at the expectant white puppy she was clearly failing to impress.

"Where's Tucker?" she asked, and Flash simply tilted his head. Not that she'd expected him to tell her.

Addie slipped out of the covers, padding past the remnants of last night's poker game—empty beer bottles, crumpled bags of chips, and their trusty deck of cards.

That was where she should've been last night. Where she belonged.

Not in some ritzy club learning flirting tricks she could use to embarrass herself.

When it came to that sort of thing, she could embarrass herself plenty without hair flips and winks—*oh holy crap, I winked at Tucker. While I pawed at his bare chest.*

His very nice, very cut, bare chest.

She ducked into the bathroom, started at her reflection, and tried to smooth down her hair. She used her finger to brush her teeth with toothpaste and then swished with Listerine until her mouth burned with a minty, bad-breath-destroying fire.

That's about as good as it's gonna get.

The scent of coffee tempted her toward the pot as soon as she exited the bathroom, and she helped herself to a mug.

Then she ventured out to the deck, and sure enough, Tucker sat having his coffee, still shirtless, although he'd pulled warm-up pants over his boxers.

While the urge to flee flooded her system, she knew she'd have to face him sometime. Might as well do it in a ridiculous dress, yesterday's eyeliner today's smoky eye.

Was raccoon chic a thing?

"Um. Good morning."

The smile he fired at her hit her square in the chest. "Mornin'." He gestured to the seat across the tiny table from him and she settled into it. "How's your head?"

"Not too bad. Minor pounding, and I feel like I drank a glass of sand." Her nerves stretched to the fraying point, and she figured she'd go ahead and address the elephant. "What I really could use is that memory-swiper from the *Men In Black* movies. If I tell you to look right into my flashy-thing, you'd do that for me, wouldn't you?"

"Not a chance. I plan on spending every spare second of the day rehashing the details of last night so I never forget them. I'll bring it up constantly to tease you, too, in case you were wondering."

"Thanks for that." She took a drink of coffee and earned seared taste buds for her efforts. "Those city girls seem all innocent until they ply you with alcohol, force you into a dress, and drag you to a dance club."

"I told you the city wasn't all it was cracked up to be, but did you listen?"

"You know me. I like to make my own mistakes. Sometimes over and over, just to ensure I learn my lesson."

He raised an eyebrow. "You've broken into someone's houseboat and tried to take advantage of them before?"

She smacked his arm, and he laughed, the sound making her heart pitter patter. "No, that was a first." She bit her lip. "Are we okay? I made it weird, didn't I?"

He set down his mug, turned to fully face her, and curled his hand around her knee. "Not as long as I can still talk to you as a friend about this crazy drunk chick who broke into my house and threw herself at me."

Her stomach sank—or it tried to. With his warm hand on her knee, it couldn't quite decide on sinking or swirling. "Sounds pretty traumatic. I hope you called the police—except not Easton. You should probably keep the girl's identity safe in case that was an out-of-character move for her, one she'd rather not have spread around town."

"Yeah, I figured that might be the case. Only now she's just made herself at home, grabbed a mug from my cupboard like she's been here a hundred times, poured herself a cup of my expensive coffee, and I'm worried she might be a stalker."

"Well…" Addie sipped the coffee, thinking that was why it tasted so yummy—he sprang for the good stuff. "You should probably buy shitty coffee if you want her to leave, so really that's on you."

"I guess that'll teach me. Also, we need to talk about this dress…" His fingers slipped up her thigh and dizziness set in. "It's pretty much the opposite of overalls and your ratty sweatshirt."

"I've never been very good at taking instructions."

"We should probably work on that." He snagged her hand and tugged. "Come 'ere."

Usually she would put up a better fight, but the intoxicating drag of his fingers had her aching all over. So she let him pull her across the small space and onto his lap.

She wrapped an arm around his shoulders, and his hand returned to her thigh, and while she used to roll her eyes at mushy gestures like sitting on laps, she understood it now.

He brought his other hand up, pushed his fingers into her hair, and then cupped her head and brought her face to his.

The mix of scruff and soft lips sent pleasure cascading down her spine, and then they were going at it like teenagers. Kissing and feeling each other up and moans and groans and not bothering to come up for air.

If she didn't stop... She broke the kiss and worked to catch her breath.

"Let me guess," Tucker said softly. "Today you're back to thinking we should take it slow."

"Is that all right?" she asked, placing her hand on the side of his face and peering into his blue eyes.

"Course it's all right."

Relief washed through her, even though she should've known he wouldn't push. That wasn't his style.

Thank goodness he'd been sober last night so at least one of them was using common sense.

Kissing him was amazing.

The cuddling thing? Sign her up.

But a small thought in the back of her mind gnawed at her, making her worry once again that they were setting themselves up for a crash.

"How many relationships have you had that lasted more than two or three months?" She didn't want to ask it—especially since she was fairly sure she knew the answer. But she needed to remember what was at stake, and what exactly she was up against.

He swallowed and reached for his coffee, and the instant his hand left her leg, she missed it. "Not a lot."

"Me neither."

A contemplative crinkle bisected his forehead as

he ran a couple of fingers across his jaw. She wanted to take over with her own fingers, forget she'd brought up such a gloomy subject, and go back to kissing.

"I'm not tryin' to make you feel bad." She raised her arm to the square. "I'm focusing on the truth and nothing but the truth, so help me God."

He rolled his eyes, but his lips hinted at a smile. "Of all the times I've heard that phrase, I think this time is the worst, because I know what you're getting at."

"In court, you didn't know what people were getting at? No *wonder* they fired you."

This time she got the full smile, along with a pinch to her side, and at least they had this. Teasing. Joking.

She wanted to believe adding sex wouldn't heap on extra complications, but how could she be that naked and that vulnerable with him without it changing everything?

Even her embarrassing failed attempt at seduction last night left her plenty raw, in spite of reassuring herself he'd been doing the admirable thing and it wasn't a true rejection.

She glanced at the two large empty pots on either corner of the deck. "Your planters are pathetic. If my grandma hears about this, she'll be breaking in next. I'll probably get roped into helping her plant the flowers, too."

"Someone should definitely call the cops on you two. Total menaces to society."

She laughed and then lifted his hand so she could see what time it was, but he wasn't wearing a watch.

He slipped his fingers between hers, and pressed a kiss to her shoulder—clearly, he was much smoother than she. "Any idea what time it is?" she asked.

He jerked his chin toward the table and she spotted his phone, partially hidden behind the mug. The fact that he trusted her with it sent warmth through her.

Then again, it was locked, so all she could see was that it was already nearly ten.

"You said you danced at the club last night," he said. "Did you dance with any guys?"

So maybe there were shaky trust items on the dating front, and did it make her a weirdo that the gruff way he'd asked sent a shock of heat up her core?

"You're not kissing other girls; I'm not dancing with other guys. To be clear, I'm not dancing with you, either. No more dancing for me—I'm banning myself, because that's where I'm a true menace to society."

"To be clear, no kissing other guys."

"I'm sure our friends will be relieved to hear you won't be trying to kiss them."

He wrapped his arms around her and dragged his whiskered cheek across her neck, and goose bumps covered her skin. "Ha-ha. You know I meant you better not go around kissing other guys."

"I think you overestimate the opportunity I have for that."

"Addie," he growled, and that zip of heat returned.

It was more fun than it should be to leave him hanging for a few seconds—to know she could even elicit that type of reaction from Tucker Crawford.

She twisted in his embrace and touched her lips to his. "The only person I'm kissing for the foreseeable future is you, 'specially since you're so damn good at it."

She bracketed his face with her hands and kissed him again—she couldn't get enough of his lips and his tongue, and how kissing him made her feel like that exciting part of a free fall.

Which happens before you hit the ground and everything hurts.

She pulled away and scooted off his lap, hating her sober thoughts for being so logical. "I better get goin'. Lexi's coming over to my house so my mother, grandmother, and I can help her organize the seating chart, and I think a shower and wardrobe change is in order."

Tucker groaned, and she lowered her eyebrows, trying to piece together where that reaction had come from. "Don't mind me," he said. "I'm just thinking about you in the shower. I was going to hold back the remark about wanting to join you, but I guess it's out there now."

Her cheeks flushed. "So you arc…attracted to me in that way?"

He stood and placed a hand on her hip. "You underestimate yourself and the effect you have on men."

"My effect usually involves sending them running in the opposite direction." She swept the strand of hair that wouldn't stay out of her eyes behind her ear. "You fled pretty fast last night."

"Not fair. You can't compare me trying to be a

gentleman to those other pricks who can't handle you."

"But you think you can handle me?"

His fingertips skimmed down her sides and her pulse skipped and hummed. "I'd love to show you exactly how well I can handle you."

She tipped to her toes and gave him a chaste peck. "That's a polite goodbye kiss meant to help us stay in check, in case you were wondering."

His hand moved to her butt, and he gripped one cheek. "That's a polite goodbye squeeze meant to do the opposite, in case you were wondering."

She braced her hands on his chest, instructing them to remain there instead of slipping up and behind his neck so her body would be flush with his. "Why are we goin' slow again?"

"You seemed to think that'd make it less of a bad idea, and I'm just tryin' to be respectful."

"Said the guy with his hand on my butt."

A crooked, mischievous grin spread across his face. "Hey, I never said I was succeeding."

To keep herself from making decisions based strictly on her overactive hormones, she reluctantly pulled away.

Rarely did she feel sexy, but as Tucker did another sweep of her from head to toe, she felt like a damn supermodel.

She wanted to make one of those awesome, confident exits, but then she remembered she'd been dropped off here, and there was no way in hell she was walking all the way into town wearing this getup, everything about her saying "walk of shame."

Not that she'd be ashamed, but without the great sex to go with it, not worth the gossip for sure. "Can I—"

Tucker tossed her the keys to his truck. "Just come get me before the game."

CHAPTER NINETEEN

Addie answered the light knock on her front door, and Lexi pushed her sunglasses on top of her head and squinted at her. "Are you hungover? I'm *so* hungover."

"That. I'm definitely that." After coffee and a shower, Addie was feeling much better, but the cringe-worthy memories that continued to pop up didn't wash down the drain quite as easily. "Come on in."

Lexi stepped inside and tucked her sunglasses in her purse. While Addie had showered, pulled her wet hair into a bun, and thrown on a T-shirt and jeans, Lexi's hungover look was pin curls, full makeup, and a summer dress. "Did you, uh, surprise Tucker like you said you were going to?"

Shoot. She hadn't realized she'd told Lexi her plans.

Hadn't she decided after she'd climbed in the back seat of the car? Apparently this girl plus alcohol turned her into an open book. "Yes, and for my next trick, I will be dying of embarrassment."

"Oh no. What happened?"

"He carried me to bed. Not in a sexy way. A gentlemanly way."

"Which is sexy," Lexi pointed out.

"True."

"And…?" A hopeful smile spread across her face as she conspiratorially leaned closer. "What happened this morning?"

Coffee and kissing and sitting on his lap, but Addie couldn't admit that.

There was no way Lexi wouldn't tell Shep, and the guys would freak. For a bunch of younger dudes, they sure hated change like grouchy old men. It was part of why they disliked everyone she dated and attempted to bring to poker night.

They'd throw out their opinions and smart-ass remarks, unable to help themselves, and it would create more pressure and drama, and besides all that, Tucker made it clear he'd rather not tell anyone.

Am I his dirty little secret or is he mine?

"Addie?" Lexi waved a hand in front of her face. "Don't you remember? And isn't that his truck in your driveway?"

"Last night is a bit fuzzy," she said, which was at least true. "I made sure things weren't weird this morning before I left, and he let me borrow his truck. He realizes I was just drunk."

Lexi frowned. "But you like him sober, too."

"Can you not mention this to Shep? I don't want the guys to know. It'd make things weird and throw things off between us and—"

"Say no more."

Luckily, the arrival of Mom and Nonna made that easier to do.

Addie did quick introductions, even though they'd all briefly met at one place or another, and then they sat and Lexi whipped out her huge guest list and a giant seating chart with tabs to write people's names on, and they got to work.

"At least the blue pulls some AU color into the mix," Addie said as she studied the color scheme along the top of the chart.

She hadn't meant to say it aloud, and she froze, hoping she hadn't accidentally offended Lexi.

"That's exactly what Will said. And if he asks, the dresses are garnet not crimson. He doesn't know the difference."

"Honey, everybody in Alabama knows the difference," Mom said.

Exasperation crept into Lexi's features. "I just like red!"

Mom patted Lexi's hand. "It's okay. Your faux secret is safe with us."

"Plus, you threw in the…" Addie squinted at the text so she'd get it exactly right. "Plum and gold along with the navy. If it was just crimson and gray, the town might revolt, but you're good."

"Yes, heaven forbid my wedding be about getting married surrounded by colors I like instead of football," Lexi said, sticking another tab in place.

Mom and Nonna chuckled and assured her it was going to be a lovely ceremony, and Addie added what boiled down to "ditto."

The colors were very pretty together, the gazebo would be decorated and all lit up, and the town center would be filled with people she'd known forever. It would be like a super-dressy town festival, and as a kid, she lived for those days.

Part of it was the lack of supervision it afforded her and the guys, and of course the food—no one cooked like a bunch of Southern women who had affinities for things like butter, jams, and pies—but those events reminded her that nosy as they may be, the townsfolk loved celebrating together.

Loved one another.

After a while of sorting through names and shuffling people around, Addie's eyes refused to focus. She stood and stretched. "I'm gonna go see what I can find for us to snack on."

"I'll help," Lexi said, heading to the kitchen with her.

She glanced around at the decor, from the floral wallpaper to the hanging wooden spoons with sayings like *Season everything with love* and *Life is short, lick the spoon* to the shelf of Bundt pans and ceramic pie holders that looked like pie, in case you wanted to get an idea of the dessert *before* lifting the lid.

"Not what I expected." Lexi gestured to the wooden sign with a mason jar and the words *You're the moon to my shine.* "You're girlier than you let on. More of a romantic, too."

"Sorry to disappoint, but it was decorated like this when I moved in. I'm just renting." Addie opened the fridge and freezer doors and peered inside. "Mr. Sumpter was actually the moon to Mrs. Sumpter's shine."

"But what if Tucker said that to you?" Lexi asked with a big smile and swoon-laced sigh.

"Then I'd be obligated to punch him," Addie said, only half joking.

While she'd appreciate the sentiment, it was way too mushy.

The frozen bag of chicken wings called to her, so she brought it out and bumped the freezer door closed with her hip. "Trust me, he'd thank me later."

Lexi's smile fell, and she blinked at Addie. "Oh. Well. For the record, I'm not disappointed. Like I said, I was surprised, is all."

Addie grabbed the watermelon off her counter to cut up and add to the strawberries and grapes she pulled out of the fridge. "No worries. It means you're gettin' to know me. After the club last night, in ways that no one else does, and I'm pretty sure it should stay that way."

Lexi swiped a hand through the air. "Whatever. You were rocking that dress, and the heels were… Well, they take some practice. But I noticed several men checking you out as we were dancing."

"Staring in shock, you mean. That was fear. They probably thought I was having a seizure."

Lexi made a *phfft* noise. "For someone who's one of the guys, you know surprisingly little about men. And, sweetie, I mean that in the nicest way possible. If things don't work out with—"

Addie lifted a finger to her lips, worried her mom and grandma might be listening, and if they caught wind of the Tucker thing, who knew how they'd react.

Probably shocked with a side of telling her not to mess it up, something she was already plenty worried about.

"With *you know who*," Lexi said, voice lowered, "then I'll take you to the city and we'll land you a man."

There was that "land a man" phrase again.

Was that what she missed out on by not taking etiquette lessons? The fancy fork goes to the—

whichever side, like she said, she didn't take the lessons—the guy runway is to the right, and here's how you force them to land there. "I 'preciate you being willin' to get me a backburner dude if Voldemort doesn't work out."

Lines creased Lexi's forehead before understanding dawned and she laughed. "Took me a second. When I was younger, I used to feel guilty because I had a huge crush on Draco Malfoy—from the movie version, of course—and clearly I shouldn't, because he was a bad guy. Isn't that silly?"

"The crush on Draco certainly wasn't. He was totally hot. Speaking of, if you ever wanna see Shep turn three shades of your wedding color, just ask him about his *Harry Potter* trading cards."

"*What?* My Will has *Harry Potter* trading cards?"

Addie nodded as she grabbed her biggest knife and sliced into the watermelon. "He has this binder that's labeled 'Baseball Card Collection,' but one day while I was waiting for my turn to play videogames, I opened it up and discovered he has way more *Harry Potter* trading cards than baseball cards. He claimed it was 'cause it was such a challenge to get 'em all and he was competing against some other kid at his school, but he sure isn't selling them." Her laugh was a smidge on the maniacal side. "He'll probably kill me for telling you, but someone's gotta let you know what you're gettin' into."

"And I appreciate it. He's always so mellow, and sometimes when I get all fired up and he's like 'whatever, baby, it'll work out,' I love it, and sometimes it makes me want to shake some emotion into or out of him." Lexi gleefully rubbed her hands together. "I can't wait to casually drop a few *Harry Potter* references and see how long it takes him to crack."

"You'll have to tell me how red he gets."

No doubt Addie would know when, because she'd probably be getting a *DUDE, not cool* text.

The spirit of camaraderie filled the air, and Addie smiled at Lexi. She hadn't felt this level of friendship for anyone outside her group of guys in a long time, and she hadn't expected it from Lexi, which deepened the squishy sensation in her chest.

"Thank you," she said. "For your tips last night, and for sticking it out with me, and for caring about me and you know who."

"You're welcome. It took me a while to understand your friendship, but I get it now, I swear. Sorry again that I freaked out."

"Sorry again that you're getting a non-girlie bridesmaid."

"Groomsman, you mean."

Addie grinned.

"Or is it groomsmaid?"

Addie wrinkled her nose. "That sounds a little too much like I clean up after him, and that honor is all yours."

"Please. That boy can clean up after himself."

"Amen, sister," Addie said, holding up the hand not wielding a knife so Lexi could give her five.

"You have a sister, right?" Lexi asked, and Addie nodded. "I always wished I had a sister. What's it like?"

"A lot of unsolicited advice. But it's also awesome."

Which reminded her, she should call Alexandria. Only she was a truth detector, and she'd realize something was up if she so much as uttered Tucker's name.

Man, keeping this a secret is gonna be harder than I expected.

By the time the fruit was cut, the wings were done, so they carried the food into the living room.

Mom frowned at the watermelon wedges. "Why didn't you cut them up in squares? They're so hard to eat this way without getting messy."

Addie grabbed one, bit as far down the wedge as she could, and then grinned at her mom as juice dripped from the rind.

Mom shook her head and sighed. "I'm gonna go cut 'em up and get us some forks. Lexi, if you wanna follow me, I have an idea I'd like to run by you."

As soon as they disappeared around the corner, Addie pulled the white bakery bag out of her purse and slipped it to her grandma.

"You're an angel," Nonna said, kissing each of Addie's cheeks.

Considering she was lying to her grandma about the cookies inside, she wasn't sure how well the angel part fit.

Maisy, who'd bought the bakery and revamped it a few years ago, found out about her grandma's high blood sugar and had concocted these chocolate brownie bites that were low sugar, low fat, and so delicious that Addie could hardly believe either of the former.

And as long as Nonna thought she was getting contraband cookies, she ate them instead of the worse-for-her versions.

She popped a few into her mouth, and Mom came back with the "properly cut" watermelon.

She and Lexi were caught up talking centerpieces, and from the sounds of it, Lexi loved Mom's idea. She even asked if she'd be willing to arrange them.

"Oh, I'd love to help," Mom said. "Alexandria got married so long ago, and it looks like this might be the only other wedding I get to decorate for."

Here she goes. The tragedy of only having one *daughter.*

"Women can marry other women now," Nonna said, waving around a hot wing that Mom frowned at. "Get with the twenty-first century, Priscilla."

"Hey, I'm perfectly happy to plan a wedding for Addie, whoever she decides to marry. But until I get confirmation that's happening, I'm gonna get my weddin' fix wherever I can."

Lexi gave Addie a confused look and she waved her hands like *don't bother going near this mess.*

They renewed their centerpiece discussion, and Lexi pulled out a couple of magazines and her laptop so they could talk options.

Thank goodness. Nobody wants me *putting together centerpieces.*

A positively evil chuckle emanated from her grandmother, who was leaned over the seating chart that'd taken hours to organize.

Addie covered the paper with her hand. "Nonna, what are you doin'?"

"I thought I'd make the reception more interesting. Wouldn't it be funny to put George Sullivan and his new wife by his ex-wife and his rumored mistress?"

Addie twisted, cutting them off from Mom and Lexi. "That's a level of deviousness that even the devil would say, 'Whoa, hold on there. Let's think about this for a minute.'"

Nonna scowled, apparently offended Addie had dared to call her plan evil, despite it being exactly that. "You used to be more fun."

Now it was Addie's turn to scowl. "Hey. I'm plenty fun. I just don't want to do anything to upset the bride. It's already complicated enough as it is, trying to be a groomsman and a bridesmaid at the same time."

Luckily, most of the groomsman duties were easy, and closer to the ceremony. She undid the seating chart damage and told her grandmother to eat her food while she could.

Her phone vibrated in her pocket and she dug it out.

TUCKER: *Remember when you showed up in that tiny dress to seduce me last night? Because I sure as hell do.*

Keeping the phone low, she typed out her response.

ADDIE: *No idea what you're talking about. How much did you drink during poker?*

TUCKER: *Not nearly enough. Maybe tonight I'LL be the one who shows up at your place drunk & frisky.*

Her body heated as she thought about it, her heart beating that much faster.

ADDIE: *Hardly a threat. Of course I'd have to be a gentleman and tuck you into my bed. Fair warning, I don't have the good coffee.*

TUCKER: *Guess I'll have to bring some.*

How's the wedding stuff going? Need me to come & save you?

Addie glanced at her happy mom and the happy bride to-be. Nonna was shoving the brownie bites from her purse into her mouth, so she was nice and happy as well.

ADDIE: *No saving just yet. I'm finding my own way of helping with wedding stuff.*

TUCKER: *You girl ;)*

Normally those would be fighting words, winky face or not. But surrounded by three strong women, she was thinking that she might just pull off being a little bit of a girl yet.

More than that, it didn't seem so bad after all.

CHAPTER TWENTY

Addie glanced around as she approached the front desk at work Monday morning, watching for her boss.

Early last week, Mr. Watkins told Addie one of their patients needed traction the next time he came in, so she'd followed his instructions, despite it not being the route she would've taken.

Then on Friday, he'd asked why Addie had put him in the traction machine, because now the patient was calling in, saying he was too sore to do his other exercises.

When she reminded him that she'd only been following *his* instructions, Moody Overlord claimed he never would've said that, and Addie wanted to scream and shout that she quit, because she couldn't deal with him anymore.

Instead she'd practiced self-control and flipped him off in her head.

Then she'd gone home, applied to the few nearby places she could find, and sent an email to one of her former professors, asking if he'd heard of any positions—he always seemed to have the scoop.

Right after she'd finished her certifications, he'd asked if she wanted to interview for a position at Bama, since he knew the coach. She'd balked for the obvious reasons and told him she couldn't be that far from her family.

Addie set down the tray with the coffees she'd

brought in for the receptionist and PT assistant and did another sweep of the area.

"Here's the chart for your first patient." Sylvie extended it to her. "He's a regular asshole."

"Oh man. I was hoping for irregular asshole this morning."

"Irregular asshole isn't in yet," the PT assistant said, glancing toward Mr. Watkins's office, and they shared a giggle.

The seniority thing was so frustrating, especially in a small town like Uncertainty. It wasn't who was best at their job, but who'd been in the position the longest, and it only added insult to injury that she often saw several more patients a day and was still paid less.

But—as he often pointed out—it was his name on the office door.

It could be my name if I ordered lettering and put it on the glass.

It would almost be worth it just to see the look on Mr. Watkins's face.

Addie pushed into the office, glancing at the file last minute, because the caffeine clearly hadn't kicked in. "Good morning, Mr. Matthews."

Ah. The asshole lawyer.

In a town as tiny as theirs, it was hard not to know someone, but he spent the majority of his time in the office, and she'd only seen him at the Old Firehouse once.

Add in his reputation, and she hadn't gone out of her way to welcome him to the neighborhood.

"Whatever," he said, his attention on his phone screen. "Just get me out of here as soon as possible.

I'm literally losing hundreds of dollars sitting here."

"Oh, I don't know. If you calculate losing the use of your"—she glanced at the file again—"shoulder for a month because you didn't take the time to let it heal, you might find taking an hour leaves you ahead of the game."

He finally glanced up, a scowl on his admittedly handsome face.

Too bad the uptight, perma-annoyed vibe ruined it.

"I'm Addison Murphy. You probably know my parents, or if not, my nonna Lucia—everyone knows her."

"*You're* Addison Murphy?"

The way he said it made her nerves stand on edge. "Yes."

"That one nosy lady who runs the craft store told me I should ask you out." He frowned as he assessed her. "You're not what I imagined when she told me you were the only single and available woman near my age in town."

"Wow. You're a real sweet talker. Lift your arm as high as you can. Stop when it catches."

He did as she asked, and she gripped his wrist, moving his arm through a series of movements as she peppered him with questions about the injury and his pain levels.

"It must be nice to dress down for work," he said.

"I'm assuming that the level of condescension you put into that sentence means you want my foot up your ass."

He cleared his throat, his eyebrows arching. "Touché. What I mean is, I guess I should take you out for dinner sometime. Seeing as you're the only available woman in town." Just when she was considering pushing his arm back and testing his pain tolerance, he added, "And that you're prettier than expected, and the feisty adds extra points."

"Well, as flattering as that is, I'm afraid I'll have to pass. I'm not as available as everyone thinks I am."

"What does that mean? That you're someone's dirty little secret?"

That time, she couldn't resist twisting—really, she needed to know what muscle needed the most work, and he could use some joint manipulation.

He let out a yelp and an "It was just a joke," and she gave him a syrupy smile.

"I'm gonna place a few dry needles around the area to help relieve the pain and tightness, then I'll send you home with some exercises to help repair and strengthen your shoulder. And if you want to prevent either of us from wasting time here, you'll take them home and do them. After all..."

She thought of her friends' teasing her about how much this hurt her dating odds, but luckily she had a guy who didn't back down so easily—halfway had a guy, anyway.

"It's somethin' my grandma could do."

Once she'd completed his treatment and paperwork and finished a quick session with one of her regulars, she stepped into the hallway and ran into her boss. *Dammit.*

"Were you nice to the lawyer?" he asked. "He, unlike most of the people in this town, actually has money to come in on a regular basis."

"I worked out his shoulder and gave him exercises so he can get to healing, which I think is pretty nice of me. It's also my job, so put a gold star on that."

Moody Overlord frowned at her, and the frown deepened when he ran his gaze down her. "I've been thinking that we should revisit the dress code for the office. We need to be viewed as professionals."

He was literally wearing jeans and a collared shirt that she guaranteed he only had on so he could hit the golf course later.

Factor in that he often made inappropriate comments about the receptionist, from what she was wearing to her body, and he was the *last* person who should be in charge of a dress code.

"I think doing our job, by definition, makes us professionals, so people should view us that way based on that."

"Starting tomorrow, I want slacks and dressy shirts. Like button down or silky stuff."

She wanted to ask if *he'd* be following the policy. People dealt with a lot worse at work, so this was totally a first world problem kind of thing, but for months she'd told herself that at least she could wear whatever she wanted at her job.

And honestly, some of the exercises she did with people meant leaning over them, and she'd rather be able to move without popping buttons off the type of shirts she didn't even own.

"Do you understand?" Mr. Watkins asked.

She gritted her teeth in an approximation of a smile. "I understand."

"Good. Push it and I'll change it to skirts."

He couldn't do that, could he? Unless he was wearing a freaking skirt, and people would pay to *avoid* seeing that.

How could she do her job if she was constantly flashing everyone? Ugh.

"My reputation is the one on the line. In case you haven't noticed, it's my name on the door."

Oh, she'd noticed a lot of things today. The lawyer definitely had a hand in this, too, so as for him? She sure as hell wasn't going to be nice to him after this.

. . .

"You've gotta be kidding me," Tucker mumbled when he went to answer the door Monday morning and saw five people lined up on his dock.

The only explanation he could think of was that they thought he was violating some town rule, but unfortunately for them, he knew the boating and housing laws better than any of them could even dream of.

They all started talking at once, and while one conversation merged into the next, he realized it wasn't about boating laws at all but that each of them had brought their legal woes to him.

"Whoa, whoa, whoa. Do any of you see a sign on my boat? One that says 'Law Offices of Tucker Crawford and Associates'?"

He wasn't sure who the associates would be. Gators and mosquitos. And Flash, of course.

"Do you need me to make you a sign?" Mrs. Jenson, his third-grade teacher, asked. "I can have my Jimmy print one up at his shop by the end of the afternoon. He does real good work."

If she hadn't been part of the crowd, maybe Tucker could've kept up the grumpy hermit act. Now he'd never know. "What did you need, Mrs. Jenson?"

"I was in line first," a lady with a huge folder of papers muttered. She looked vaguely familiar, but he couldn't place her.

"Just call this international waters—there are no rules."

Mrs. Jenson stepped forward. She held up a finger, then dug in her purse and pulled out two crisp dollar bills. "There's your retainer. Now, do I just say what I need, or do we go into your…" Her brow furrowed. "Office?"

As much as he loved Addie's grandmother, he was going to have to… He struggled for what mental threat to make, even though he'd never act upon it.

Not just because he was nice, either. The woman would somehow sense it and come scold him, and he couldn't have his very first client in Uncertainty unhappy, or she might send *even more* clients his way out of spite.

"We'll head around to the front deck." He turned to the rest of the people in the group, noticing one couple in the mix. "I'll be with y'all shortly."

This probably fell in the *if you can't beat 'em, join 'em* category.

"You really should have some chairs if you're going to make us wait," the stickler-for-rules lady said, and he blew out an exhale, hoping it'd help his thinning patience.

He settled Mrs. Jenson in a deck chair and sat across from her. "I've gotta be upfront and tell you that I don't have a law firm here in town."

"So you're not a lawyer? I thought you just got fired, not… What's the word?" She snapped her fingers, the same way she'd done when she was teaching them state capitals and lost the name of the city herself. "Disbarred."

"I didn't…" While he wanted to metaphorically stomp his foot and say it was no one's business and he didn't care what they thought anyhow, he figured it was time to clarify he hadn't been fired. "I actually quit my old job, and I still have my license. But I'm not the only lawyer in town—just the only one not currently practicing."

"Those other two…" Mrs. Jenson shook her head. "One's so old he falls asleep halfway through a meeting, and the other is a…" She glanced around and then leaned in. "He's an asshole."

"Mrs. Jenson! I should send you to the principal's office."

She appeared mildly reprimanded before cracking a smile. "There's no other word for him. Some city guy who thinks we're all gullible idiots. He doesn't even try to hide he feels that way about us, either."

Righteous anger immediately surged forward. The thought of some prick moving in and taking advantage of people like Mrs. Jenson grated at him.

One of the reasons he'd gone into law was to see justice served. It wasn't until so little of it went to those who deserved it that he'd fallen out of love with it.

And as far as the townsfolk went, well, it was sorta like how you could pick on your family and friends, but heaven help anyone else who crossed that line.

Some of them could be right pains in the ass, but they looked out for one another, and Uncertainty held several of the most genuinely nice people he'd ever met. "Let's hear the case, and I'll see if I can help."

She withdrew a file folder with several medical bills and told him that her insurance company claimed they wouldn't cover the things they previously said they would, and now she was looking at having to sell her home so they wouldn't have the pleasure of foreclosing it out from underneath her.

That last part hit a nerve. "I won't let that happen," he said, despite the fact that the first rule in Legal Club was not making promises. That was promises you might not be able to keep, and he'd be damned if he let Mrs. Jenson lose her home.

"Does that mean you'll take the case?"

Honestly, he didn't know how restoring boats would go, and with the first one done, he found himself antsy.

This case meant defending someone who deserved it. "Yeah. I'll take the case."

Her relief was so palpable, and he could hardly handle the flow of gratitude aimed his way.

He showed her off the boat and turned to the next person in line—the woman who'd insisted she was first.

"All right. Come aboard and let's hear it. But if it has to do with suing a pig, I'm warning you that I'm not the right lawyer."

"How about taking a cheating pig's money?"

He scrunched up his eyebrows, wondering if the town would ever have a shortage of weird cases. But the angry glare in her eye helped him put it together. "The cheating pig in this scenario would be…?"

"My ex-husband. He's trying to get out of paying child support, and I need someone who's not going to tell me that I should either let it go or find a new man, but that would probably require a makeover."

The angry heat returned, and he suspected he knew the answer before he even asked the question. "Who told you that?"

"That asshole lawyer who's moved in to drain the residents in Uncertainty of their money while he insults them."

"Not on my watch," Tucker said.

Apparently he'd resorted to cheesy sayings that only grown men in tights and superhero capes uttered on TV shows or movies.

But as he sat back and listened to the woman's case and what she'd been dealing with over the past three years, the words echoed through his head again.

Not on my watch.

CHAPTER TWENTY-ONE

Easton and Ford rained dollar bills on Tucker the instant he stepped inside the community center Wednesday night for the dance lessons they'd been instructed to attend "or else."

"What the hell is this?" he asked.

"We hear you're working for dollar bills now," Ford said. "And we are about to witness your dance moves, so…"

Sputtered laughter came from Addie, who covered her mouth with her hand when he pinned her with a look.

It didn't hide the sparkle of humor in her eyes, though.

"Oh, you think that's funny? This is your grandma's fault, and since I don't have the heart to yell at her for it, I'm gonna make you pay."

"Jeez, a couple days of havin' dollar bills thrown at you, and suddenly you need to be constantly showered or you go getting all kinds of grouchy." Addie pulled a couple of bills out of the pocket of her jeans and smacked them to his chest. "There you go, you diva. But later tonight, I'll expect a performance."

He caught her wrist as she moved to withdraw her hand, and her sharp inhale made it hard to not yank her flush to him and whisper in her ear that if anyone would be stripping later tonight, it'd be her.

"Take it off, Murph!"

Tucker turned and glared at Ford, who jerked back and raised his hands. "Dude, it was a joke. Murph wasn't actually going to strip you of your shirt."

His blood pressure slowly returned to normal—his friend hadn't been demanding *Addie* strip.

Funny how hollering for him to lose his shirt in a crowded room seemed much better.

If Addie was losing her shirt, Tucker wanted it to be at his place, himself as the only witness, where he could also kiss her until they were both gasping for air.

He peered down at her, fighting the urge to haul her against him and relive the sensation of her soft lips opening under his demanding ones.

The image of her lacy bras flickered into the mix and then he was thinking of running his hands over every inch of her, and he should definitely derail that line of thinking before it got him in trouble. Next thing he knew, he'd be accused of getting turned on by the idea of stripping for everyone.

Hell, if Addie was the one relieving him of his clothes, he might say go for it, audience be damned.

He released his grip on her, and she let out a shallow exhale. "I don't think we have enough dollars now that he's in such high demand," she said.

Oh, he'd make her pay for all these jokes later.

Ten tongue lashings at least.

He reclined against the wall next to his friends. Several of Lexi's friends were there as well, and when Brittany waved at him, Addie tensed at his side. He gave her hand a quick, subtle squeeze.

"So, are you gonna tell me whether or not the

rumors are true?" Addie shot him a sidelong glance. "Are you, or are you not, practicin' law from your boat?"

"Guilty as charged."

"Wow. That was ridiculously easy to get you to admit. I guess *I* should be a lawyer. After the past few days, I'm beyond ready for a job change, too."

"Bad day?"

"Make that days—plural. My boss made a dress code edict on Monday. Slacks or skirts."

Tucker leaned closer. "Is that all it takes? Making an edict? I choose skirts."

Skirts meant easy access, and he shouldn't think about that right now, but his thoughts were very one track tonight.

He hadn't seen Addie in days, and it felt like months since he'd kissed those tempting lips of hers. Since he'd run his hands over her.

She lifted an eyebrow. "Funny, I remember you demanding baggy overalls."

"And instead you're wearing those tight, holey jeans." The knees had gone out of them long ago, and he'd noticed the back pockets were fraying at the corners, one good tug from coming off completely.

Damn did he want to give them a tug.

Her chin hitched a notch higher. "Because I don't take instructions."

A loud whistle pierced the air, cutting him off before he could come up with a retort—probably for the best, considering their back and forth was only revving him up more and more.

"Everyone," Lexi said. "Gather round so we can get started."

Addie walked toward the center of the floor, and he couldn't help teasing her. "Looks like you're taking instructions pretty well to me."

She stuck out her foot and tripped him, and he stumbled before catching himself.

Just like that, this dance practice he'd been dreading since getting the text became that much more fun.

Addie had always challenged him, but she was smart and quick-witted, and he was seeing a new, flirty side of her that he couldn't get enough of.

The eccentric woman who had on a colorful skirt and a scarf tied around her head like a rainbow version of Rambo cleared her throat and began giving them the details about how the first dance at the wedding would go.

The music would start, and at first, it would be just Shep and Lexi waltzing in the middle of the floor to Tori Kelly and Ed Sheeran's "I Was Made For Loving You." As soon as the song moved to the second verse, the bridesmaids and groomsmen would join in and dance around the couple, who'd remain in the middle.

Lexi gave Tucker and Addie an especially wide grin when she paired them up, and Tucker scooted closer to his sexy dance partner. "Does she know?"

"She knows that I… You know."

"Gonna need more details."

If Shep's girl was onto them, there was no way she wouldn't tell him. It was surprising his friend hadn't cornered him yet and asked what the hell.

Then Easton would know he'd gone ahead and crossed the line, and Ford would join in, and they'd land in that unnecessary drama they'd worried about.

Part of him wanted to say *so what*.

So what if they knew that he wanted to kiss the girl they all claimed wasn't one?

So what if they didn't know how to plan for or solve every complication?

Those complications were why, though.

It'd only be a matter of time before everyone they passed on the street was adding their opinion. About how they always knew it'd happen or how it would never work. They'd make bets on if it'd last and gather information that could double as ammunition, in order to better decide whose side to be on if it went south.

When news of his parents' divorce broke, their mutual friends acted supportive and promised to remain neutral, but as it turned messy and more of what they assumed were facts came out, most of Mom's friends turned on her, judging her for moving on so soon.

Sides were taken, and people who'd come over for countless barbecues and birthday parties through the years were suddenly arguing in the street over who was "in the right" and making decrees about never talking to one another again.

As Addie pointed out, neither of them was great at making long-term relationships work.

It was easy to say things would stay the same, but they never did. If they failed and bitterness and resentment crept in and they couldn't be around each other—like his parents couldn't be in the same room without arguing to this day—what would that do to their group of friends?

Uncomfortable pressure built in his chest, and on top of that, he couldn't stop worrying people would end up talking about Addie the way they'd talked about Mom.

I'll do whatever I can to keep that from happening. And if they don't know, they won't have any ammunition to use against her.

"Lexi noticed something was up between us after the football game," Addie whispered, bringing him back to what'd started his mind down the anxiety-filled path in the first place. "Since it made it easier for her to be cool with me being in the wedding, and I was caught anyway, I admitted that my feelings for you had changed. But I haven't told her anything happened because we agreed to keep it a secret."

Shep walked up behind them, placing his hands on both of their shoulders and sticking his head between theirs. "Are you two paying attention? Because if this doesn't go well, Lexi will be upset, and I need her to be happy when I get her home, if you catch my drift."

Addie opened her mouth—Tucker would bet money to make a smart-ass remark about his code being way too cryptic—but then Shep squeezed their shoulders harder.

"Not to mention that thanks to agreein' to have the weddin' here, Lexi's had to deal with a whole bunch of crazy shit involving the people in town, and pressure from her mom and friends, so she's getting her damn waltz. You guys copy?"

"We copy, we copy," Addie said, shrinking away from his vise grip. "Also, uncle already."

"Oh, and thanks for spilling the *HP* beans to Lexi, Murph. Don't think I won't pay you back for that." Shep clapped them both on the back, and then stepped between them and toward Lexi so he could help demonstrate the steps.

"*HP* beans?" Tucker asked, and Addie shrugged, her expression equal parts self-satisfaction and false innocence. After making sure Shep was preoccupied learning the "proper form for the waltz," Tucker draped his arm around Addie's shoulders and whispered, "How good a mood do you need to be in, if you catch my drift?"

Addie elbowed him in the side, grinning when he grunted. Then they got another stern glare, and just like when they were kids, they assumed the instinctual stick-straight posture that only ever pronounced your guilt.

The dance instructor raised her voice to address the room. "Okay, now we're all going to try it."

Most of the time, Tucker would be tempted to fake an injury to get out of anything involving learning dance steps. Since he now had a perfectly good excuse to put his hands on Addie, he was unexpectedly all about it.

Her forehead crinkled as she watched the woman at the front laying out the steps while rattling off foreign terms. "I just vowed to never dance again, and look where that got me."

"As I recall, you even told me you wouldn't dance with me."

A threatening grin stretched her lips. "If I break your leg, that can still apply. Hell, break *my* leg." She curled her fists in his shirt and jostled him. "I'm actually *asking* for your help here."

He wrapped her tighter in his embrace, splaying his hand on her back. "But what you get is my protection."

"What good are you to me, then?"

He lowered his lips to her ear. "Once I get you alone, I'll present my case, and trust me, it's a strong one. With lots of impressive demonstrations."

He gently bit at her earlobe, and her fingers dug into his shoulder. Her chest rose and fell against his, and then he was thinking about her lacy black bra, which led to thoughts of getting his hands on the curves he'd gotten a peek at.

As soon as she was ready, he'd make sure he followed through on his promise.

Lexi approached, and he froze and tried to temper his body's response to being smooshed up against Addie as the bride-to-be surveyed them with a critical eye.

"Addie, you probably want to practice in heels," Lexi said. "Lucky for you, I brought a spare pair in case you forgot."

"I'm starting to suspect that you don't know what the words 'want' 'lucky' or 'forgot' mean. You're not seriously expecting me to keep my heels on for the whole wedding *and* reception, are you?"

While Lexi had remained a fairly mellow bride, that comment brought out the crazy-eyed diva.

"I'll wear heels," Addie quickly said. "It's cool."

The laugh he'd tried to hold back escaped and Addie elbowed him in the ribs again.

He was going to have a bruise there by the end of the night if this kept up, and his mind conjured images of rough foreplay, with him pressing Addie against things, and her pushing right back.

Once Lexi crossed the room to get the shoes, Addie sagged against him. "I'm going to be hanging on you, making you carry all my weight, just to save my poor feet and their circulation."

He slid both hands low on her back and secured her tighter against him. "Not as much of a threat as you might think. Especially if the dress you'll be wearing is as revealing as you claim."

Lexi returned with the shoes, and as he helped her into them, Addie gripped his hand and mouthed "save me," while the rest of the guys snickered.

They all got the bird, which she quickly folded down when Lexi straightened and asked how they fit. "So comfortable, I thought they were my sneakers."

Lexi pursed her lips, not buying it for a second. "Your sarcasm makes me feel less bad about forcing you into them."

"I think we just crossed into the next phase of our friendship—brutal honesty. Go us," Addie said, and she lightly punched Lexi's shoulder.

Lexi flashed her a grin and then returned to Shep, who gave them all threatening behave-or-else glares.

If Tucker ever fell so hard for a girl that he willingly went along with the idea of waltzing, he'd ask one of the other guys to put him out of his misery.

The music swelled, and the instructor shouted the steps as she clapped out a loud rhythm. Then it turned into the blind leading the blind. Addie stumbled as he went back and she stepped right, and he barely caught her. She let loose a string of swear words that raised a lot of eyebrows and unhinged a lot of jaws, and the guys snorted out laughs.

"How's it goin' over there, Murph?" Ford asked, and if her eyes could shoot the lasers she was clearly trying to fire from them, he'd be dead.

"You want me to tell 'em to be nice?" Tucker asked, voice low.

"No, then they'd know something was up. You've never defended me before."

Offense tweaked his gut. "I have, too. Plenty of times. Like when they were plannin' on lettin' the air out of your boyfriend's truck so he'd miss poker night. *I* was the one who stopped that—you're welcome."

"When was that, and with who?"

"After the regional game senior year, and that prick you dated way too long. None of us wanted him at the party, but I argued that then *you* wouldn't be at the party because you'd be too busy changing the tire for his pansy ass, and I wanted you there, even if we had to deal with the douche."

Now he was thinking of the way the guy hurt her, and then he was worried that he'd be the next douche who did, no matter how hard he tried to prevent it.

I'm not even supposed to be getting anything near to serious right now. I have no business pretending I'm in a place to.

"I never knew that, although I can't say I'm surprised. He *was* sort of a douche," she said, then she tripped on the heels again.

Tucker steadied her, but she reached down and unbuckled the strap around her ankle, the hole in her jeans stretching so wide that her knee and a couple inches of her silky-smooth thigh made an appearance.

"That's it," she said. "Sorry, Lexi, but I'm going to have to learn without the shoes first."

She kicked one off, hitting Ford square in the back. The other one got aimed at Easton.

Then everyone was laughing again. Correction, make that everyone on the groom's side.

The bride's family and friends wore scandalized expressions.

Brittany strolled over, her heels clicking against the floor. She hit him with a flirty grin as she extended her hand. "Here, Tucker, lemme teach you so you can learn the steps before you attempt to use them with her."

Addie wrapped herself around him, her body heat soaking into him and giving him more dirty thoughts to keep the others company. "He's learnin' the steps just fine."

"I'm just saying—"

"I'm dancing with him, so thanks for your totally nonsuspect desire to suddenly help, but we're good."

With a huff, Brittany stormed back over to where she'd come from.

The amused grin he couldn't hold back brought out Addie's disgruntled glare. *"What?"*

Tucker lowered his lips to her ear again, and her perfume flooded his senses. "You're jealous."

"I can't be jealous when I'm the one still dancin' with you."

His grin widened, and she rolled her eyes.

He found he liked that she got jealous over the thought of him dancing with someone else, especially since he'd experienced so much of that toxic heat thinking of her at that club.

Addie readjusted her dancing stance. "While you're bein' three kinds of smug over there, I'm not getting any better at this, and you're the one who has to waltz with me in front of everyone at the weddin', so maybe you want to lead me instead of mock me?"

She batted her eyes, deceptively sweet.

"Your wish is my command." He tightened the arm he had around her waist and dipped her, and while the people in the room were undoubtedly going to wonder what this was all about, he didn't care.

Tucker slowly pulled Addie back up, securing her against his chest. She gripped on to his biceps and swallowed, her pupils overtaking the brown of her irises.

Oh yeah, dance practice was way more fun than he'd thought it'd be.

"Holy shit, Crawford," Easton said. "Were you really working in a law firm, or do you have a secret competitive dance side we should know about?"

"You probably shouldn't waste those moves on Murph," Ford said, and Addie frowned.

If the moves worked, he couldn't help thinking that they wouldn't be a waste.

• • •

Round two with the high heels had been brutal, and the instant Addie sat down to take off Lexi's shoes, Brittany approached Tucker, and she couldn't possibly talk to him without her hand on his arm.

What part of "he's seeing someone" don't you understand?

Probably the part where he can't be seen with that person he's "seeing."

Yes, there were complications, but that didn't stop her from wanting to go over and claim him as hers.

"Thanks for being such a good sport," Lexi said as she sat in the chair next to her. She must've noticed the eye daggers, because she added, "Want me to try to call off Brittany? She's a bit aggressive when it comes to guys, and I wouldn't have given her Tucker's information if I would've known that you…" She glanced around. "You know."

"*You know* seems to be the new code word. But it's okay. He can make his own decisions."

I just might have to castrate him if he chooses wrong, so it's convenient that that won't make our friendship weird or anything.

The other bridesmaids were over there as well, chatting with the rest of the guys, so it was more of a group thing, and as soon as her feet regained circulation, she'd go join them.

Addie rubbed at her aching muscles, hitting the pressure points to help provide relief and wishing they worked magic instead. "I can't believe you willingly submit yourself to wearing heels."

"I *love* shoes."

"I love shoes, too, but I love ones that love me back."

Lexi laughed, then slumped down in the chair and let her head fall back with a sigh. "It's all coming together. I was seriously about to have a nervous breakdown last week, but your mother is a godsend. She has a ton of connections, as well as an eye for design, and we might actually pull off this wedding in time."

"Of that I have no doubt." Addie glanced at Tucker again. Brittany was going above and beyond in her flirting attempts, slowly licking off the frosting from the cupcakes Lexi had provided from Maisy's Bakery for an after-dance-torture treat.

"I thought she'd be more help when it came to the wedding," Lexi said, clearly talking about Brittany again, "but she always claims to be too busy. When she was so excited tonight, I thought it was for the waltz, probably because I love the waltz. Have ever since I saw it in *Beauty and the Beast* when I was a little girl. It's so classic and romantic, you know?"

There was that "you know" again, and although Addie didn't know, she nodded.

She got the gist and why Lexi would like it, even though during that movie, her main thought had been wondering if her parents would let her get a pet wolf.

"Why are you even still friends with her?" Addie brought her hand over her mouth. "Sorry. My filter's obviously broken today."

Lexi simply shrugged it off. "It's okay. I get it. But she and I have been through a lot together."

Just like Addie and her group of guys had been through a lot together.

Maybe too much to realistically throw romance into the mix.

Whoa, that makes me sound like the one girl in the middle of an orgy.

Make that romance with *one* guy. Maybe if she was a different girl, and circumstances were different, and ugh.

Although Tucker's posture was closed off, his arms crossed, and he was only politely nodding here and there, Addie hated how much watching the pretty brunette flirt with him brought out her insecurities.

Not like she needed proof that she'd never be smooth, but the other night certainly proved it, and she'd never be able to lick frosting off a cupcake without either smearing it across her face or inhaling at the wrong time and choking on it.

I wish she'd *choke on it.* Immediately guilt flooded in. She shouldn't be aiming bad wishes at anyone.

How could she compete with that, though? Brittany was exactly the type of girl Tucker had always gone for, too, which so didn't help.

Addie was just make-believe sexy, playing in fancy clothes and makeup for a wedding. It wasn't her.

Would never be her.

Once she stopped dressing up, would Tucker think she'd gone back to boring Addie, the plain girl he grew up with?

They had chemistry to spare right now, but part of that was probably the mystery. The excitement of the unknown.

There'd been times she'd thought she and a guy had crazy sparks in her past relationships, and then they'd finally have sex and it'd be meh, and all of a sudden she wouldn't have a relationship anymore.

And still she'd feel disheartened and slightly rejected at the end of it.

If things were meh with Tucker? Her stomach knotted. She wasn't very worried on her end, but— as she'd been thinking about way too much lately— most of his girlfriends exuded sexiness without even trying.

If the spark misfired, would that cause a chemical reaction in their friendship, and would it be bad enough to destroy it?

Could they honestly go from seeing each other naked and adding that whole new level of intimacy, to fizzling out, to sitting in his houseboat and joking around and playing poker with the rest of the guys, things completely easy and normal again?

Seemed highly unlikely, with a side of nearly impossible, which had her wondering if she should hit the brakes now, before they could crash.

All her worries buzzed through her head, and then she wished that if she had to doubt something, it wouldn't be the one thing she was starting to want more than anything.

CHAPTER TWENTY-TWO

It'd been ridiculously hard for Tucker to see Addie this week. There'd been dancing on Wednesday night, but earlier that day he'd finally pulled the trigger on announcing he was open for boat repairs—i.e., he'd told Lottie, and the woman was nothing if not efficient at spreading the word.

With the news also out about him taking on clients, a surprising number of Uncertainty citizens had come to see him.

Mrs. Jenson made him a sign, one he stuck on a post and placed at the end of the houseboat dock. Legal clients on the right, boat repair inquiries on the left.

Funny how many people ignored the huge sign, but between that and digging into the cases he'd taken on—and piecing together the stack of files that Flash had destroyed one night—he'd been nonstop for days.

At the end of each night, Addie texted him questions that'd become a running joke between them. "Which department have I reached? Boating or legal?"

His replies varied. "What needs repaired, ma'am, because I'm sure I have something that'd fix it," "Would you like to debrief me?" "Do you need a conjugal visit arranged?" etc., etc.

So far, there'd only been one day where he'd had more boat inquiries, but legal still outweighed it four to one.

Then, after a guilt-trip phone call from his mom about how he was so close now and still hadn't come to see her, he'd gone down to Montgomery to have dinner with her and her husband. It was nice enough, and it was good to see Mom, even though she'd been less than enthusiastic when he told her he was taking on some legal cases in Uncertainty.

She, like Dad, thought he should at least commute to somewhere he could "actually make enough money to support a family." As if he hadn't already been stressed enough about how far he was from his goals.

Meanwhile, he and Addie had continued to flirt via text, and he'd called her last night on the drive home just to hear her voice, because it turned out he was sappier than he'd realized.

The way he practically skipped toward the Old Firehouse on Sunday night only made a stronger case to support that theory.

The second he stepped inside the bar, he scanned the tables, anticipation zinging through his veins.

The rest of the guys had already arrived, and Addie sat right in the middle of the group, wearing those fucking overalls.

She glanced up and gave him a smile that sent him from revved to supercharged.

"Are you Tucker Crawford?" came from his right, and he was all set to ignore it, unable to hear another case or boat request or any other damn thing until he got his hands on Addie. But then the guy stepped into his path. "I asked if you're—"

"Yeah, that's me." He cataloged the button-down shirt, designer jeans, and shiny shoes that must require constant maintenance with all the dust around town. The air of superiority that the guy propagated himself. "You must be the city-slicker lawyer I've heard so much about."

"Justin Matthews," the guy smugly said, clearly proud his reputation preceded him.

The nerve, thinking he could come in and make a name for himself by being a shark in a small town of friendly folk.

"I suppose I should thank you. Since you only care about winning, I have more clients than I can shake a stick at. Now if you'll excuse me, I also have a game to catch."

The guy thrust out his hand and slapped it to Tucker's chest as he started by—evidently, he had a death wish.

"Runnin' short on patience here, buddy," Tucker said. "Spit it out or get outta my way."

"They might come to you now, but I have a better case record. I know all about your stint in Birmingham, and I'm not letting go of my practice here. Henry Pike's supposed to retire in two years and leave me to it."

"Well, you know what they say in the lawyer biz. Shit happens. But sure, do your worst and all that. I'm real scared."

Addie walked over and shoved her hands deep in her oversize pockets, and he could see through the gap that the shirt underneath was tight and black and 100 percent in need of removal later tonight. "You guys done with your pissin' contest yet? I'm about to order food and drinks."

The lawyer looked her up and down, and his pinched features left Tucker selfishly glad she'd worn the overalls. "Addison Murphy. And I thought you dressed down at the office."

"Not anymore, thanks to something I'm sure you said. Need me to check on your shoulder?" She cracked her knuckles. "I'd love to."

"I'll pass. I was just informing Mr. Crawford that I don't plan on letting go of the law practice, and that I don't want a partner."

Addie nodded at him and then turned to Tucker. "Bet you took that pretty hard, considerin' you don't wanna work at that law office anyhow."

He curved his hand around the bill of his trusty, worn Saints cap. "Real broken up about it."

"Come on, then. I'll buy you a beer." She took his hand, and a calming warmth washed through him.

To see the stunned expression on the asshole lawyer's face, he would gladly ask her to swoop in and "save" him any day.

"You'd better be doing your exercises on that shoulder, Matthews," she fired back. "I have ways of finding out if you're not."

With that, she tugged Tucker toward the bar.

He wanted to lace his fingers with hers, curl her close, and kiss the hell out of her.

Unfortunately too many people were giving them curious looks. She dropped his hand and leaned her forearms on the bar, calling out an order for a pitcher of beer, wings, and a giant order of onion rings.

She glanced back at him. "Uh, make that French fries please."

He hoped that meant there'd be a lot of kissing in their future.

It was going to take every ounce of his self-control to suffer through the game without getting his mouth on her. It'd been so long he could hardly remember the taste of her lips, and that simply wouldn't do.

They headed to the table and caught up with the guys, and as the game got going, they ate and hollered at the TV and did the usual Sunday afternoon thing.

He'd stuck to one beer in the first quarter so nothing would hamper their getting the hell out of Dodge the second the game was over.

The Falcons pulled ahead of the Pats halfway through the third. It was the one matchup where he reluctantly cheered for Atlanta, and a happy Addie added extra motivation to join in on the celebration.

Among the cries and cheers, Tucker circled around behind Addie in the name of seeing the game better. The table was at least partially blocking them, so he slipped his hand inside the large gap in her overalls.

She sucked in a breath, and he pushed closer to her stool as he leaned over and braced a palm on the table. "These aren't really working at keeping my thoughts out of the gutter," he whispered, and then he slipped his hand under her T-shirt and dragged it across the smooth skin of her stomach.

He spread his fingers until his thumb brushed the bottom of her bra, and his rapid pulse pounded through his head.

He swallowed, hard, his desire moving into need

territory. "Bonus, they provide excellent cover."

She reached in from the other side, covering his hand with hers, and he thought she was going to stop his progress or tell him they needed to be good.

But instead she tipped her head to the side, and when everyone else was busy cheering for the wide receiver who was running the ball, her lips brushed his jawline. "Your hat's not as much of a deterrent as I thought it'd be, either. Then again, you're still wearing it on your head, and not—"

He pushed against her, his arousal lined right up with her ass, and she gripped the edge of the table.

His pinkie skirted the top of her panties, and when he arrived at the spot over her hip, all he felt was one blessedly tiny string of fabric. "You're not wearing good girl underwear," he said low in her ear, and if he didn't keep himself in check, he'd throw caution to the wind, capture her mouth with his and kiss her in front of everyone, and then drag her into the bar bathroom.

Their first time couldn't be in a bar bathroom.

Then again, who was he to go pretending he had scruples? Kinda hard to do with his hand down Addie's pants.

• • •

Delicious, intoxicating heat danced across Addie's skin, and the ache forming between her thighs demanded she do something about it, and soon.

She batted her eyes at Tucker, feigning inno-cence, and then she shrugged a shoulder and said, "Oh. I'm not really a good girl."

His harsh exhale stirred her hair and zapped every single one of her nerve endings.

She'd never expected to feel sexy in the overalls. She'd worn them as an inside joke.

Right now it felt like the best inside joke *ever*.

Tucker's calloused fingertips dragged over her hip bone, and her nipples strained against the lacy bra she'd worn, just in case. *Screw slow*, her body said, and her brain began saying it, too.

They'd known each other forever and you only lived once and—she bit her lip against the hum of pleasure that tried to escape when he stroked the spot where her hip met her thigh.

The guys turned back to comment on a play, and Tucker's hand stilled. He managed to say something that sounded about right, but all she could do was nod.

Shep glanced at her, obviously expecting commentary that for the life of her she couldn't come up with, even though Tucker had covertly withdrawn his hand. "Are you okay?"

She shot to her feet, so quickly the stool rocked. "Tucker and I have to go."

Ford's confused expression joined Shep's, but Easton's spoke to suspicions and the desire to turn an interrogator's spotlight on them.

Or maybe she just felt guilty.

"You're leaving before the end of the game?" Ford asked.

"I, uh…" She struggled for words, cursing them for being so damn slippery when she needed them most. "My grandma texted, and I have to go check on her. It looks like Atlanta's going to pull off this win, too, so…"

Crap. That didn't explain why Tucker needed to come.

"She's had too many beers to drive," he said, placing his hand on her lower back. Then he quickly dropped it. "So I'm going to take her."

"Right. Because we're responsible adults."

"Well, I'd hate to arrest two of my best friends, so that's good," Easton deadpanned.

Yeah, he was definitely onto them, which almost made her hesitate to follow through, but they were already neck deep in the lie, and when it came down to it, she was too turned on to care.

She *needed* Tucker's hands on her and for him to kiss her, and if she allowed her thoughts to continue down that path much further, she'd spontaneously combust in the bar.

If the Falcons hadn't set up to kick a field goal, they would've been busted for sure, but as the attention swiveled back to the game, she and Tucker took the opportunity to call out their goodbyes and rush out of the bar.

Tucker guided her to the driver's side of his truck, then practically launched her inside with a firm hand on her butt.

He slid in right beside her, fired up his truck, and peeled out of the parking lot.

"I'm totally going to hell for using my grandma as an excuse to go have sex with my best friend," she said.

He circled her thigh with his big hand, slowly drifting higher and higher. "As the best friend you're about to have sex with, I'm okay with that."

"*Ah!* You're okay with me going to hell?"

"Addes, I'm way too turned on for trick questions."

"It's not a trick question, it's—"

He kissed her, slowing the truck as they turned down the winding dirt path that led to the houseboat. Even with half his attention on the road, he kissed better than anyone else.

The second he threw his truck into park, she climbed onto his lap and slanted her mouth over his. He gripped her hips and arched against her, and then she was cursing the bulky denim between them.

"Too many clothes," she said.

"I agree." He quickly undid the straps of her overalls before his mouth recaptured hers.

His fingers slipped under the hem of her shirt, and when his hand moved up to palm her breast, his thumb brushing the lace over her hardened nipple, she let out an embarrassingly loud moan.

The groan that ripped from his mouth as she rocked against him came out even louder, and then it was almost like a competition. Whose sounds of pleasure could outdo the other.

The nice thing about this competition would be that no matter what, they both won.

Sticky, humid air hit her as he pushed open the door of his truck. He readjusted his grip on her, and she wasn't sure how he got them both out of the vehicle without them tumbling to the ground.

As far as she was concerned, the ground was as okay a spot as any, as long as more clothes came off.

Thanks to the straps of her overalls sliding down,

down, down, her pants were barely hanging on, and most of that was due to the fact she had her legs wrapped around Tucker's waist.

Flash greeted them with barking and jumping and general pay-attention-to-me tactics the second they came through the door.

"He's gonna be relentless," Tucker said, setting her down. "Lately he's taken to tearing everything apart, too, so just give me one second."

He grabbed treats and Flash's toys and led the hyper dog onto the deck. He scratched the puppy's ears and tummy and then tossed him a treat and stepped back into the cabin, closing the door behind him.

He looked so big and sexy, taking up all the space and the oxygen, and she'd just thoroughly groped and made out with her best friend. He'd had his hands on her breasts and she'd felt every inch of his hard body.

Weird.

Or maybe it was weird that it wasn't weirder.

What if it waited until tomorrow to show up and it was too late to do anything about it? Apprehension rose up to poke at her now that her body wasn't plastered to his.

He grabbed hold of one of her fallen shoulder straps and reeled her over to him. "Check-in time?" he asked, and she nodded, worried he thought it was weird and even more worried that following through would bring more weirdness—or worse, disappointment. "We don't have to rush, and we don't even have to do this tonight." He cupped her cheek. "No pressure, okay?"

She nodded again, because that was all she could seem to do. "Is this weird to you?"

"'Weird' isn't the word I'd use. Unbelievable. Intoxicating. Amazing—take your pick. We always have a great time together, no matter what we do, so I shouldn't be surprised at how addictive kissing you is, but *damn*."

His gaze raked over her, fanning the still-burning embers and sending need pinging through her once again.

"Clearly I have trouble keeping my hands off you," he said. "I got a little carried away in the bar."

"Me too. I guess I'm really not a good girl."

Tucker moved his thumb under her chin, using it to tip her face up as he brought his mouth down over hers.

He drew out the kiss, paying attention to her top lip and then her lower one, and then finally sliding his tongue against hers.

The world spun out of focus, everything narrowing to the feel of his lips and whiskers and his strong hands and his muscles and the way they twitched underneath her fingertips.

She wound her arms around his neck and kissed him until the necessity for air overtook everything else.

A quick sip of oxygen and she'd dive back in.

Tucker pressed his forehead to hers and sucked in a deep breath. "You make me want things I'm not sure I'm ready for."

"I'm not sure I'm ready for them, either," she whispered.

He brushed his mouth over hers, not kissing but

leaving it there as words fell from his lips to hers. "What I do know is, if there's anyone I want by my side when I try something crazy, it's you."

"So kissing me—being with me—is crazy?"

"Hell yeah," he said, and when he reclaimed her lips, everything inside her went so crazy she couldn't disagree.

Give her more crazy.

He backed her up against the nearest wall, his large body pinning her in place. His tongue swept inside her mouth and every other thought besides, *mmm*, *yes*, and *more* fled right from her head.

She circled his wrists with her hands and peered into those familiar blue eyes. Eyes that'd been a comfort to her for so long she couldn't remember life without them. "I'm done going slow. I want this. I want us."

A heady smile curved his lips, sending her heart fluttering.

She reached up and knocked off his hat.

He yanked down her overalls, the metal buttons and fasteners jingling when they hit the floor. Then he peeled off her T-shirt, leaving her in the same bra she'd accidentally flashed him in and the matching black panties.

She undid her ponytail and shook it out, and he continued to stare.

She heard every one of her thundering heartbeats, and right as self-consciousness started to seep in, Tucker stretched out his fingertips and swept them over her collarbone and down between her breasts. "Holy shit, Addes."

"I know I'm not like, overly sexy or girlie, or—"

He cut her words off by pressing his mouth to hers. "You're effortlessly sexy."

She curled the bottom of his T-shirt in her hands, and he assisted with a tug to the back of his collar, pulling it up and over his head.

Then he drew her to him, the skin-on-skin contact enough to send the world spinning again. He moved his lips to her neck, kissing and sucking and driving her wild with desire.

She fumbled with the button of his jeans for a second, and he groaned as he sprang free of the tight fabric. His hands skimmed down to her butt and he boosted her in his arms.

They knocked into just about every surface on their way to the bed—counter, cupboard, table, chair—and then he laid her back on the bedspread and took another long look at her as he ran his hand over her stomach.

He reached around to unhook her bra, and when she felt the clasp give, she placed her hand on the center of his chest.

"It's…it's been a while," she said, heat crawling up her neck and settling in her cheeks.

He covered her hand with his, his gaze catching hers. "For me too."

She didn't want to say it, but she felt like just in case this went wrong, she should put it out there. "I don't think I'm very good at this. I might even need some practice. Think of this as, like, warm-up. Or preseason."

Tucker gave her a crooked grin that held a hint of *you're-a-little-crazy*. "Don't worry. I'm good enough for the both of us."

She smacked his arm. "You cocky—"

He cut her off with a kiss, his weight pressing her into the mattress. She moaned and arched against him, wanting more friction, more of his weight, more of him on more of her.

He arched an eyebrow as he toyed with the strap of her bra. She nodded, and he slowly slid it off her shoulder, dragging his fingers over her skin as he did.

The other strap received the same treatment, and then he tossed the bra aside.

He swallowed, his Adam's apple bobbing up and down, and when he spoke, his voice came out deeper and huskier than usual. "In case I haven't made it clear yet, your body is insane. Like I said, effortlessly sexy."

Her heart swelled, and he moved his lips over the fluttering pulse point in her neck.

"I'd say I'm worried this is all a dream, but I'm afraid you'll pinch me again," he said, and while she meant to come up with a clever retort, he began kissing his way down her body and words didn't seem to matter anymore.

He slipped off her panties and put his mouth on her, and then she was adrift in a sea of bliss. He drove her right to the edge, torturing her for amazing eternal minutes.

She twisted her fingers in his hair and whimpered his name, a combination of a threat and a plea, and just when she didn't think she could take it anymore, he finally gave her exactly what she needed to experience that euphoric free fall her body had been begging for.

As he rolled on the condom, all she could really do was make unintelligible *mmm* noises.

Tucker laced his fingers with hers, kissed her, and pushed inside her. For a moment they remained like that, breathing as one, basking in how perfectly they fit together.

Then he began moving, gradually bringing her higher and higher. She wrapped her legs around his waist, anchoring her entire being to him.

A shudder racked his body as he struggled to keep a grip on his control. Watching his powerful body move over hers, seeing the way every muscle flexed and tensed—it took her breath away, and now she was the one worried she was dreaming.

"This right here. You and me…?" He swept her hair off her face and locked eyes with her, providing a lifeline in the swirl of emotions currently overtaking her. "This feels right, Addie. More right than anything ever has."

His words sank in, washing away her earlier concerns.

She was naked and underneath him, and it felt amazing and full of possibilities, and as he'd said, it *did* feel right.

She completely let go, crying his name as she let the incredible sensations she'd never experienced so strongly before wash through her, and he followed right after.

They'd crossed a huge line, but instead of it feeling like the end of anything, it felt like the beginning to something even more amazing.

CHAPTER TWENTY-THREE

Tucker curled Addie onto his chest and ran his fingers up and down the line of her spine, basking in the glow of having her warm, naked body pressed against him and her smooth skin under his fingertips.

It'd taken him longer than usual to catch his breath, and he still wasn't sure he'd totally caught it.

"You good?" he asked, knowing she'd feel better with a check-in.

Her eyelids drifted halfway closed as she smiled and sank her teeth into her lower lip, and he felt a hundred feet tall. "I'm amazing. You?"

"Also amazing. I do have to call you out on something, though. You lied."

She lifted her head off his shoulder, her forehead crinkle in full effect. "Okay, I think your ratty old baseball hat is sexy as hell on you, even though I maintain the Saints logo needs to go."

"And I'll be fantasizing about you wearing those damn overalls, although I won't bother with the shirt underneath. But I wasn't referring to that. I'm talking about when you said you weren't good at sex. You're really fucking good at it."

A blush crept across her cheeks, and she brought her hand to her mouth. "Yeah?"

"*Hell yeah*. Now that's not to say I couldn't use more demonstrations on how good you are at it. Just to, you know, make sure I can fully attest to it."

"Oh? Are you gonna be my witness in court?"

"If it means bragging about tonight? For sure."

She laughed. "I think you're crazy. We both might be crazy."

"And after sex that good, we should be."

He dragged his hand down her back again. He was never going to get enough of touching her.

He guided her mouth to his because he was never going to get enough of that, either.

A canine whimper carried through the silence, followed by scratching at the door. "Looks like Flash's patience for our alone time is up."

Addie sat up, her hair mussed, holding the sheet over her breasts. "I still can't believe you named your dog after one of my most embarrassing moments."

"Can't say as I'm sorry, considering it was one of my top five moments." He tugged on the sheet, getting another peek, since he'd been in too much of a hurry earlier to get his fill. "A few minutes ago is number one, in case you're wondering."

She tugged the sheet back up. "What's number two?"

"Flash pulling down your shirt. Three would be movin' back to Uncertainty and seeing your legs sticking out from underneath that truck—totally countin' that as one amazing day—and four would be passing the bar."

"And five?"

"Not sure. Probably the other night on my boat."

"I think you're buttering me up."

"No, but I like where your head's at. Some people go for whipped cream and chocolate, but if you like butter, I'll do whatever kinky thing you like."

Addie rolled her eyes, but she was also fighting back a smile.

As if he sensed whatever was going on might leave him outside for even longer, Flash renewed his pawing and whimpering, putting more volume behind it, and Tucker reluctantly forced himself out of bed.

When he turned to find his underwear, Addie was unabashedly checking him out, and it made him want to dive back in bed with her all over again.

While he'd tried to play it cool, a tiny part of him *had* been worried it might be weird afterward. Luckily they transitioned right back to friends, but with more ogling.

"If you want, I have ice cream in the freezer." He took a few steps and then spun around. "Not that I'm opposed to dripping it over your body and eating it that way, but I more meant you could grab a couple of spoons and we could watch a movie or somethin'."

"Well, my truck is back at the bar, so I guess I am sorta stranded. Might as well make the most of it and watch a movie with you."

"I'll take it," he joked, and then he went to let Flash inside.

By the time he'd opened the back door and semi–calmed down his puppy, Addie had moved to the kitchen. She stood in front of the freezer, sheet wrapped around her like an extra-long toga as she peered inside.

Flash bounded across the floor, nails clicking against the hardwood as he went right for Addie. She'd reached inside for the ice cream, and with only one arm to secure the sheet and Flash sinking in his teeth and tugging on the other end, she didn't stand a chance.

She squealed, and then she was standing buck naked in the middle of his kitchen area. An area that was way too small for everything he wanted to do to her.

"You've gotta be kidding me," she said.

Tucker gestured toward the puppy, who was now happily fighting the sheet. "See? His name practically chose itself."

She had one arm covering her breasts and the other covering his own personal heaven. "Some assistance, please. There's naked and then there's bent-over naked, and it's way too soon for the latter."

"I don't see a problem with you just staying right there for a while." He leaned a hip against the nearest wall. "I might suggest dropping the arms, though."

She fired a dirty look his way, and he didn't have the heart to tell her it was hardly effective while she was standing there with all that tempting skin on display.

He snagged his shirt off the floor, stepped over the *best dog ever*, and pulled it over Addie's head. If she had to wear clothes, they might as well be his.

Bonus, it left her killer legs nice and bare.

"I'm starting to think it's a conspiracy," she said. "You trained him to do that, didn't you?"

He gave her a crooked grin. "I plead the Fifth."

The cold ice cream carton hit his chest and the drawer opened with a rattle of silverware.

Addie grabbed two spoons and they retreated to the bed, where he arranged the pillows against the headboard so they could face the flat-screen TV he'd recently installed on the opposite wall. He brought up the menu to order a movie and typed in *Lake Placid* to mess with her.

"That's it, I'm outta here." She acted like she was going to hurdle over him and leave, and he caught her around the waist and tugged her back to him.

"Wait. I was going for guaranteed clinging and cuddling, not fleeing."

"What if I guaranteed those things if we *don't* watch a movie with killer alligators?"

Tucker relinquished the remote, figuring whatever she picked, he'd enjoy. "Choose whatever you want."

She resettled into the spot next to him and aimed the remote at the TV. "I feel so drunk on all the power."

As she scrolled through movies, he dug into the ice cream. When the first bite was loaded with the mini peanut butter cups Addie mined for whenever they had Moose Tracks, he extended it to her.

Her eyebrows drew together, and then with a shrug, she leaned forward and ate it off the spoon.

"Was that weird?" he asked.

"Weird. Delicious. I kinda dig it. Saves me time from unearthing them myself and"—she patted his arm—"gives you something useful to do with these biceps. I was starting to worry you were strictly eye candy."

Now he was the one rolling his eyes. "Stop or you'll make me blush." He ate a bite and extended the next one to her.

"So…" Her lips wrapped around the spoon, and he got lost in that for a second or two. "Since you know my secret fear, I think it's only fair that you tell me yours."

"I fear nothing," he automatically said, puffing out his chest, and she tilted her head.

"At least tell me one of your secrets—something I don't already know."

That narrowed it down quite a bit.

He also didn't want to say anything too deep or too real that would ruin the happy mood, and he searched his brain for a tidbit to satisfy her.

"I mentioned I love working with my hands and fixing up the boats…"

She nodded.

"Once in a while when I'm out in the shed, I wonder what it'd be like to do that to a whole house. To either take an old one and breathe new life into it or to build one from the ground up."

That'd make it harder for someone to take away, too, right? Or maybe it'd leave him with more to lose, but he wasn't going to think about that.

Part of him simply wanted to prove to himself he could do it. Then, sure, he'd love to plant a flag and claim it as his forever.

Addie picked up the hand not holding the spoon and ran a tingly line down his index finger and palm. "A house built by these hands? I have no doubt it'd be incredible."

Her unwavering faith in him sent the zipping sensation from the center of his palm to the center of his chest.

He lowered his voice. "But I might need the tiniest bit of help while working on the roof—I'm not a fan of heights. My office had that nice view, and I couldn't get too close to the windows or I'd think about cracking the glass and falling two dozen stories."

She beamed at him. "Not to rub it in or anything, but statistically, gators are responsible for more deaths than people falling through office windows."

"And where are you pulling these statistics? From your ass?"

"Possibly," she said with a laugh.

"Well, I'll give you some statistics that came from a reliable—if not as nice to look at—source. You're way more likely to be attacked by a cow, horse, or some other mammal than a gator."

"I'll still take my chance with the cows, thanks. Now, stop hogging the ice cream."

She reached for the spoon, and he quickly dug a bite out and shoved it in his mouth. But he offered her the next one.

A few minutes later, they were cuddled up watching a movie with gratuitous explosions over mini peanut butter cups, and he couldn't speak for her, but he was experiencing the best slumber party of his life.

• • •

Gentle shaking accompanied her name. Addie clung tighter to the warm body she was wrapped around, not yet ready to let go or open her eyes.

"Isn't that your alarm?" Tucker asked, and now

she heard the familiar chiming sound that woke her every weekday morning, a good hour or so before she preferred to climb out of bed.

Addie nuzzled his neck, taking a moment to inhale the scent of cedar and musky cologne and all things Tucker. "Nuh-uh."

"Funny…" The roughened pads of his fingertips dragged across her skin, waking up her libido as the rest of her body fought to stay asleep and immobile. "It's not *my* alarm."

"It's cool," she said. "My boss is super chill about me being late."

"I thought he was an asshole."

"Yeah, he is. An old school, misogynistic one at that. I made up the super-chill part so you'd let me sleep." With a sigh, she stretched, gradually forced her eyelids up, and found herself peering into stormy blue eyes.

She ran her hand down Tucker's scruffy face, enjoying the way his whiskers tickled her palm, and he gently pressed his lips to hers.

"Morning."

"Morning." Gathering her strength and what little motivation she'd managed to summon up, she slid over him, planning on silencing her alarm and climbing out of bed. But then she felt his erection pressing into her, awakening all the places that were pleasantly sore from last night, and she only made it halfway off.

Or all the way on, depending how one looked at it. "Oh, um. You're…"

He rocked against her, and she shuddered, bracing her hands on his firm chest so she wouldn't fall right back to the mattress. "Yeah," he said. "I woke up next to a hot naked brunette."

A ragged moan escaped as he rocked against her again, and her oddly happy alarm still chimed out, now on to its loudest setting. "But we don't have time for—"

He tugged on her arm, bringing their bodies flush together, and gave her a hard kiss on the mouth.

"Mmm, that is a rather compelling argument. Just a sec…" She scooped up her phone and tapped the screen. "You've got till the snooze goes off."

The next thing she knew, she was on her back, Tucker's delicious weight pinning her down. He peppered kisses across her jaw and her neck and then lavished attention on her breasts, while she arched against his hard length and grew hotter and wetter.

Tucker made quick work of a condom wrapper, and then he was moving inside her, hitting that spot that drove her crazy. It was fast and furious, intense and euphoric, and when her muscles tensed, her release so close, he reached between them and pushed her right over.

His orgasm came on the heels of hers, and for a quickie, she felt very thoroughly satisfied.

Chiming music rang out again, and she fumbled around for her phone and shut it off. She desperately wanted to sink back into Tucker's embrace, but since she'd never have the strength to leave again, she forced herself to sit up.

Soft lips brushed her bare shoulder. "As much as I'd like to hop in the shower with you, I don't think I could behave, so you go ahead, and I'll make you breakfast."

"If you feed me, you might never get rid of me."

He grinned and nudged her toward the bathroom, and moments before the rush of hot water hit her, she heard him talking to Flash.

The guy was ridiculously adorable, although she doubted he'd appreciate her using that adjective.

She rushed through the shower and came out wrapped in a towel.

Sunlight streamed through the windows, highlighting every dip and groove in Tucker's gloriously bare torso, and she nearly melted at the adoring expression he aimed her way.

Flash came bounding over, and despite the fact that he'd have to really jump to get it and she didn't think he could hit that height yet, she secured the towel tighter.

She eyed the clothes still strewn on the floor. "What am I going to wear? It's not like I can wear my overalls to work."

Tucker lifted the skillet off the stove and divided the scrambled eggs between two plates. "What if you added a tie? I've got a shit-ton of ties." His eyebrows knitted together as he glanced around. "Or did I put that box in storage?"

"Somehow, I'm thinking a tie won't help. Not with Moody Overlord's new obsession with a dress code." She gathered up yesterday's clothes and made do with a too-big pair of Tucker's warm-up pants.

Even after cinching the drawstring as tight as it'd go, she had to roll the waist twice, and one good tug from Flash and she'd lose them for sure. Which meant she'd better have Tucker drop her at home before going in to work, which was going to make her late, not to mention might raise a few eyebrows.

Hopefully people would think they'd just been playing crack-of-dawn football or fishing or something.

After shoveling down breakfast, the three of them climbed in his truck—Flash insisted on coming along, and as Tucker drove into town, the puppy couldn't decide if he wanted to be on Addie's lap getting petted or if he wanted to balance on the window and get a face full of fresh air.

With him being so tiny, Addie worried he might fall out, so she gripped his back legs the entire time, despite it leaving his wagging tail right under her nose.

"Remember how Casper wouldn't let me sit between you and him?" Addie said. "But he'd try to climb on your lap while you were driving, so then I tried to get him on *my* lap so you wouldn't wreck us, but he'd only stay there if I sat bitch. He was freaking heavy, too."

One corner of Tucker's mouth lifted. "And if I put him in the bed, he'd cry the entire time."

"Oh, and then there was that day we played baseball in the rain. He'd been out digging, and the three of us were coated in mud, so you decided he might as well join us in the cab anyhow. He'd gone from a white lab to a crusty chocolate one."

She laughed, but her sense of humor over the incident faded as she remembered walking into Tucker's house the same way they'd done hundreds of times, only to hear a huge fight between his parents.

Her mom and dad had argued here and there, but she'd never heard insults quite so cutting, with so much venom behind them that they stung her, too.

Then they'd been discovered, and that anger got turned on them.

"You're thinking about how my dad yelled at us, aren't you?"

"No," Addie quickly said, and at Tucker's skeptical look, she came clean. "Yeah. I'd never seen him like that. Either of your parents."

She'd frozen, unsure what to do, and Tucker had stepped in front of her, acting as a shield as his dad ripped into them.

Then Mrs. Crawford had yelled at Mr. Crawford, telling him he could stuff his "my roof, my rules" lecture, since he couldn't even pay the mortgage.

"They'd hidden it pretty well before that— usually I was the only one lucky enough to hear it." Tucker tightened his grip on the wheel, and his words came out careful and measured. "Dad was months late on the mortgage yet again, and they'd discussed trying to sell even though my mom never wanted to, and the mud we'd tracked in was the last straw, I'm sure."

"Well, we were crazy muddy. My mom wouldn't have been happy, either."

"Yeah, but she'd hose us off and offer us food while she continued to scold us."

Not embarrass her and then ground her, Tucker meant, which was his punishment, along with her being banished from his house for what seemed like forever.

It was summer, and two weeks without being allowed to hang out was torture—especially since he'd already spent so much of it with his grandpa.

Even after the ban lifted, he'd been withdrawn, and rumors about his parents' divorce followed shortly after. She'd tried to be there for him, but there'd been times when she wondered if she was ever getting her friend back.

Or if he'd have to move away before that happened.

The bank eventually foreclosed on their house and he and his dad—who never appreciated Tucker enough for what a kind, strong person he was, in her opinion—had to move into a cramped, rundown one-bedroom apartment.

One night she and Tucker had an intense talk where he confessed to feeling homeless, even though he'd added he was grateful he had a roof over his head and knew plenty of people had it worse.

Since Addie could sense him drifting from her at the memory, going to that place where he closed himself off, she quickly changed the subject. "Did you have any pets in Birmingham? It seems wrong to think of you without a dog by your side."

Tucker cracked a smile and reached over to scratch Flash's back. "Nah. I didn't have time for a goldfish, much less a dog. I didn't want to get one, only to have it be cooped up all the time."

"Like you were cooped up?"

"Exactly. Flash and I need space."

She hoped that was literal, countrified space.

Thanks to pushing the speed limit, they made it

to her house in record time. Instead of driving off, Tucker insisted on taking her to work, since he had errands to run in town anyway.

One quick wardrobe change later, and they arrived in front of the clinic that housed the physical therapy office. Addie wanted to lean across the bench seat for a goodbye kiss, but way too many people were out and about, and while she was starting to care less and less if they knew, Tucker had made it clear he wanted to keep them a secret.

So she kissed the top of Flash's head and said, "Pass it on." She pointed to Tucker, and the puppy bounced over there and licked his hand.

"For the record, mine wasn't that sloppy." She pushed out the door and rounded the front of the truck.

"Not sure I believe you," Tucker called out his open window. "I might need to collect more evidence later. In fact, why don't you text me when you take your lunch, and if I'm still around, we can grab a bite."

"Sounds good." With that, she gave him one more wave and rushed into the building, hoping and praying her boss wasn't in yet. Usually he came in on the later side.

Of course she wasn't that lucky.

The instant she stepped inside the office, a whole twenty-five minutes late, her boss crossed his arms.

"Nice of you to finally join us," Mr. Watkins said.

No excuse seemed good enough, and yes, it was unprofessional to be late, but it was the first time in years, and she had a really sexy excuse.

Mr. Watkins launched into a lecture about what

he expected from his employees, and how he'd taken a chance on her, and asked his favorite question about if her name was on the door.

And while she would've loved to turn and walk right back out, not even the Moody Overlord could put a dent in her mood.

A nod and a few answers he wanted to hear, and she managed to escape to a quiet room.

While she checked out the day's schedule, Addie relived last night in her mind. Tucker feeling her up in the bar; she and Tucker ripping each other's clothes off; sex and ice cream and a movie and waking up to more sex and breakfast and *gah*…

Happiness filled her up, head to toe.

We slept together and it wasn't weird and we're better than okay, and maybe…

She was almost scared to think it, as if that might summon some unforeseen issue.

But they'd been friends for a lifetime, and last night was amazing, so she went ahead and let herself finish the thought.

Maybe this could turn into a whole lot more.

CHAPTER TWENTY-FOUR

Tucker had looked at two different boats, and he answered Tula Brigg's question about whether she could force the town to give her a new address, considering high school kids were always posting pictures in front of hers: 69 Ultimate Court.

At first she was flattered, thinking they were showing off her beautiful floral landscaping on those "instachat snap things" to all their friends, but then her neighbor Gertie told her why—apparently because she was jealous *her* flowers never did as well—and now Tula wanted her address changed ASAP.

When he'd told her he couldn't change an address because it was, well, a set place on the earth, she muttered "and they say you're a good lawyer" before storming off.

From there he'd picked up supplies from the local hardware store to complete the boat repair jobs he'd taken on, and while he was in there, the owner asked if he would take a peek at his lease agreement and find some wiggle room so he could move the store to a different location, one that wasn't so "damned expensive."

By the time Tucker pushed into the diner, it felt like it'd been hours since breakfast.

He inhaled the mouthwatering aroma of food on the grill, and since he had Flash in tow and he was hardly a well-behaved dog, he headed to the patio area to find a table.

He momentarily worried having lunch with Addie would get tongues wagging, but considering they'd eaten enough hamburgers and fries at the diner to feed an army through the years, he realized he was being ridiculous.

After how well things went last night, he was thinking that maybe it wouldn't be so bad for people to know. Let them talk.

Plenty would claim they always knew he and Addie would happen, even though neither one of them had.

A grin spread across his face as he thought about Flash stealing that sheet from her. Surges of heat immediately followed, as the image of her naked and in the middle of the houseboat cabin popped into his mind.

Then he was thinking of her naked and underneath him, her dark hair spread out on the pillow.

The sounds she'd made. The way she kissed.

And that was only the start of the amazingness.

Last night he'd felt deeper things than he'd ever felt with anyone before, and the fact that afterward they could alternate between laughing and talking and cuddling and kissing while they watched a movie made it even more amazing.

It was everything he didn't even know he was looking for and more.

Could we really have it all? An amazing easy friendship on top of a passionate, ridiculously fun relationship?

Eventually he'd need to find a long-term place

to live, but that would require fully establishing his business. He wasn't sure how long he could run a law office out of his houseboat, although that would certainly help cut overhead.

And when he and Addie wanted to have some fun without bumping and bruising themselves along the way, they could go to her place.

"They said you were out here." Addie bent over and ruffled Flash's fur. "I assume that's because this guy can't behave?"

Tucker's gaze lingered on Addie's ass, right there in front of his face, and it seemed a shame not to do something about that. He glanced around, and when the coast was clear, he gave it a quick pinch, gratified when she squealed.

"I guess neither one of us can behave." He pushed out the chair next to his with his foot, and after she settled into it, he squeezed her knee under the table. "Did you get in trouble for bein' late?"

"I got a lecture that I would've gotten for one reason or another. You'd be so proud of me, though. I was so happy I just let it roll right off me."

He dragged his thumb across her knee. "I'm happy, too."

The waitress came out to take their order, then brought their food shortly after. Other than that, thanks to the unseasonably warm afternoon, they were alone, save the people who wandered past on the sidewalk, most of whom they exchanged a friendly nod or hello with.

But then a familiar figure strode down the sidewalk, and everything inside of Tucker turned to stone.

This was the perfect example of speak of the devil, a few hours late or not.

Addie cocked her head, obviously noticing the mood shift, and as soon as she saw his dad, he could see she'd pieced together why.

"There you are," Dad said. Admittedly, Tucker had been ducking his calls ever since he'd returned to town. "I ran into Lottie, and she told me you two were here at the diner. Guess some things never change."

Apparently the town busybody's comment about wifi and smartphones hadn't been a bluff—news traveled even faster than it used to, and that was almost as impressive as it was alarming.

Instead of bothering with going through the diner, Dad stepped over the short wrought-iron fence and pulled out one of the seats. "Mind if I join you?"

"Fair warning," Addie said, "I have to get back to work in about five minutes, so don't think I'm leavin' on your account."

Considering the reason Dad most likely showed up unannounced, Tucker might leave on his account.

Dad flashed her a wide smile, and Tucker wrapped his fingers tighter around her knee. "Good to see you, Addison."

"You too, Mr. Crawford." She did a good job of pretending she'd forgotten the past and that afternoon they'd recalled earlier today, but after Dad yelled at her, she was cautious around him, and she'd once sworn that if he moved Tucker away, she'd never—*"and I mean never"*—forgive him.

She covered Tucker's hand with hers and gave it

a reassuring squeeze, a silent way of telling him she was fine and—as usual—could take care of herself.

Dad made small talk, asking after her parents and grandmother and her job. Tucker would never say he and his dad were especially close, but they used to be closer before he was forever pushing him to make more money.

His constant attempts to get him to sell the houseboat and Grandpa's shed and boat, including the rough plot of land they sat on, only widened the rift between them.

After he'd started his job at the law firm, it seemed like all Dad ever asked about was the salary and what he could do to move up the ladder faster.

Tucker had once asked if he needed money, figuring that was why he kept on mentioning it, but he'd said that now he was happily divorced, he could make it just fine.

Although Tucker had never made an official stance on which side he took in the divorce, he'd accidentally taken Dad's the tiniest bit. Probably because he was the one left behind when Mom bounced back so quickly, and maybe even because the rumors made him wonder, too.

"I'd better get going," Addie said, scooting out her chair. She twisted toward him, cutting Dad off from the conversation, and voice low, asked, "Will you be okay?"

Just her asking made the amount of trepidation he'd experienced since Dad took a seat across from him feel silly.

He was a grown man. He could make his own decisions.

He brushed his thumb across the top of her cheek, warmth winding through him that she knew him that well and that she cared enough to check on him.

"I'm fine. Have a good rest of the day, and I'll call you later." He wanted to kiss her, but now he was thinking once again about the town gossip and how corrosive it could be.

It'll make it that much sweeter once we no longer have an audience.

Addie also forewent going through the diner, easily launching herself over the fence and then muttering, "Damn, I miss my yoga pants and sneakers."

Tucker watched until she rounded the corner, and when he returned his attention to Dad, his expression had *gotcha!* written across it.

"I guess I spoke too soon when I said some things never change. I'm surprised Lottie didn't tell me you were dating Addison Murphy. Seems like big news."

"We're not…" Denying it didn't settle right with him, although if they were going to make it official, there were a handful of people who needed to be told before it spread through town. "It's no one's business, but it's new, and I'd appreciate if you kept it to yourself."

"Is she the reason you came back?"

Now that he thought about it, he wondered if his subconscious knew something he hadn't when he'd decided to quit his job after one amazing night in Uncertainty. "She's one of them. Along with the rest of the guys, and the town. The people need me here,

Dad. I can make a difference."

"You'll never make as much money here as you could pretty much anywhere else. Just pick a law firm, one in a closer city, and you can visit here on the weekends."

"I know money is important to you, but it's not everything to me."

"That's easy to say until you don't have any. Until you're struggling for every penny and running out of money halfway through the month, and the stress eats at you day and night. And what about if you and Addison get serious? The houseboat might seem charming now, but it'll get old fast."

His chest tightened, his unmet goals pressing in to remind him yet again he hadn't come close to meeting them yet.

To gaining the financial security he'd craved since he and his family had to live without it—the same security he'd sworn to have *before* jumping into a relationship. "Addie doesn't care about that stuff."

Dad laughed, a mirthless laugh with a sharp edge of cynicism and cruelty. "Oh, son. All women care about that. Her tastes might be simpler, and yeah, that'll work in your favor in your current situation, but she wants stability just as much as the next girl."

"You don't know her."

He's wrong, Tucker's brain screamed. Not about wanting stability, because who didn't, but she would understand that it'd take some time, and they'd find ways to make it work when and if it reached that point.

"Your mom once told me she didn't need anything besides me, and look how that turned out.

Now she's living in that big ol' house with another guy, bragging to her friends about how rich and important he is."

Flash whimpered like he hated Dad's words as much as Tucker did.

Tucker untied his leash and sat him in the seat Addie had abandoned. He showed how well he was going to behave by licking Addie's leftover puddle of ketchup.

"How's that any different than you wanting to brag that you have a son who works at a big law firm and rakes in the money? *You're* the one who constantly brings up how much money I make, not Addie, and not anyone else in this town."

"I'm not doing it to brag. Like I said, I know what it's like to try to make it on a meager salary. What it's like to wonder how to feed and clothe your family, and I know exactly what it feels like when that shelter you've worked so hard for gets ripped right from over your heads." Dad placed his forearms on the table and shifted forward. "I'm trying to give you a reality check, son. This town tends to make people all shiny-eyed with its laid-back charm, but when those nice people don't get paid, they turn mean as the next guy."

"I've seen the next guy," Tucker said. "I've gotten him out of charges he deserved, and no thanks to doing that again. These people need me. I might never make a lot of money, but I can support myself."

"Right. *Yourself.* Not a wife, not a family."

"I'm well aware of what I need to accomplish before I can think about those things."

How many times had he reminded himself? A down payment on a house and $40,000 in a 401K—so his future wife and kids would never have to worry about their home being taken away—and the plan was to have that accomplished by the time he was thirty.

He'd let those goals disappear in the happy haze of moving here, and spending time with Addie pushed them even further back in his mind.

He and Addie had barely started dating, so he tried to tell himself there was no reason to freak out over how short he fell just yet. Maybe his goals would need to be adjusted, and it might take a year or two, but he could still find a way to be a good provider.

"I've made my choice of where I want to live," he said, "and I choose here with my friends and people who need someone who'll stand up for their rights without price-gouging them while doing it."

Dad held up his hands like he was surrendering. "I didn't come to fight. I came to speak my piece and because I was driving through. Good thing, too, because where would I stay? The couch in the houseboat?"

"There're a dozen people who'd offer you a place to stay, I guarantee it."

"So they could gossip about how I can't afford a room at the inn and add that to the list of reasons why your mom left me? At least they'd get that part right. But I'd rather not end up as fodder to discuss over coffee."

"And a few of them might add that it's a shame I got fired from my law firm, in spite of the fact that

I didn't, and even though it doesn't keep them from coming to me for legal advice. The grapevine is part of small-town life, but the beauty is, I don't care what they say. You should try it."

"Yeah, but Addison, you care what she says. What she thinks. You want her to have the best, right?"

Of course he cared, and of course he did. That was like asking if ice cream was delicious.

"I have a feeling you and I would disagree what's best for her," Tucker said.

"Probably. But it wouldn't kill you to learn from my mistakes so you won't have such a hard go of it. Your mom and I foolishly believed love would fill in the gaps, but it doesn't work like that. Stress wears on everyone, and money's one of the biggest stressors there is, not to mention one of the top reasons couples fight."

Dad pushed his chair out but didn't stand. Genuine concern flickered through his features, and that was what dug at Tucker, even as he told himself, yet again, that Dad was wrong. It didn't have to be that way.

"Addison's a great girl, and I hope you two work it out, I truly do. It'll just be a lot easier to do if you're not constantly fighting about money."

• • •

Addie stared at the email until the words swam together, and then she blinked and read it again.

Her former professor, the one she'd emailed after one of her especially crappy days at work, did know of a job. An amazing job.

The University of Alabama had an opening for a sports therapist. It was similar to the one he'd told her about right after graduation, but this position was higher up in the pecking order.

It was the type of job she'd dreamed about back when she was forcing herself through difficult classes.

Not only did they have the opening, he'd already talked her up, and they'd agreed to an interview, so she'd have to travel to Tuscaloosa and meet with them.

He warned it was a competitive position, and there were a few other applicants, but he thought she'd be a good match, and with the in he had with the team, her odds were even better.

Could I really abandon my War Eagle cry and cheer Crimson Tide?

Her friends and family would tease her endlessly about being a traitor, but now that she was older and wiser—and had experienced working for Moody Overlord—she recognized how huge this opportunity truly was. She'd be working for one of the biggest football organizations in the state.

Hell, in the country.

A two-and-a-half-hour drive was long enough that commuting on the daily was out but close enough that… Well, weekends would be tricky with games.

Her heart sank. Maybe it was stupid to even consider it. She had her family to think about.

Mom often needed help with Nonna, this was her home, and Tucker had barely moved back—from a place a lot closer to Tuscaloosa, nonetheless, which seemed a lick mean on fate's part— and things were going so well with him.

She placed her hands on the keyboard and tried to think of how to respond, but it was a big decision and she didn't want to do anything rash. She'd sent a few other résumés out as well and ought to give other people time to respond so she could better assess her options.

The interview was already set up, though, so she didn't have a lot of time.

No reason to drive up there if she didn't plan on taking the job. Then again, she had nothing to lose by going to the interview and seeing what the job entailed, if she'd be a good match.

If she'd received this email a couple of months ago, she would've been jumping on her couch, Bama or not.

Sure, most of the same worries would've come up, but with Nonna stable, Addie's main worry now was that taking the job might mess things up with Tucker.

Tucker, who didn't want people to know they were dating.

She mentally batted away that errant thought.

They'd *both* decided it would create extra drama, and she knew how much he hated having people in his business. With his dad in town, reminding him of why, the timing for the going-public discussion wasn't great.

But last night, things had changed.

Then again, here she was, considering ignoring a huge opportunity without *knowing* how much. If he wasn't ready to become an official couple, or at least take some steps in that direction, then she needed to know that, too.

Ugh, this means we're gonna have to have a serious discussion about it.

I hate serious discussions.

That went double for relationship ones, and she worried about coming across as too clingy, especially since it was so new—with a side of already being complicated—and she'd never been great at talking about her feelings as it was, so the chance of messing it up was that much higher.

The question is, do I talk to Tucker before or after I respond to the email?

Since a beam of heavenly light didn't pop up to point her in the right direction, she slammed her laptop closed and punched on the TV.

When in doubt, procrastination always made a nice alternative.

A knock came at the door, and she checked her phone to see if anyone had texted about coming over. No messages, and if it was Tucker, she planned to tease him about being in booty call range, and how she thought he was opposed to that.

Not that *she* was opposed to that. Bring on the booty.

Her emotions nearly gave her whiplash as they thrashed from dirty thoughts to *OMG, don't let your face show your grandma that you were thinking about Tucker.*

Or sex. Or sex with Tucker—especially not that.

Engage robot mode.

"Hello, love." Nonna kissed both her cheeks, and Addie couldn't help noticing that one arm remained behind her back. "I was at bingo and decided to stop by and see how my favorite granddaughter who lives in town is doing."

"And if she'd let you eat your contraband take-out in her house?"

"No?"

"Nonna, I can smell the fries."

Her grandmother closed the door with her body and held it in place like someone might come crashing in after her at any second. Then she brought forward a brown bag with grease splatters, and the scent of french fries grew stronger. "The youngest Bartlett boy was working the cash register at the diner, and he's the only one Priscilla hasn't gotten to yet. I saw an opportunity and I took it."

"My casa is your casa. Bonus, we'll get to have a double funeral when Mom finds out."

"She take it too far! This week we had jackfruit masquerading as pulled pork, and she replaced the noodles in my Nonna Cavalli's lasagna recipe with zucchini. That recipe has been passed down for generations, and I swear I sensed my nonna rolling over in her grave."

Addie bit back a laugh, and they settled onto the couch, where she charged a fry tax for her troubles.

Then she was thinking about the job offer again. The excitement and possibility and being on the sidelines during the big football games, followed by the downer thought about how she'd live too far away for her grandmother to stop by unannounced.

Maisy would continue to provide her with treats that were secretly low fat and low sugar, but who'd trespass with Nonna in the middle of the night to plant flowers? She could get into real trouble, some that her sexy lawyer might not be able to get her out of, especially if it came down to her health.

"Didn't you have a follow-up doctor's appointment today?" Addie asked, and Nonna nodded without providing further information. The fries made her suspect she'd been told something bad about her cholesterol or blood sugar.

The woman was so stubborn that she'd formed a conspiracy theory about how they "rigged" tests so they'd have a reason to see you more.

"How'd it go?"

If it went well, Addie would feel less guilty about considering moving away from Uncertainty.

If it went badly, that'd be another reason she should stick close, and right now, she didn't know which one to cheer for—the one where Nonna was doing well, of course, but she meant more which effect of the cause.

"I'm perfectly healthy."

"And your cholesterol and blood sugar levels?"

Nonna chewed a little faster and glanced toward the window. "They fine."

"You know that with a couple of calls, I can find out just how fine they are, right?" Half bluff, but Nurse Hays could be won over with muffins from Maisy's bakery, and she was concerned enough about people's health to the point that most of the time it didn't even take that.

"Those doctors are in cahoots with the drug companies! They team up and tell you that you need medication that you no need." Nonna jammed several more fries in her mouth. "I thinking of having my lawyer sue."

She straightened, and the look she gave Addie sent a prickle across her skin.

"Speaking of my lawyer, why did Tucker drop you off at work today? Is your truck broken? I keep telling you to take my Buick. It's reliable car."

Oh, I'm not much for boats, she wanted to say, but she was fully aware of how much Nonna loved her Buick and how sad it made her that she rarely got to drive it these days.

"Sometimes I forget how wicked-fast the grapevine is here. He had to get a bunch of supplies for his boat repairs, and he stopped by for a few minutes and then took me to work. We also had lunch," she added, since everyone in town had probably heard already.

Addie watched for signs that her grandmother suspected more was going on between them, but she either had the best poker face ever or she didn't have a clue.

What did it say that not a single person jumped to that conclusion? She wanted to think it was a good thing, but maybe it meant…

Nope, not going there.

Tucker was the one part of her life that felt perfectly right at the moment. His words replayed through her head: *You and me…? This feels right, Addie. More right than anything ever has.*

And it did.

"I so happy he's back in town where he belongs," Nonna said. "And just tonight, as all my friends were talking about how many of their grandkids have moved, I was thinking about how glad I am that you live here."

Guilt bubbled up. It wasn't like she *wanted* to live far away.

Addie spent a lot of time trying to counterbalance Mom's and Nonna's strong personalities. She liaised and encouraged them both to compromise, and without her here, who would do it?

Dad had washed his hands of it, claiming he didn't want to pick sides between his wife and his mom, and Addie wondered how bad it'd get before he decided to step in.

Her thoughts continued to tug back and forth. For and against the job.

Yes, she needed to talk to Tucker about it, but at the same time, she wanted to figure out how she even felt before she did.

Then maybe she'd know what to say. How to start.

A dozen other things she didn't know now.

"You okay, love?" Nonna asked, tipping the bag toward her. "Need more fries?"

Addie snagged several and slumped against the couch cushions. For once in her life, it seemed like everything had finally aligned. She no longer felt lonely, the gang was back together, and instead of messing up things with Tucker, crossing lines had brought them closer than ever.

It'd given her hope that they had a shot at something amazing.

She'd barely gotten to enjoy the afterglow before life threw her a curve ball, and she wasn't sure whether she should swing or try to catch it, and the pressure of the huge decision left her unsettled all over again.

CHAPTER TWENTY-FIVE

Addie's breaths came right on top of each other and she could feel her pounding pulse throbbing through every inch of her body, but in this type of situation, none of that mattered.

"I think I hear someone," Tucker rasped out, and the two of them immediately crouched low, the harvested peanut plants in the field they'd been sprinting through far better at tripping them up than providing decent coverage.

The night sky and clouds obscuring the moon helped, but they were sitting ducks out here if they didn't find somewhere better to hide.

"I swore I heard the four-wheeler's engine," he added. "They might've shut it off to listen for us."

Shep wanted to go unconventional for his bachelor party with a throwback game from back in the day, one they hadn't played in nearly a decade. Possibly because they were too old, even though Addie's competitive spirit begged to differ.

Fugitive involved splitting into teams, running through fields, and a home base. The "fugitives" were escapees on the run from the law. The "US Marshals" had to search them down via four-wheeler and/or foot and capture them. If they did, they won, but if the fugitives made it to home base before the Marshals, they won.

Mostly bragging rights on both sides, but tonight's losing team had to pay for dinner and drinks.

As usual, Addie and Tucker had teamed up. Easton and Shep were the lawmen, and Ford had paired with Shep's cousin who was in town and probably currently reexamining his life choices.

Addie's thighs burned, screaming for some kind of movement besides squatting, and she scanned the area, squinting as she tried to regain her bearings.

"We should break for the next field." She placed her hand on Tucker's arm. "Just remember the fence has claws."

One night he'd run straight into the wire fence and flipped right over it, and besides the hard landing on the other side, he'd shredded his shirt and ended up with long scratches up his abdomen from the barbed wire across the top.

They'd cleaned out the cuts once they got around to it, but that was after going to a party and building a bonfire, and now that she was older, she marveled he hadn't ended up with tetanus.

They should all know better than to run through fields late at night without much light or cover now, too, but the whole point of a bachelor party was to revert to feeling like a carefree group of friends with no responsibilities, right?

And if Easton failed to catch them after his extensive cop training, and she got to rub that in his face, even better.

Obviously "maturity" wasn't the watchword.

The whine of the four-wheeler's engine cut through the air, and they held their breath. Then it grew quieter, signaling it'd headed in the other direction.

Addie and Tucker exchanged a wordless glance

and raced toward the next field, leaping over mounds of dried-up peanut plants. This time, Tucker slowed well before the fence.

He wrapped his hands around the stretches of wires without barbs and motioned for her to hop over. Then she held the wires down so he could cross.

She'd barely made it a step before she was yanked down to the ground. Tucker rolled over her, covering her body with his. "Someone's close," he whispered. "I saw figures. I'm just not sure if it's the other fugitive team or the marshals."

Addie tried to remain perfectly still, watching and listening—well, listening. It was so dark she could hardly see Tucker, and he was plastered against her.

She shifted, squirming against the unforgiving ground, and then gasped as his hard length pushed into her, sending another form of adrenaline into the mix.

"No, I don't have anything in my pocket," he said, "and I *am* happy to see you."

Her fingers dug into his arms, and her body automatically arched against him, craving more of the delicious friction. His groan made her do it again, and his lips came down on hers, urgent and demanding.

Pure physical need took over, and then they were making out with reckless abandon in the middle of the field, winning no longer the name of the game.

Although there would definitely be winning.

Tucker slid his hand under her shirt, skirting her sports bra with his fingertips before finally breaching the barrier.

He tugged on her ponytail, angling his mouth over hers, and swept his tongue inside.

The *moo* made her jump and was immediately followed by another low bellow.

Addie squinted through the darkness and vaguely made out the large bovine shapes. "Um, those figures you saw are cows. Did you know that when you tackled me to the ground?"

"Nope, but while you're down there…" Tucker kissed her again, and she got lost in having his lips on hers, his hands on her body.

The mooing came closer, along with the sounds of hooves on hard dirt and a wet *splat* that meant the air was about to get a lot more aromatic.

"You sure know how to woo a girl," Addie teased, running her fingers through Tucker's hair as he kissed her neck.

"Don't say I never take you anywhere fun."

Obviously he was joking, but it made her wonder if they ever would go on an official date.

She should really stop being a wimp and talk to him about how official things were, not only for herself but because she was starting to feel guilty keeping it from the rest of their friends and from her family.

Then again, maybe I'm rushing.

It's only been a week since we've slept together, and suddenly it feels like things are going too fast and too slow, all at the same time.

Since that wasn't enough complications, she still needed to talk to him about the possible job with Bama. It'd been a crazy busy week, though, and she wanted to find just the right moment to bring it up.

She'd given up on figuring out exactly how she felt about it.

More hoof beats sounded, accompanied by a *moo* so loud it vibrated across her skin, and while she maintained that she'd rather face a cow than a gator any day, she wondered about those statistics Tucker had thrown at her over ice cream.

Lying here and waiting to be stomped on hardly seemed smart, and on top of that, the whine of the four-wheeler grew louder.

"Sounds like our time is up." Tucker gave her one last hard kiss on the mouth, pushed to his feet, and helped her up. He jerked his head toward the lights that marked home base, and she nodded.

Then she ran, hoping that his last statement didn't end up being too true.

• • •

The group of them looked like they'd been playing football in the mud, and Shep had twisted his ankle enough that he had to limp into Hooters.

Tucker halfway expected the hostess to examine their mangy group and turn them away, but she greeted them with a flirty smile and led them to a table. Ford made sure to mention that it was their friend's bachelor party, and she promised they'd take good care of them.

"Is there any way we could get a bag of ice?" Addie asked. "Or a cup if you can't wrangle up a bag?"

The hostess seemed to notice Addie for the first

time. Her ponytail had turned from brown to dusty gray, and heat and a smug sense of pride wound through Tucker when he thought about how he'd been partially responsible for that and the caked-on mud on her sexy backside.

His competitive nature demanded they win the game, but he'd temporarily forgotten that when he'd had Addie pinned underneath him in the field, her enticing mouth his for the taking.

Right until being trampled by cattle had become a reality.

The four-wheeler had stirred them up and made them nervous, and so he and Addie had made their big break for the base.

Easton and Shep had come flying down the road, a cloud of dust kicking up behind the four-wheeler. Tucker had screamed for Addie to run, even though she needed no prompting, and Shep leaped off the back of the four-wheeler like some kind of crazed stuntman.

He'd landed wrong on uneven ground, but all of them had crashed and burned plenty through the years. Since Shep was the king of the fake-out, Tucker and Addie had run to base.

They'd only realized he'd truly hurt himself when he remained on the ground, a grimace on his face.

"I'll, uh, ask if we can do that," the hostess said.

"You've gotta get some ice on it now," Addie said, her *I'm-dead-serious* expression aimed at Shep. "If you have to limp down the aisle, Lexi's gonna kill us." She glanced at Ford. "Back me up here."

"Ice your damn ankle, Shep."

The two of them had combined their sports

medicine and paramedics skills to determine it wasn't broken but sprained, thank goodness, but when they'd suggested they cut the party short, he wouldn't hear of it.

Not because of their dinner location—which Ford had picked out after it'd been made clear there would be no strippers—but because he'd had a great time so far, busted ankle and all, and he'd insisted on one last night with his boys before he married the "most amazing girl ever" in two weeks and had to become an official grown-up.

The hostess brought a lumpy bag of ice, and Addie lifted Shep's leg up on her chair and held the makeshift ice pack over the swollen bump. Three waitresses arrived to take their order, and there was a lot of mutual ogling on the other side of the table between Ford, Easton, and the waitresses.

A few glances drifted his way, but he kept his gaze solidly on Addie. This situation had potential for disaster written all over it, and he was trying to be respectful, not to mention Addie was the only girl he wanted right now, and he wanted her to know that.

One of the waitresses kept giving her quizzical looks, so Addie winked at her.

Tucker covered his mouth with his hand to keep from busting up. It also made him think of the night she'd broken into the houseboat and winked at him while drunk.

That night it was more of a twitch than a wink, but both times were just as damn cute. He placed his hand on Addie's knee and gave it a quick squeeze, figuring he could get away with it between the table and other distractions.

The waitress Addie had winked at circled the table, and at first he thought she must be into Addie's flirting. Only then she leaned her entire body against his side and asked for his order in a low, husky voice.

A muscle flexed in Addie's jaw, but she managed to keep her cool.

As soon as the waitress left, Addie shifted closer. "Did she have to shove her boobs in your face while she took your order?"

Tucker met her fiery brown eyes and whispered, "Yours are way better. Especially in that sexy black bra. Or without a bra. It's all win."

"And now I'll never trust anything you say."

"It sounds like I'd better pay them more attention tonight, so you see just how big of a fan I am."

"Mm-hmm," she said, and he could tell while she was trying to be cool with the situation, she was far from it.

Every time the waitresses came over and flirted with him, Addie's shoulders tightened even more, and it was the first time since crossing lines that things were a bit weird and tense because of it.

During the entire meal, he could hardly relax, afraid his gaze would accidentally drift and Addie wouldn't believe him. Not that he blamed her for being irritated—if a bunch of ripped dudes were paying special attention to her right in front of him, he'd hate it, too.

Worse, toward the end of the meal, she seemed more sad than mad, and he'd take pissed over that any day.

It'll all be okay once we're alone again. Then I'll follow through with my promise and prove she has nothing to worry about.

• • •

Since every male ever always claimed Hooter's simply had the best wings, Addie stifled her comment about them not being that good—the ones at the Old Firehouse definitely tasted better.

But then she'd be the girl, and not only did she feel like the girl tonight, she felt like the bitter, jealous girlfriend.

Which was also stupid because she would've felt left out if they hadn't brought her along.

Watching the waitresses flirt with Tucker had been akin to torture, and it sucked she couldn't just loop her arm over his shoulders, kiss his cheek, and make it clear they'd better back the hell off.

If I land the job, I'll be gone a lot, and with how many pretty women hit on Tucker…

Her insecurities flared and she bit the inside of her cheek to redirect the ache in her chest. Who wanted a relationship with someone who needed constant reassurance?

At the same time, how many times had she been left behind once those types of girls stepped onto the scene?

They wrapped up dinner, and then Tucker and Easton helped Shep into Ford's truck. Addie tugged off his dirt-crusted shoe, gently palpated around the outside of the ankle to check the swelling, and rolled it through a series of movements to check his range of motion.

"Elevate it as much as you can, take some more ibuprofen as soon as you get home, and ice it again before you go to bed. You'll need to stay off it as much as you can the next few days."

Shep saluted her, the smart-ass. "Got it, doc."

"What she said," Ford so helpfully added.

She rolled her eyes but then noticed something was off about Ford. He was distracted and subdued—rare for the guy with the larger-than-life personality.

Instead of climbing into the truck, she held back. "What's up? Did you not get the waitress's phone number?"

"I got it," he said, his voice monotone. She didn't even know he could do monotone.

"You're usually happier after something like that. I feel like if I lifted my hand for a high five, you'd leave me hanging."

He opened his mouth, clearly trying to summon some of that Ford charm, but then he sighed. "I know. I've been off my game lately. It's not a big deal."

When she focused on their past few interactions and tried to pinpoint when things had shifted, a lightbulb went off in her head. He'd gone down south to help after a storm had flooded several towns. "Did something happen on your last job?"

"It was definitely one of my rougher jobs. Saw more devastation than usual and... I've held people's lives in my hands before, but this time, with this certain woman..." Some kind of emotion flickered in his eyes before he shut it down, so quickly she couldn't read it—she almost wished for a deck of cards, because she could read him easier when it came to poker. "Things just feel different now is all."

She gave him her most serious *spill-it* look and he returned his obstinate *ain't-gonna* one. "Fine. I can't pretend I've experienced anything like that, but lemme know if you need to talk about it. I know I'm not the best with emotions, but—"

"I appreciate it, Murph," he said, patting her on the back and effectively ending that conversation.

She tried not to let it bother her. Usually she was the first to hear about his ventures, mostly because they turned into medical talk and the rest of the guys tended to tune out the "boring" or "disturbing" details.

When things got heavy, like with a hiker his team found on the brink of starvation, he came to her as well.

While she desperately wanted to dig, she respected his boundaries and wouldn't push—not unless it grew worse. Instead she'd watch him and reiterate he could talk to her anytime, about anything.

After one last look to convey that, and a nod from him, Addie climbed into the back of the truck along with Tucker and Easton so Shep could stretch out his ankle. His mostly silent cousin sat in the middle of the front seat, and Addie wondered if they'd traumatized him or if he was always that quiet.

Or maybe he had a lot on his mind. Now that she had a moment to think, her brain started bringing up all the things weighing on it, and concern over Ford tumbled into the rest of the messy mix.

What if she left and *he* needed her? The rest of the guys would be there for him no matter what, but he'd never open up to them the way she might eventually force him to open up to her—their macho egos would get in the way of admitting any kind of weakness.

Not that she was much better…

What if she rushed things with Tucker because of her possible job opportunity and they weren't ready for the big talk? Why couldn't they simply enjoy the beginning stage? When things were light and fun?

Because you know each other too well and you have to be a grown-up, even if it sometimes sucks.

She tapped out an anxious rhythm with her fingers on her thigh, working to keep those thoughts on silent, at least until she could do something about them.

Unfortunately, it didn't work. If only it was as simple as flicking a switch, like on her phone.

Thinking about her phone gave her an idea. She lifted it and thumbed out a text to Tucker.

ADDIE: *Maybe we should tell them about us.*

Tucker shifted at her side, slipping his phone out of his pocket, and she fought the urge to peek over his shoulder while he read her message. A moment later her phone buzzed, and she tipped it so that Easton wouldn't see.

TUCKER: *Let's talk about it later.*

In other words, no.

Since her brain hated her, the asshole lawyer's comment popped into her head: *Does that mean you're someone's dirty little secret?*

The guy was a tool, but right now, covered in dirt and grime, the dirty part definitely fit.

But it's not like that with Tucker and me. I'm just freaking out. Once we're alone, we'll talk about it and the job and everything will be fine.

Then I won't have these annoying thoughts constantly buzzing at me.

Ford pulled up to her house first, and of course Tucker couldn't get out with her without raising suspicion, and he clearly still cared about that.

"Night, guys. It was fun." She shot Easton a smile. "It also makes me sorta worried about the safety of the town, considering you couldn't even catch four fake fugitives."

"Next time I'm going to pepper spray you and see how funny you still think you are."

She laughed and scooted out his side—she couldn't just brush past Tucker and keep on pretending her chest didn't feel too raw, her emotions too close to the surface.

He'd see right through her, and she needed to gather her wits and figure out how to curb feeling hurt over things they'd both agreed on.

But if he wanted to continue to keep them a secret, that made her wonder if he thought she wasn't worth taking a risk.

And if he didn't, why was she factoring him into her decision about applying for a job?

"Poker tomorrow," Shep reminded her. "We're gonna cram in all the fun this weekend."

"Sounds good. It'll also give me a chance to check on your ankle. Once the swelling goes down, I'll give you some exercises to do to get you up and running ASAP." She climbed out of the truck and dragged her tired, dirty self into her house.

Admittedly, now that she had to clean up the mud she tracked in, she better understood why Tucker's and her parents had yelled and lectured so much over it.

In order to prevent as much future cleaning as possible, she kicked off her shoes, stripped down to her underwear, and left the messy pile in the entryway. She padded into the bathroom, turned on the shower, and stepped underneath the steady stream of warm water.

A few minutes in, she swore she heard her name. Weird, especially since she should be alone in her house.

She pushed the curtain aside and paused to listen. Yep, definitely hearing things.

She turned back to the spray of water and began to sing, the way she only ever did when she was in the shower.

• • •

Tucker froze in the doorway of Addie's bathroom. The front door had been unlocked, and while they lived in a safe town, he was going to mention he'd feel better if she locked it.

Of course at the moment, he was extremely glad she hadn't.

He'd never heard her sing before, and he loved

hearing her so uninhibited, slightly off key or not.

Plus, her shower curtain was sheer enough that he could see her sexy profile. Since he didn't want to scare her, he called her name again. "Addie? Did you hear me come—"

"Ahh!" She plastered the curtain over her body with one arm and wielded a shampoo bottle with the other, as if that'd stop anyone with bad intentions, and right now he definitely qualified. "You scared the crap out of me."

"The door was unlocked. I called your name, but…" He swallowed, his words gone.

The curtain didn't just *hint* at her profile anymore. He could see nearly every detail.

He closed the distance between them, took her head in his hands, and kissed her.

He'd left his shoes at the door, and while he'd wanted to add his dirty clothes to her pile, he'd worried she was upset about the restaurant thing, and he hadn't wanted to be too presumptuous.

Her tongue rolled over his, and then he presumed the hell out of the situation. He tugged off his clothes as fast as he could and stepped into the shower with her.

"You're lucky I didn't maim you," she said.

"With the shampoo bottle?"

"Don't say it like I can't pull it off, or I'll have to show you how dangerous I can be with it."

"This whole threat-based foreplay thing you do?" He took the bottle from her fingers and set it aside. "I'm totally into it."

He backed her up against the wall, groaning at the amazing way her skin slipped against his.

Earlier tonight in the field had merely been a prelude, and as promised, he planned to lavish extra attention on her breasts.

He dipped his head and flicked one of her nipples with his tongue.

"Tell me how you like it, Addison."

A whimper escaped her as he sucked her breast into his mouth, and her fingers drove into his hair. "A little rougher," she panted, and he lightly scraped his teeth over the sensitive skin. Goose bumps traveled across her body, and she gripped his hair in her fist. "Ohmigosh, yes. Just like that."

He dragged his lips to the other breast and repeated the move, holding her to him as she shuddered and writhed against him. Then he pressed a kiss to her rib cage, her belly button, lower…

He knelt in front of her and worshipped her with his tongue, teasing her and letting her ride right along the edge of her orgasm.

"Tucker…" she whispered, a pleading note in her voice that had him increasing the speed and pressure until she came undone. Her cries of pleasure bounced off the tile and settled deep inside him, and he wanted to hold on to this perfect moment.

She slumped back against the wet wall, her eyelids half closed as she worked to catch her breath. Then she mumbled something about having condoms in her medicine cabinet, and if he ended up maimed tonight, it'd be from jumping out to grab them so quickly that he slipped and injured himself.

A couple of seconds later, he was back under the warm spray of water with her. Then their bodies were gliding together again, things completely in sync between them now that nothing else was in the way.

The future didn't seem so scary anymore. He didn't need to know exactly how or when he'd figure his life out, as long as Addie would be there.

"Addie, I…" It was too fast. He couldn't say the thought that popped into his head.

So he kissed her instead, doing his best to show her how much he cared about her that way.

As they circled higher and higher, he tethered her to him, dragging out the euphoric high as long as possible.

And when they tumbled over the edge together, he held tight to her, letting her know that no matter what happened, he'd always be there to catch her.

CHAPTER TWENTY-SIX

Tucker's eyes were drifting closed when Addie lifted her head off his chest and said, "We need to talk."

Usually those words would strike fear in his heart, but this wasn't one of those relationships where surprises came out of the woodwork. This was Addie.

He sat up against her headboard so he could wake himself enough to focus. Her bed was definitely more comfortable than his, and he planned on taking advantage of all the room inside her full shower again and again.

"What's up?" he asked. "Is it about telling the guys? We can, but I'm thinking maybe we should wait till after the wedding. Just to keep the drama as low as possible, because you know they'll all have an opinion about it."

Easton certainly did, and Shep and Ford would undoubtedly feel the same way about anything that might mess with the group dynamic.

In time they'd get used to it. Hopefully.

They'd have to, whether they liked it or not—now that Tucker had Addie, he didn't plan on letting go.

She opened her mouth, and then she scrunched up her forehead. Which meant she was holding back instead of spitting it out, and trepidation and doubt crept in.

"What's up? You're starting to worry me."

"That was one of the things I wanted to talk about, but I have news, actually," she said. "It's not bad news, exactly. I mean, it might be good. But there are bad aspects, I suppose, just like there are good ones. It doesn't matter, though, because I'm rethinking everything again."

"Okay, now you've gotta tell me." He grabbed her hand and laced his fingers with hers, trying to brace himself, although without knowing why, he didn't know how. "Spill."

"I've got a possible job lead." She swiped a section of her still-damp hair behind her ear.

"That's great. And a huge relief. I thought you were gonna tell me you didn't want to do this anymore."

"I do want to. It's just the job is…well, it'd be a sports therapy position with…the University of Alabama. Working with their football team. Can you imagine me having to cheer 'Roll Tide'? It's enough to make my stubborn side stand up and say hell no, but it's one of the biggest sports organizations in the country, and the pay would be a lot more."

His stomach sank, his relief doing a quick one-eighty spin.

For all his talk about Addie not caring about money, there it was. *She wants more out of life than this tiny town. Than someone with a meager salary could give her.*

Than I could provide her.

And it wasn't like he could say, *Who cares about a big bump in pay? Just live on hopes and dreams with me in my tiny-ass houseboat.*

She tucked up her knees and looped her arms

over them. "As I'm sure you know, considerin' how you lived near there not all that long ago, Tuscaloosa is also two and a half hours away."

He'd been so focused on the money angle that he hadn't thought about it.

He'd finally returned to where he belonged, and she was thinking of leaving. Timing was such a bitch.

He'd be back here working on small cases, and she'd be working for one of the biggest football teams in the country.

Which also meant she'd be around football players day in and day out, guys who wouldn't be the type to get easily intimidated and run. Unless it was running toward her, racing to see who could ask out the sexy new physical therapist first.

She'd be taping up their knee or helping them work their muscles, her hand on their leg…

"Apparently the thought of that makes you have murdery feelings?" she asked.

Yep, you touching other guys, other guys touching you. Murdery applies to both.

"I'm just processing." Honestly, the players were a bit young—okay, they were practically kids, hardly competition.

The blood in his veins cooled for all of two seconds before he realized there'd be a lot of coaches and other staff members around her as well. Guys closer to her age, who pulled in impressive salaries, no doubt.

"Tucker, I really need you to say somethin' right now."

He shoved away his personal feelings and focused on how good this would be for her.

Ever since he could remember, she'd talked about working for a professional team, and she hated her job here. She dealt with it, and she'd continue to duck her head and bear it if she felt like she had to, but it'd grate on her more each day, until she was completely miserable—he had too much experience with what that was like, and he didn't want that for her.

"You'd be crazy not to go for it."

Addie bit at her thumbnail. "I know. Or anyway, I tell myself that. But then my grandma came over the other night and was talking about how nice it was to have me so close, and my family totally flipped when Alexandria moved so far away—do you remember how upset they were? They took her leaving personally, and considerin' who I'd be working for, they'd take mine *extra* personally."

Obviously she was attempting to make a joke, but there was too much truth in there for it to land.

"You deserve to have the kind of life you want, not the one other people think you should have."

"But I don't know which kind of life I want. I thought I did, but now…"

The temptation to tell her he wanted her here—that he *needed* her here with him—nearly overpowered him. Which meant he had to make it clear she couldn't stay because of him.

Later she'd regret it, and as she grew more and more discontent with her job, resentment over his asking her to stay would seep into their relationship, whether it was simply friendship or more, and it would end up doing major damage.

Possibly enough to ruin them completely, and

not having her in his life was the worst thing he could think of.

He shut down his emotions the best he could, ignoring the twinge in his chest. "It's good timing. Or as good a timing as this kind of thing could be. It's not like I can get serious with anyone right now anyway."

Two creases formed between her eyebrows. "Wait. So you're saying that what we're doing *isn't* serious? Because it felt pretty damn serious crossing those lines. Why would we even risk that if we weren't going anywhere? If you didn't see a future?"

Breathe in, breathe out.

As long as he stayed calm, they could hopefully keep this from devolving into the types of screaming matches his parents used to have. "I'm saying that I'm in no place to settle down right now. We haven't gotten that far into the romance part of our relationship—not so far things will be messed up between us—which is why I'm glad we agreed to take it slow."

A fissure formed in his chest as everything he'd tried to convince himself of came unraveled.

"Let's just get real for a minute," he continued. "I live in a houseboat and get whopping two-dollar retainers, for hell's sake, and until several of the cases are wrapped up, I see no end in sight to that. You have a chance to go make some decent money and add more impressive experience to your résumé."

"*Now* you care about money? I thought you left your job because you *don't* care about it."

"No, I left because I hated it like you hate your

job, and to be honest, the fact that it's left me without a steady income terrifies me. I can't even think about settling down until I have a down payment for a house in the bank. I'd also hoped to have a large chunk of change in my 401K first, but again, I'm trying to get real here."

The line of Addie's jaw went rigid, and she gathered the covers tighter around her. "I'm starting to notice a pattern. We'll tell people we're dating *after* the wedding. We can get serious *after* you have a down payment. Just say what you really mean. You don't want to get serious with me."

She started to pull away and he caught her arm.

"Dammit, Addie, that's not what this is."

She whipped back to face him, anger and hurt flickering through her expression. "What do you think will happen to us, Tucker? You sure didn't mention anything about trying to make the long-distance thing work, and even though it wouldn't be easy, I at least hoped you might consider it. Then again, why bother, right?" She shrugged and her words came out icy and sharp. "We could hardly keep up a long-distance friendship, and that was with me only bein' a little hurt when you didn't call or visit when you said you were going to. If we were dating, it'd be harder for me to say, 'Oh well, he's clearly busy. No big deal.'"

Thanks to the fact that he knew her so well, he could tell she wanted him to deny it. Or fight it.

But she was right, and what good would it do for both of them to pretend it'd somehow be magically okay?

Crashes were always bigger, uglier, and a lot

more painful after you got your hopes up.

"Let's take it a step at a time. You go interview for the job, and once we find out what's going to happen with that, we can take it from there. But I'm sure they're going to love you and offer you a position with the team. Why wouldn't they?"

A sardonic "Ha" came out, so at odds with her usual infectious laugh. "At least you have some faith in me, even if I'm afraid it's in the wrong place."

He grabbed her hand and sandwiched it between both of his as he peered into those big brown eyes. "I have all the faith in you, Addes. Which is why I don't want you to say no to your dream job because of me."

Tears formed in her eyes, and a hollow, sucking pit opened up in his chest.

"Please don't cry," he said, and she swiped at her cheeks as the tears broke free.

"I'm afraid I'm not going to be able to stop them, so if you don't want to see, maybe you should go."

"No." He wrapped his arms around her, holding her as she sniffed and blinked at her tears.

He felt her slipping through his fingers, and that pit in his chest opened wider, sucking away all the happiness they'd experienced the past six weeks—and especially the last two.

She tugged free from his embrace and turned her face away, and as much as he wanted to pull her right back and refuse to release her, he wouldn't force her to let him hold her.

"I really wanna be alone right now," she said.

"Addie—"

"Please, Tucker." Her voice cracked, and pain lanced his heart. "Please just go."

• • •

Addie woke up and looked at the empty spot next to her, and then she immediately wanted to throw the covers over her head and give up on the day.

Last night she'd asked Tucker to leave, and he'd kissed her goodbye on her forehead, way too softly, and it felt way too final.

Then she'd cried some more, because apparently dating her best friend had turned her into a girl who cries over a boy, and she didn't even know what they were anymore, and that made her want to cry again, so she wasn't going to think about that right now.

Last night, sorrow had gripped her, not leaving room for much else; this morning, she felt like an idiot on top of her turmoil.

She'd thought she and Tucker were getting serious. That they'd been on their way to something that might surpass serious.

That was a problem she hadn't foreseen about being friends first. Everything automatically seemed more intimate because you already knew each other so well.

Part of her realized she had to go for the job—a big part of her—but she'd also hoped Tucker would tell her that he didn't want her to move.

Instead he'd immediately encouraged her to go for the job that would take her hours away from Uncertainty, and while she told herself that his words didn't mean he didn't want to try to make them work, it still felt like that.

This was fun while it lasted was what she'd heard.

I don't want to get serious with you.

Don't count on me, and don't count me in.

Her friends were good-looking guys who got hit on a lot. Not a newsflash by any means, but experiencing it last night while caked in mud, her insecurities flaring, took it to a whole new level.

She'd already been wondering how she could compete with that, and if she was over two hours away…well, that'd be that.

Say she didn't get the job. Then she'd get to remain in her beloved hometown, but she'd get to do so with the knowledge that a few hours could make or break her and Tucker.

That wasn't any better.

Now she had to go on with her day and pretend the illusion of her happy, far-from-lonely life where she was crazy about her boyfriend hadn't been shattered. Not just pretend alone in her house, either, because once the clock struck six, she forced herself into her truck and started the drive to Tucker's place so she could fake being okay in front of all her friends.

Big freaking yay for poker night. Good thing I've had so much practice perfecting my poker face.

Since the thought of another one-on-one conversation where Tucker conveyed how not-serious they were made her want to vomit, Addie purposely showed up ten minutes late.

Everyone was already settled, as she'd hoped they'd be, and she slid into her usual seat to the left of Tucker.

"You clean up nice, Murph," Shep said, and she smiled at him.

"Thanks. How's the ankle?"

"Black and blue and hurts like a bitch, but I think I can at least walk down the aisle in two weeks."

She urged him to lift his pants leg so she could check on it. She grimaced at the swelling and colors but also thought he'd be mostly healed by the wedding.

"What did Lexi say?" she asked, tossing in the ante so the game could get going.

"I've only talked to her on the phone since it happened, so I didn't exactly tell her."

Addie shook her head. "Of course you didn't. You know she's gonna find out."

"Tonight when she comes over, I'm sure." Shep tossed a couple of chips into the center of the pile. "I was hoping if I gave it extra time, it'd miraculously heal some more."

"Just remember one thing…" Addie picked up the cards Easton had dealt her and peeked at them, keeping her expression carefully neutral. "It was all Ford's idea."

"Thanks, Murph," Ford said. "I appreciate it."

She winked at him. "Anytime."

Tucker nudged her with his elbow. Despite knowing it was going to hurt, she'd have to look at him eventually, so she figured she might as well get it over with.

Sure enough, misery surged forward, rushing through her beat-up heart and trying to break the barrier she'd erected around it to prevent her emotions from spilling out.

He didn't say anything, and when she arched her eyebrows, he pressed his lips into a tight line and cocked his head, like *she* was the one being difficult.

What was she supposed to do? Come over all broken and red eyed and beg him to try? To give them a real chance?

So that he could repeat how not-serious they were. A big no thanks to that.

Ignoring the fact that she *did* feel broken inside, she smothered those weak emotions the best she could and reached for a beer.

After their second round, Tucker stood and announced he was grabbing more drinks, and that Addie was helping him. She opened her mouth to beg off, but before she got out the words, he snagged her arm and hauled her to her feet.

In the name of keeping the peace, she went along with it, following him over to the kitchen area before tugging free.

"You're ignoring me," he said.

"I *wish* I could ignore you," she said, since she was super good at comebacks.

"Can we just get through poker, and then, after everyone else is gone, we can talk it out?"

"Why? We already talked it out. I told you I had a job opportunity and that it would mean moving away, and you practically did cartwheels over all the freedom you'd have. I had no idea being with me was so confining."

He gritted his teeth. "You're being ridiculous."

Her blood pressure skyrocketed. Did he actually just call her *ridiculous*? "Yep, that's me. It was ridiculous to think you and I could cross lines without everything getting all screwed up. Even more ridiculous to think that you'd want to be with me, even if it wasn't convenient."

"If you think what we've been doing is convenient, you need a vocabulary lesson."

She jabbed a finger at his chest, the angry heat surging to the forefront getting the best of her. "Well, if you think liking you is super easy, then I've got news for you, buddy. You're a regular jackass sometimes. I'd count now as one of those times."

"You're hard to read and stubborn as hell."

"Like you're an open book? I have to hand it to you, that 'this feels right' line was a nice touch."

"Ouch. I'd never feed you a line."

"And yet I ate it up anyway."

Tucker dragged a hand down his face, frustration etching his features, and he could join the freaking club because she was right there with him. "Addie, you asked for my opinion on the job, and I told you that you'd be crazy to give up an opportunity like that. And you would! You should take it and run with it."

"You're *literally* yelling at me to leave. Don't you see how that might hurt?"

"I won't be your excuse to not take a risk."

The band around her chest tightened even more, no longer allowing for breaths. "And see, the difference is, I wanted to take a risk on you."

"You are!" Tucker flung up his hands. "I'm a huge risk. That's why you should go."

"This arrangement doesn't allow you to tell me what to do."

"Then what good is it?" he roared back, and everything inside of her shattered. The barriers broke and the pain spilled out, flowing everywhere until every inch of her hurt.

Then she noticed they'd gained the attention of the guys, who were watching the exchange with mostly confused expressions. Somehow she'd managed to forget they had an audience.

Too bad the damage had been done, no chance of simply shoving it away and faking her way through being okay now.

"Um, why are Mommy and Daddy fighting?" Ford asked, and she wanted to be able to laugh it off, but more stupid tears pricked her eyes.

"Great." Tucker raked a hand through his hair. "The nightmare continues. This is exactly what I worried would happen."

"Yep. Now people are gonna know that you were actually interested in me, even if it was just for a little while. That must be horrifying."

"Addie." He reached for her, but she jerked her arm away—it made it too hard to think straight when he touched her, and this wasn't something he could hug away.

Luckily, the glare she fired at him effectively stopped him from trying again.

Pull it together. Just for a few more seconds.

"Sorry, guys," she said past the giant lump in her throat, and there was no hiding the quiver in her voice. "I've gotta go."

She rushed out of the houseboat, and as soon as she was safe inside the truck, the roar of the engine drowning out every other noise, the tears broke free. How could she even have more?

She needed someone, someone who she could talk to about the situation without judging or momentary excitement followed by crushing disappointment.

But all of her someones were in that houseboat.

Then she realized that wasn't exactly true.

She fumbled with her phone and tapped the name she'd pulled up.

After two rings, Lexi answered, her voice as chipper as ever, and Addie sniffed, gratitude mixing with the sorrow. "Lexi, it's Addie. I need someone to talk to, and I was wondering…hoping, really…" She sucked in a deep breath, not sure why it was so hard to spit out. "Could you meet me at my house?"

Lexi didn't miss a beat. "I'll be right there."

CHAPTER TWENTY-SEVEN

Tucker stood across the room from three of his best friends, unsure where to even start. He'd lived in that magical world without consequences for a while, but it was time to face the music, and he doubted it'd be nice music.

It didn't help that the pit that'd opened up in his chest last night was now a gaping hole filled entirely with despair, and Addie was driving away after they'd said awful things to each other.

"What the hell just happened?" Shep asked, his voice dangerously low. "That fight didn't look like a fight between friends. It looked and sounded like the type of heated discussions Lexi and I get into."

The wheels were turning, all of them slowly coming to the same conclusion, though Easton had some insider information.

Ford was the one who voiced it. "Did you sleep with Addie?"

"I…" His shoulders sagged, everything inside him deflating. *"Shit."*

Shep shot to his feet, sending the table and the poker chips wobbling. "You. Did. *What now?*"

"Now why would you go and do that?" Ford asked, so much disappointment in his tone, and seeing how everyone considered him the reckless one, it stung even more.

The ache pushed deeper, down to his bones. "Because I like her."

Like was way too weak of a word, but his head was still spinning, and *damn it.* How had it spiraled out of control so quickly?

Ford pushed to his feet and stepped around the table. "We all like her. And it's not like she's exactly hard to look at, but there are lines. You don't see me sleeping with her."

Tucker surged forward, his finger pointed at Ford's chest. "And you better not, or I'll kick your ass so fast—"

"I'd like to see you try." He advanced, and Tucker lifted his fists, and then Easton stepped between them, one hand braced on each of their chests.

"Everyone just calm down," he said, his cop voice in full effect. *"Now."*

Calm? There was no calm.

He and Addie just had one of those huge, damaging fights he'd worked so hard to avoid, and then she'd left and Ford made that remark about her looks, and he'd seen red.

Was still seeing red.

"Crawford." Easton gave his chest a mild shove, and Tucker dropped his arms but kept his fists clenched, and Ford did the same. On the rare occasion, they'd gotten on each other's nerves, mostly for dumb shit like taking a joke or prank too far, but he'd never genuinely wanted to take a swing at any of the guys.

Not to mention those times had never been accompanied by this overwhelming sense of anger and adrenaline.

But how could they make light of such a shitty situation? How could they talk about Addie like there weren't a hundred other amazing things about her besides how beautiful and sexy she was?

She was smart and funny and easy to talk to, and the best person to have by your side, ups, downs, and everything in between.

She made life better. Made him better.

"I warned you," Easton said with a shake of his head, and variations of "you knew?" came from Shep and Ford, but Tucker ignored those.

"And I told you that I was aware it was a bad idea." He'd wished so hard that it wasn't, that he'd convinced himself he and Addie could figure out a way for it to not be.

"Seriously? You guys honestly didn't see it?" Easton asked, which brought out offended scowls, and he held up his hands again and sighed. "Let's not get into this. What I need to know is why Addie stormed out of here like that."

Never before had Tucker struggled so much to rein in his emotions. He dug deep, not allowing himself to break in front of the guys, especially not with them so pissed at him. "Because I told her she should go for a really good job."

"Doesn't sound like our Addie," Ford said, and it sent a toxic burning through Tucker's gut—she was his more than theirs. "I feel like you're leavin' out a few details."

The calm-breathing shit didn't work yesterday, so Tucker forewent it and stuck to the basics. "If she gets it, she'll be working at the University of Alabama. For their football team."

"Addie's gonna go redcoat and work for Bama?" Shep asked, brow furrowed.

"She should, and don't act like any of you wouldn't jump at the opportunity. She'd be working for one of the best teams in the nation, doing what she was trained to do. She'd make more money than she ever could here, and while we all cringe at the thought of any of us yelling Roll Tide—"

A uniform groan carried through the room.

"—she wouldn't have to deal with her asshole boss anymore, and she'd be doing what she loves."

"In Tuscaloosa," Ford said, his voice softer.

For all his brash ways, Tucker could tell it dug at him to think of her far away, and that made his anger and desire to punch him cool.

"Yeah. It'd mean a move." The weight of everything it meant hit him again.

He knew how this story ended. She'd head out there and they'd love her. Weekends would go by where she couldn't visit, or he couldn't get to her, and she'd fall in love with the benefits and working with such successful, driven people, and they'd grow further apart.

They'd have uglier, more devastating fights.

Things sucked right now, but they could get over it. If they gave it everything they had and dragged it out, it'd only hurt more in the end.

Only do more damage to their relationship.

If he was even sort of financially stable, maybe then he could find a better way to make it work, but he wasn't, and he never should've crossed lines. The risk had been too high, and he'd known better.

Now look at the mess—it'd torn the group apart, just like they'd worried it would.

"You think I want her to move?" Tucker asked,

to no one in particular, and in fact, he found it easier to stare at the knot of wood in one of the cabinets. "Think I want her that far away? She's worried about not being here for her family. For her grandma."

"I'll help with her grandma," Ford said, and Shep and Easton added they would, too.

"And so will I." Tucker cleared his throat. "Opportunities like this don't come along very often, and she needs a nudge to get her to go for it, so I'll be the asshole who gives her the nudge."

"Still don't understand why you had to go and sleep with her," Ford mumbled.

So I could get that much more attached, and experience how amazing we could be together before life ripped her away.

Life didn't care about fair, and the timing seemed extra cruel, coming right when he'd gripped hold of that fickle bitch, hope.

He replayed her rounding the cabin of his boat and throwing her arms around him all those months ago, minutes before Shep had announced his engagement. She'd hugged him so tightly and something inside of him whispered, *There you are. Exactly what I've been missing.*

He'd loved her in a different way then, but over this past month of spending more time together, and going out on the water, and kissing, and…so much more—and he didn't just mean the sex, although it'd been incredible—their relationship had deepened and morphed into something else entirely.

None of that changed anything, though.

"I crossed a line I shouldn't have; I get that." It

tasted bitter on the way out, and even though it'd made a mess of things, Tucker couldn't bring himself to regret it.

"You'd better make it right," Shep said.

"I wish I could. But I'm willing to have things not right if that means she's happier in the long run."

Ford shoved his hands in his pockets and hung his head. "This blows."

Amen, Tucker thought, but because things were still too volatile, he didn't say it.

If he voiced it, he might also add that it sucked way more for him, and *he* was the one who had more to lose.

Everything to lose.

Then again, with his center of gravity suddenly off-kilter and misery streaking through him, deadening every organ it touched, it felt like he'd already lost it all.

CHAPTER TWENTY-EIGHT

Addie stepped out her front door and threw her arms around Lexi. "Thank you for coming."

Lexi patted her back, the paper bag in her hand crinkling as she did so. "Okay, you totally initiated the hug this time, where usually I have to sorta force them upon you, so now I'm extra concerned."

Addie half laughed, half sobbed.

"I gotcha, girl. I even brought reinforcements."

Panic tore through Addie as she cast her eyes toward the street, terrified Lexi's bridesmaids would be storming in, and then she'd have to pretend she had a normal problem that didn't involve falling for her best friend.

Because yeah, she'd fallen hard, and the landing freaking sucked.

Lexi moved into the living room and lowered her bag onto the coffee table, then she reached inside and pulled out a large bottle. "See, I brought wine…"

Wine. Right.

Maybe she could just choke it down to help numb the pain.

"And, ta-da!" She brought out a six-pack of Naked Pig Pale Ale. "I know you guys like this stuff. And if you need something harder, I also grabbed Will's bottle of Jack."

Addie blinked back tears and initiated her second hug of the night.

Then they settled on the couch, and the entire story spilled out of her. About how she and Tucker had kissed after he'd taken her for a ride in his renovated boat, and then kissed some more, and how they'd slept together and it was amazing, but he didn't want anyone to know. Then she covered the way everything had fallen apart so quickly, leaving off with the awful screaming match at the houseboat.

Lexi listened, nodding and patting her shoulder, and at the end, she opened the Jack Daniel's and passed it over.

Addie took a burning swig and handed it back. Lexi tipped it to her lips and then coughed, her eyes going watery.

"That's *horrible*. Even worse than I imagined."

Addie shrugged. "You get used to it."

Lexi wrinkled her nose and shoved the bottle at Addie. "No thank you."

After everything that'd happened, Addie hadn't expected to be able to laugh.

She sank into her couch cushions as a maelstrom of emotions hit her, the sad and happy fronts meeting and leaving a tropical storm with the kind of hail that cracked windshields.

The cushions shifted as Lexi propped her elbow on the back of the couch. "I'm sure he cares about you—I can see it in the way he looks at you. That's why I kept pushing for you to say something."

"Then we both said something, and we took a risk, and now that our friendship is in ruins, I'm not sure it was worth it. Everything's broken, and it feels like the kind of broken that can't be fixed. How can we ever come back from this?"

"That's what people say after every bad hurricane that hits. Then we rebuild and we do."

"I get what you're sayin', but the hurricanes have never been our friends. They haven't cozied up and promised it'd be okay before suddenly changing course and laying waste to everything." Addie pinched the bridge of her nose. "Oh jeez, now I'm getting all sappy and overly dramatic, and I'm glad you're the only one here to witness it."

Lexi wrapped her in a side hug. "It's okay. I promise to never reveal that Addison Murphy not only has emotions but actually lets them out once in a while."

The half-laugh, half-sob thing happened again, accompanied by a snort.

Addie drank another glug of Jack, and then Lexi took the smallest sip before reaffirming her stance against it and opening the wine.

In a shocking move, she didn't bother with a glass, either. Simply tapped the bottle to Addie's and downed a healthy gulp.

Addie picked at the label with her nail. "I know Tucker cares about me. There are years and years of history and ups and downs where he was there for me. He sometimes gets protective to the point someone should protect *him* because I'm considerin' throttling him, and he claims he just wants what's best for me. I get all that. But I could tell the thought of at least tryin' a long-distance relationship never occurred to him, and then he tells me he can't get serious anyway, like we weren't serious. As if that wasn't enough, he gives me some spiel about having a certain amount of money in the bank before he settles down. Like I'm the kind of girl who'd demand financial security from a guy instead of taking care of myself.

"I actually considered skipping the interview so I wouldn't have to choose the job over him. My family factored into that, too, but leaving him behind was my first thought."

The giant lump she'd finally managed to rid herself of lodged in her throat again.

"And it was his last," she continued. "I know he'd never move back to the city, either. I just thought…" Her lungs tightened, deflating instead of filling with air, and pain radiated through her chest. "But he doesn't want me. Not for good, not to settle down with. In the end, all the reasons I worried that he wouldn't came true."

"Oh, hon," Lexi said, and she covered Addie's hand with hers. "I wish I knew what to say. I'm still sort of holding out hope that he'll burst in at any moment and tell you he's been a complete idiot."

The knock at the door made both of them jump. Addie shot to her feet, her heart pounding with so much hope—too much.

Then Shep walked in.

He strode over, still favoring his right ankle, gave her a hug so tight her feet left the ground, and asked, "You okay?"

Addie squeezed him back, the crack that'd formed inside her filling in a bit when Lexi turned the hug into a group one.

"Hey, babe?" Lexi asked. "Were you limping?"

"I, uh. Funny story…"

A loud knock cut him off, then Ford barreled inside like he'd been called over for some type of emergency. He glanced from Addie to Lexi and Shep, back to Addie. "I came to check in. And to give you shit about Bama, you traitor."

Right now, Addie needed someone to treat her like she wasn't fragile, same as she'd needed the talk and drinks with Lexi and the hug from Shep. "Don't act like you won't be begging me to sneak you in and meet the players."

"The cheerleaders maybe. Probably getting a little too old for that, though." Ford crossed the room and squeezed her shoulder. She knew what he was asking, even if he didn't say the words.

"I'm okay," she said, and she prayed that if she said it enough, maybe one day she would be.

CHAPTER TWENTY-NINE

Flash tugged on the leash as Tucker walked across the town square. While his puppy was forever in a hurry to get to wherever they were going, lately Tucker didn't feel excited enough to rush anywhere. Or to even get out of bed in the morning.

He forced himself to so he wouldn't turn into one of those pathetic has-beens, the anecdote people told their kids to scare them into sticking with it, or else look at what they might become. Day in and day out, he went through the motions, digging through files and talking to people about their broken boats.

Mere weeks ago, he'd found a newfound love for legal cases, no matter how odd or how small. He'd taken on boat repairs and renovations, and he'd thought he was building something. That he could make life in Uncertainty work, even if it meant shifting his goals and how he'd once envisioned his life.

As Flash dragged Tucker past the gazebo, he automatically glanced inside. But Addie wasn't up on a ladder risking life and limb in the name of helping her friend's fiancée with her wedding planning.

She always went above and beyond, putting herself last, which was why he'd tried to force her to put herself first.

And in return, he'd lost her.

It'd been ten days since their awful fight in the houseboat. She didn't answer his calls. Didn't answer her door. She'd started locking it, too, so he'd have to go the breaking and entering route, and he'd be lying if he said it hadn't crossed his mind.

He did happen to have a cop friend, although he wasn't sure Easton would let him out of anything right now, and no matter how much legal jargon he could spout and spin, B and E wasn't exactly a gray area.

In desperation, he'd driven to the soccer field and caught the tail end of the last game Addie had coached. As soon as it ended, her team and parents surrounded her, and then she'd managed to give him the slip.

She hadn't gone to her house, either—he'd swung by to check.

This morning he'd finally received a text, in reply to the one he'd sent asking how things were going in Tuscaloosa.

He told himself not to look at it again. And yet he pulled out his phone anyway, as if the words might've changed and would mean something different this time.

ADDIE: *It went great. Gee thanks for not thinking I had a mind of my own and for making sure I followed this possible job lead. Now you don't have to worry that those few times we had sex didn't do any good. Feel free to commence with the freedom cartwheels.*

To say she was still pissed would be an understatement. If he could take back that stupid "Then what good is it" comment, he would. He'd been frustrated, and everything had been falling apart, and now she wouldn't even listen to his apologies.

How did it get ugly so fast?

Everything he thought they could avoid because they were friends first didn't matter in the end. They disagreed; they fought. They...

His lungs collapsed in on themselves.

They broke up.

Tucker walked past the fabric shop, and of course Lottie was standing outside, hands on her hips. You'd think helping her daughter with her divorce would've put him in her good graces, but nope.

She sighed, nice and loud, and he experienced that urge to hurry he'd been missing. "Mornin', Lottie," he said in the name of not being rude.

"You think another girl will put up with you the way Addison Murphy does? Because I'll tell you right now that you'll never do better." Another huff. "The nerve, coming back to town only to tell her to leave. Who's going to help rehab my bad knee now?"

Logical answers about seeing Mr. Watkins or how Addie didn't have to live her life for the people of Uncertainty wouldn't do him any good, so he simply walked on, and this time he had to tug on Flash instead of the opposite way around.

At first, Tucker thought one of his friends must've spilled the beans as some sort of payback. Probably because his head hadn't been right in over a week.

Apparently what signaled suspicion was the fact that his truck *wasn't* parked at Addie's anymore. The town had accepted they were friends, so once they began avoiding each other, everyone speculated they'd had a falling out.

Maisy, the pregnant woman who ran the bakery shop, didn't say anything, but the purse of her lips made it clear she was Team Addie. And as he was leaving the coffee shop, someone muttered, "And he claims to be a War Eagle man."

That was too far, and nearly enough to make Tucker turn back and say something, but again, no use.

Once tongues started wagging about the rift, everyone jumped in to speculate why. Turned out he and Addie weren't as discreet at the bar and diner as they'd thought. Once those juicy pieces of gossip were added, the whole town realized they'd attempted a romantic relationship, and several blamed Tucker for it being no more.

He didn't bother defending himself, because unlike the rumor about him being fired from his big-city law firm, this one was true.

He'd screwed it up.

There were a hundred better ways he could've handled it.

He'd forgotten how silly the town could be when sides were drawn, and yet it didn't dim the love he had for it, the slower pace, and the different lifestyle. They protected their own, and he admired them for standing up for Addie without bothering to gather things like all the facts.

The problem was they hadn't a clue about what was best for her. She thrived on challenge and deserved a job she loved, one she'd dreamed about since forever.

She needed to go meet someone who could provide her with the life she deserved.

By the time he got his act together, she'd probably be running the whole damn organization up in Tuscaloosa and be engaged to a burly football coach who also raked in the dough.

The idea of it ate at him, and he was getting sick of being the bigger person.

He froze in place when he spotted Addie's grandma coming down the sidewalk. Lucia flashed him a sad smile as she approached. She threw her arms around his neck, and he bent lower so she could kiss one cheek and then the other.

While it'd taken him a few seconds that first night back in town to get re-accustomed to her greeting, he'd been afraid she wouldn't bother now that things between him and Addie were so screwed up.

"How you doing?" she asked.

"I've been better." He wasn't sure why it was easier to admit to her, but it came right out, and then he found himself needing to explain further. "I just want the best for her. I'm sorry it means she might live in another city, but she hates her job here."

"I know. You've always looked out for her. You're a good boy."

He wasn't so sure, but it was nice that all of one person in town thought so. "How is she?" he asked, holding his breath as he awaited the answer.

Lucia sighed, her shoulders getting in on it. "She's sad. She tries to hide it, but she can't from me. Whenever she stops fighting to be okay, the sorrow hits her." She flattened a hand to her chest. "It breaks my heart to see her so sad."

His heart didn't feel so great, either, and that news cracked it right open. "If she'd just let me talk to her…"

Lucia shook her head. "She's too stubborn. And she got a good arm. I worry about the things she'd throw at your pretty head."

He laughed. "Yeah, me too."

"I've watched you two circle each other for years. I always wondered what'd happen if you fell into the same orbit at the same time. You have something between you that not many have, so I knew it'd be explosive bad or explosive good. Either way, lots of banging."

He clamped his lips, working not to react to the way she'd phrased it—he was relatively sure she didn't mean it like that… But with her, he couldn't be 100 percent sure.

"You see, friendship is easy. You add fire, it gets tricky. But if you find a way to have both…?" A smile curved her lips, and she tapped a finger to them. "My Seamus was like that. My best friend. My love. Some days he make me so angry, but on days I so angry, he pull me into his arms and love replaces it all."

Tucker glanced across the square like he could peer through the row of houses and see whether or not Addie's truck was parked in front of it.

"She no home right now. She has more interviews. Lots and lots of interviews—my granddaughter's in high demand, you know." The woman took his hand and squeezed it. "I'm not sure if she coming back today or tomorrow, but she'll for sure be back for the wedding stuff."

"Oh good, so she can throw decorations at my head and everyone can cheer when she hits me. Then they can also get mad that I messed up the wedding. Can't wait for that."

She chuckled. "Sounds about right. But if you try real hard, maybe you can fix it. Maybe you only get one black eye," she teased.

He ran his fingers along his eyebrow, his mind whirring.

He wanted to fix it more than anything. He needed Addie in his life, even if all they'd ever be was friends.

Even if he'd always have to suppress the desire for more.

"I don't know how," he admitted.

Lucia pinned him with a serious look. "Well, you have three days to figure it out. I suggest you stop feeling sorry for yourself and get started."

He admired her enthusiasm and how she managed to be on his team as well as Addie's. Unfortunately, it wouldn't prevent their lives from heading in two separate directions, and he refused to be dead weight.

Even though he was sure that Lottie had been right when she'd said he'd never find anyone better.

• • •

Relief flowed through Addie the second her interview with the Auburn athletic department was over. Not only because she'd made it through without botching it, but it also meant no longer having to fake being okay.

She wanted to be excited when she'd received a call from the boisterous athletic director who'd insisted she come in for an interview since he'd "be damned if I let Bama steal one of our alumni."

For a brief second, a spark *had* lit inside her, but then all she could think about was how much she wanted to call Tucker with the news but couldn't, because she wasn't currently talking to him, and that made it hard to be excited.

Hell, it made it hard to get out of bed.

Then there was the other insane thing she'd thought during the interview. If both football teams offered her a position, she might pick UA.

She couldn't very well stay in Uncertainty knowing that Tucker might *settle* for her. Or worse, have to watch him date a Barbie and suddenly decide his financial situation wasn't that important after all.

No, if that were going to happen, she'd rather be hours away, trying out a new life.

It'd be less lonely not knowing anyone than knowing too many people and still feeling lonely. Anyway, she assumed.

She didn't want to not take a job because of a guy, but she also didn't want to take a job just because of one, either.

The fact that Tucker was that guy made everything a hundred times more complicated.

She climbed into her truck and glanced at her phone. A text from her mom asking how the interviews went, as well as a voicemail from Nonna.

Addie tapped the screen and put the phone on speaker, worried something bad might've happened, and her grandmother's voice filled the car.

"Your mother force-fed me squash in place of noodles today," Nonna said, forgoing a typical greeting. "In case you ever wonder, spaghetti squash is no the same as pasta. My nonna *make* her own pasta from scratch, and she'd be rolling over in her grave if she saw the way people have bastardized Italian food here."

If Great-Nonna Cavalli rolled over in her grave as much as Nonna Lucia claimed, the groundskeeper at the cemetery would've called in those hot brothers from *Supernatural* by now.

Don't get her wrong, Addie would definitely stop and take a second to appreciate the eye candy, but what she really wanted was to get her hands on that car. To take it out on the back roads and see how fast it'd go.

"It a good thing I still had those brownie bites you smuggled from the bakery for me, or I would have starved," Nonna continued, and affection and sorrow clashed through her.

Missing her funny, overdramatic grandmother would be hard, but at least Addie could still hear her voice when she needed to. The drive to Tuscaloosa and back wouldn't be too bad, even if she could only buzz down and buzz right back.

"This no mean I don't want you to move, although I don't. It just mean I appreciate you, and you're such a good girl. But if you do move, you have to find me a replacement smuggler. I happen to know a guy who might do it. I ran into him in town today."

The vise that'd held Addie's heart hostage for a week and a half tightened.

"That boy is about as miserable as you. Just thought you should know."

About as miserable?

Probably like he was *about* as serious as she was about crossing lines, and apparently there was a lot of wiggle room in what "about" meant.

He'll get over it. Me…?

The ache in her chest bloomed, spreading throughout her body.

She texted her grandma to say she'd call later and, on reflex, checked her phone's screen again, figuring she'd take one last look before starting the car.

Nothing.

As if it had a mind of its own, her finger tapped Tucker's name.

He'd stopped calling and texting, and while seeing his name brought too much pain and conflicting emotions, it hurt even worse to not see it.

She hated how the weight of everything that'd happened sat like a giant wall between them, making it too hard for her to simply call and start a casual conversation and let his sexy voice carry her cares away.

To be able to ask how Flash was, as well as which side of the dock had more customers this week, boating or legal?

To ask him which job she should pick if they offered them to her, even though a big part of their fight stemmed from him doing exactly that.

I just wanted to know he'd be with me, no matter

what I chose.

Hell, I just wanted him to hold my hand in town and tell everyone I was his so that I'd *believe it.*

"This love stuff is bullshit." Addie froze. She hadn't meant to say it, but it didn't make it untrue.

She'd loved Tucker Crawford for so long, and she'd realized the love was changing and deepening, although she hadn't stopped to analyze it.

The knowledge burned through her now.

I fell in love with him.

How could I let myself fall in love with him before being sure he'd love me back?

Driving the thirty minutes home seemed overwhelming, not because of the time or the distance but because of everything she'd have to face there.

The rest of her friends were constantly checking in on her like she was some kind of sad, broken girl, and while she was, she couldn't handle it anymore.

A quick swipe sent the contacts on her screen rolling, and she tapped the name that took her first spot, her heart in her throat as she pleaded for the person on the other end to pick up.

"Alexandria? Would it completely put you out if I came and stayed with you for a few days?"

CHAPTER THIRTY

It was funny how three days away from home could make everything look so different.

The fact that the town square had been transformed for a wedding probably had something to do with it.

Tulle had been draped like curtains in each section of the gazebo, white lights twinkling through the fabric, and floral arrangements arched over the spot where the couple would be wed.

Basically, the beautiful execution made Addie's attempt seem even more pathetic, and she was definitely deleting that picture off her phone.

She parked her truck and observed the bustle of people going back and forth. The rehearsal dinner was about to start, and she needed to get out of her truck, but once she did, she'd have to see the guys — and then she'd have to see *the* guy — and she still didn't feel ready.

Not now that she knew she was madly in love with him.

The last few days were exactly what she needed. She and Alexandria had talked like they'd never talked before. About the reality of making relationships work and about Addie's two job options, which were officially options now, and about anything and everything.

Addie had expected her sister to tell her that if the closer job meant a better chance at landing her man, she should do that. Instead, Alexandria had shocked the hell out of her by saying that until Tucker put himself in the equation, Addie needed to take him out of it and then make her decision.

"I've always admired how strong you are," Alexandria had said. "Eli's been working so much over the past few months and honestly, I felt completely lost without him for a month or so. Then I wished I'd been more independent like you, but I'm too stubborn to come out and say it. That's also why I got a bit too invested in the dentist."

"Well, the fancy underwear worked for a little while, even if it worked on the wrong guy," Addie said, then frowned. "I mean the right guy. You know what I mean." The pain that'd become her constant companion rose up to remind her it was still there, raw and achy. "In the end, I guess it takes more than that to be sexy."

Alexandria shook her head. "He's an idiot if he doesn't see how amazing—and yes, sexy, too—you are."

"Thanks. Same goes to Eli."

"Oh, he knows," Alexandria said with a smile, going all dreamy eyed. "We've been working on us, and things are really good. And now that we're over the rough patch at his work, I'm going to take online classes and see about finishing my degree."

"Wow."

"Yeah, so girl power and all that jazz."

"Wait. Am I a girl in this situation?" Addie asked with exaggerated shock as she pointed at herself. "Because you always said that—"

Alexandria had shoved her, and they'd laughed,

but then her sister had told her again that she was a strong, independent woman, and Addie felt like she could face anything.

Until she was looking out across the square and a familiar head came into view.

Coppery brown hair with one stray wave that wouldn't behave.

Just like that, the rush of memories hit her. Of summer days catching baseballs and footballs. Climbing fences and trees and returning home scratched, bruised, and blissfully happy.

Of being out on a boat with him, back in high school, a few times in college, and that night a month ago, when the sparks between them fully ignited and spread until there was no ignoring them.

Her fingers went to her lips as residual butterflies stirred in her gut.

No thinking about that.

Addie took a deep fortifying breath and left the safety of her truck.

Out of respect for Lexi, she'd dressed up, which meant borrowing her sister's pink dress again. Two more days of wearing a dress, and then she might never put on another.

Then again, while she still didn't love them, she'd gotten more accustomed to them, so she supposed on the rare occasion, it wouldn't be the worst thing ever. Heels would never be her thing, but she'd put on the same ones she'd have to wear tomorrow with her bridesmaid's dress so she could do the waltz and break them in.

Be strong, be strong, be strong...

Lottie intercepted her before anyone else, which

was remarkable considering Addie swore she'd been on the other side of the square a minute ago. "I just want you to know that the Craft Cats are on your side."

Addie lowered her eyebrows. "My side of what?"

"You and Tucker."

Addie stopped midstride, her spine going stick straight. "What do you mean, me and Tucker?"

"We all know that y'all were a thing for a while and that you're not anymore." She leaned in and whispered, "He kissed one of those other bridesmaids, didn't he? They say cheatin' isn't genetic, but sometimes I wonder…"

Addie wanted to defend Tucker's mom, despite hardly knowing her side of the story or if she had cheated, and this was ridiculous. "I really don't wanna talk about it," she said, but couldn't help adding, "and for the record, no, that's not what happened."

A few other people gave her encouraging nods and nonsarcastic *bless your hearts* as she walked toward the center of the action, and how did she end up as the scorned one? The brokenhearted one?

Just because she was a girl?

Never mind that she was, in fact, nursing a broken heart.

Now she wished their plan to keep things under wraps had worked. It was worse now that everyone knew they'd tried and failed.

A couple more people mentioned it, which made it damn hard not to think about.

"Addie." Tucker strode right up to her, and since she was a strong, independent woman, she stifled the urge to run and instead put on the best poker face of her life.

"Hey," she said as she continued toward the table that held the rest of their friends.

Tucker caught her arm and slowly spun her to face him. "You can't ignore me forever, you know. At some point, you're gonna have to talk to me."

She nodded like she was perfectly okay with that. "I'm sorry everyone knows that we…" She made a sweeping gesture between them to fill in the blank because saying the words would hurt too much.

"You think I care? I don't give a shit. I care about you." He lifted his arm like he was going to cup her cheek, and she gripped his wrist, stopping him a few inches short of contact.

"Please don't. I don't wanna do this here. Let's get through tonight, and then we'll talk."

"Will we? Or will you just find new ways to avoid me?"

A sharp pang went through her chest as she peered into those familiar blue eyes, and the last thing she felt right now was strong.

So much for her pep talk.

"Addie, I'm goin' crazy not talkin' to you."

"You managed just fine for a couple of years. I'm sure you'll get used to it again." Yeah, it was below the belt, but she'd also been telling it to herself for days, and what good had holding back done before?

Tucker stepped closer and curled his hands around her shoulders. "I never got used to it, and don't act like things are different now than before I left for Birmingham. Addes, I messed up. I miss you so much I can hardly think straight, and then I look at you, and…"

His gaze drifted down, and she wanted to believe the gleam in his eyes would last, but she was done with letting her delusions get the best of her.

"Let's face it, Tucker. If holding your puppy hadn't caused me to flash you, and if I wasn't wearing sexy underwear that my sister had to talk me into buyin', this never woulda happened."

Sometimes she wished it hadn't. But the thought of losing those amazing kisses and those heated nights between the sheets, nothing and everything between them, hurt too.

"You never woulda decided you wanted me like that."

Tucker adamantly shook his head. "That's not true. If we want to get technical, it was seeing your legs in that very dress, sticking out from underneath the hood of that car. That was the moment I thought, *That's my type of girl right there.*"

"So I put on a dress and what?" She shrugged as if her words didn't weigh a thousand pounds. "You suddenly want me again? Or maybe it's because I seem like a challenge, like back when the dentist was interested and you wanted to see if you could win."

The line of his jaw tightened, and his fingers dug into her shoulders. "It's because I'm a selfish bastard even though I'm trying not to be."

"After tomorrow, I'll go back to plain old Addie, and I don't want you to pretend to want more, just like I don't want to pretend to be someone I'm not."

"That's what you think of me?" His voice bled misery, and it seeped into her and joined the surplus she already had.

"I think that if we keep goin' down this road, it'll be impossible to repair our friendship, and I wanna get over this so we can get back to how things used to be, if that's even possible anymore. I do know that it's gonna take some time and space."

"I guess it's a good thing that you're moving away, then. You'll get all kinds of space."

"Hey, you were the one who pushed me as far away as you could. Don't act like you care about me leaving town now."

"I never *not* cared. Things started moving so quickly, and then they were spiraling out of control, and it got all messed up along the way." He raked a hand through his hair and let out a frustrated growl. "Can't we just—"

"I hate to break this up," Shep said as he hesitantly encroached the bubble they'd formed, "specially since I can't tell if it's going good or bad. But everyone's staring and speculating, and we need to begin the rehearsal."

Tucker loosened his grip on her and trailed his hand down her arm, and the cascade of tingles that followed, even after such a gut-wrenching conversation, were so not fair. "I'll talk to you during the waltz."

Addie's throat tightened, and she had to force out words that didn't seem to want to come. "I'm doing the waltz with Ford now—Lexi's the one who suggested it, actually. No drama during the wedding, remember? Which is why he's also pairing up with me on the walk down the aisle."

She blinked away the threatening tears and then

forced her feet into motion, not stopping until she reached her new waltzing partner.

And when Ford punched her shoulder instead of asking how she was, she nearly hugged him, totally defeating the point.

• • •

A buzzing numbness overtook Tucker's body as he watched Addie walk to Ford. He'd had a speech prepared, but the second her mask slipped and he could see the raw pain in her features, he knew it wasn't enough.

"Sorry, man," Shep said. "I don't have to tell you that the girl holds a grudge—I'm still not allowed to eat food in her truck. The end comes out of a burrito *one time ten years ago* and the trust is gone, just like that." He snapped his fingers. "And that was just a burrito."

Tucker swallowed and worked to keep his voice even. "Big help with the pep talks as ever, Shep."

"Well, what did you expect? To say, 'Hey sorry, dude,' and she'd punch you in the shoulder and say, 'It's all good'?"

"Not gonna lie. That'd be pretty awesome."

"Too bad. Once line-crossing happens, that option's over. That's why you respect the line."

"It wasn't as simple as that. Like I said, I tried. Sometimes there are stronger forces than lines."

Tucker expelled a breath, and a different type of exhaustion settled deep into his bones.

"I'm so miserable without her. It's all I can think about—all I've thought about for nearly two weeks.

But being this close to her and still having so much distance between us? It's the worst kind of torture."

The weight of the situation hit him again, and he took a heavy step toward the gathering crowd so they could get this over and done with and he could retreat to his houseboat and drink himself into oblivion.

Shep stopped him with a hand on his chest. "Wait. You're saying it's more than foolin' around?"

"Of course it's more than fooling around," Tucker said. "It's *always* been more than that—I never would've crossed the line if it wasn't."

Shep gaped at him. "Why didn't you say so before?"

"I don't know. Because it'd be weird as shit. For one, it involves Addie, and you know how we can get when we talk women—I almost took a swing at Ford for saying she was nice to look at, so tread careful. And two, it's not like we usually talk about this stuff."

Three, he didn't feel like he deserved to defend himself, but he was keeping that to himself—his skin was already too tight after what he *had* admitted.

"Well, buckle in, 'cause we're gonna talk about it now." Shep crossed his arms and studied him as if he was getting ready to cross-examine him on the stand. "Do you love her? And I mean in a different way than the rest of us love her."

He glanced at Addie, felt every inch of physical distance and the emotional ocean between them, and it crashed over him all at once. His brain had whispered it before, but he'd tried to ignore it because he couldn't already be that far gone, and it would make her moving away and what'd happened between them even more painful.

But now everything in him screamed the truth, no way he could deny it. "I love her. I'm *in* love with her."

"Dude."

His chest tightened, and he tugged at his tie. No amount of loosening would make it easier to breathe, but he needed something to do with his hands anyway. "What good does it do me? The timing's all off. She's leaving, and I don't have enough money saved up to even think of settling down and getting serious."

"What does that have to do with anything? You can't tell her you love her because you don't have enough money?" Shep looked at him like he'd lost his mind. "Have you met Addie? Does she seem like the type of girl who cares?"

"I don't want to pull her into a life where we don't know how or if we can pay the bills. I watched it tear apart my parents, and I won't put Addie in that position."

"You holding back is what's tearing you two apart."

Tucker knew Shep was right, but he also knew things wouldn't magically work out simply because he wanted them to.

He didn't want Addie to have to make do. Hell, he didn't even have enough saved to rent an apartment in Tuscaloosa.

What was he supposed to do? Squat at her place while he struggled to start over yet again? Then she wouldn't just be making do, she'd have to support him on top of everything else.

"You think love follows rules?" Shep asked. "If it did, there'd be no way Lexi would be marrying me. Look at her, man. She's pretty and smart and funny, and for some reason, she's crazy about me. She agreed to have the wedding here, despite her country club parents and their friends. And I warned her the entire town would invite themselves to the rehearsal, and they're all standing around on the outskirts, and she's taking it in stride. Which is why I don't even care that we have fucking crimson as one of our wedding colors."

"At least there's some AU blue in there."

"Exactly! It's about compromise. It's about putting the other person first. It's hard work, but you'd be a fool to walk away from something that's right, just because of some idea or rule. You dig in your heels and you find a way to *make* it work."

Lexi came over, a concerned expression on her face. "I don't want to be a diva bride, but we kind of need to get started. Minus the 'kind of.'"

"Tucker's in love with Addie," Shep said.

"I knew it!"

"Thanks for keeping it in the vault, bro," Tucker said.

"Are you kidding me? Do you have any clue how much help you need to dig yourself out of this mess? I'll fully admit I'm not qualified. But my sexy fiancée right here?" Shep wrapped his arm around her shoulders, curled her closer, and kissed her cheek. "If anyone can help you now, it's her."

"Okay, but we can figure it out later," Tucker

said. "I don't want to steal your thunder or mess up your show."

"Now it's my turn to ask if you're kidding me," Lexi said with far more sass than he'd expected from her. "I can't watch you two avoid each other all through my wedding tomorrow, knowing I could've done something to help. It breaks my heart to see Addie so sad, and the thought of you two walking down the aisle with other people? It's not right."

"You didn't even flinch at the walk-down-the-aisle talk." Shep clapped him on the back. "Oh yeah, he's definitely in love."

"That question has been asked and answered, and while I appreciate the enthusiasm, I can't even get the girl to have a full conversation with me."

Lexi tapped a finger to her lips. "Then we've got to do something she can't ignore." He could see the wheels turning in her head. "We're going to have to call in reinforcements. I'm thinking all the groomsmen, save the one who needs the convincing."

"On it," Shep said. "As we go through the rest of the rehearsal, I'll give 'em a heads up."

This was what Tucker got for having that thought during the waltz, about how if he was ever that gone over a girl, he should have one of his friends put him out of his misery.

Now here he was, eating his words, begging for help instead.

He was about to be part of some big shit show, no doubt about it, but he couldn't care less, as long as it meant he might be able to make things right.

Hope was calling to him, and despite the

indisputable fact that he'd crash all over again if it didn't work, he went ahead and let it in anyway.

"Now…" Lexi placed her hand on his shoulder and locked eyes with him, the way so many of his coaches had done before they sent him out to attempt a big play that usually ended with him getting crushed. "How do you feel about groveling and a little public humiliation?"

CHAPTER THIRTY-ONE

They'd gone through the schedule and choreography of the ceremony, Addie had danced with Ford—whose waltzing skills were fine, although she couldn't help reminiscing about being in Tucker's arms and the way he'd dipped her…and then she was struggling to keep it together.

Naturally, they'd had to go through it four more times.

In general, she was counting down the minutes until she could go home. She'd definitely need to rally and reinforce her heart before the wedding festivities tomorrow.

At least they'd finally reached the sitting portion of the evening.

Shep grabbed the microphone and took over going through the schedule for the reception, and Addie kicked off her shoes, sighing as her feet hit the cool grass.

She wanted to tuck up a knee, but then she'd be flashing everyone, which volleyed her back to her earlier stance of never wearing a dress again.

"…and then there will be some speeches. We won't go through all of them right now, but Tucker's gonna come up and say a few words."

Addie tensed at his name, which was ridiculous. And devastating.

How could they ever recover their friendship if she couldn't even hear his name without hurting?

Knowing his voice was about to be amplified, she began silently chanting her new mantra: *Be strong, be strong, be strong.*

"Hey, everybody. I'm Tucker Crawford, one of the groomsmen. Hardly the best man, as I'm sure plenty of people here could attest."

Did he mean her? He shouldn't talk about himself like that.

The guy worked for two-dollar retainers.

She loved him for that. His determination to make sure justice was served versus his need for financial security made it that much more admirable, and damn him for being admirable and lovable and so dang sexy that she hadn't managed a full breath since their earlier conversation.

"I feel like I should apologize in advance to all the innocent bystanders for what's about to happen. The truth is, I'm going to do something crazy. I'm up here tonight to put myself on trial." He switched the microphone to the other hand and made a *there-there* gesture. "Don't worry, I'm a lawyer, which makes me semiqualified."

Most everyone in the vicinity exchanged confused looks, and several of the townspeople gave her suspicious glances, as if *she* knew what was going on.

Obviously everyone thought they were pulling one last big prank.

Considering Easton rushed up front with a Bible, of all things, in his hand, maybe they were.

Lexi sidled up to her on one side, and Ford scooted his chair closer on the other, both of them effectively blocking her in.

"I'm totally here for you, and if you need a hug

or a hand to hold, I'm your girl," Lexi said, and then she made a face best described as an unapologetic grimace. "Full disclosure, I'm also here to make sure you stay long enough to hear him out."

"Hear him out?" Addie glanced from Lexi to Tucker, who was placing his hand on the Bible Easton was holding.

Ford put his hand on the back of her chair. "And I'm here because if you say the word, I'll get you outta here."

"You're not being helpful," Lexi hissed.

"I made my choice," Ford shot back, and seriously, what the hell was going on?

A *Twilight Zone* sensation crept over her.

She'd love to determine if she was dreaming or not, but Tucker wasn't next to her, so she could pinch him and he could tell her.

No, he was lifting his arm to the square and speaking into the microphone.

"I swear that the evidence that I shall give shall be the truth, the whole truth, and nothing but the truth, so help me God."

Easton stepped back and sat in one of the three chairs lined up beside him. Shep took the other one. A quick glance at Ford left her sure he was meant to be in the last one.

With all the weirdness going on, she was glad he'd stayed by her side. If she was the hand-holding type, she might've grabbed his, but she gave him a nod, and he returned it, and that said enough.

"These guys to my left are my character witnesses, should I need 'em," Tucker said. "So let's get started, shall we? Here's a rough list of everything

I've done wrong since arrivin' in town…"

He cleared his throat, and the townspeople and groom's side leaned in, practically salivating, while the bride's side squirmed in their seats, clearly not sure they wanted to hear.

Addie wasn't sure she did, either, but she leaned in all the same—must be something in the swampy lake water.

"Since moving back to Uncertainty," he started, "I've stared at my best friend's legs. *A lot.* Now the first time I didn't exactly know they belonged to her, but if you've seen Addie's legs, they certainly make an impression. She was underneath a car, trying to figure out what was wrong with it, which made the whole thing even hotter, let me tell you."

Hot. Yep, with that statement in the air and people giving her sidelong glances, hotness was definitely happening—embarrassed heat with an edge of interest in what more he had to say.

"I went to a soccer game that she coached and checked her out again, and more than her legs this time. I vowed to chase off the other guy who'd been staring at her, and I did. I also stand by my claim that he never would've been able to handle her, and let's remember I'm under oath."

Two different kinds of anxiety went through her, about what he'd say next and if it'd wreck her, but intrigue and the tiniest pinch of flattery joined the tornado of emotions twisting up her insides.

And since she liked to be prepared, she contemplated the objects in the near vicinity, weighing which ones she should throw if he went too far and she needed to stop it or create a distraction, at the very least.

Candles would probably break, and she couldn't destroy the fancy centerpieces before the wedding.

The metal napkin holders, maybe? Heavy enough to go far and do some damage.

Same went for the battery-powered tea lights.

"From there," Tucker continued, "in spite of tellin' myself numerous times to keep things strictly platonic, my thoughts constantly strayed to what it would be like to kiss her. In my defense, she's funny and smart, and she does this unbelievable fake-out move on the field…"

"I can attest to that," Shep said, standing and leaning over Tucker to speak into the mic. "It's why I feed her the ball so much. You get her in her *natural habitat*"—he grinned, obviously proud of himself for throwing that in there—"and there's no stopping her."

"You okay?" Ford whispered, and Lexi grabbed her hand, gripping hard enough to convey she planned on thwarting any attempts at leaving.

"I'm okay," Addie whispered to both of them. She wasn't precisely sure where this was going, or if she'd be okay afterward, but now that Tucker had started talking, she couldn't not hear what else he was going to say.

Especially since his eyes locked on to hers, anchoring her to this spot, to him, to everything they'd been through the past two months.

Her heart picked up speed, revving to hummingbird levels and leaving her a tad dizzy.

Shep nudged Tucker with his elbow. "I believe you were listing the things you've done wrong."

"Right." Tucker ran his fingers through his hair, and that one rebellious wave stuck out even more. "I also started feelin' super protective, somethin' she hates, and she made sure I knew it."

He flashed her a smile, and her heart went from beating too fast to forgetting how to function altogether.

"I took her out in gator-infested waters on a boat I hadn't tested and thought some more about kissin' her. I'm sure thoughts about her legs and the rest of her body were mixed in, especially since…well, let's just say she loves my puppy as much as I do, and there was something about the way she picked him up and cuddled him that I'll never forget."

Addie's fingers wrapped around the napkin holder, testing its weight. Yeah, if he went there, he'd have a black eye for pictures tomorrow.

Sorry, Lexie, but if he mentions the flashing incident, it's happening.

"I kissed her that night," Tucker said, "and after that, I couldn't stop kissing her."

Time ground out as he looked at her again, and then she was reliving that night, too. His lips on hers, the way he'd pulled her close and molded her body to his…

A torturous amount of longing annihilated every other emotion, and she wanted to run to him and fling her arms around him and kiss him again. But as fantastic as that moment and the days that came after had been, things had still fallen apart.

Rehashing the good parts only made the subsequent crash that much harder to bear, and her brain reminded her that he was putting himself on trial for those kisses. That he was listing the things he'd done *wrong*.

Addie stood on shaky legs, making it a few inches off her chair before Lexi tugged her back down.

"Okay," Addie said, "I think you've proven your point. You shouldn't have kissed me."

"But you see, that's not where I went wrong," he said. "I kissed you before telling you that you're the coolest person I've ever met, hands down. My witnesses will definitely back me up on that."

Easton and Shep muttered their agreement.

"And I should've told you that I love how competitive you get, whether it's poker or football or control over the remote. I love that I hardly have a childhood memory without you in it. But these past several weeks? They've been the best weeks of my life, Addie.

"You have no idea how much I appreciate your reassurance that it didn't matter that I walked away from a perfectly good, high-paying job, and the way you encouraged me to try something new when I really needed someone to believe in me. I love that you always texted to check on my dog and ask me if I had more legal or boating clients. Love that I can talk to you for hours and hours and still have more to say. You're the first person I want to talk to when anything good or bad happens.

"I shouldn't have kept us a secret. I worried other people would mess it up, and in the end, *I* messed it up. I should've told you that you're beautiful and smart and sexy—for you to not think you are is ridiculous. You're sexy as hell in that dress right now, sure, but you're also sexy in that ratty Falcons hoodie or your farmer overalls or any damn thing you put on."

He looked at her now. "You're especially sexy when you're covered in dirt and your cheeks are flushed and you get that competitive gleam in your eye that gets my heart pumping double time. You're the whole package. I'd be so lucky if you'd be willing to do the long-distance thing. But after this past shi—crappy week, I'm not willing to have that much space between us.

"There's too much space between us now."

Tucker started down the walkway leading from the gazebo, his intense gaze leveled on her, and her stomach rose up, up, up.

"Crossing lines with you is the best decision I've ever made. When you told me about the job, I should've said I wanted you to go for your dreams *and* that I'd do whatever it took to make us work. I had this idea in my head of how it had to be before I let myself fall for someone, and now I see that once you find the right person, those kind of things no longer apply, the way the rest of the rules never applied to us."

"Those rules *did* apply to you," one of their former teachers said. "Heaven help us if y'all actually work this out and have children."

Tucker ignored the comment from the peanut gallery, his long legs eating up the distance between them, and then he was right in front of her. "I love you, Addison Murphy. Which is nothin' new, but being in love with you is, and I couldn't let you go without at least telling you so. But I'm hoping I won't have to let you go at all. If it means we get to be together, I'm goin' with you."

"With me to live in Tuscaloosa?" she asked, because of all the crazy thoughts spinning through her head, it seemed to be the only one she could catch hold of. The safest one to ask, as well, considering the others might mean her crying in front of the entire town.

"With you wherever you go."

"But you hate the city. You never wanna live in one again. You don't deal well with being cooped up, remember? And I don't want to be the one to rip you away from your home."

He reached down and cupped her cheek, and everything inside her came undone. "I think you missed the part where I said I love you. That overtakes everything else. You're what I want more than anything else. You make me happier than anything ever has."

He brushed his thumb across her cheekbone. "*You're* my home."

Her heart pounded so hard she was sure it was bruising her insides.

"And if you wanna go back to just being friends, I'll…" He blew out a breath. "Man, I'll be so miserable, but Addes, I'll try it for you."

"Ah, hell." Ford stood next to Tucker and crossed his arms. "I'll be a character witness." He looked down at her. "Still on your side, and the promise to get you outta here if you say the word stands."

Tears were forming, such a rush of them that it left her useless to fight them. She bit the inside of her cheek and nodded. "Thank you, Ford." Tucker's features blurred as she turned her teary-eyed gaze on him. "As for you, Tucker Crawford…"

Addie stood, and Lexi jerked her back down. Half a second later, she seemed to realize what she'd done and gave her a shove up.

Then Tucker was mere inches away, so close and so familiar, this big guy who'd just poured out his heart with the entire town watching, something he wouldn't normally do. "You know everyone's gonna be all up in your business after this. You'll never live it down."

"Guess that's a point for me moving to the city with you."

He obviously didn't mean it, but she could tell he was trying to.

"Can you lift up the mic?" a voice called out. "We can't hear you anymore."

Addie grabbed the microphone, put it right next to her lips, and looked her best friend in the eye. "I declare Tucker Crawford guilty of everything he said, and there's a whole lot more I could add. But right now, y'all might want to avert your eyes because I'm about to do somethin' terribly unladylike."

She handed the microphone to Lexi, gripped Tucker's tie, and yanked his lips down to hers.

Then she looped her other arm around his neck and kissed him for all she was worth.

And when he lowered his hands to her butt, she jumped into his arms and wrapped her legs around his waist.

Hooting and hollering carried across the square. While her group of friends were the loudest by far, most of the town was cheering for them, reminding her of why deep down, this was her home and always would be.

Later there'd be stories about how people had to cover their children's eyes, and her mom and Lottie—and probably a whole mess of other women in town—would congratulate her in one breath and then, in the next, give her a lecture she'd heard every variation of before, but she didn't care.

She cared even less when Tucker's tongue grazed hers. "I'm sorry I was so stupid," he said. "If you give me the chance, I promise I'll spend the rest of our lives making it up to you."

"The rest of our lives, even?"

"You think I'm ever letting you get away again? But if you need to take it slow, I—"

She cut off his words with another kiss. "No more going slow. Because I'm in love with you, too. I'm all in."

Relief flooded his features. Then he glanced around. Lexi was thanking everyone and instructing them when and where to be tomorrow, but they were still getting a mix of scandalized and hungry-for-more looks.

"I think I'd better take you home so we can talk more about this love thing."

"Oh, no. I know how this ends. You get a crazy idea that you then talk me into, and we both land in a heap of trouble."

"There's no one else I'd rather be in trouble with." Tucker slowly lowered her to the ground, and she tugged her skirt back into the respectable range.

Then he took her hand, and after a quick wave at their friends, they rushed off to get started on seeing just how much trouble they could get into.

CHAPTER THIRTY-TWO

"Pinch me," Tucker said to Addie, who took all of two seconds to slip her hand inside his suit coat and pinch his side.

"Did it hurt?"

"I've had worse."

She pinched him again, harder this time.

"Uncle, uncle." He wrapped his arms around her and squeezed her to him to prevent further injury. And because he loved being able to hold her and kiss her and they should've gone public weeks ago.

Maybe he could've saved himself that crazy trial, although he'd never felt like he'd so thoroughly won a case before.

He ran his hands down to the curve of her butt, and he copped a generous feel as he swept his tongue inside for another taste. The red dress was sexy as hell, as was the fact that she'd been wearing only his T-shirt around her house this morning as they'd rushed to get ready.

"Seriously, guys?" Shep asked, and Tucker wasn't going to take his eyes, hands, or lips off Addie to see, but he was probably still working on getting his bow tie right. "Get a room already."

"Had one last night, thanks," Tucker said.

"Nice!" Easton held up his hand, and Tucker smacked it.

Addie raised an eyebrow. "Really?"

"Don't get all huffy. I'm getting to you, too."

Easton extended his open palm to her, and she smacked it.

"Does anyone know how to tie a damn bow tie?" Shep asked.

Everyone turned to Addie, and she pulled out her *go-to-hell* glare. "Tell you what, I'll trade you. I'll wear the tie; you wear the dress and heels."

The gang quickly returned to working on their ties, and Addie tugged him off to the side. "Hey, so I know we got distracted with other things last night…" Her cheeks flushed, and he was reliving carrying her into her bedroom and making up for two weeks without her.

Thankfully, Ford had been willing to go puppysit Flash so that Tucker could stay the night. Waking up with Addie in his arms was something he could definitely get used to—and he planned to.

"Anyway, about Bama," she said.

"*Boo,*" Easton said. The guy must have bat hearing.

"I'll ask for all y'all's opinion in a few minutes, but for now, shut it." She hooked her thumbs in the top of her dress and tugged, and for a second he got distracted watching the way it emphasized her cleavage. "They've officially offered me the job."

He'd prepared himself for that.

He couldn't believe how sad he was to leave a practice that'd started on a fluke, all because the woman across from him had a grandmother as stubborn as she was. He found he liked how different one case was from the next, even though it was a challenge and took a lot of brushing up on laws he wasn't familiar with—and some he'd never even heard of before.

The boat business would never be a big money maker but a good side hobby, and he'd hoped…

But he could find a firm to work for in Tuscaloosa. The other option was straining his relationship with Addie with too much distance, and he wasn't willing to risk it. "I'm not surprised. They'd be crazy not to want you. I'm just warning you that I plan to be super protective, and to go down to the stadium all the time to remind the guys that you're already taken."

"I don't so much mind the letting everyone know I'm yours and you're mine, but if you plan on going overboard with the overprotective thing, I hope you also plan to get into a lot of fights about it."

"Hell yeah. That'll be half the fun."

She tried to fight back her smile, and he grinned and dragged his thumb over her jawline, teasing it out of her. "I suppose, though, that we could just as easily have that fight in Auburn. It'd cut out those extra hours driving home to see our family and friends, and a good group of guys for poker night is hard to find."

"Wait. Are you saying…?" Tucker schooled his expression, too afraid to let the glimmer of hope that'd flashed before his eyes get the best of him. "What exactly are you saying?"

"I think she's saying that Auburn University also offered her a job," Shep said, coming over and slapping Tucker on the back before reaching for his cologne.

Addie rolled her eyes. "Oh my gosh, you guys are the biggest eavesdroppers ever."

"Hey, this involves us, too," Ford said, moving closer instead of pretending not to be listening. "Like you said, poker night is at stake. Plus, we kinda like you."

Addie glanced at Easton. "You wanna throw in your two cents?"

"Mine's worth ten, and I'd like to sound all selfless and tell you that I'll support whatever you want. Which is true. But it'd make it a hell of a lot easier to support you if I actually got to see you once in a while."

"You wouldn't feel like you were giving up your dream?" Tucker asked Addie, needing to be sure it was what *she* wanted.

"Are you kiddin' me? I have a sexy boyfriend—"

"Blech," Ford said. "You guys are so mushy. I'm not sure if I can be around this much longer."

"And a big burly friend who does search and rescue—"

Ford grinned. "Now you're talkin'."

"And a cop who can get me out of speeding tickets—"

"I hope you don't mean me," Easton said with a laugh.

Addie turned to Shep. "And a friend who's stood up for me time and time again, who's also marrying this awesome girl who likes me enough to let the aforementioned boyfriend overtake her rehearsal in order to help get us back together. All that, plus getting to be a sports therapist for the team who shouts 'War Eagle'? I don't think it gets any better than that. It's like whatever the level past wildest dreams is."

"Then I say AU, baby." It was the first time he'd tried a pet name, and he liked it more than he thought he would.

A squeal escaped her lips a few seconds before they were on his, and just when the guys were backing away to give them space, Addie reached out and blindly tugged on suit jackets. "A group hug is happening right now. I suggest just going with it."

If anyone but Addie had suggested it, he had a feeling the guys would balk.

Instead, they brought it in for one big mushy huddle.

• • •

"I now pronounce you husband and wife."

The second the words were out of the preacher's mouth, Shep enthusiastically kissed his bride. Then he lifted a fist in the air and everyone cheered louder.

Addie glanced at Tucker, and he gave her a smile that sent her heart racing.

They followed Shep and Lexi back down the aisle, over to the reception area. The couple was announced, and then Mr. and Mrs. Shepherd stepped onto the portable dance floor for their first dance as husband and wife.

The song Addie now had memorized swelled, and as the first verse wound down, Tucker locked his arm into place around her. "You ready for this?"

"I sure hope so. Promise you won't let me fall."

"I promise to never let you fall," he said, and then they were off and waltzing to a song about being meant for loving each other.

Countless pictures followed. Comments from everyone in town. Food and drinks. Laughing. So much laughing.

"Excuse me," Mr. James Lindley said, stopping in front of her and Tucker. "At the trial last night, you didn't let the audience say anything."

Tucker's brow furrowed. "Oh-kay. And you had something to say? To help me win over Addie?"

Mr. Lindley glanced at her. "No, not about that. I mean, congratulations, I guess. But you won't take my case. I wanted you to answer to that."

"James, you need to talk to your brother already. Do you want me to raise my voice and ask everyone if they agree?"

Addie squeezed Tucker's hand under the table, trying to silently signal to him that under no circumstance should that happen. They'd already upstaged the rehearsal—with Lexi's blessing, but still.

This was Lexi's day, and if anyone tried to ruin it, Addie would personally take them out.

Even if she had to hurdle the table in her short dress and tackle Mr. Lindley to the ground.

Tucker winked at her, making her think he knew what he was doing—she certainly hoped so. Especially since she now had that twitterpated light-headed sensation that made it hard to think straight.

Mr. Lindley hung his head. "No."

"Just talk to him. If you need a mediator, I'll help. I'm not going to bring a frivolous lawsuit against him."

He shuffled away, and Addie leaned against

Tucker's side, loving the way he automatically curled her closer.

"You're a good lawyer," she said.

"Thank you."

"I like that you care about the people here. Quitting your other job was the right choice, and if it means we live in the houseboat for all our lives, it will have been worth it."

"Oh, now you're inviting yourself to move in with me? Talk about a total stalker." He shook his head and lowered his lips to hers. "I had all those signals, too, and I just ignored them."

"Very funny. You know what I'm saying."

"I do. I was thinking maybe someday we'll build a house on my grandpa's land. It's a bit out of town and it'll need a lot of work, and I'd like to completely pay off the loan against it first. It might also add another ten minutes to your commute, but…" He waved a hand through the air. "We can talk about it later."

"But you've thought about it?"

He twisted a strand of her hair around his finger. "Definitely thought about it."

Affection and desire swelled within her, and if she got any happier, she might float right off. "I'd like that. And I can't wait to see what an amazing house you can build with your own two, very capable hands. Don't worry," she said with a wink that was still closer to a one-and-a-half-eyed-blink. "I'll take care of the roofing."

He let out a soft laugh and brushed his lips across hers. "Then I'll make sure to gator-proof the place."

"Deal."

"There you two are." Nonna Lucia rounded the table, and they stood and exchanged hugs and cheek kisses. She beamed at them. "You make such a handsome couple. I so glad I called it. I knew eventually you'd find your way to each other."

"Was this gonna be before or after you set me up on dates with girls?" Addie asked, and her grandmother clucked her tongue at her.

"I just know. Maybe it take me a while to see it, like it take you two a while to see it. But once I do, I tell this young man to fix it. He's a good boy, so he fixed it."

"Yes, ma'am. I do what I'm told."

"I'll have to remember that," Addie muttered under her breath, and the hand he had on her hip gripped her a little tighter. "Love you, Nonna."

"You too." Nonna patted both of their cheeks. "Both of you."

The celebration went on for a few hours, with more pictures and music and toasts that focused on how wonderful the bride and groom were. If someone would've asked Addie a couple of months ago what she thought of weddings, she might've said, *A big no thanks to that*.

As she sat there, soaking in the love and the joy between the happy couple—as well as among the family and friends and a town that was way too involved in everyone's business but also showed up for one another—she changed her mind about weddings and love and the whole crazy thing.

Well, the jury was still out on the fancy clothes, although admittedly, the guys looked good in their matching suits.

Finally, things settled down enough for Addie to steal a moment with the bride. She gave Lexi a hug and told her how beautiful she looked, which she did, then said, "I also wanted to thank you. For letting me be in the wedding, for taking the time to understand my relationship with Shep, and for last night—*especially* for last night. You went above and beyond."

"What can I say? When I see two people are meant to be together, I'm willing to go above and beyond."

"You're also surprisingly strong." Addie shook out the hand Lexi had gripped last night. "I have no doubt you would've tackled me to get me to stay, dress and all."

"Oh, I would've." Lexi bumped her shoulder into Addie's. "I learned from the best, too. Admittedly, you and Tucker did have me a bit worried. It was right down to the wire, and I get invested, okay? Do you have any idea the kind of stress that puts on a person's heart?"

"Girl, I'm a hardcore football fan. I know all about getting invested and heart palpitations and down to the wire."

Lexi sighed and shook her head. "I don't think I could do it every week."

"But that's the thing. Every week you get another chance. Every game. You can have this amazing play, but it could go to shit the very next. Or you have three crap plays, but you make that one perfect pass and *bam*! Everything's possible again."

"I like that. I'm going to stick to…not football, but yeah." Lexi leaned closer. "I'm a little afraid to point out this just proves you're more of a romantic than you claim to be. Even if it's for a game. And for one guy."

"As long as you don't spread it around, you have nothing to fear."

They shared a laugh, and then the guys drifted over.

Tucker's arms circled her waist as he tucked his chin on her shoulder, and she relaxed into his embrace and pictured what their future might bring, several extraordinary possibilities stretched out in front of them.

Even better, she knew that in every single one, they'd be together, and that meant no matter which path they chose, they'd all have happy endings.

Hmm. Maybe she was a romantic after all.

EPILOGUE

It was all Addie could do to keep her poker face in place as her friends squeezed around the table in the houseboat. Lexi had also come at her request, and Addie reached underneath the table and linked her fingers with Tucker's.

In the past they'd used tables—and even overalls—to hide their affectionate gestures, but tonight it effectively hid something else.

Any emergency meeting text, or one about a change in plans, would've brought suspicion. The invite to Lexi happened enough to avoid too much of that, and for some reason Addie couldn't recall, she and Tucker thought it would be more fun this way.

To just spring the news on them.

It was nice to be back at the houseboat, too, where their biggest adventures always seemed to begin.

One new beginning several months ago, when Shep announced his and Lexi's engagement; another after a football game where she and Tucker had gotten a little frisky and then come back here and fully crossed all the lines.

Countless new beginnings through the years.

These days, Tucker and Flash spent most nights at her place, but they spent their Monday through Thursday workdays here in the houseboat, where Tucker took client meetings and occasionally agreed to fix up boats, and Flash alternated between making messes and taking naps.

Fridays and Saturdays were for working on boats or for taking them out on the water, or for sleeping in and watching football when it was on and complaining about the lack of it when it wasn't.

Tucker looked at her, and she nodded, silently telling him to go ahead. "Guys, before we get started, Addie and I have some news…"

"We already know you drew up plans for the house," Ford said. "People in town have been talking about it for the past week. Lots of opinions. Some have voiced their hope that the place won't be an eyesore like Nellie Mae's fuchsia house that she built herself; several think you're crazy to build on land that needs so much work; and a few people asked me why you think you're too good to live in town like everyone else."

"Actually, it's somethin' else," Addie said, ignoring the urge to defend herself against that eyesore claim.

Their house was going to be modest and beautiful and 100 percent their business and their business only.

"Did you get a promotion?" Easton asked, addressing her. "If you guys are telling us the house plan is off and you're going to work for Bama, I might have to flip this table. Just saying."

"No, I… Well, I did sorta get a promotion." Working with the AU football team was amazing. She loved her job and helping the athletes, and then during the off season, she also did a few personal visits for her former clients or people in town who weren't fans of the guy whose name was on the door of the physical therapy office. "Same building, but now I'm number two instead of number five on the sports therapy totem pole."

"Nice!"

Flash came up on Addie's left side and nudged her hand with his nose, and Addie scratched the top of his head in that way he liked. Lexi glanced down, and her eyes went wide as the diamond on Addie's finger caught the light.

"I think they have other news," Lexi said, and her voice went up a few octaves, but apparently not high enough for Flash to hear because he flopped down on the floor, evidently bored with the conversation already.

And the jig is up.

"So, you guys might recall that Tucker and I have been friends for a while now," Addie said, thinking again of the night Shep had announced his engagement.

Tucker slipped his arm over her shoulders and kissed her temple. "Well, I asked her to marry me the other night, and she said yes. We're gettin' hitched."

Lexi let out a squeal and started rattling off wedding-planning details, and Addie blinked at her for a moment and then smiled. "Thank goodness I have you to help. You probably don't know this about me, but I'm not exactly the wedding-planning type."

"Noooo," Lexi said, as if she was all shock, and the rest of them laughed and offered their congratulations.

"Which brings me to my next point." Addie sat up straighter in her seat and grinned at her guy friends. "You all are gonna be my bridesmaids."

The expressions went in waves. Twitching eyebrows, forehead crinkles, pursed lips.

"Don't worry," she said. "I won't make y'all wear dresses."

"Are you sure?" Ford asked. "I don't know if you know this about me, but I got real sexy legs."

He propped his foot on the table and pulled up his pants leg to display a few inches of his hairy calf, and Addie whistled and yelled for him to "take it off."

"Wait," Tucker said, twisting to face her. "I get some of them, right?"

"We'll do it like when we split into teams. Or maybe we should do a quick draft—like fantasy wedding party. Quick, guys. Give us your stats."

They all started rattling off their strengths and weaknesses, a few of which made Lexi blush, and Addie sat and soaked it in.

This was going to be so fun.

She glanced at Lexi. "I'm using my first pick on you, by the way. Will you be one of my brides-maids?"

Her eyes went watery as she nodded and lunged over Flash to give Addie a hug. "You shouldn't use your first pick on me, though. I'm kind of a shoo-in."

"Too late. Things move fast in the draft, and you've just gotta go with it."

Between Lexi and her sister, she could probably only justify one bridesman, but one of the awesome things about marrying your best friend who was also friends with the rest of your group, was that they'd all be there for the shenanigans, every step of the way.

They toasted the engagement with their favorite beer before they got down to playing poker, talking crap, and enjoying a night off from their worries and cares.

And at the end of the night, after everyone else had left, Tucker drew her to him and kissed her. "Man, I love you."

"Good thing," she said. "I'd hate to be marrying someone with lukewarm feelings for me."

"Not an issue. Right now they're feeling very, very hot." He peeled her shirt up over her head, tossed it aside, and walked her backward toward the bed. "I thought we should stay here tonight. For old times' sake."

Addie took his ratty Saints hat off his head, almost tossed it aside like she usually did, but then got an idea and tugged it on. "I'm game."

The desire in his eyes flared hotter as he yanked her to him. His mouth captured hers, and then they were kissing and tumbling onto the bed, and it was one of those perfect nights that she'd add to her ever-growing list of perfect nights with her best friend.

Boyfriend.

Fiancé.

ACKNOWLEDGMENTS

Usually I end up thanking my family near the bottom, but after a year of huge changes, I want to thank them right up front. Thanks, guys, for pitching in and helping out around the house. For asking how my writing's going, understanding when I can't make all the things, and for basically helping me live out my dream of writing stories about people kissing.

Big hugs to Gina Maxwell and Rebecca Yarros for being my anchors in both calm and crazy waters (although the crazy seems to be pretty constant lately-lol). Not sure what I'd do without all the brainstorming sessions, writing sprints, the chats and the laughs. Love you, wifeys!

Thanks to Stacy Abrams and Liz Pelletier for believing in me and this book and working so hard to get it out into the world. To everyone at Entangled Publishing, thank you for all you do. Thanks to my publicists, Holly Bryant & Riki Cleveland, the marketing team, as well as Melanie Smith, Jessica Turner, Katie Clapsdl, and Heather Riccio. I'm constantly blown away by all of you.

Big shout out to Kerrie Legend for organizing my chaos, making my stuff look pretty, and for being such an awesome high-energy cheerleader. I also have to thank my agent, Nicole Resciniti, for all her hard work, often on projects that dated before she and I even started working together. You rock!

Huge thanks to my readers for supporting my books and sending me messages that keep me going. My FB group, Cindi Madsen's Banter Babes, is full of awesome people. Come on over if you'd like to join us—we mainly talk about books and life and how books make life better.

And thank YOU! Whether it's the first book of mine you've read, or if you've read several, I appreciate every time a reader gives one of my novels a chance.

Turn the page to read start reading

The Trouble with Cowboys

by *NYT* bestselling author

Victoria James

Want more from Cindi Madsen?!
Sign up for her newsletter and get

Just Jilted
for free!

Just visit: https://tinyurl.com/CindiNewsletter

The *Trouble* with *Cowboys*

CHAPTER ONE

Ty Donnelly would rather be knee-deep in cow manure than back in his hometown of Wishing River, Montana.

He pulled his trusty Chevy into an empty parking spot outside Tilly's Diner, a long-standing town landmark, and sat still for a minute. Steady rain hammered against the roof of his truck and streamed down his windows as he peered out at the familiar sights of the town he hadn't seen in eight years. It was too early for stores and most businesses to be open—except Tilly's. Some things didn't change.

They probably still had the best coffee, the best breakfast, and the best gossip on Main Street.

He'd never been one for nostalgia, but it crept up his arm like a fast-moving spider, startling him. It was the damn town. It held too many memories, too many friends, too many secrets. He should just keep on going to the ranch and face everything he was hiding from. But after driving all night, he needed a coffee. Or maybe he needed an excuse to delay seeing his father. Even facing a diner full of gawking townspeople was more appealing than seeing his father.

Their final day together, his father's last words to him had changed his entire life, and he'd been running from them for eight years.

Hell. He ran his hand through his hair and glanced over at Tilly's again before putting on his cowboy hat and finally pushing his door open. Cold rain soaked him as he ran up the steps to the diner. He pulled the door open, and a blast of warmth and a good dose of reality greeted him as he stepped inside. His past slapped him in the face, a little too harshly for a guy going on no sleep. Flatware clanked against dishes, and the animated conversation dwindled to that of a whispering brook. He walked forward, sure to keep his head up but eye contact to a minimum in the packed diner.

Making his way around the round tables with their vinyl-backed chairs, he gave an occasional nod and tip of his hat but made sure not to stop. By the time he reached the long counter at the far end of the diner, he felt as though he'd walked through fire. He took a deep breath and held on to it for a moment as he recognized the man sitting at the counter. Dean Stanton. One of his former best friends—and now his father's doctor. He hadn't expected to see him this soon.

"Dean," he said, bracing his arms on the counter. Dean gave him a nod like he was a stranger. He hadn't seen him in eight years and hadn't had any contact until Dean had called, telling him his father had suffered a stroke. He could still hear the censure in his friend's voice. Dean had also made it pretty clear he was calling as his father's doctor, not as his old buddy. He looked the same—older, sure. Judging by his clean-shaven appearance and expensive-looking clothes, he seemed like he had his life together, too. Ty was the one still in faded jeans and an old cowboy hat.

He kept his eyes trained on the kitchen door and sure as hell hoped Tilly would come out of there soon, because he needed a coffee and then he needed to get the hell out of Dodge. When the door swung open a minute later, it wasn't Tilly. He didn't know who the waitress was. He may have been driving all night, his eyes sore and tired, but there was no stopping the instincts he was born with as he gazed appreciatively at the woman in front of him. Her honey-colored hair was pulled back in a ponytail, and she had familiar, large chocolate-colored eyes. She was wearing a T-shirt with *Tilly's* scrolled across the front, the shirt clinging to very nice curves. Her jeans were dark and showed off nicely rounded hips. When his eyes traveled back up her curvy length, her brown eyes were on his, and any of the warmth he'd detected was replaced by an unapologetic disdain.

"What can I get you?" she asked, now wiping the counter and not making eye contact with him.

"Large coffee to go?" He ignored the various glass-domed cake stands filled with muffins, doughnuts, and pies, even though he hadn't eaten in twelve hours. Tilly was known for the best and freshest baked goods for miles. He just wasn't in the mood for eating.

She didn't actually give him an answer, only sort of gave a nod. He noticed she glanced over at Dean before grabbing a white paper cup and pouring the coffee. She handed him the drink and a plastic lid. "That'll be a dollar and fifty cents. Cream and sugar are over there," she said, pointing to the far side of the counter.

He laid the correct change out in front of him. "How's Tilly?"

"Dead," she said, walking away with the carafe of coffee in her hands. Damn. He hadn't expected that. He'd kinda assumed Tilly would always be here. He glanced over at the waitress again, studying her profile as she refilled Dean's cup. Hell. He knew her. Tilly's granddaughter. She'd always been at the diner with her grandmother. As a little kid and then later as a teenager. Now she'd turned into this gorgeous woman. It was well known that Tilly's daughter had saddled her with her baby and taken off. No one really knew much about her after that.

It was sad to hear Tilly was gone. She had always had a warm smile and a kind word for him. So maybe some things did change.

He put the lid on his steaming coffee and turned around, no need for cream or sugar. Of course, the entire damn restaurant was still staring at him like a lame cow being judged at the county fair.

Pushing open the front door with his palm, he jogged out to his truck, happy to be away from there. Now the last thing separating him from his past was the drive to his father's ranch. He pulled out of his parking spot and drove down Main Street, Wishing River.

Eight years and barely a thing had changed.

The old buildings still had that charm that beckoned tourists and artists, especially during the summer and fall. But this wasn't his home anymore; that much was clear.

He made the drive out to the ranch in record time, the need to get this over with encouraging him to drive faster. The winding country roads were virtually empty, and the rugged beauty of the land hit him—as a kid he'd sworn he'd never leave Montana. Wishing River was nestled between the jagged peaks of the Bitterroot Mountains to the west and the Sapphire Mountains to the east. The valleys held the fall foliage like a secret prize from the other areas of Montana that couldn't boast the range of color they had here.

The rolling green hills, the towering trees, the pastures, the wide-open sky, they were as familiar to him as breathing. But something wasn't right.

Easing his foot off the gas, he slowed as the old three-rail wood fence bordering his family's sprawling ranch came into view. A couple of the posts were down, some in need of maintenance, but it was fall, and that's when all the maintenance usually happened around the ranch.

He pulled into the long gravel drive, dust and pebbles kicking up behind him, and he didn't bother avoiding the potholes, the mud splashing onto his already filthy truck. The pit in his stomach seemed to grow exponentially, knowing his mother wasn't at the door, knowing his father...was ill.

Once parked, he grabbed his keys and coffee and went to face his past.

His boots crunched against the gravel, and he took a deep breath. The red barn in the distance was just screaming for a coat of paint, and he couldn't make out any movement around there or the bunkhouse way in the distance, but he knew all the cowboys were out by now. He was the only one not working this time of morning.

The large, sprawling covered porch didn't have a single plant. The paint was chipping on the railing and spindles, and the shutters and windows looked like they hadn't been cleaned in years. His mother would have been mortified.

He rolled his shoulders as he stared at the faded red front door. He gave a knock and then walked inside. The smell of coffee greeted him as he did a quick survey from the front rug. The house was the same. Except it didn't have that welcoming, shiny clean feel from when his mother had been alive. Now it was obvious a bachelor lived here. The curtains weren't drawn, there was a fine layer of dust, and no fresh flowers.

"Is that you, Tyler?" Heavy footsteps approached, and he stood like a stranger in his childhood home.

"It is," he called out.

Mrs. Busby—one of his parents' close friends— appeared from the door to the living room. "Well, aren't you a sight for sore, sad eyes?"

He took off his hat and smiled. "Hi, Mrs. Busby."

Her hand was on her chest, and she gave him his first smile since coming home. "It's been a long time, child. I'm so happy you're here. I prayed for this, for you to return to Wishing River. You are just what your father needs. Better than any kind of medicine."

He swallowed down the lump in his throat,

along with a hefty dose of guilt. He wasn't so sure he was going to do his father any good, but he was facing his responsibilities. His father was now his responsibility. All of it was. He owed it to him; despite everything, the man had raised him, and now it was his turn to take care of his old man.

"Well, I hope he agrees," he said, shoving his free hand into the front pocket of his jeans.

"Of course he does," Mrs. Busby replied, placing her hands on her hips. The older woman was almost exactly how he remembered her, maybe a little wider in what had already been ample hips.

"How's he doing?" he asked, feeling awkward in his childhood home.

She stepped out into the hallway, shutting the French door that led to the living room, where he assumed his father was sleeping. "He's stable. It could have been much, much worse. I'll let Dr. Stanton fill you in when he comes tonight for his daily visit."

Dr. Stanton—aka Dean. How the hell had his friend gone from troublemaker to doctor? But he'd always known Dean was going to do big things. He'd come from a long line of doctors and successful ranchers, and the guy had never strayed from his goals, no matter the amount of trouble they'd gotten themselves into as teens.

He stared down at his worn boots for a second as a wave of insecurity washed through him. "Dean comes every night?"

She nodded, her oversize gray curls standing still despite the motion. "Yes. On his way home from the office, he stops in and checks on your father."

Ty gave a nod. "You mentioned on the phone that you have a nurse who comes by?"

"Yes, yes. Two different nurses, one for morning and one for night. I usually drop by in the morning before church. But I'm only a phone call away, and if you need anything, you call me. We've rented a hospital bed for him so he can rest comfortably, and it helps with sitting up and such."

"Thank you," he said, following her into the kitchen when she motioned.

"You don't have to thank me. Your father and I go way back," she said. He knew they did. When Mrs. Busby's husband had been alive, the couple would often come over and have dinner or drinks with his parents. They had all been best friends. He could still remember hearing laughter into the late hours of the night. He hated thinking how things changed, how quickly time passed.

"I'd offer you coffee, but I see you already picked up a cup," she said, placing her empty mug into the dishwasher.

"It was a long night." He glanced in the direction of the living room, dreading having to go through with this but wanting to get it over with now. "Is he sleeping, or can I go see him?"

Walking forward, she placed a hand on his arm. "Of course you can. Now, don't expect him to be… like the man you remember. Martin is holding his own, and Dr. Stanton said he's very lucky that Lainey found him when she did, or it could have been much worse."

He cleared his throat. "Lainey?"

She angled her head. "You remember—Tilly's

granddaughter?"

The image of the gorgeous blonde with the pissed-off gaze flashed across his mind. "Yeah. Right. Lainey. Where...did she find him?"

She shook her head and then did the sign of the cross, her dark-brown eyes filling with tears. "By the fence close to the road. I think he was trying to fix it. Apparently, he was unconscious when she found him, called the paramedics, and they coached her on what to do until they arrived. That sweet girl rode in the back of the ambulance with him and didn't leave his side." She sniffled and produced a handkerchief from those velour pants and blew her nose loudly.

Staring down at the top of her gray head, not capable of words yet, his mind flooded with questions and guilt and images of his father unconscious outside. Fixing the damn fence. There should be hired help for that. When he left eight years ago, there were thirty-five employees—any one of them could have done it. *He* should have done it. He should have been the one to help him, to be by his side in the ambulance. "He's in the living room?"

She nodded. "We did the best we could, finding a spot for him on the main floor. We figured that'd be the best place, since there's a door for privacy and it's close to the washroom. It's not perfect. Of course the house isn't exactly welcoming; I'm sorry for that. My arthritis is bad in the fall and winter, and we haven't really had time to get the place all spick-and-span."

"Don't worry," he said, wincing at the harshness in his voice. He tried to speak softly. "You've done more than enough. I can take it from here."

Her eyes softened, and she smiled at him with such sympathy and acceptance that she reminded him of his mother. She reached out and patted his arm again. "Oh my dear, we aren't going anywhere. You're going to need us. But I'm happy you're home to take the lead... And your father needs you, Tyler."

He swallowed hard against the emotion simmering inside. "Does he know I'm here?"

Her full cheeks reddened. "I...didn't know... I wanted to wait until you had arrived. I didn't say anything."

A pit formed in his stomach. She hadn't believed he'd come home. He gave her a nod. "That's fair enough. I understand. I, uh, I guess I should go see him," he said, looking toward the door.

She squeezed his arm. "Tyler, he's not the same man. He can't speak. He can't stand. He can't use his arms to eat or drink."

He was biting down hard on his back teeth. "Okay."

"The day nurse is Sheila; she's just on a call in the office. I always tell her to take a little break when I come and visit. She'll get him all washed up for the day. He's already had breakfast. Sheila stays until seven. That's when Lainey gets here. She usually stays for an hour, brings him dinner, until the night nurse, Michelle, comes in. Oh, and of course Dr. Stanton drops in after work, so anywhere between five and eight at night."

So the entire town was taking care of his father. Except him. He didn't bother asking why Lainey was bringing him dinner when he knew there was a cook in the bunkhouse for the men.

"I should probably get in there."

She nudged him forward. "I'll leave you two, then. You won't be on your own long. All our numbers are on the fridge in case of anything. I'm here if you need me, Tyler."

"Thank you," he said, forcing a smile. "I really appreciate what you've done."

She waved a hand. "Don't have to thank me—that's what friends are for. Now go on and say hi to your papa. I know seeing you will cheer him up."

Standing there, watching her gather her purse and keys, he desperately tried to figure out what the hell he was going to say to him. Eight years ago, his father had stood tall and proud. He'd been fit, the ranch keeping him active and strong. But the death of his wife had brought the man to his knees, and it had been the first time Ty had seen his father as something other than invincible—and then everything had unraveled after that. After his mother had died, he realized just how tenuous their relationship had been. But it wasn't until that last night, that last argument, that he realized why his father could let him go.

Tyler rolled his shoulders, braced himself, then slowly walked over to the living room door. Regardless of their argument, he owed his father. Tyler had always considered himself a pretty rational person, but the situation with his dad, his emotions about everything were irrational, and he didn't like that. He didn't like being at the mercy of his feelings.

He gave the door a knock and then opened it.

Nothing could have prepared him for seeing his father like this. He was lying in the hospital bed, his once-strong face now weathered and hanging loosely on one side. His eyes were closed. His hair had thinned out, the gray having given way to the white. He wasn't the man Ty knew. His father was strong. This man lying in the bed was broken.

He blinked, forcing the emotion away, not letting himself dwell on it, the passage of time, the stroke, the regrets.

Walking forward a little, he cleared his throat. "Hi, Dad," he said.

There was no indication he'd heard him. Ty walked around the bed slowly, noting the way all the old furniture had been piled up at the other end of the room. It was nothing like the living room he remembered. The plaid curtains his mother had painstakingly sewn were all closed up, hiding the large picture windows she'd loved. They had remodeled the house to his mother's liking, and she had made sure it was perfect at all times. It was nothing like the house of his childhood.

Taking a deep breath, he sat in the chair beside the bed. His gaze traveled from the disturbing image of his father sleeping to the slew of medication bottles on the nightstand. And the picture of his mother. He turned away quickly as emotion hit him in the gut.

He ran his sweaty palms down the front of his jeans and leaned back in the chair. His father's eyelids flickered but didn't open. Did his dad know he was here? Had he heard him? Heat washed over his body at the idea his father knew he was there and just didn't want to see him.

"Dad?"

His father's good hand moved slightly, and Ty stared at it as a wave of memories tumbled into his mind. He'd held that hand. As a child, he'd clung to it, hadn't given it a second thought. He'd reached for his father's hand so many times growing up, in the pastures, in the barns, when learning to ride a horse. It had always been powerful, rough, large, and Ty thought his father could save him from anything. The hand lying on top of the blanket wasn't a hand that could save him anymore. It was thin, without his tan, and with age spots and wrinkles.

He blinked past the pool of moisture in his eyes. Hell. This was hell. When had everything changed? His childhood was over in a blink of an eye. The family of three that they had been no longer existed. He'd walked out on the man who had raised him, who had given him everything of himself, who had taught him all he needed to survive in the world. Their years together had meant nothing when the center of their world died. They hadn't been able to hold it together after she'd passed. They'd said harsh words to each other his last night at home.

They each blamed the other for her death.

But it was the last thing his father had said to him that had sent him packing, though, because the knife had been too deep.

Ty tried to breathe despite the heaviness in his chest. He cleared his throat and whispered his father's name, but it came out sounding more like a plea.

This time, his father's eyes did open. Faded

blue ones, which he'd once thought so similar to his own, latched onto his. It was clear his father's mind hadn't been affected by the stroke, because the animosity shining in them took his breath away. Ty sat there, staring at his father, silently hoping for something—a softening, an indication that he was happy to see him.

"I, uh, came back as soon as I found out what happened. I'm going to stay as long as you need me. I'll help you get back on your feet, Dad." The words poured out of him, like when he was a kid and had done something wrong, how he'd always try and get out of whatever punishment was coming by making a million promises and speaking as fast as he could. His dad had never bought it.

He didn't question calling him "Dad" even though he swore he'd never do it again. But that's what this man would always be to him, regardless of their argument, of the words that had been exchanged. He had raised him; he had loved him. He was the only father he loved.

Tyler held his breath, waiting for something from the man, just the tiniest sign that he had done the right thing by coming home.

Instead his father just shut his eyes, but not before he let him know, more powerfully than words could ever speak, that it didn't matter. None of it mattered. He didn't matter. His promises, his presence. It was all too late.

nothing but trouble

By Amy Andrews

For five years, Cecilia Morgan's entire existence has revolved around playing personal assistant to self-centered former NFL quarterback Wade Carter. But just when she finally gives her notice, his father's health fails, and Wade whisks her back to his hometown. CC will stay for his dad—for now—even if that means ignoring how sexy her boss is starting to look in his Wranglers.

To say CC's notice is a bombshell is an insult to bombs. Wade can't imagine his life without his "left tackle." She's the only person who can tell him "no" and strangely, it's his favorite quality. He'll do anything to keep from leaving, even if it means playing dirty and dragging her back to Credence, Colorado, with him.

But now they're living under the same roof, getting involved in small-town politics, and bickering like an old married couple. Suddenly, five years of fighting is starting to feel a whole lot like foreplay. What's a quarterback to do when he realizes he might be falling for his "left tackle"? Throw a Hail Mary she'll never see coming, of course.

How to Lose a Guy in Ten Days meets
Accidentally on Purpose by Jill Shalvis in
this head-over-heels romantic comedy
with a hot-as-hell flame.

the aussie next door

by *USA Today* bestselling author
Stefanie London

When American Angie Donovan discovers the tiny
seaside town of Margaret River, Australia, she feels at
home for the first time. And nothing, especially not a
little thing like a green card, is going to keep her from
staying past her six-month visa. It only took two days
to fall in love with Australia. Surely she can fall in love
with an Australian—and get engaged—in less than
thirty. Especially if he's as hot and funny as her next-
door neighbor…

Jace Walters has never wanted much—except a
bathroom he didn't have to share. The last cookie all
to himself. And solitude. But when you grow up in a
family of seven, you can kiss those things goodbye. At
least now he's finally living alone and working on his
syndicated comic strip in privacy. Sure, his American
neighbor is distractingly sexy and annoyingly nosy, but
she'll be gone in six months. He can make it that long.

Except now she's determined to date every eligible
male in the area, and her choices are even more
distracting. He doesn't want to, but he's going to have
to intervene and help her if he ever hopes to get back
to his quiet life again. It's a sacrifice, but, well, his
parents raised him to never leave a lady in distress…

*An emotional, touching
story for fans of
Nicholas Sparks...*

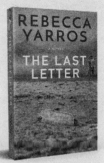

"A stunning, emotional romance."

—Jill Shalvis, *NYT* bestselling author

"Yarros' novel is a deeply felt and emotionally
nuanced contemporary romance…"

—*Kirkus* starred review

"*The Last Letter* is a haunting, heartbreaking and
ultimately inspirational love story."

—*InTouch Weekly*

"I cannot imagine a world without this story."

—Hypable

AMARA
an imprint of Entangled Publishing LLC.